# Kathryn must  about their union absolutely clear this very moment

She might never be able to muster the courage to approach the subject later. Especially when this newly regained confidence of Jon's wreaked havoc with her body's needs. He was terribly appealing at his worst, and this looked as though it definitely might be one of his better days. With a sharp intake of breath, she prepared to speak.

He interrupted. "There can be no further incidents like last evening." Kathryn noted the blunt determination in his voice as he continued. "If we are to succeed in this endeavor, nothing personal must get in our way. Do you understand what I'm saying?"

Kathryn raised her chin and stared. Damn him, that was supposed to be *her* line. She had expected him to argue when she refused him his rights, but apparently he didn't even want them…!

Dear Reader,

Lyn Stone's first book, *The Wicked Truth,* was one of the featured titles in this year's March Madness promotion and earned the author a favorable review in *Publishers Weekly.* Her second book, *The Arrangement,* is another unique and touching story about a young female gossip columnist who sets out to expose a notorious composer and winds up first agreeing to marry him, *then* falling in love with him. Don't miss your chance to enjoy this exciting new talent.

Kit Gardner's *The Untamed Heart,* a Western with a twist, has a refined English hero who happens to be an earl, and a feisty, ranch hand heroine who can do anything a man can do, only better. And this month also brings us a new concept for Harlequin Historicals, our first in-line short-story collection, *The Knights of Christmas.* Three of our award-winning authors, Suzanne Barclay, Margaret Moore and Deborah Simmons, have joined forces to create a Medieval Christmas anthology that is sure to spread cheer all year long.

Our final title is Susan Amarillas's new book, *Wild Card,* the story of a lady gambler who is hiding in a remote Wyoming town, terrified that the local sheriff will discover she's wanted for murder in Texas.

Whatever your tastes in reading, we hope you enjoy all four books, available wherever Harlequin Historicals are sold.

Sincerely,

Tracy Farrell
Senior Editor

Please address questions and book requests to:
Harlequin Reader Service
U.S.: 3010 Walden Ave., P.O. Box 1325, Buffalo, NY 14269
Canadian: P.O. Box 609, Fort Erie, Ont. L2A 5X3

# THE ARRANGEMENT

## Lyn Stone

# Harlequin Books

TORONTO • NEW YORK • LONDON
AMSTERDAM • PARIS • SYDNEY • HAMBURG
STOCKHOLM • ATHENS • TOKYO • MILAN
MADRID • WARSAW • BUDAPEST • AUCKLAND

ISBN 0-373-28989-8

THE ARRANGEMENT

**Books by Lyn Stone**

Harlequin Historicals

*The Wicked Truth* #358
*The Arrangement* #389

## LYN STONE

A painter of historical events, Lyn decided to write about them. A canvas, however detailed, limits characters to only one moment in time. "If a picture's worth a thousand words, the other ninety thousand have to show up somewhere!"

An avid reader, she admits, "At thirteen, I fell in love with Brontë's Heathcliff and became Catherine. Next year, I fell for Rhett and became Scarlett. Then I fell for the hero I'd known most of my life and finally became myself."

After living four years in Europe, Lyn and her husband, Allen, settled into a log house in north Alabama that is crammed to the rafters with antiques, artifacts and the stuff of future tales.

For my mother, Louise Pope, who encouraged
me through all those years of music lessons.
You were right—no bit of learning is ever wasted.
This one is for you.

# Chapter One

*London, September 1889*

"Follow that carriage," Kathryn Wainwright ordered as her coachman folded up the steps and closed the door. "Make certain the driver doesn't notice. When he gets where he's going, drive on by without stopping. All I want is his destination."

"Yes, ma'am," the man answered, climbing up to his seat.

Two hours later, they passed through a tatty, run-down village. A mile past the outskirts, the carriage ahead turned off onto a small side road through the trees. Kathryn knew she couldn't follow it without revealing her presence, and probably her purpose, if the rutted track was no through road.

She tapped on the inside roof and stuck her head out the window. "Drive on up that rise, Thom, and see if we can look down and see where that road leads."

When the carriage reached the top, she could indeed see quite clearly, with her father's old field glass to one eye. In the moonlight, an old manor house rose out of the summit of the adjoining hill.

No welcoming lights shone in the windows, nor could

she see anyone about the place. She watched until she saw his carriage pull up to the wide circular drive. Jonathan Chadwick alighted, spoke with the driver, and then strode into the dark house. Kathryn collapsed the spyglass and clapped her hands in glee. So this was his lair.

She had followed him before, always to a modest set of rooms near the theater district. And she knew from trying to bribe her way past the landlady that he rarely stayed there, except on the nights when he was performing somewhere in town. He disappeared for days on end, sometimes a week or more, the woman had said. Now Kathryn knew where he had gone.

This must be his family home, she guessed. From the deserted look of the place, he must live alone.

Kathryn smelled a fine story here. Perhaps there was something to the gossip that he was of some impoverished noble family. No one seemed to know very much about him, except that he had once been a child prodigy, traveling Europe since he was in short coats. Then, on reaching manhood, he had dropped out of sight. He had returned this summer with a vengeance. London's drawing rooms and concert halls fought to book him, while he stubbornly played hard to get. The ploy had worked nicely for him. He accepted only the plummiest offers.

Even if his music was not as marvelous as it was, the man's mystique would have put him in demand. Yes, there was a grand old mystery about Jonathan Chadwick and she meant to uncover it.

Excited by the prospect, Kathryn knew exactly what she had to do. "Turn around, Thom, and let's make for the village. We'll see if they have an inn."

They did indeed, a squalid little two-story hovel that barely deserved the name. Its sign, vaguely resembling a starving rabbit, swung precariously from uneven chains. The Hare's Foot Inn.

Kathryn quickly dismounted, went inside, and secured a room—the only private one available.

Thomas Boddie, her driver, protested in a loud whisper, "Ye can't be stayin' here, Miss Kathryn. Look at th' place! More 'n likely got bugs." He glanced around again, *tsk*ing and scratching his head to emphasize the warning.

"Buck up, Boddie. You're getting soft in your old age." Kathryn giggled when he looked indignant and a sight younger than his twenty-four years.

She waited until the innkeeper disappeared upstairs to change the linen before she spoke again. "I want you to bring one of the coach horses around after they're fed and rested. Oh, and get me your breeches."

"Breeches, miss?" he squeaked.

"Yes, and the shirt, too. I know you keep a change in the boot for when you stash your livery. We're about the same size, don't you think?"

"Ye can't wear me breeches! That's scan'lous! Indecent!"

Kathryn smiled at his outrage. "No, it's necessary. I need to get to that house and do some snooping if I'm to get this story. I can't ride bareback in an evening frock." She swatted behind her at her cumbersome bustle.

Thom groaned and rolled his eyes. "Oh, Lord save us. Your uncle Roop will skin us both. I'll have t' come, too."

"No. You'll wait here with the coach." When he started to argue, she placed a hand on his skinny arm to silence him. "If I should get caught, somebody has to get me out of this. Agreed?"

"Might as well," he grumbled. "You'll sack me if I don't."

"Precisely," she admitted cheerfully. Then she punched him playfully on the shoulder. "Ah, c'mon, Thom. Where's your sense of adventure? You used to dare me to do things like this!"

"We was children then, Miss Kathryn. Yer father—God rest 'im—was a sight more understandin' about yer pranks than yer uncle will be. Stealin' round a strange man's home ain't no game. He'll have th' law on ye. Worse yet, shoot ye fer a thief.''

"That prissy wretch wouldn't know one end of a pistol from the other." Kathryn hoped he didn't, anyway. Somehow, the composer didn't strike her as the type to wield a firearm. In the only duel that she knew anything about, Chadwick had used a sword. Apparently he'd been rather young when it happened, but a French immigrant attending the last concert evening had resurrected the story. Probably embellished it, as well. He'd said Chadwick was the best swordsman in France at the time.

Well, the silly rogue wasn't likely to run her through without getting close enough to notice she was a woman.

"Calm down, Thom. He won't even know I'm there, and I'll be back before you can blink. All I want is a look around.''

"Lord save us," Thomas groaned, and went for the breeches.

Kathryn decided the third time would be the charm. Twice before tonight she had attended Chadwick's performances. And twice she had failed to find out a thing about him other than how well he could compose and play.

He was a genius, and an odd duck all around. Everyone said so. And everyone came to see, as well as to listen. His appearance intrigued his audience as much as the music. The cream of London society talked of little else these days, when the subject of music arose. He could do no wrong, no matter how hard he tried. And, no mistaking it, he certainly did try. Tonight he had been haughty to the point of obnoxiousness. Arrogant, even insulting.

The social scale apparently meant nothing to the man. Kathryn wondered whether she might have been the only one in attendance tonight without a title. Certainly she was the only member of the press, though no one admitted knowing what she did to earn her keep. They *did* know, of course. If the hostess, Lady Ballinger, was not an intimate friend of Uncle Rupert's, Kathryn knew she'd have been snubbed at the door. Even then, her welcome had felt distinctly cool. Female news writers, even those who published discreetly under a male nom de plume, hardly qualified as guest-list material in the upper echelons of society.

Given the usual content of her column in Uncle Rupert's popular gossip sheet *About Town,* she could certainly understand why the elite kept up their pretense of ignorance in regard to her occupation. They wanted to stay on her good side. So far, her barbs had nicked only those in the professional limelight, but they all knew that could change overnight.

If only she could become self-supporting, she would much prefer doing novelettes or short stories to the entertainment column. But Uncle Rupert insisted on her articles for his paper, and he did pay the bills. *About Town* rated only a jot above the scandalous rag *Tit Bits,* but both were avidly read and both competed fiercely for the latest *on-dit.* Kathryn supposed she should be happy for the opportunity to be writing anything so eagerly received.

However, this latest assignment worried her. She had nothing substantial for the article on Chadwick. Apparently he had been the darling of the Continent during his youth, performing privately, as well as in concert halls in Milan, Rome, Vienna, Paris, even Germany. But never in London, until now. She wondered why? As far as she could determine, there were no lurking scandals, and no social life apart from performances such as this one. Rumor had it he was working on an opera.

Kathryn had interviewed a few people who recalled seeing him perform as a child and a young adult. He certainly appeared to be a man of the world now. She'd covered all the back issues of the major publications from around the civilized world, and the last mention of Chadwick had been over five years ago in Florence, Italy. Then he seemed to have vanished.

If she meant to get any kind of story out of the rascal

for *About Town,* she needed a personal interview. He had refused her in no uncertain terms, the belligerent lout.

Who would think a head like his could conjure all that beauty? Well, it *was* a beautiful head; she had to give him that. That unfashionably long hair looked quite the rage on him, its wild mahogany waves tumbling over his brow as he played, the back locks negligently clubbed with red velvet. Except for that scarlet ribbon and white ruffles at his throat and wrists, he dressed all in black, as had been his custom the two times she saw him. It set off the false whiteness of his skin to a fare-thee-well. That mask of powder he wore only emphasized the stark handsomeness of his features.

His eyes were remarkable; cold and arctic blue, much too light, even for his powdered paleness. One expected them to be black, like his rotten attitude. The nose was noble—it was the only possible description—with its straight prominence and slightly flaring nostrils. And he did flare the things at every opportunity. His lips were slightly redder than Kathryn thought natural, wide and finely chiseled, almost voluptuous in repose. If one could ever catch him relaxed long enough to notice. Usually he set them in a forbidding line that defied anyone to question his overwhelming superiority.

Well, his size would take care of establishing that, even if his looks didn't. He was enormously tall, with shoulders like a dockworker. She'd bet her last farthing he worked as hard at keeping those muscles fit as he did at perfecting his music. His apparel, the face paint and the long hair only served to underscore his masculinity. He obviously concocted the whole getup as a bizarre private joke on the public. They knew, of course. And they loved it.

She loved it, as well. The thought surprised her.

Considering her attraction to the man, wisdom told her to forget the story on Chadwick. Reason stopped her. She had a job to do, if she wanted to continue life as more than a decoration for Randall Nelson's arm and a broodmare for his nursery. God forbid she should forget that. Uncle Rupert certainly wouldn't. If she failed in this assignment, Kathryn figured, she might as well use that wicked little pen of hers to start addressing her wedding invitations.

It wasn't that she was diametrically opposed to marriage—only to marriage to a man like Randall. Aside from the fact that her skin had crawled the few times he touched her, there was also the matter of his having mentioned all those children he would give her. As though that might encourage her to accept his suit. Ha!

Randall wanted only to use her. Perhaps all men were users; certainly all the men she knew were. Her father had expected her to take her mother's place in ordering his household at an age when most girls still clung to their dolls. When he died, she'd had to argue with his old solicitor until she was blue in the face for funds to attend college. Thank God the will had provided that she complete her education without specifying where or at what age. They'd had to sell her father's house to finance it, but she'd won in the end.

Uncle Rupert had righteously insisted on her moving in with him after graduation and put her straight to work editing copy. Until he found that she could write better than his best reporter. Now the only suitor she'd ever had, with her uncle's eager blessing, wanted to station her in his bedroom and only let her out to push a pram full of babies around the park? Not bloody likely.

Surely, somewhere in the world there lived a man willing to share her life, rather than direct it like a dictator. Love wasn't a necessary requirement, though a modicum of physical attraction certainly was. If she had to bear the indignities she and her school chums had discussed so thoroughly, it would damned well be with a man who didn't turn her stomach.

She smiled as an image formed in her head. The man she chose would be witty, above all. And handsome as sin itself. Maybe he'd fill out his evening clothes as did Jonathan Chadwick. Lord, that man cut a sharp figure! She could well imagine submitting to certain indignities with a fellow built like that. Oh, never Chadwick himself, of course. No woman in her right mind would choose him, a pretentious performer with a penchant for rudeness.

When Thom brought her those breeches of his, she'd go and get that story, all right. She would ride right out to that old estate and find out what the man was really like. By the time she finished with him, Jonathan Chadwick wouldn't have a single secret left out of print. Make sport of her, would he?

"Damn that female!" As if he didn't have enough problems right now, without having to dodge her curiosity.

Worrying about that only augmented the familiar roiling in his gut that always followed a performance. Stage fright—his old and dreaded bugaboo. Every time he stepped up to or held an instrument in public, he became that terrified eight-year-old he'd been the first time he played to an audience. He remembered thinking at the time that it must be a bit like taking all one's clothes off in the middle of Trafalgar Square during the noonday rush. Well, he had decided then that, if forced to do it, by God he would do it with a flair. Did the Wainwright woman suspect it?

He couldn't stand much more of this. If the past five years as a soldier hadn't proved such a bloody fiasco, he'd never have returned to performing. Most composers hired the best musicians they could afford to present their work to possible investors. A pity he couldn't. Every ha'penny he earned had to go directly to his creditors. The army paid better; perhaps he shouldn't have sold out when Long San died. But the whole thing seemed wrong to him, this killing of men who were only trying to hold on to what was theirs. Too late for second thoughts, anyway. The commission money was spent and there was an end to it.

If he didn't cultivate some backers soon for the opera,

he'd find himself bereft of his precious collection of instruments and taking up space in debtor's prison. He must get past his damnable shyness and make some real contacts. Rich ones.

God, he wished he had a head for business, or at the very least a compulsion to perform that matched the one to compose. Useless to try to escape that driving need to put down the notes, though. He'd tried that, without success, so he figured he might as well use it. In the best of worlds, he'd stick to composing and live a regular sort of life, whatever *that* was. Unfortunately, everything hinged on money. Always had.

Discounting the soldiering skills he hoped never to use again, music was all he knew. It was all he had ever studied, all that could save him now. *Maman,* relentless as she was, had been right about one thing; he couldn't live without music and the music couldn't live without him. He wished to hell he'd been born a bloody banker.

The playing should be a private thing, an opening up of his soul. At rare times, he could forget the audience was there—all those fawning, simpering faces, with their cow eyes, staring and judging—but usually, as tonight, he simply endured. Pretended. Held back. Threw up. *Suffered.* And still blushed at applause.

*Maman* had solved the problem of his beet red face by powdering it white. That had worked when he was eight; it still worked. The dark wig looked a bit much, but it was necessary. His own hair, bleached near-white by the African sun, combined with the white face powder, made him look like an albino. He knew very well that the strange stage image he presented lent a certain mystique, an added attraction.

Tonight it had proved a massive drawback. The Wainwright woman had studied him like a sparrow hawk poised to swoop. A female predator. Those quick brown eyes of hers missed nothing. For the past two weeks, she'd been everywhere he looked. If he didn't keep away from her, she would pick him apart like the puzzle he was and destroy him with a single swipe of her pen. God knew she was capable. And eager.

Her pieces in the *About Town* news sheet were caustic as lye, the praise rare as chicken's teeth. She never even pretended to be other than what she was, either. As though working for that rumor rag were a thing to take pride in.

She didn't even have the grace to look like a destructive force. That wispy halo of golden curls escaping her oh-so-proper hairstyle gave her heart-shaped face an angelic appearance, despite those dangerous chocolate eyes.

What the hell was a woman doing writing for a newspaper, anyway? And such a beautiful woman, at that. Damned unnatural.

Tonight's confrontation had destroyed every vestige of pleasure he'd found in her appearance and any hope that she might choose another victim.

Immediately after the performance, Jon had hurried down the front walk to his hired carriage. The sweetness of lilacs had hit him full force as he climbed into the dark vehicle, and he had very nearly squashed the source of the scent by sitting on her.

"Get out!" he ordered, placing the perfume immediately. He shoved her skirts aside as he twisted around and plopped down across from her.

"Come now," she answered calmly, fiddling with her gloves. "I only want to ask you a few questions. Why do you refuse to talk to me? It's not as though I'll bite."

"Nonsense. You bite quite regularly. You chew people up and spit them out like a mouthful of bad fish. And you wonder that they run from you? Get the hell out of my carriage."

"Your music is marvelous. What harm could it do to let people know what you're really like as a person? You took a long hiatus in the midst of a brilliant career. Why don't you share what occupied you in the interim?" she suggested, pausing to purse her lips for a second, "Assuming, of course, that you have nothing to hide. Do you?'' She smiled sweetly and cocked one brow.

*Tenacious little bitch.* He relented a bit, not by choice, but out of trepidation. If he continued acting the ogre, she would write just that. The persona that intrigued an audience might not look so good on paper. ''Look, Miss…?'' As though he didn't recall her name.

''Wainwright. Kathryn Wainwright.''

''Yes, well, Miss Wainwright, I'm very tired right now. Exhausted and really out of sorts. Perhaps another time. If you would, please?'' He gestured toward the open door, not offering to assist her. She'd climbed in by herself; she could jolly well climb out.

She didn't move. ''Shall I call you *Lord* Jonathan? I heard an odd rumor that your late father was a peer. Is that true?''

Jon stiffened and sucked in a deep breath. *Damn.* If she'd managed to unearth that much, what next? She might even stumble on the worst of his secrets. No, not if he kept his wits about him. She knew nothing definite, and was merely fishing. He exhaled with a sigh and gave her his most withering look. ''Chadwick's my name. If you're to call me anything, it must be that.''

''Ah, that's right, you claim the famous Sir Roald of Chadwick as an ancestor, do you not?''

''Yes,'' he answered carefully. Admitting that much couldn't hurt him. He had used it for all it was worth most of his life.

''The noble one who penned all those lovely poems and songs about his liege, the Black Prince? Well, that certainly lends a note of credence to your choice of careers, doesn't it?'' she asked, smug laughter evident in her every word.

Who did this chit think she was to mock his ancestry, even if this part of it was one of *Maman*'s outrageous fabrications? If the old minstrel hadn't been an ancestor of his, then he bloody well should have been.

Jon summoned up all the hauteur he had left for the

evening. "And you are a *Wainwright,* you say? Judging by the origin of *your* name, your ancestor was likely nailing someone's wagons together at the time. Just what are you trying to construct for me, my dear? Perhaps a trundle cart to your paper gallows?"

She gasped in outrage. Her hands flew up in frustration and then slapped angrily against her silk-swathed knees.

He laughed. And he continued to, louder and louder, as she scrambled down from the coach, muttering what sounded vaguely like obscenities. Jon leaned his head out the window and watched as she marched along the street to another coach, parked three back from his own.

When he realized what he had just done, the laughter died a quick death—almost as swift as the fatal blow she would deliver to his career when tomorrow's papers hit the street. "Damn!" he said through clenched teeth, then drew his head back in and knocked it sharply against the back wall of the coach. The driver obviously took that bump for a signal, and the coach started with a jolt.

He had found it impossible to force thoughts of Kathryn Wainwright from his mind on the trip home. Even as he paid the hired coachman and watched him drive away, he had imagined her watching, imagined her wearing that knowing grin. A plaguing fancy, that was all. For the moment, he was safe at Timberoak.

Next time he'd be ready for her, he thought as he climbed the stairs to his room. Next time he would have some cock-and-bull story ready for her. Next time he would charm her knickers off.

He jerked off the stupid wig and gave it a shake. More mindful, he removed his evening clothes and hung them in the armoire. Raking both hands through his damp hair, he leaned over the basin of cold water and soaped off the powder and accumulated sweat.

But the heat inside him did not abate as he replayed the night's events in his mind. Events condensed into images: Kathryn Wainwright absorbing his music from across the crowded room, Kathryn Wainwright leaning forward, her umber eyes wide with questions, Kathryn Wainwright smiling at some inner thought. Images gave way to notes, and the notes to a pervasive melody.

God, there would be no sleep tonight. None. He gave up without a struggle and slowly made his way downstairs, eager despite his exhaustion.

# Chapter Two

**J**on's eyes stung from lack of sleep and the soap he'd used earlier to scrub off the rice powder. He blinked, shook his head, and picked up his pen again to get the notes down before they escaped him. They ran through his head like a string of crystal beads, tinkling against each other, winding around full circle, twisting playfully here and there. They'd been doing that ever since he arrived home.

He stopped scribbling to test their possibilities on the violin. Pleased with the results, he laid the instrument aside. Ink-dotted paper crinkled under his bare legs and feet as he wriggled out a comfortable spot. Stretching out full-length, his head on a threadbare cushion, Jon closed his eyes and let the music in his mind flow through him.

*Last scene. The tenor returns.... Soprano greets him. Ahhh, a lyrical tease, a sly, dark-eyed cat... Dark-eyed?* That woman's face flashed through his mind, likely because she was the last one he'd seen. Jon lifted one hand toward the cracked ceiling plaster and waved in time with the imagined aria. *Sforzando, now. Tenor offers final tribute to his lady. Now up, swiftly, like a cock...pounding, surging, reaching...*

Jon's voice joined in the process, using only pure sounds instead of words, bel canto, now rising in volume to return, almost unrecognizable, to his ears. *Ah, yes...* Slowly, on a burst of feeling that reached a crescendo, Jon rose to a sitting position and lifted the Stradivarius to repeat himself.

Then it came, profound as a lover's cry, powerful as the urge itself, the whole of it sweeping over and through him, ending like the little death. Culmination, climax, ecstasy! *Done!*

He had finished! All but the finale with the entire ensemble, a mere repeat of the overture, with a few adjustments. At last!

Jon spared but a moment to savor the exhilaration, then laid down the violin and located his pen. He scratched madly with the pen, humming with his bottom lip caught between his teeth.

The ink trail crawled left to right in a wavy line, broken by myriad squiggles and curlicues. When it reached the right edge of the paper, it curved down and tracked right to left in a continuous scroll to the bottom of the page. *Jon's code,* as *Maman* had laughingly called it, had developed when he was only five and untutored in the intricacies of the music staff and individual notes. She had quickly taught him to put down the music correctly, but suggested he keep to his own invented method for the first drafts when he wrote. No one could decipher the childish chicken tracks but himself, when he translated them later.

Poking a hole in the paper at the excitement of penning the last sound in his head, Jon sailed the pen across the room and boomed, "Bravo!"

A sharp "Ouch" jerked him off his cloud of euphoria. The shock of reality struck him dumb, and he stared, disbelieving, at the shadows surrounding the old grand piano. Out of the semidarkness crept a small figure nursing an ink-stained cheek.

"How did you know I was there?" she asked, rubbing the spot and smearing the black fluid down the side of her face.

Jon still stared, his mouth open. *Good God, it was her!* For a long moment, he feared he had conjured her up out of his imagination. How the hell had she gotten in? He looked around, seeing the open casement, feeling the cold night air for the first time. The candles in the broken candelabra next to him threw their wavering shadows on the peeling wallpaper.

He looked down in horror. He was sitting on the floor in his short flannel drawers, surrounded by a mountainous tangle of ink-scribbled papers. His lute, an ancient lyre and the Stradivarius lay about like scattered bodies on a battlefield. Frantically he snatched up the violin, worried she might step on it.

Hair tumbled across half his face, several frazzled strands caught on his lips. Jon winced, thinking how wild he must appear in this condition. Sweat from God knew how many hours of work wafted its scent upward from his body. He cringed. What a story this would make. *Nasty, mad musician assaults female reporter with inky nib pen.* He felt sick, and swallowed hard.

"Don't be afraid," she said softly, inching toward him. "I'm a friend. It's all right now. Just be calm." He recoiled as she crouched down and gently touched his bare foot.

Jon made himself meet her eyes. They held no sign of recognition, only compassionate warmth. Well, except for his size, he couldn't possibly bear any resemblance to the man she had watched perform. The dark wig, nothing like his own light hair, was safely tucked in the armoire with his suit. He recalled scrubbing off the itchy powder and shucking his clothes to go to bed. But then the "ladies" had called him downstairs. At the memory, he stroked the Strad's strings—it was his treasure of treasures, his most inventive lady, the most beautiful of his harem.

Maybe the woman thought him an interloper like her. She might take him for a village lad who'd broken into the main house to play with the instruments. Hope flared. He swallowed heavily again and nodded like an imbecile.

"You poor fellow. He keeps you here, doesn't he?" Her voice held a wealth of pity as she patted his ankle.

Jon wiggled his foot, sniffed loudly and looked away. The dust from his hair made him sneeze. So, she thought he was mad. He fully agreed with her.

"You're the one who makes up the music, aren't you? I listened to you singing and playing. It's all right to tell me about it. I know you have to be the one who creates it. No one, even Chadwick, can match what you just did."

What a hypnotic voice she had. And she looked even lovelier than he had realized when he was trying to intimidate her. Her hair, loose from its pins, rippled over her shoulders like a mass of fine gold filament. She had very wide, dark-fringed eyes that reminded him of rich Dutch chocolate. He licked his lips at the thought. The eyes held such pity, though, that it was hard to meet them for any length of time. Her skin gleamed like porcelain, just the right amount of sheen to it. Her small breasts heaved with indignation now—for him, he realized—or at least for who she thought he was.

Jon shook his head to break the spell, but it didn't work very well. When he squeezed his eyes shut, all he could see were the slender curves of her hips and legs in those too-tight breeches as she crouched beside him.

"No need to pretend with me," she said sweetly. "What is your name, dear? Can you tell me your name?"

"Pip," Jon answered reluctantly. It was the first thing that popped into his mind, his father's childhood name for him, one he hadn't heard since he was eight years old.

The woman obviously believed him some sort of idiot, from the way she spoke to him. Small wonder. If he had come upon somebody wallowing in the middle of a cavernous ballroom, dressed—no, undressed—the way he was, and in the throes of a musical stupor, he would have thought so, too.

Oh, God, how was he going to get out of this?

No recourse now but to play out the scenario and hope to hell her sympathy was genuine. First, he had to find out how much she had already uncovered about the public

Chadwick's background. This could be tricky, but the alternative of a full admission would definitely be disastrous.

He plucked idly at the Strad's strings with two fingers. "Where's Jon?" he mumbled.

She looked vastly relieved that he could string two words together. "Gone again," she said. "At least his coach was gone when I got here. The place looked deserted, but then I heard you playing, so I came in."

Ah, so she'd seen the hired conveyance leave, he mused. She'd braved his den believing the bear had left. He wondered for a moment if she might be after more than his life story. The only thing of great value here was his collection of instruments. Only a few knew of his "ladies" and fewer still would know how to go about selling such traceable treasures once they took them. No, she was probably just what she appeared to be, a female writer from a third-rate publication devoted to gossip.

His only hope was to persuade her not to print anything too derogatory. As it stood now, she would either expose him as a horrible pockets-to-let slob with delusions of grandeur, or as a pompous fraud who had enslaved a gifted simpleton and used him to ghostwrite his music. The situation didn't look good, to say the least.

*Play dumb and think.* He drew his knees up and rested his head on them, letting his tousled hair curtain both his face and the violin.

"By chance, is Jon your brother? Your eyes look like his." She explained her assumption with a tender smile. Jon started violently when she touched his head. "Don't!" he muttered, jerking away.

"I won't hurt you, Pip," she crooned. "I can help you."

He faked a shiver. "Go away," he whispered. With feeling.

She responded immediately by scrambling to her feet. He hoped she would take herself on back to London now and let him be. It would be his word against hers if she guessed the truth. He would sue her frilly drawers off if she printed a single word of this.

And he would still be ruined. Jon sighed heavily.

"Don't you worry, Pip. You're coming with me! Come on, get up now. We're going to find you some clothes and get you out of here. Your brother's very wrong to make you stay in this dismal place." She shivered, more with disgust than from a chill. "Aren't you cold? Are you hungry? Did the wretch think to feed you?"

Jon waved toward a discarded rind of cheese and the remainder of the coarse bread loaf Grandy had left for his midnight supper. He kicked at the empty wine bottle peeking from beneath the first page of the overture. "You eat?"

"Oh, you dear thing! You'd share it, wouldn't you?" She sighed and squatted down again to lay her hand over his. He thought he detected tears swimming around those rich brown orbs. "Oh, Pip, how can he do this to you?" she moaned.

"Jonny likes me," he said defensively, thinking a large lie from him was no more damning than allowing her to make up her own. And it *was* a lie. He certainly didn't like himself much at the moment. On second thought, he didn't like himself at all.

She pulled a wry face and sniffed. "No doubt he likes you very well, since you're making a bloody fortune for him. I simply can't believe this, even of someone like him."

Jon felt a small swelling of warmth in his chest at the thought that anyone would really care if he was used and mistreated. Even though she thought him a half-wit, he could tell she meant what she said and wanted to do all she could to right the situation. It had been so long since anyone bothered about his feelings. He couldn't even recall the last time. However, he reminded himself, in this case he was also the villain of the piece.

The whole predicament was so ridiculous, he felt like laughing. Until he remembered his whole career hinged on whether he could keep up the Pip act and retain her sympathy.

Jon needed to get rid of her so that he could think about this. Keeping his thoughts straight was proving difficult. Lack of sleep and that marvelous scent of hers were making him dizzy.

*Lilacs.* The fragrance cut right through the smell of his own sweat and the rancid wax of the cheap candles. Even the odor of the mildewed walls retreated behind it. Heady stuff, in spite of its subtlety, maybe because of it. Way too distracting. It made him want to take her to bed. Now? Ha! She'd love that, wouldn't she! Hell, maybe she would.

"Sleepy?" he asked, blinking up at her stupidly, savoring a wicked inner vision of sharing Kathryn with old Morpheus.

She squatted down very near him and put one of those expressive little hands on his bare shoulder. He felt the heat shoot right through her glove, his skin, and into his bloodstream. God, he was hot. And hard, of all things.

Jon squirmed a little and tried to recall the last time he had bedded a woman. A month? Two? Too long ago, apparently. His appetite never flared up so rapidly as this, at least not since he'd grown old enough to control it. No way to approach her with any kind of proposition now, though, without revealing his identity. He shifted the violin to cover his lap.

"Poor fellow, you look exhausted. Where does he make you sleep?"

Jon let his eyes wander around the chaos of the room and then up. He motioned toward the ceiling.

"Upstairs?" she asked, and took the hand that was still raised to point. "Come on, Pip. I'll just see you settled for the night and come back with my carriage first thing in the morning. You'll like where we're going. All right?" She smiled in a reassuring way and tugged on his hand.

Jon got to his feet rather clumsily; no task to fake, really, considering how long he had gone without sleep. He never got a wink the night before a performance, and tonight's sudden inspiration had kept him from collapsing afterward. It had been at least forty-eight hours since he rested. That, in itself, wasn't unusual. It might not hinder his creativity, but it certainly didn't provide a clear head for dealing with disasters.

He ought not to continue this stupid charade. Even in his current muddled state, he knew it was madness. But, hell, almost everything he did was mad.

His mother, his tutors, his old bodyguard; every one of them had always drummed into him the necessity of thinking before he acted. "Look before you leap" had become a litany. So he'd looked. And usually leapt anyway. The failing persisted, in spite of all their best efforts and his well-intentioned promises.

Jon tugged at the fourth finger of his left hand, a crooked reminder of the impulsive act that had almost destroyed his budding career. He massaged the souvenir of the bloody fistfight that had settled the outcome of the wildest horse race in history.

*Maman* had brought them home to Timberoaks to sell off the paintings and silver. He had been a strapping thirteen then, drunk with freedom in one of those rare, stolen moments away from *Maman*'s watchful eye. His stallion, Satan's Imp, had carried him to a closely-won finish with Bick Wallerford. Old Bick had conceded the race only after Jon broke the fellow's nose with a powerful left hook. An hour or so later, at the sight of his mangled hand, Jon's mother had collapsed. So had his racing ambitions, when she reminded him of his vow to his dying father. That had been when he knew without doubt his father had made a dreadful mistake, demanding that Jon give total obedience to *Maman*. The man couldn't have wanted a son who quailed at a few fisticuffs. Jon had told her as much, and *Maman* reluctantly agreed.

A lad of his size and build—especially one who admitted to being musically inclined—couldn't swear off fighting

even if he wanted to. Fortunately, *Maman* had agreed with
him and hired a strong dockworker as a bodyguard soon
after the incident.

Sato Nagai, a young Japanese expatriate, relished his
new post, anglicized his surname, and became Long San.
Understanding Jon's need to fend for himself and yet protect his hands, Long San had taught him to fight with his
feet. The method of fighting had come easily to Jon. Learning precaution and avoidance of a confrontation had proved
a much harder task, one he wasn't certain he had mastered
even yet.

Judging by his reaction to Kathryn Wainwright and the
threat she posed, he must have regressed farther back than
lesson one in sidestepping a conflict. He sure as hell had a
conflict here. And his well-trained feet weren't going to
help him at all.

Jon laid the Strad and the haphazard stack of music on
the table by the door and led the way upstairs to his bedroom. Stumbling over a broken riser, he grunted his frustration and kicked aside the debris that had fallen or been
dropped on the stairs during the past few years.

"Good Lord, this place is a wreck!" Kathryn muttered,
following in his wake. "I wonder how *he* would like to
have to live in this mess. Poor Pip. Don't you worry, I'll
take care of you."

Jon bit his lip to keep from answering. Through her eyes,
he noticed the state of the master bedroom when they entered. He rarely paid any attention to the squalor, since his
stays were brief and his thoughts glued to his music. The
only things he took care with were the tools of his trade—
his instruments, his one good suit, and the blasted wig.
There was little point in worrying about housekeeping,
since he hadn't the extra cash to hire a cleaning woman.
Tidying things up himself had never occurred to him. Until
now.

The grayed sheets lay in wadded lumps, mingled with
yesterday's discarded clothing. One drape hung askew, rot-

ted half off its sagging, tarnished rod. A mouse scurried off a blackened apple core and into its hole near the ash-heaped fireplace.

"Whew!" She grimaced and turned away toward the door. "You can't possibly stay in here. Is there another room furnished?"

Jon nodded, remembering his mother's chamber. He'd never been welcome there in the best of times. He hadn't touched it, hadn't even opened the door, since she died. Five years ago now? Yes, just before his twentieth birthday.

She patted his shoulder. "It's all right, Pip. Let's have a look at the other room."

He dreaded facing memories he had wanted buried along with his mother, but Jon led her down the hallway to the very end. In front of the dusty oak panel, he stopped.

She brushed past him, opened the door and walked right in. "Oh, much better," she said brightly, and promptly threw open the windows. "Needs to air out, but at least it looks clean."

Her pert nose wrinkled when she approached him, and he knew very well why. He needed a long, soapy soak in a hot tub, but Jon knew he couldn't stay awake for it. His lids drooped over what felt like a spoonful of sand in each eye. "So tired," he exhaled on a sigh, and collapsed on top of the embroidered coverlet of his mother's tester bed. Maybe if he feigned sleep, she would go away.

Jon felt her efficient little hands tuck something around him as he wriggled out a niche in the softness beneath him. A smile of sweet contentment stretched his lower face. He drifted toward sleep with the feel of her lips on his brow, thinking that at this moment, being Pip was better than being Jon.

Infinitely better.

Morning dawned gray and dreary at the Hare's Foot Inn. Autumn had arrived overnight. Chill rain plinked on the roof above Kathryn's head as she drowsed, reluctant to rise just yet.

A sharp staccato of knuckles against the flimsy door roused her fully. Annoyed, she crawled out of bed and dragged the tattered blanket around her like a robe.

"What is it, Thom?" she answered as she padded to the door and swung it open.

"He's gone and it's your fault!" The massive figure of a black-clad Jonathan Chadwick filled the doorway.

"You!" Kathryn blinked sleepily and shrank back from his furious, heavily powdered countenance. "What? Who's gone?"

"Pip, that's who!" he thundered, twisting half away from her and then back again, in a frustrated movement that spoke of violence barely leashed. "You frightened him half to death! What makes you think you can prey on *him* just for the sake of a damned newspaper piece about *me?* It's unconscionable, that's what it is!" He slapped his gloves against a bare palm and pushed past her into the room.

Kathryn exploded, anger bringing her fully alert. "I? *I* preyed on him? Why, you ill-mannered thief! How dare you accuse *me,* when you keep the poor boy locked away in that crumbling excuse for a house and steal every note he writes!" She clenched both fists, releasing her grip on the blanket, but she didn't care. "If I were a man, I'd..."

"But you're certainly not that, now are you?" he said, leaning his head back and raking her with those piercing blue eyes of his. "Not by a very long chalk."

"Don't you try distracting me with your nasty leers," Kathryn warned, well aware that she stood dreadfully exposed in her flimsy knee-length chemise. "If you think I'm going to let you get away with what you're doing to your own brother, you are wrong! Dead wrong!"

Chadwick seemed to drop his anger as if it were a wet cloak. He slumped down on the rumpled bed, shaking his head as he looked up at her. "Pip's not really my brother."

Kathryn scoffed, crossing her arms across her half-bared bosom. "Of course he is. He looks so much like you, it's unreal, except of course for the hair and…" Then it dawned on her what he meant. "Oh, I see. He's your father's bastard, then?"

The dark head inclined, and he stared at her, nodding slightly. "He's a bastard, all right."

Kathryn narrowed her eyes and gave him her sternest look. "You must know what you're doing is wrong, Chadwick."

He sighed soulfully. "Yes, I know." His wonderful hands uncurled, and their long agile fingers lay open in supplication, bearing traces of the powder from his face.

"What would you have me do, Miss Wainwright? Stick him in some crofter's hut to tend the sheep? Bury his music?" She watched him unfold his large body and pace the confines of the room with a catlike grace. He stopped and pinched the bridge of his nose. "Or I could banish him to Bedlam, where he could while away his days in like company. You tell me what I should do."

Kathryn felt confused, thrown by Chadwick's admission of guilt and obvious distress over the dilemma. "At least he ought to receive some credit for his talent," she suggested.

"Ha! Credit, of course. We surely ought to advertise his talents. I could parade him about London, maybe even Paris and Rome. Introduce him as the calf-witted composer, the nimble-fingered numbskull. How do you think he'll do in polite society, Miss Wainwright? Will you applaud him as he drools on the ivories? Perhaps you could stand by with his bonbon rewards and wipe the spittle off his chin."

"Oh, God," Kathryn groaned, clenching her eyes shut as she turned away toward the window. The silence grew, broken only by Chadwick's harsh breathing and the increasing patter of the rain.

"Has he always been…that way?" she asked gently.

"An unfortunate accident," he explained, "and I've

dealt with it the only way I know how. Look, I know you only want to help improve Pip's circumstance, but Timberoak is his home. God knows I can't afford to improve on the old place, but to sell it from under him would be unthinkable. Impossible.'' His voice grew soft and imploring. "Believe me, Miss Wainwright, he's usually quite content there. He needs his forest and the lake. They provide his inspiration, and what precious snatches of peace he can find.''

"Is that where he's gone now, do you think? To his forest?'' she asked, suddenly fearful that she might be the cause of Pip's venturing too far from his haven and into danger.

"That's where he usually goes when he's troubled. When I returned this morning, he told me you planned to take him away today. He ran off to hide from you. He'll probably come home before dark. I apologize for my temper, but you did upset him, and therefore me.''

Then Chadwick did the strangest thing. He rose and offered her his hands and a look of sad entreaty. "Will you please not expose us, Miss Wainwright? I ask this for Pip's sake, as well as my own. We cannot let his music die, and a few words from you in print could slay it outright.''

Kathryn reached out to him in spite of herself, grasping the hands that brought such wonder to the world. Pip's wonder. "What kind of monster do you take me for, Mr. Chadwick?''

"A benevolent one, I hope,'' he answered, with a pale, dimpled smile. His eyes sparkled with light azure fire and wry humor. Her knees turned to pudding when he did that.

Kathryn forced a laugh and squeezed his fingers gently. "I'm no monster at all. And I no longer believe that you are, when you speak so eloquently on Pip's behalf. I believe I've misjudged you, sir, at least this private side of yourself.''

"I do promise to take better care of Pip,'' he offered sincerely. "Rest assured, I shall.''

His gaze grew even more heated as it wandered down the length of her, reminding Kathryn that she stood half-naked, unchaperoned, holding his hands, in the middle of a sleazy bedchamber. What must he think?

"Perhaps you'd better excuse me now, Mr. Chadwick."

"Please call me Jon. I feel we've become friends in the space of our visit. May I call upon you when next I'm in town? Perhaps the interview was not such a bad idea after all."

Kathryn pulled away from the handclasp and backed up a bit to put a decent distance between them. This beguiling charmer was almost as different from the Chadwick she knew as his brother Pip. "I'd be honored. No doubt I'll see you again when I call on Pip. I'll worry till I know he's safe."

Chadwick looked wary, as though he hadn't considered that she would pursue the matter farther than this conversation. "Oh, that's not necessary. Not even wise, under the circumstances. He was so frightened, he'll take a bit of calming down, I expect. Tell you what, I'll send word to your offices when I've found him, so you needn't fret." He reached for the door handle.

Kathryn laid a detaining hand on Jonathan's arm. "I never meant to upset Pip. It's just that when I found him there, so engrossed in his music, practically naked and shivering, all I wanted to do was help. Your resemblance is so remarkable, it was obvious to me you were brothers. I feared you had mistreated him."

"And that I'd stolen his compositions. A natural assumption. I just regret you discovered him in such an embarrassing condition." Chadwick touched his fingers to his temple and sadly shook his head. "The lad simply doesn't know any better. Will you consider, then, not writing about it? Your article could destroy the only outlet for pleasure the poor wretch has. Music is all he knows. All he's able to comprehend." Silvery eyes, so like his unfortunate brother's, pleaded for compassion. His beseeching smile melted her heart, a heart long dedicated to exposing all entertainers for the arrogant, self-centered scoundrels they were.

She offered no definite promise about the exposé, but gave his arm a reassuring squeeze. "Your concern is admirable, Jonathan. You are not at all the man I first thought you to be."

He glanced down at her hand and Kathryn felt the hard muscle flex beneath his carefully tailored coat sleeve. The ice-crystal eyes had darkened a shade when he finally returned her gaze. "Indeed, Miss Wainwright," he said, "I am not."

Kathryn stood idle for a long time after Jonathan Chadwick left, her mind sifting the new information for stones of hard truth. He pretended to be a cocksure genius looking down his gifted nose at the rest of the plebeian world. Instead, he gave his protection to a baseborn, disadvantaged half brother and provided an outlet for the man's creativity.

True, Chadwick performed Pip's music as his own, but what other option had he, other than to ignore it? He benefited greatly by claiming authorship, of course. But where would Pip be without Jon's support? Somewhere cleaner, perhaps, but likely no happier or better off.

Men thought little about their surroundings, as a rule—at least the men she knew did. Ought she to judge it Jonathan's fault if the manor house was a wreck? How much time did he spend there? she wondered. Apparently not enough. He had promised to do better by Pip. She meant to see that he did. The least she could do was ensure that the place was cleaned and sufficient food laid by.

Something about Pip stirred maternal instincts Kathryn hadn't realized she possessed. Children didn't interest her much at this point in her life. But Pip, the overgrown child with a mind full of beautiful sounds, had uncovered something tender in her heart. Something beyond ordinary compassion. She wanted to hold him and protect him against a world she knew could be hostile and cold.

Kathryn began dressing for the trip back to London. As her hands worked the bodice of her dress over her breasts, she suddenly recalled Pip's long-fingered hands, ink-stained and tanned, clutching a violin to his chest, caressing it as tenderly as a lover.

She shoved the errant thought away. Heavens above, what had happened to her propriety and good sense? First she'd gone weak-kneed over Jon Chadwick, a world-weary cynic who probably wallowed in depravity, and now she was lusting after his innocent, younger brother. Pip was just a child, not a man to think of in such a way. He was a large, precious boy in a rather perfect adult body. A body she must learn to overlook, not look over.

Pip needed motherly care and nurturing. The haughty Jonathan Chadwick could hardly be expected to understand that. Men simply were not born to nurture. In his overprivileged, autocratic way, Jon probably did all he knew how or had time to do.

He simply needed help with Pip, Kathryn decided. Her help.

# Chapter Three

Jon spurred his stallion to a lather on the way home, his feelings a jumble of agitation, anger and embarrassment. Riding full tilt failed to calm him as it usually did. Truth told, he felt more like Miss Wainwright's Pip at the moment than he had last night in the ballroom.

He despised the feeling. Trust a woman to twist a man's guts like taffy. Just when he had everything more or less worked out in his life, she had to come along. Now she had tangled him up in a lie that could grow to impossible proportions. Almost worse than that, she had stirred up the lust he needed to have lie dormant. And she threatened his career, all he had left in the world at this point.

At least all he could *claim* as his. His survival as a composer was definitely at stake. If Kathryn Wainwright ever found out he *was* Pip, she'd crucify him in print, if not in deed. His career would stop dead in its tracks. Then he might as well *be* that slowtop bastard writing ditties in his underwear.

*Damn.* He hated that anyone—especially a woman—held that kind of power over him. Female influence ought to stop when a man shucked off his mother's control. But even then, he'd been unable to get out from under that completely. Thanks to the promise he'd made his dying father,

Lady Caroline Chadwick had kept him partially under her thumb right up until the hour she died.

Women wielded guilt, love and old promises like weapons of war. The time had come to erect some defenses, before this new battle got out of hand. He would see Kathryn Wainwright once more, on neutral ground in London, and make it abundantly clear that she was to leave him, and that simple fellow Pip, alone. He would charm her first and, if that didn't work, he would employ a few threats of his own.

Jon lifted Imp's reins, shouted a command and leapt the high stone fence by the brook. Imp sailed over the barrier, landed solidly and jerked to a halt. The mighty Chadwick sailed over his head as though weightless and landed facedown in the mud.

"Ah, hell!" he groaned and rolled to one side, nursing his stone-bruised temple. Immediately he checked his hands for damage. God, he had twenty fingers! He'd cracked his head for certain, to be seeing double like this.

Slowly, carefully, he staggered to his feet and caught up the dragging reins. Imp whinnied and snuffled, nudging for an apology. "All right, then! It was a damn stupid jump. And the next time you dump me, dog meat, I'll sell you to the knackers." He mounted after three tries to find the stirrup with an unsteady foot.

This was the last time, he promised himself as he rode home, the very last time, he would leap before he looked.

With Imp stabled and fed, Jon dragged himself to the back entrance of the house and into the kitchen. This morning's bathwater, now cold as a frog's ass and scummy with soap, stood waiting to be emptied. Without pausing to dread it, Jon peeled off the wig and muddy clothes, draped them over a chair for Grandy to clean later and stepped into the tub.

He submerged his head and came up shuddering. When he cleared his eyes, a long-haired tortoiseshell feline greeted him with a perfunctory growl and an angry green glare.

"Dagnabbit, I just fed you not two hours ago. God knows there's enough four-legged food in the house to keep you busy if you weren't so damned lazy." He slung a spray of water in the cat's direction. "Get out of here or I'll give you a bath. And it's bloody well cold, I can tell you!" Jon rose and grabbed for the still-damp toweling draped over a rickety chair.

When he was mostly dry, he wrapped the length of cloth around his hips and scrabbled through the pie safe, searching for bread and cheese.

"Aha, look, Dag! Grandy's been and left us some grub. Here." He tore off a mouthful of a mutton pasty, swallowed greedily, wolfed another bite and tossed the rest on the bare floor for the cat. The lone bottle of stout was emptied with a few noisy gulps.

His hair dripped, sending chilling rivulets down his chest and back. Taking the stairs two at a time, he dashed to his room and shrugged into his old velvet robe. The ash-coated coals in the fireplace leapt to life when he added kindling and poked them up.

Jon peered warily into his small shaving mirror. At least only one of him stared back. Maybe no concussion, then. He probed the bruise on his head, wincing as he touched it. Ah, well, it could have been worse, he supposed.

He whistled Mozart's "Queen of the Night" aria from *The Magic Flute*, changing a few notes as he went along. While he snuggled into his overstuffed wingback, he looked around the bedroom at the years of dirt and clutter. The Wainwright woman had a point. He ought to take better care of Pip. The thought prompted a lazy smile.

Exhausted and comfortably warm, he drifted into a half-waking dream of a furious Kathryn Wainwright prancing around in her diaphanous little underthing. Sassy little baggage. He could even imagine her scent of lilacs.

A clatter downstairs brought him upright and onto his

feet in an instant. Good God! She was back! He tore downstairs to see what she'd tripped over. God help her if it was one of his ladies. Had he left the Strad on the floor?

As he rounded the corner into the ballroom, a fist connected with his jaw and sent him spinning backward. Hands caught and pinned his arms behind him while a blow to the midsection took his breath away. Gasping he lifted his head and got another fist in the mouth for his trouble.

"Now that I have your attention, Chadwick, let us get down to the business at hand. All your markers are mine. I'll have five thousand pounds or the Stradivarius. Now!"

"Bunrich." Jon spat blood out of his mouth, aiming at the man's feet. "I should have guessed." Jon cursed his luck. Ned Bunrich had approached him several times about buying the Strad. His best guess was that the man had a wealthy client hot to add it to a collection. Fat chance of that. He slumped between the goons holding him and played for time until his head cleared.

The violin in question, his most beautiful lady, lay on the table near the door, where he'd stuck it last night on the way up to bed. The shuffled-up sheets of his opera score camouflaged it, thank God. No one with his wits intact would be expected to treat such a treasure so casually. Scattered amid the pages of music left on the floor lay the antique lyre and his precious lute.

Damn Kathryn Wainwright. Anyone who could make him forget his ladies, even for a moment, was dangerous. He glanced toward the large wall safe where he usually stored them. Standing wide open and empty, just as he had left it.

The two instruments on the floor looked forlorn and helpless. There was no way he would fight the bastards in this room and risk shattering his ladies. Somehow, he had to move the conflict to another place.

If only he'd saved the old violin he had dragged around while on campaign. Perhaps he could have fooled Bunrich with a switch. Suddenly a plan formed. Not a perfect plan, but with a bit of luck, it could buy him time to raise the money.

He coughed and spat again. "You're too late, Bunrich. I pawned it months ago."

Bunrich growled and drew back to hit him again. "This will flatten that pretty nose, fancy boy." He hesitated. "Unless you want to give me the pawn chip."

"All right." Jon heaved and nodded frantically. "Let me go, and I'll get it. Just don't break my nose." He felt the hands on his arms relax and drop away. As soon as he could straighten himself, he staggered to the door, the assistant "collectors" at either side and Bunrich just behind him.

Maybe a fight wouldn't be necessary after all, he thought as they cleared the ballroom. The outcome of one might not be favorable, anyway, since he could see a blurry six of them, when he knew very well there were only three. His head pounded, and several of his ribs felt cracked. Given that, Jon wasn't altogether certain how high he could kick.

Entering the study, he strode to the only piece of furniture left in the room, a large cherry desk he had kept because it once belonged to his father. Retrieving a wrinkled pawn ticket from the right-hand drawer, he held it out, faking a frown of regret as Bunrich snatched it up and read it.

"You idiot! You pawned the thing for two hundred pounds? Are you mad? And in Edinburgh, of all places!"

Jon shrugged painfully and fingered the cut just inside his bottom lip. "Needed the blunt."

Bunrich hissed through his teeth and clenched the paper in his fist, shaking it under Jon's nose. "You'll still owe me whatever it takes to get it out of hock. Plus travel expenses. I'll be back, Chadwick. Depend on it." Jon nodded as Bunrich turned to leave.

When the sound of hooves faded away, Jon sank to the floor and lay there groaning. Jesus, life was getting too complicated First, Kathryn Wainwright's poison pen threatened his livelihood, and now *Maman*'s creditors were beating down the door. Not to mention her son.

Best he could recall without checking accounts, he thought he owed Ned Bunrich a bit less than three hundred quid after last month's payment. *Maman* had owed the man less than she did the others. He'd offered to purchase the Stradivarius outright, less the amount of Jon's debt. Now he had gotten altogether too serious. Maybe Bunrich Antiquities's business depended on whether old Ned could produce the Strad. Well, the bloody Thames would dry up before Jon let him have it. If Bunrich had bought up all the other markers now, Jon would simply have to find the money somewhere to pay him in full.

He turned his head to one side. The desk could go next, he supposed. Then maybe the little harp. She was a scaled-down child's instrument, designed for his fifth birthday, virtually useless for present purposes and valuable only because she was unique. But how could he part with her? He couldn't. Not on pain of death. Rising on one elbow and gasping with agony, he rapidly reconsidered. Well, *maybe* on pain of death. He lay back down, drawing shallow breaths to ease his ribs.

Jon figured he should have at least ten days until Bunrich found the obscure little pawnshop, got the fake Strad appraised and returned. Maybe, with luck and bad weather, a fortnight. What would happen then was anybody's guess, but the options were not that hard to imagine.

From the amount demanded, Jon knew Bunrich must have bought up every one of *Maman*'s debts, and he could bring the law with him next time he came to collect. That could mean debtor's prison or transportation, but the greedy toad would get nothing for his trouble but the satisfaction of seeing the mighty Chadwick brought low. Somehow, Jon didn't think Bunrich would bring the law. He wanted the Stradivarius too badly to settle for revenge on a reluctant seller. In that case, Jon knew a broken nose might be the very best he could hope for.

Within ten days, he had to amass five thousand pounds and a bit extra for Bunrich's trouble, or face music not of his making. Not a pretty tune to dance to, either.

Few knew that the house was entailed. He couldn't have sold it even if he wanted to. If Jon produced no heir in his lifetime, the property would revert to the Crown. As if Queen Victoria would want the damned thing, in the condition it was in.

He doubted anyone knew he held the Lyham title, either. *Maman*, in her dubious wisdom, decided to let it rest with her elder son, Edward, who lay in an unmarked grave in America. An earl, even an impoverished one like Jon, didn't make his living playing in parlors and concert halls around the globe. *Maman* had known society would never condone a titled gentleman taking money for his talents. But a second son made his way as best he could, and more power to him. So, when they received word of brother Edward's death in Charleston eight years ago, the news had remained a closely guarded secret. Anyone who cared enough to inquire would think the earl was still adventuring abroad, squandering what was left of the Lyham wealth.

There never had been much of it, and what little there was, Edward had spent long before he died. *Maman* had taken every farthing Jon made from performing and tried to increase it the only way she knew how. Only she hadn't known how very well at all. It amazed him still, how deeply mired she had gotten them. Some days he despaired of ever reaching solvency.

Now, nearing the age of twenty-five, Jon owned a broken-down manor house he couldn't sell, an aging stallion nobody in his right mind would try to ride, a collection of instruments he'd rather die than part with and a tortoiseshell cat too stupid to chase mice. Oh, and the mountain of gambling debts, he added with a grimace of pain. Mustn't forget *Maman*'s debts. His wonderful inheritance.

Success with the opera he'd just finished seemed his only hope for survival. And, hell, he didn't even like opera all that much. The libretto he'd concocted was trite—idiotic drivel about thwarted love and such—but then, that was the expected thing. The recitative stank like rotten eggs. The music, however, was magnificent, if he did say so himself, the episodic fugue in the second act, truly inspired. No point entertaining any false modesty there. If he could do nothing else—and he had fairly well proved that true—he *could* damn well compose.

If only someone else could promote the cursed thing. God knew he suffered the agony of the damned every time he forced himself to a keyboard in public, every time he lifted a bow to the strings. This knock on the head and a few cracked ribs seemed nothing compared to it. Not that had much choice in the matter.

Well, he thought as he ran a tentative hand over his injuries, he had been thoroughly trained in one other thing. But killing people—in legal battle or otherwise—didn't seem a viable alternative. England had no real war at present, and life as an assassin certainly held no appeal. If he were inclined that way—and he almost wished he were—he might have started with Ned Bunrich. Hell might well be his destination eventually, but he didn't intend to pave his way with any more bodies if he could avoid it. He'd left enough of those on battlefields in Africa. Stage fright ran a distant second to the sleep terrors he had endured after wielding his weapons at Abu-Klea and Khartoum.

He had to get the damned opera produced somehow, even if that meant playing it for every backer in London and on the Continent. The time had come to admit his limitations; without the music, he was nothing. Nobody. A shell of a man, full of imposing sounds. And a load of guilt for what he'd almost become, the one time in his life he tried to abandon the curse for a soldier's life. With another groan, he tried to roll over.

"Jon? Are you there? Pip?" The door knocker echoed only twice through the hall before he heard her shoes clicking on the tiles.

"Oh, Jesus Christ in a manger, this is all I need!" he moaned, and curled his knees to his chest, hoping to God he would go ahead and die before she found him.

Her sudden scream he could have done very nicely without. It scraped over his brain like sharp fingernails. The flurry of silk skirts over his naked legs, and the enveloping scent of her, almost made up for it.

Well, hell, he ought to get some small pleasure out of today, whether it be the whisper of silk ruffles on his skin or a laugh at her expense. The little wretch wanted to spend her sympathy? Why not let her, then? A private joke on her was better than dwelling on his misery.

He opened one eye and peered up at her through a wild tangle of sun-streaked hair. "Hurt," he said, enjoying the tears that sprang to her eyes. Lord, he wished he deserved them.

"Oh, your poor face! Who did this to you, Pip? I'll send Thomas for the constable right now! Did Jon hit you?" She touched two gloved fingers to his swollen temple.

He jerked away. "I fell down." God's truth, several times, he thought with a wince.

Her face softened, and she pulled off her gloves, tossing them aside. "Can you get up, dear? Come, I'll help you. We should get you up to bed so I can tend you."

Jon sat up, holding his side and trying to keep his robe together at the same time. He felt torn between wanting to send her packing and needing sympathy from any quarter where he could get it. So far, it had not been a good day. The need for sympathy prevailed.

When they had struggled up the stairs, she turned him automatically toward his mother's old room. No sooner had she seen him stretched out on the unmade bed than she began to tug at the neck of his robe. He was bared to the waist before he could yell, "Stop!" He clutched the fabric close.

"Don't be silly, Pip. You're hurt, and I need to see where, so I can help you."

"Bad! You can't see that part." She'd better not see that part, he thought, or she'd get the shock of her life. Those gentle hands touching his waist, her firm little shoulders beneath his arm on the way upstairs, had wreaked havoc on the lower part of his anatomy, in spite of the headache and pain in his side. He felt fit to burst.

The sight of his erection would definitely get her out of here, but he wasn't at all sure he wanted her to go just yet. The longer she stayed, the more he pretended with her, the worse it would be if she found him out. He knew that.

He also knew that some part of him—the Pip part, maybe—needed her softness. Acting the village idiot was a small price to pay for something he'd always craved and rarely found. Sex was easy enough to get, if he wanted it. Sometimes he had even run from it, when the supply exceeded his demand. But real caring was scarce as summer snow.

Surely he could risk acting the part she'd presented him with for a little while. Just long enough to grab a bit of solace. Comfort was all he would take from her, he decided firmly, no matter how she fired his loins. He could be noble if he tried, even if he hadn't been trained to it.

"Will you tell me where it hurts you, Pip? Just point to the places, and Kathryn will make them better."

*Oh God, I wish!* he thought, and rolled his eyes. "Here," he said, pointing to his temple and his mouth. There was nothing to be done for the ribs, and he doubted very much she'd be willing to ease the other, lower part that was aching like the devil.

"Are ye up there?" a too-familiar voice called up the stairs. The voice of doom, Jon thought with a clenching in his gut. Grandy *would* show up now, of all times. He could *never* find the blasted woman when he needed her. Now she'd ruin everything.

"In here," Kathryn sang out. "Hurry, Pip's been injured."

A thud of heavy footsteps promised the death knell of

his hopes. He watched with a fatalistic languor as Grandy's pudding face peeped around the doorframe. "What is it, lad? Who's this woman wi' ye?"

Good, she hadn't called him by name yet. Jon thought he might as well go for broke. He stretched out his arms and groaned, "Grandy, Grandy, I fell down!"

"And dropped yer pie all over th' floor, too, ye clumsy oaf. I near slid down in it. Ye know I canna see worth beans."

Kathryn's mouth dropped as she rounded on Grandy, shoulders squared in a militant manner. "Now you see here…"

Jon grasped her elbow and gave it several yanks. "The ladies! I want my *ladies!*" There, that distracted her. And it wasn't a bad idea to have them up here where they'd be safe.

"Ladies?" Kathryn asked, thoroughly confused, as he had known she would be. Jon widened his eyes, trying his best to look innocent, as he met Grandy's curious gaze.

"He's meanin' th' fiddle and 'is other dulcies," Grandy said to Kathryn. Then her pudgy finger pointed at him. "Ye'll have to go find 'em yerself, rascal. God only kens where ye left 'em layin' this time."

He gave Kathryn a piteous look and whispered, "Please."

She patted his hand tenderly and squeezed it. "Of course. I'll go find them for you. Lie back and rest now."

"Don't fall down," he added as she started for the door.

As soon as he heard the stairs creaking, he beckoned Grandy closer. "She doesn't know I'm Jon, and you'd better not muck me up here, old woman. Do you understand?"

Grandy snorted. "I ain't helpin' ye trick no gel into yer bed, Jonny."

She had not been a decent nursemaid when she really was one, and he certainly didn't need her services. He held on to her faded sleeve. "That's not it, Grandy, I promise. Now listen to me carefully. Bunrich has bought up *Ma-*

*man*'s markers, and if I don't come up to scratch in a week or so, I'm cooked. This Wainwright woman writes for the newspaper, and if she learns Jonathan Chadwick is up to his ears in gambling debts, it will be all over London with her next column. There won't be any more concerts, for the nobs or anybody else. No patrons for the opera, either. Neither of us will *eat,* do you understand? If I can turn her up sweet on Pip, she won't go after Jon.''

"What's all th' *Pip* business, then?'' she asked, rubbing her bulbous nose with a callused forefinger.

"I told her that's my name. Can't you imagine what a joke all of London would make of it should she describe Chadwick looking like an overgrown pig boy? She thinks I'm Jon's dim-witted brother, and she feels sorry for me. As long as she believes I'm Pip, she won't write anything bad about me—us. Just bring the meals and see you don't give me away, or I'll have your hide. And then you'll starve!''

"Don't ye threaten me, ye wee turd. I'll pin yer ears back to yer head wi' roofin' nails!'' She gave his hair a tug for emphasis.

"All right, *please,* then. C'mon, Grandy, help me out here.''

"What about this Bunrich? He th' one what kicked ye around today?'' Grandy asked, poking roughly at his head.

Jon winced as he endured her prodding. "Uh-huh. I'll have to worry about him after I get her out of here. Shhh, now, she's coming. Mind your mouth.''

Kathryn sailed into the room, her arms full of his musical instruments. "Here are your ladies, Pip!'' Carefully she laid each one on the bed beside him. "Now lie back like a good boy and let Kathryn see to your hurts. Mrs. Grandy, would you heat some water and bring it up? Also, he'll need a towel and some soap, if you have it....''

"Humph, no chance o' that. Canna see t' take th' stairs totin' nothing. He'll live.''

Jon watched Grandy shuffle out of the room with her

usual rolling gracelessness. "Bye, Gran," he said, as lovingly as if he were her very favorite grandchild. He ought, by rights, to go trip her on the top step, the fractious old wart.

At least she wouldn't give him away. Grandy's instinct for survival surpassed even his own. And, deep down in that mass she called a body, Jon suspected she had a heart.

"She's a mean old woman!" Kathryn said, brushing his hair back out of his eyes. "You rest a bit and I'll go get something to wash you up."

"Kathryn?" Jon said, grabbing her hand in both of his. Her tender smile nearly stopped his heart. He had to close his eyes against it so that he could think of something to say.

When he opened them, they felt unfocused, rolled around like marbles in a bowl. Maybe he did have a concussion after all. It wouldn't do to have her here after he gave in to sleep. He had to get rid of her now. Discounting the secrets she might unearth by snooping around the house, there was always a chance Bunrich would begin to suspect the trick Jon had planned. He might come back and finish what he had started.

"Go get Jon," he said. "Please?" He knew that was the only way he would get her out of the house.

"Where is he?" she whispered, leaning over him to examine the lump on his head more closely. Her soft palm slid down to the uninjured portion of his face and rested lightly against his left cheek.

Jon breathed in her scent, hoping to hold it until he could fall asleep and dream.

"Town," he answered. His need for sleep battled with his reluctance to make her leave. "Go to town."

"Will you be all right until he gets here?"

"Um-hmm. So tired," he mumbled, and turned away from her.

Ten minutes later, Jon relaxed for the first time since entering her room at the inn that morning. The sound of her carriage wheels crunching down the driveway provided much-needed relief. And a surprising sadness.

Why did he yearn so for her to stay, when he knew it was impossible? The woman could wreck his life, for pity's sake. He ran a tentative finger over the swelling at his temple. That fall on his head must have left a severe dent in his brain. It had definitely mangled the section dedicated to self-preservation. Too bad it hadn't numbed the region that ruled his nether parts.

He wanted her. Craved her. Not like the tasting of a sweet roll or a snifter of fine brandy. More like drawing his next breath. *Damn.*

But would he be satisfied by a mere tossing-up of her skirts, if and when she ever allowed it? He let his fingers drift down the side of his face, where she had last touched him.

Probably not.

# Chapter Four

Kathryn set aside her lap desk, glanced out the window of her second-story room and wondered again how poor Pip was getting on today. She didn't think he had been seriously injured, but Chadwick surely would want to know about it.

She had left word with the landlady at Jonathan's rooms the moment she arrived in town the day before. Since midmorning she had searched for him. She'd sent Thom to the servants' entrances of the gentlemen's clubs with questions, and contacted everyone Chadwick had performed for in the past few weeks. By midafternoon, Kathryn had decided to give it up and come back to Uncle Rupert's. Either no one had seen Jon or they were helping him avoid her.

Perhaps she should have mentioned the reason she wanted to find him in the inquiries she made. Even then, everyone would probably believe she was only after a story for the paper. Her "secret" occupation was hardly a true secret.

Working did nothing to alleviate her worries. The article on Chadwick was a futile effort, anyway. All the way back to London yesterday, she had thought of little else. Aside from his obnoxious public arrogance, she had found nothing derogatory to write about. Of course, she could expose his secret about using Pip's music. That, coupled with his nose-thumbing superiority, would have everyone believing him as reprehensible as she had at first. Such a story would set London on its collective ear. But it would destroy Jonathan, and probably Pip, as well.

She laid the pen aside and crumpled the paper in her fist.

Where the devil had Jon gotten to, anyway? She had turned the city upside down, and he was nowhere to be found. As far as she could discern, he wasn't performing anywhere in town tonight. Kathryn thought again of poor Pip, wounded and waiting in that sorry excuse for a home, with no one but that crotchety old crone to look after him. She had half a mind to go back there tonight and make certain he didn't go hungry. If there was no word from Jonathan Chadwick, she'd go first thing in the morning, she promised herself.

Right now, she had problems enough of her own to face. Uncle Rupert would fly into a rage when she told him she had decided not to make Chadwick her subject for the week.

If only she could beg off doing the column for two months, she wouldn't have to write anything about anyone. She would be twenty-five and financially independent. Well, just how independent remained to be seen. But however much she received from her inheritance must suffice. Maybe she should be grateful to Uncle Rupert, but living under his thumb was becoming increasingly intolerable. There were times when she thought him a bit unbalanced, especially when he nagged her so about the articles. Chadwick did not seem to warrant ruining, as the others had.

In the beginning, she had reveled in the chance to knock some entertainer off his golden perch. If only she hadn't done the exposé on Thackery Osgood six months ago, she wouldn't be in this mess. The wretch had ruined three young singers fresh off the farm. Three in a row! Those poor girls hadn't had a clue what the lecherous old sot was up to when he offered them parts in his musicale. Promises of fame and riches had turned to shame and degradation

within days of their respective arrivals. Luckily—or maybe
not so luckily, given her present predicament—Kathryn had
virtually stumbled on one of the unfortunates, a vicar's
daughter, trying to throw herself into the Thames. Osgood's
admirers had nearly lynched him from the theater marquee
after Kathryn's column revealing what he had done appeared. She couldn't regret having a hand in that. Hanging
was too good for the bastard.

Then there had been Theodosia Lark. *Lark,* indeed! Sang
more like a goose with a bad throat, Kathryn thought. The
woman had abandoned her own children, infant twins, on
the steps of a local orphanage just so that she could resume
her career unencumbered. Lark's return to the stage had
lasted only until the next edition of *About Town.* The pathos
Kathryn injected into the piece about the babies had inspired their subsequent adoption by a wealthy merchant's
family. Now the singing doxy had neither career nor motherhood to worry about. Public outrage had forced her retirement.

Other scandals had followed, dutifully penned by her alter ego, K. M. Wainwright. Kathryn knew that targeting
entertainers had everything to do with her own mother's
profession. Maria Soliana's operatic career flourished even
today, but Italy's darling had better not dare a return to
London. Father had never quite recovered from his wife's
abandonment. Kathryn had adjusted to being motherless,
but it had left her bitter. How could any mother put her
career before her own child? No, Kathryn didn't regret
dashing Theodosia Lark's career. Not for a moment.

Kathryn knew there were good and talented people in
the business, but most of them were self-centered and uncaring. What began as a small crusade against the worst
evils of the stage had simply gotten out of hand. She
thought perhaps she had run out of truly ignominious in-
dividuals. Uncle Rupert would have to find himself another
writer with a grudge. Hers had spent itself, at least for the
present.

He could threaten all he liked, but Kathryn didn't really believe her own uncle would set her out on the street without a farthing. And if he still intended to thrust her into a marriage with that pompous Randall Nelson, he could jolly well think again.

With her shoulders squared and her mouth firmly set, Kathryn went down the stairs to confront him with her resignation.

When she stopped on the first floor landing to brush out the wrinkles in her skirt and bolster her flagging courage, Randall's voice drifted up from the open door of Uncle Rupert's study. His words were indistinct, but his tone sounded angry. The fact that he was here wasn't out of the ordinary. He owned a part interest in the paper and he and Uncle Rupert had been friends for years, despite the difference in their ages. This was no ordinary conversation between chums, however. Kathryn had been a reporter just long enough to heed her instincts. Quietly she descended just far enough downstairs to overhear without being seen.

"You ought to keep a tighter rein on her, Rupert," Randall said. "I don't like the idea of her haring off about town unescorted. Her reputation's already in shreds since you let it be known she's the one doing those columns in the paper."

Rupert laughed; it was a nasty sound. "Hey, you can't blame me for taking full advantage of her talents, now can you? She's good at what she does—subscriptions have doubled! And you won't mind all that talk when you get your hands on her inheritance, will you? Not every day a man comes into a fortune like that. Eighty thousand pounds can sugarcoat the foulest little pill, can't it?"

"Eighty thousand? But that's only half! You said a sixty-forty split in my favor, Rupert."

Kathryn grasped the stair rail. Her knees wobbled so violently she thought she would collapse right there, in a heap. *One hundred and sixty thousand pounds!* Never in her wildest dreams had she imagined her father had accrued so much in his lifetime! Ten or fifteen thousand at most, she had figured. She was a bloody heiress! She could live forever on that amount. Like a queen! Drawing in a shaky breath, she made herself listen further.

"What if she refuses? We only have two months left to convince her, and so far she hasn't given me a speck of encouragement," Randall complained. "She won't marry me."

"Don't you worry about it, my boy. A little laudanum in her wine will do the trick. I've got the parson in my pocket already. Old Tim Notchworthy's not above a hefty bribe. We'll have this marriage sewn up right and tight in a few days. All we need do is keep her groggy afterwards. Ain't that unusual for women these days to fall slave to the opiates."

Kathryn heard the clink of glasses. Good God, they planned to drug her, concoct a sham of a marriage and take over her inheritance? Her own uncle, for heaven's sake!

Outrage overcame her shock, but, fortunately, not her prudence. Confronting them with their heinous knavery could be dangerous. With a quick shake of fury, she crept back upstairs to her room and stuffed a few clothes in a small carpetbag. Obviously, Uncle Rupert hadn't heard her come home this evening. If she hurried, she could be away again before he knew she had ever returned. But where could she go that he or Randall wouldn't find her and drag her back to complete their plans?

She had no close friends living near London, and no funds with which to travel far. Tearing open her reticule, Kathryn counted her money. The pittance Uncle gave her for fripperies wouldn't hire fare to the next county. Taking Thomas and the carriage back out would draw attention. She would have to ride. With an angry sigh, she tore off her day dress and donned her sturdy blue riding habit.

With all the stealth of a practiced thief, Kathryn stole down the servants' stairs and made a dash for the stables. Thomas was nowhere about, thank God. Not that he'd ever tell, but Uncle might dismiss him if he thought they had conspired in her getaway. Her stout little mare whinnied a greeting.

"You're about to become a racehorse, Mabel," Kathryn said as she struggled with the sidesaddle. "And God help me, you'd better go the distance!"

A plan began to gel as she threaded Mabel through the back streets at a steady clip. She would call in a favor, or resort to blackmail, if necessary, but Jonathan Chadwick was going to be her savior, one way or another. He was the only one she knew with a great place to hide. If no one had discovered Pip in all this time, no one would be able to find her, either.

Jon exited the lane onto the main road, carefully keeping Imp to a walk. Wouldn't do to arrive at the Turkingtons' affair covered with road dust and sweat. As it was, he would probably smell of horse, but there was no help for it. He hadn't been able to scratch up enough to hire the coach this time. Perhaps his smell would keep the female leeches at a distance. He resisted the urge to wipe his forehead. Already the powder was beading up there and threatening to run down his face in rivulets.

A rider approached and stiffened in the saddle as he watched. The woman sped to a canter, and he recognized her, even at a distance. Kathryn Wainwright.

"Chadwick?" she called, reining to a halt several lengths away. "Thank God it's you. I need your help!"

He dismounted and strode over to assist her down. She pushed herself away from him and brushed tousled blond ringlets out of her eyes with the back of her hand. He wondered if she knew how fetching she looked in her disarray.

"If it isn't Miss Wainwright! To what do I owe the pleasure?" Jon inclined his head in a mocking bow.

She drew in an unsteady breath and looked at her feet. Even in the fading light of sundown, he noticed the fierce blush on her cheeks. "I really need your help."

"So you've said. My wish is your command, of course, but I'm in rather a hurry. An engagement, you see." He took her hand and felt it trembling. "Come now, speak up. I haven't got all night."

Her hand turned palm up to grasp his in a death grip. "Let me hide in your house, sir! Please!" She rushed on before he could think what to say. "If you will, I won't write a word about you. Ever. My oath on it. Just let me stay for two months. I can look after Pip for you, cook, clean, whatever. Please say I may!" Her other hand joined the first and worked frantically over the stretch of his ostrich-skin gloves. "I will pay you, too. Soon I'll have lots of money and I'll pay you well."

Jon looked down into the wide, teary eyes. They darkened to near black. Deep, rich chocolate. Her brow furrowed and her lips trembled as she waited for his response.

While nothing in the world would have pleased him more than holing up in his house with this spicy little morsel, Jon knew he couldn't allow himself that. How could he explain Pip's absence? Even if he could concoct an explanation, Grandy wouldn't keep her mouth shut. She'd give away the whole ruse, and Kathryn would have the story of his life. So would all of London. "That's not such a good idea, Miss Wainwright."

Her face crumpled. Two giant tears trickled down her cheeks and dripped off her chin before she got herself in hand. He led her over to a large boulder just off the road and settled himself beside her. "Now then, why don't you tell me what's prompted this unseemly suggestion of yours?"

Kathryn cleared her throat. She drew her hands away from his and smoothed them over her corseted waist. "My uncle plans to marry me off to his wretch of a partner. They want my inheritance, and I don't mean to let them have it."

"Inheritance?" Jon hoped his greed didn't show. Not greed, he reminded himself. It was need that prompted his interest. Need, and his healthy sense of self-preservation. "They cannot make you wed if you refuse to."

"Yes! Yes, they can! I overhead them planning to drug me and bribe some minister to perform the deed. Oh, please, Mr. Chadwick, you have to help me!" Her breath shuddered out, and he feared she was about to begin weeping in earnest.

"Your own uncle is party to this scheme? It must take a frightful amount of money to inspire that sort of thing," Jon said, probing none too tactfully.

She didn't seem to notice his lack of subtlety. "One hundred sixty thousand pounds!"

Jon's mouth dropped open. "Good Lord! I'll marry you myself!"

Her wits seemed linked to her anger. At least they both returned to her at the same time. "Ha! What makes you think I'd let you get your long-fingered paws on my money, when I just ran away to prevent such a thing?" She stood up and paced furiously back and forth in front of him, twisting her fingers and shaking her head.

He hadn't really believed she would entertain his half-baked proposal, but perhaps it wouldn't hurt to push a little further when the time was right. For now, he would be the helpful friend. "Well, then, it seems to me you should simply take your fortune and make yourself scarce," he suggested amiably.

"No, I can't do that," she declared. "Father left it in trust to me, and I can't touch it until I'm twenty-five. He didn't trust me to manage it until I'd passed my youth. Not even then, if you want the truth. He thought I needed a husband, of course."

Jon smiled. He wanted to jump up and down. "Then take a husband you can manage, sweetheart. I promise I'll be the soul of cooperation. You call the tune, and I'll play it. What say?"

She stopped pacing abruptly and faced him. A light came on in her eyes, turning them almost amber. An unsteady little laugh escaped, and she clapped her hands. "Genius! I knew you were a genius, Jon Chadwick!"

"So you're proposing to me now? I accept!" He laughed, too, amazed at how easily he had solved both their problems.

"Dream away, Chadwick," she said smoothly, and raised that square little chin of hers. "You're going to arrange a marriage for me, all right, but not with yourself. I'm going to marry Pip."

His speechlessness lasted for five whole seconds. "Over my dead body!"

"What's your objection?" she asked. "I could look after him for you while you're away performing. It wouldn't be a marriage in the real sense, of course. I understand that he has a child's mind." Her face grew earnest. "I do feel affection for him, Jon. He would never want for anything, I promise. You must know I'd never take advantage of his..." She faltered and dropped her head.

"His idiocy?" Jon finished, with a dark look. He felt a sharp pang of guilt for what he was about to do, but he had learned long ago to grab an advantage wherever and whenever it presented itself. This one had virtually fallen into his lap and screamed, *Take me!*

"Please, Jon," she implored, resting a hand on his arm. "If you have one scrap of compassion in that black soul of yours, do this for me."

He sighed. "All right, Kathryn. I'll do it, but I want something for my trouble."

"Anything!" she promised, and then obviously thought better of the offer. "What?"

"Six thousand pounds," he stated baldly.

Kathryn's mouth worked soundlessly. She looked irate.

Jon tried to explain, "It's not so mercenary as it sounds. I'll never ask you for another groat, and I'll pay you back with interest before year's end. Five percent. My word on it."

She looked doubtful, considered in silence for a few moments. "Eight percent," she countered.

"Six."

She bobbed her head once. "Done."

Jon held out his hand, and she gave it a firm shake. He tried to disregard the disappointment in her eyes.

"Come with me," he said. "I've a friend in Lakesend who'll perform the ceremony without the banns. He owes me a favor. It's probably best if I stand proxy for Pip."

Kathryn hesitated, tugging her hand away from his and remaining where she stood for the moment. "Well, I suppose that would do. Are you certain that will be legal?"

"Binding as a hangman's noose. Sure you really want to do this, Kathryn? Pip's not exactly every lass's dream come true."

"I think it's the only solution," she said with a sigh.

"We'd best get on with it, then," he said, ushering her toward her mare and providing a boost up. "If we hurry the ceremony, I can still make the Turkingtons' do by nine o'clock, and you can put your bridegroom to bed by ten. Let's ride."

All the way to Lakesend Jon watched her with a wary eye. She could call the whole thing off at any second. He prayed. He promised whatever gods were watching that he would make this up to her. He would face her wrath when she discovered what he had done, and give her her freedom whenever she asked for it. And, in the meantime, Pip would be the most docile, undemanding husband any woman ever had. No, Kathryn would never suffer because of this night's events. She would be saved from the machinations of that avaricious uncle, and Jon could pay off Bunrich. A perfect scheme.

Kathryn was right. This was the only way.

Darkness had fallen and the full moon risen by the time they arrived. "You wait outside and let me talk to the vicar first," Jon suggested as they reached the outskirts of the village. The old stone chapel snuggled comfortably at the edge of Lakesend Common. Unthreatening moon shadows bathed the churchyard that flanked the parsonage. A weak light shone through the window signaling the presence of Reverend Carl Lockhart. Thank God Carl was home tonight. Jon thought it a good omen.

He dismounted and looped his reins over the spiky wrought-iron fence. "I'll be back in a few moments," he promised with a pat on her knee.

Lockhart answered immediately, and after a perfunctory greeting, Jon stated his case. "Carl, I need a hasty wedding performed. The lady outside doesn't know she's to be a countess, and I'd as soon you didn't make any reference to it. For my sake, just do the pretty and say only what's necessary, will you?"

Duplicity didn't sit well with the good reverend. "I don't know, Jonathan. Doesn't seem right, somehow."

*If you only knew,* Jon thought with a grimace. He lounged negligently on the corner of the parson's desk. "Why? She needn't know just yet about my title. She's perfectly willing to marry me thinking I'm Nathan Chadwick Lyham, a simple musician. If she knew the rest, she'd balk. Her attitude toward the nobility could make this marriage impossible, and then I'd be done right out of my heir. The chit has no notion how difficult it would be to rear a bastard. Her parents will throw her out. No telling what she might do then. Best we marry and have done with it. I promise I will tell her the rest when the time's right."

The vicar shot him a suspicious look and began to shake his head.

Jon held up a gloved hand to forestall any denial. "Bear with me on this, Carl. We were fast friends as children. Still are, eh? Didn't I see that Edward gave you the living here when your father died?"

Lockhart snorted. "Such as it is. You're a sporadic landlord, at best. Better than Edward was, but still..."

Jon brightened. "Well, you've the best music in three

counties, haven't you? Draws 'em in like flies. We'll build that school of yours by next summer, too. Things are looking up.''

''Sounds like bribery, milord,'' Lockhart replied with an infectious grin.

''We always did understand each other, Carl,'' Jon said. ''You fix the papers. I'll get the bride.'' He turned on the way out. ''Don't mention the child. She's dreadfully embarrassed about it.'' Again he paused. ''And thank you, friend. I won't forget this.''

Kathryn took the whole thing rather well, Jon thought with relief. The words were said in a rush, witnessed by Carl's sleepy housekeeper and the resident gravedigger. Jon punctuated the ceremony with a brief kiss he dared not prolong.

The taste of her soft lips lingered in his mind as he handed her the pen to sign her name on the church register. When she had done so, he handed her the marriage lines. She pored over the document for a moment and then scratched her name with a flourish.

Her eyes rested on his hand as he boldly wrote *J. Nathan Chadwick,* dropped down a space and wrote *Lyham* a little to the right. He handed her the paper. She looked at him then, with a helpless little smile, as though she'd only just realized what Pip's real name was. No mistake there, Jon thought with a wry twist of his lips, only a few letters missing. A lie of omission.

He waited until Carl drew her away to congratulate her and then turned back to the church register. *Jonathan Chadwick, Fifth Earl of Lyham,* he wrote clearly beneath Kathryn's signature and quickly closed the book.

God help him, it was done. He had wed Kathryn Wainwright for her wealth, an act of desperation and wicked deception. Hell was too good for him, but at least he had postponed that destination for a while. Ah, well, he'd march along the path of survival, as out of step as ever, and hope one day to find the rhythm that always eluded him. This was only another stumble.

"We must away now, Reverend. Our thanks to you," Jon said with a nod to the housekeeper and the gravedigger. "Come, my dear, and leave these good people to their rest."

Kathryn laid her hand on his arm and preceded him through the door. "What now?" she asked as they reached their mounts. She placed her tiny boot in his hand and let him boost her up.

"I'll ride back with you as far as the Hare's Foot Inn, and then you're on your own. Say what you will to Pip, but see he gets to bed at a decent hour. If I don't show at Turkington's affair tonight, he'll let his stork of a daughter sing. The whole county will heave up its supper, and they'll be blaming me for it."

She laughed hard, leaning forward in the saddle and almost unseating herself. Jon grinned up at her, wishing it was him she would be putting to bed later on. Actually it would be, but certainly not in the manner he fantasized. Curse his luck.

As soon as they reached the village inn, Jon blew Kathryn a kiss and waved goodbye. He kicked Imp to a gallop and cut through the woods to the manor. Old Turkington would have to hum for his guests tonight. There were only moments to spare before his wife arrived at the house, expecting a wedding night of some sort. He supposed music would have to suffice.

Kathryn took her time approaching Timberoak Manor. Moonlight did nothing to disguise the ragged condition of her new home. Half-dead vines hugged the stones as far up as the second-floor windows. The ivy appeared to be all that was holding the place together. Paint-peeled shutters hung precariously, threatening to drop to the ground with the first strong breeze. Knee-high grasses probably concealed all manner of debris around the weed-infested gravel of the driveway. Still, one could clearly see the ghost of former grandeur. Perhaps, with care and a hefty portion of her inheritance, she could resurrect that ghost.

Kathryn clung to the newly realized ambition. Such as it was, she now had a home to call her own. She had always craved a home, a family and a husband. Timberoak, Jon Chadwick and Pip weren't exactly what she'd had in mind during all those wishing sessions, but at the advanced age of almost twenty-five, she could hardly hope for much more.

After she located the stable and fed Mabel, Kathryn walked around front again. The heavy door swung open at a touch. She strode down the entrance hall and entered the littered ballroom with forced confidence and determined hope. She had always heard it was best to begin as one meant to go.

Pip sat on the floor with his back to her, humming along with the small harp he strummed. His tattered green robe was bunched around his hips, and his outstretched legs were bare. "Pip," she called softly, afraid she would startle him. "It's Kathryn."

He turned with a wide, vacant smile. Simply beautiful, she thought with a catch in her breath. And beautifully simple. Regret and sympathy streaked through her, leaving in their wake a need to do something, anything, to improve the quality of his life.

"May I join you?" she asked as she knelt beside him.

"Want to play?" Pip handed her the child's harp.

She pushed it back into his arms. "I don't know how, dear."

"I play. You sing," he ordered, and began to pluck a folk tune she vaguely remembered from childhood.

"'Winnowing Away,'" she remarked as the title came to her. Her mother had sung it to her when she was little. Before...

"I don't sing. Ever," she said. The words came out more

sharply than she had meant them to. His mouth drew down in a pout.

Before she thought what she was doing, Kathryn reached up and brushed his hair back, uncovering the dark bruise on his temple. He had scrubbed it nearly raw. The whole of his face and neck looked freshly washed, his sun-kissed hair still damp around it.

She wondered whether he shaved his own face. Perhaps Jon or Grandy did it for him. At least he made some attempt at cleanliness on his own. She caught a faint whiff of cologne and smiled. He must have dabbled in Jon's things out of curiosity.

"Sing to me," he mumbled, stroking the harp strings.

Kathryn sighed. She hadn't sung in thirteen years. The last time had gained her the only beating her father ever gave her. After that, even humming had drawn dark scowls from him.

"My mother used to sing," she said, almost to herself and noticed Pip's head cock to one side as though he were interested.

Kathryn realized then that she now had a confidant. Pip could listen to all her woes and would promptly forget them. She had talked to her cat when she was small and had no one else to listen. Whiskers had probably saved her sanity after Mother left and Father grew morose and distant. Come to think of it, Pip's curious expression had a certain similarity to her feline friend's.

She smiled and clasped her hands together in her lap. "Mother sang like a nightingale, Pip. Still does, I expect."

"Mother died," Pip said bluntly, catching a bass string with one fingernail. The note bonged and then faded to silence.

"Your mother died? Mine went away. Sad, isn't it?" Kathryn leaned against his shoulder, and Pip grunted softly in assent.

He began to play again, this time a piece she didn't know—one of his own, she suspected. The soft music soothed as a maternal caress was meant to. Perhaps Pip had invented his own consolation for the loss of his mother and was sharing it with her. What a lovely thought that, despite his disability, he possessed such sensitivity, such natural goodness.

She lay back on the chilly floor and covered her eyes with one arm. Pip's sweet, comforting sounds enfolded her, warmed her, and eventually lulled her to sleep.

## Chapter Five

Strong sunlight and the smell of coffee greeted Kathryn when she woke. She blinked and rubbed her eyes, groaning as her corset bit into her rib cage.

She was in Pip's room. Or at least the one she had assigned him when she saw the pigsty he usually occupied. The covers lay tangled half about her, half on the floor. Otherwise, the place looked much as it had the last time she was in it. The dust was more evident, and the furnishings seemed a bit more faded than she recalled. How in the world had she gotten here?

Searching her memory, Kathryn vaguely remembered strong arms beneath her, the shifting movements of being carried like a child. She lay back and sighed. So Pip was looking after her. The future didn't look half so bleak as she had expected it would this morning.

Once she had her money, she would restore his home and make it livable. Maybe even as beautiful as it had been in its glory days. And she would give him a life of comfort and ease. Her Pip would have no worries at all other than what note to play next. Her Pip. *Nathan.* She remembered the name Jon had written on the marriage certificate, but she could never think of Pip as Nathan. He probably wouldn't answer to that name, anyway.

So what if Pip wasn't her ideal husband? Not likely she

would ever have found the man she'd envisioned anyway. She had imagined a somewhat older fellow. Handsome, naturally. Virile and experienced, worldly, sure of himself, the master of all situations. And rich. Well, now she didn't require a rich man. Love had never been on her wish list. She'd seen what *love* did to her father when he lost it. She wasn't even certain what love meant; passion, supposedly, coupled with obsession. She would gladly settle for a different, safer kind of affection with Pip.

She couldn't deny that she felt a strong physical attraction to her brother-in-law, Chadwick. But then, she had experienced a stirring toward Pip that proved nearly as strong. The failing was one she'd have to combat until she got over it. Desire might be new and unsettling, but she could deal with it until she got used to the near proximity of two extremely handsome men. Once they became familiar in a family setting, she would surely come to think of both in a sisterly way.

They could live a pleasant life here at Timberoak. Jon would come periodically, of course, to get the music Pip wrote. They would make him welcome and be a real family. Even old Grandy might fit in, once Kathryn set her straight about showing Pip the respect he was due. Just because a childhood accident had stolen some of his reason, that gave the woman no call to grump at him the way she did. Everything would work out beautifully. Kathryn meant to see that it did. They were all her responsibility now.

She listened to the steady thump of footsteps on the stairs and the firm knock at her bedroom door. "Come in," she called, fully expecting Pip.

"Good morning, Kathryn," Jon said as he entered. "You slept well, I trust?"

Kathryn shifted uncomfortably in her wrinkled riding habit. He looked too wonderfully decadent, still in his evening clothes. Powder lay thick on his face, its pallor interrupted only by his dark brows and lashes, and the natural color of his expressive mouth. Most of his dark, wavy hair had escaped from its scarlet thong, as though the wind had pulled it free. Was he just coming in from last evening's affair at the Turkingtons' or leaving for another? The night had passed, but she had no idea what time of day it was.

Or did he never allow anyone to see him without this ridiculous mask of his? One would think he was hiding something. Scars, perhaps? La, men could be more vain than women!

His appearance ought to have set her teeth on edge, and in a way it did just that. It was as though he were daring anyone to challenge his eccentricity. He wore his trappings like a badge. Kathryn stifled a sudden urge to rip away the pretense and discover the real man underneath. She supposed most women felt that way, and that it was precisely what Jon intended.

"You have a performance today?" she asked, assuming the coolest voice she could manage.

He handed her a mug of steaming coffee. "Actually, no. I thought we might go into the city and announce the marriage."

"And collect the money," she said acerbically.

"Yes."

"No."

"What do you mean, *no?*" At least he had the grace to look embarrassed.

Kathryn shrugged, took a sip of the over-sweetened brew, and shivered with disgust before she answered. "I told you I can't have it until I'm twenty-five."

"But you said a husband would make all the difference. You said…"

Kathryn saw where this was going. "I said no such thing. I still can't get the money until my twenty-fifth birthday. Nor can anyone else. Why do you think my uncle waited this long? If I could have collected merely by taking a husband, I'd be long married by now, with my brain pickled in laudanum syrup. You'll just have to wait along with me, I'm afraid." She finished the coffee in two swallows and winced again at the sugary taste.

Even under the pallor of his powder, Kathryn imagined, Jon looked ashen. He just stood there wearing one of Pip's blank expressions. Odd, aside from their hair color, she hadn't realized just how close their resemblance was until now. She had a strange urge to reassure him, the same urge she usually felt toward his brother. "Don't worry, Jon. My birthday's in two months."

"You'll be twenty-five?" he asked, visibly shaking off whatever troubled him. "I'd thought you much younger."

"Thank you. The blush is off, though." She flashed him a quick grin. "At least I'm no longer an old maid."

His eyes registered surprise at her sally, and then resignation. "No, no, I suppose not." He stepped back toward the doorway, stumbling a bit on the edge of the rug. "Well, then... Well, I'll be off to town. If you don't need anything else, that is."

"Where is Pip today?" she asked as she stood up and placed her coffee mug on the bedside table.

"Uh...he goes down to the lake most mornings. Sometimes the woods. Look, Kathryn, I have to leave now."

"Wait awhile, if you're going into the city. I'd like you to take a message to my uncle. Even if I can't collect the money yet, I'd like to make at least one announcement."

He shook his head and looked eager to be on his way. "I'm afraid I haven't time to wait."

"Oh, I promise you it will be short and to the point," she assured him.

When he stood back, she preceded him down the stairs and into the ballroom. Amid the scatter of music sheets, she located a blank page and sat down on the floor to write.

Dear Uncle, On Tuesday night, the fifth of September, I was married to Mr. Nathan Lyham. We are residing at his country house until my birthday. Your niece, Kathryn

Jon peered over her shoulder until she had finished. He cleared his throat and rocked back on his heels when she looked up. "Is that all?"

"It ought to do the trick. His plans are definitely foiled. Will you post it for me?" She folded it in thirds and handed it up.

"I shall have it delivered. Will he come looking for you, do you think?"

Kathryn laughed as she took his hand to get up from the floor. "He won't know where to look, now will he?"

Jon crouched and picked up the little harp Pip had played the night before. He stuffed her letter in his pocket and tucked the harp under his arm as he rose.

"Won't Pip mind if you take away one of his ladies?" she asked.

"He will weep buckets, Kathryn, but there's no help for it." The look on his face was pure grief. She knew then that he felt the same affinity for the instrument that Pip did.

Kathryn took his free hand in hers. "You will sell it? Are we really so desperate for funds, Jon?"

He squeezed his eyes shut and blew out a long breath through his nose. "Everything will come right, Kathryn. Not to worry."

Then he shifted the harp to a more comfortable position and offered her a rather forced smile. "Leave Pip to his own devices today. He'll wander for a while and then return late this evening to work in here. Food's in the pie safe and there's fruit in the orchard out back. Make yourself at home."

Kathryn followed to the back door and watched him stride across the yard. "Anything else I should know?" she called out.

He turned and walked backward as he answered. "The cat's name is Dagnabbit, and he bites. So does Grandy. Have a care!" Then he laughed and disappeared into the stables.

Kathryn felt deserted, but she also felt rather adventurous. Never since she was a child had she been quite so free and left to her own inclinations. She could do whatever she wanted!

After wolfing a few slices of bacon and a handful of biscuits, she washed it all down with the remains of Jon's ale. Next thing, Kathryn thought, was to get rid of the corset.

The freedom of it all went right to her head, and she laughed aloud as she ran up the stairs. Married life was wonderful already, Kathryn thought, even without the money!

A midafternoon message caused a crisis at the Wainwright town house.

Rupert Wainwright crushed the letter from Kathryn into a wad and threw it into the grate. "The little fool! She's gone and got herself wed!" He raked his hand through what was left of his graying hair and scratched his bushy side-whiskers.

"That's it, then," Randall Nelson said, slumping his gangly frame down on the horsehair settee.

"You limp-wristed nodcock! You're giving her up? Just like that?" Rupert threw up his hands, wondering whether he had chosen the right man after all. He needed Kathryn wed to someone malleable enough to go along with the scheme. And someone stupid enough to share the wealth. Pity the lad didn't have more gumption, though, when it came to overcoming obstacles.

"What we have to do is find the bastard she married and get rid of him!" Wainwright settled himself behind his scarred oak desk and pounded a fist on the blotter. "Now then, think hard, boy. Do you know any Lyhams? Unusual name. Can't be many of 'em. Check the census records first. The fellow has to be from here in town, or she'd never have met him, eh?"

Nelson's gray eyes widened and his head came up with a start. "You mean to *kill* the man, sir?"

Rupert snorted with disgust. "You have a better idea?"

Nelson winced. "I hadn't thought to do murder, Roop."

"How else can we pull this off? You think she'll simply divorce him and fall in your lap for the asking? We'll have to make it look an accident, of course."

Nelson stared out the window, saying nothing.

Rupert nodded and breathed out a gusty sigh. "Shame we can't just do away with *her*. Wouldn't get anything that way, though. Charities would get it all. Damn that brother of mine!"

He noticed Nelson's brooding silence. "What is it?" Then louder. "What is it, man? I know that look! You're hiding something from me, I can tell. Let's have it."

"I knew a Lyham once. Was up at school with him. Eton, when we were just lads." He shook his head. "Couldn't be the same one."

"And why not? Well, spit it out." Rupert wanted to cuff him, but he held off. No sense in alienating his only hope.

"Name wasn't Nathan. Edward, I believe we called him. Surname was Chapton, or something like that." Nelson nodded, satisfied he'd remembered correctly. Yes, I believe it was Edward Chapton, or perhaps Chudwyn."

Rupert threw up his hands again and rolled his eyes. "Well, if his given name wasn't Nathan and his last name wasn't Lyham, what's the bloody point, man?"

Nelson folded his hands and returned Rupert's glare. "Lyham was his title, Roop. The fellow was a lord. Father was an earl, I believe. Left school when the old man died."

"Christ's nails! An earl?" Rupert's voice dropped to a whisper. "The gel's gone and got herself an earl?"

"No, no. I told you this fellow's name wasn't Nathan. And besides that, wouldn't Kathryn have thrown the man's title at you if he had one? That would make her a countess, and I doubt very much if she'd forget to mention *that*."

Rupert thought for a moment. Randall was right for a change. The lad hadn't much in the way of fortitude, but he had a head on his shoulders. A fine-looking head it was, too. Rupert had been banking heavily on Nelson's good looks to snag Kathryn's attention. Bugger that idea now; they would simply have to resort to elimination and force.

"You find out, boy. I want to know who this rascal Lyham is by week's end. Get on it first thing in the morning. Better yet, tonight. Ask around, check the peerage books just in case. Hire a detective, whatever it takes. We have to know who we're dealing with and get rid of him before the girl turns twenty-five."

Very late that evening, Jon stopped in the village and stabled Imp with the smithy, Ike Noblett. He then trudged through the woods to Grandy's cottage, where he left his suit and the small case containing the wig, mirror and stage paint. After scrubbing himself in the lake, he donned the rough work pants he had brought with him. His heart had gone out of the charade, but he had little choice but to continue now that he was in it up to his neck.

The chilly night air revived him a little, but nothing could restore the bit of his soul he had left with his harp at Graythorne Antiquities. With a huge dose of luck, he might retrieve her someday, but that would rest with fate and the whims of Ned Bunrich.

He approached the house and noticed candles flickering in the ballroom windows. Had Kathryn waited up? "Halloo th' house!" he called, so that he wouldn't frighten her.

"Pip! Where have you been? It's so late!" She caught his arm and shook it gently. "I was worried about you."

Jon patted her hand and fought the urge to raise it to his lips. There was a stupid thought. He had always hated kissing hands. Pretending attentiveness. Watching women simper. But Kathryn's hands were so small and so soothing, even when she was berating him for being late.

"Hungry," he mumbled. And not just for food, he thought.

She sighed and pulled him toward the kitchen, where she had obviously been sitting. One of the chairs stood out of place. Usually they all did. Someone had scraped away his huge mound of candle wax from the center of the table and replaced it with a dish holding a fat new taper.

Kathryn nudged him to sit. "There's a bit of the bacon from this morning. Your Grandy brought a tin of biscuits, and I cooked some of the apples I picked out back."

Jon looked around while she gathered the food on a chipped plate. The whole room seemed different. The floor had a near shine to it. The cobwebs had disappeared, and the window glass reflected the light clearly. He didn't recall ever seeing it do that. "It's clean!" he exclaimed.

"You noticed! I worked all day, but I only had time for the kitchen and your old bedroom. There's plenty to keep me busy while I'm here!" She smiled as though she relished the prospect.

Jon stared at her face, really looking at it for the first time tonight. Shadows underlined her eyes and a smudge of dirt marred her stubborn little chin. Her hair had accumulated a coat of dust that dulled its golden sheen. Small gold curls had escaped the sensible knot at the back of her head and were trailing down her cheeks and neck. With dismay, he noticed something else. Her corset was missing.

Without allowing himself to explore the ramifications of that, Jon ducked his head and began to devour the food she had placed in front of him.

Only after he had stuffed his mouth completely full did he realize what he was doing. He never bothered with manners at home. He had let himself run wild here. Only when he performed—and he considered the performance begun when he alighted from the carriage at a patron's home— did he make any effort to be civilized.

With *Maman* gone and military life a thing of the past, the home place had become his refuge from polite society and all the niceties forced on him since early childhood. Lord, Kathryn must think him a pig! Jon swigged the cold water from his chipped mug and choked down the mouthful of biscuit and bacon.

He dared a glance at her and saw she wasn't paying him the slightest attention. Kathryn was concentrating on a slice of raw apple, apparently the only foodstuff she had saved for herself. His gaze dropped to his own plate, which she had filled with the bacon, salted biscuits and a huge mound of applesauce. She had given him all the food, all but one late-summer apple!

Something caught in his chest and stuck there. It wasn't what he had just swallowed, though. It was more like a wad of indigestible feelings, all tangled together. Tears rushed up to the back of his eyes and threatened to spill over. He blinked hard, sucked in a deep breath and held it.

Women were supposed to take, not give. Every woman he had ever known was obsessed with taking. True, some had been kinder about it than others, but they had all wanted something from him; his body, little pieces of his soul, or money. Even Grandy expected her pound a week, outrageous pay for the little she brought around to eat. Now here came this girl with her sharp tongue and pushy ways, giving him all the food left in the house, when she must be starving herself. Look at all she had done for him already today! A giving woman. God, he was in trouble. He hadn't an inkling how to deal with this.

Jon shoved the half-empty plate toward her and heaved himself out of the chair. Just in time, he recalled who he was supposed to be. "You eat now," he said, and pasted a stupid grin on his face. "I play."

He left her sitting there and hurried down the hall to the ballroom. He prayed she hadn't cleaned in there.

Thank goodness. His sheets of music lay on the floor, undisturbed. She had placed the lute and violin on the table by the door. He subdued a renewed pang of loss for the harp. Somewhere in the deep recesses of his mind, Jon recognized the significance of his attachment to the instruments he held so dear. He couldn't bestow his care and protection on the living objects he should be responsible for. But these creations of fine wood, wire and gut, imbued with the loving voices he drew forth from them, had become his family. At least he'd been able to know them, hold them, keep them safe and near. Until now, anyway.

Kathryn approached with his ratty robe in one hand. With a smile, she stood on tiptoe and draped it around his shoulders. "The night grows cold, Pip. I think autumn's here to stay." She tugged the fabric close around his neck before stepping away.

He grabbed her hands before she could leave. "Wait!" Then he released her, to see if she would.

She lifted her eyebrows in question, a hesitant smile on her lips as she leaned back against the doorframe and crossed her arms.

Jon picked up the violin and spent a few seconds tuning while Kathryn watched. Then he met her curious gaze with one he hoped looked childlike. He began to play the tenor's tribute he had written the night she first came here. She had heard it then, of course, but not in its entirety, and never the way he felt it now.

In seconds, he closed his eyes and lost himself in the music, but somehow Kathryn became the music. All the emotion she had stirred with her caring, her unselfishness, her touch, her giving, permeated his soul and sought a sharing.

This, he thought, was the only way he could repay her. No, not repay. She asked for nothing. To suppose she did denigrated her offering. This was his gift to her, the outpouring of his purest self that he had never given to anyone before. Not his teachers, not his audiences, not even *Maman*. Especially not *Maman*.

Absolute accuracy and exquisite technique, a moving arrangement of notes, were not adequate tonight. He imagined his heartstrings stretched along the length of the Strad and offered everything he had held inside for the space of nearly twenty-five years. This might be the only physical expression of the need he felt for Kathryn that he would ever be allowed, and Jon played accordingly.

*Pure magic!* Jon felt it flow. Some force within him broke free and released the magic he had always doled out sparingly, afraid of its full impact on his own senses, unwilling to waste it on others. Perhaps Kathryn was the catalyst, the only deserving recipient. He could not have held it from her if he tried.

When he drew the bow down with a last quivering caress, he opened his eyes and looked at her. He felt as wonderfully spent as she looked. Her hands were clasped together under her chin, and tears streaked her face. The deep brown of her eyes shimmered in the weak candlelight. It was almost enough.

A soft, soundless sob escaped her. She reached out and touched his right hand with two tentative fingers. Reverently they slid along the length of the bow and rested on the Strad's belly for the space of several heartbeats. Then she drew her hand away and touched it to her trembling lips.

The silence of mutual acceptance surrounded them; a sweet shared lethargy after consummation, sweeter than any Jon had ever imagined possible. God, how he wanted to hold her. Unable to resist the pull, he enclosed her in the circle of one arm. She rested her head on the plane of his chest, and he felt the brush of her lashes as she closed her eyes.

How long they stood that way, he could not have said. He released her reluctantly when she finally raised her face to his. "Good night, Pip," she whispered, and touched his chin with her lips.

Jon knew then, as surely as he knew his scales, that the whole matter of wanting Kathryn had progressed far deeper than desire. Before he recovered enough to speak, she had slipped out of the ballroom and up the stairs.

He sank to the floor and laid down the violin. God help him, he had leapt again without looking. And fallen harder than he'd thought a man could fall. Resting his elbows on his knees, he pressed the heels of his hands to his forehead and blew out an unsteady breath.

Christ, what was he going to do? As much as he wanted to deny it, what he felt for Kathryn could only be described as love. Damn. The best he could hope for was that it wouldn't last. But, against all reason, he wanted it to last. He wanted it to go on forever, in spite of what it would cost him. His chest ached like an open wound.

Surely he could get over this in time. Calling a halt to it in the early stages would be the wisest thing. Perhaps he ought to admit his deception now and send her running.

Another, darker thought knifed through him. He had dragged Kathryn into danger, just by allowing her to stay here. He should tell her the truth and make her leave. But where would she go?

Bunrich would be back in less than two weeks to collect. And he'd be mad as hell about the wild-goose chase Jon had sent him on with that pawn ticket for the fake Stradivarius. Perhaps he could stall the man if he told him about the amount expected from Kathryn's inheritance. That, plus the five hundred pounds he'd received for the sale of the harp, might serve to placate Bunrich.

Lord, Jon had hated to sell the harp, but the pittance he'd have gotten for pawning her wouldn't have helped at all. He dismissed the sorrow; it was a small price to pay, if the money could satisfy Bunrich for a couple of months. The cad wouldn't hesitate to hurt Kathryn if he found her here with Jon, especially if he found out they were married.

The ladies must take second place in his worries now. He would sell them all to keep Kathryn safe. All but the Stradivarius, he amended with a determined frown. Somehow he would keep both Kathryn and the Strad out of Bunrich's reach.

Jon rose and lifted the violin. He wrapped it carefully in a frayed piano shawl, gently tucked it inside the cavity of the grand piano and closed the lid. No point in making Bunrich's job easy, in the event he got the upper hand. The first place he'd demand to search would be the safe. An empty safe would look suspicious, though. Jon placed the lute and lyre inside it and left the door standing open.

He shut down the creative side of his nature and drew on his training as a warrior. He faced the fact that the money he had to offer Bunrich probably would not suffice. Defense might be required. Organization usually eluded Jon, but Long San had taught him well how to plan and marshal his thoughts when in a crisis. Jon silently thanked the old bodyguard for those valuable lessons.

Methodically Jon arranged the scattered sheets of scribbles in perfect order and stored them along with the ladies in his safe, closed the door and spun the lock. Shutting away his music in this way provided a symbolic, as well as actual, dismissal until he could afford to return to it with an unencumbered mind.

Jon frowned at that last thought. He knew he would have to deal with more than just his financial problems to ensure an unencumbered mind. No use denying it; Lady Kathryn Wainwright Chadwick, new countess of Lyham, invaded practically every thought he formed.

With dread, Jon recalled the primary lesson in life his mother had taught him, possibly the only one of hers that he truly believed. She had learned by her own experience that love ate creativity like a hungry shark, gobbled it away until there was nothing left but a husk of grief and anger. And that anger, in turn, devoured the love. One was left with nothing in the end. Hadn't he watched it happen even before he was old enough to understand?

Jon knew he would be forced to choose in the near future: Kathryn or the magic. Either one would destroy the other.

And, eventually, him.

# Chapter Six

Kathryn dipped a rag in the bucket of suds and scrubbed at the years' worth of grime that encrusted the ballroom floor. The only place that revealed the true color of the oak parquet was the circle in the middle where she had first seen Pip writing his music. He had polished that little island of clean with his behind, she thought with a smile.

Dear old thing, he certainly wasn't a great one for conversation. Despite that, Kathryn thought they were getting on well enough. Pip seemed to be a rather self-contained fellow, but he did have moments of infinite sweetness. He answered her questions with one or two words, when he bothered to respond at all. Most of the time, she didn't think he noticed her much.

Apparently Jon had some sort of arrangement with the Grandy woman to supply food. She brought simple fare in amounts to last the day before Kathryn came down each morning. By that hour, Pip had usually eaten and gone about whatever it was he did all day. He came home for a late supper, which they ate together, Pip intent on his food and she chattering on about this and that.

Today, she had needed company, and had managed to catch Pip before he left the house. Kathryn scrubbed harder as she stole a surreptitious glance in his direction. Sprawled on the piano stool, he supported his head with one hand while he dragged a damp cloth over the ivory keys with the other. The discordant sound of the instrument seemed to mirror his mood.

Maybe she shouldn't have put him to work. Dusting looked to be a new experience for him. *Despondent* didn't begin to describe the way he looked right now. Well, he had been on his way out for his daily wandering when she enlisted him. Perhaps he was just disappointed that she'd delayed his outing. "Why don't you play for me, Pip?" she asked in a bright voice.

"No," he snapped, putting a bit more effort into his task.

"Come now, you're pouting. I could ride to town on that bottom lip of yours. A happy tune would make my work go faster."

"Stop it!" he shouted, jumping to his feet and kicking the stool backward. "Just stop working! I *hate* this!"

Kathryn scrambled to her feet and dropped the rag in the bucket. She raced after him as he stalked toward the hall and grabbed his arm. "Pip! Calm yourself. You needn't work if you don't wish to. I simply thought you might want to help."

He turned then and stared into her eyes, with an incredibly lucid expression that silenced her. For a second, Jon's haughty arrogance superimposed itself over Pip's face, totally obliterating the usually vacant features. Before she could gather her wits, his mouth descended on hers, hungry and insistent.

Shock, as much as his forceful grip on her shoulders, held her still. Fear rippled through her as his firm lips grew soft and persuasive. His tongue traced her lips, seeking entrance. She struggled against him, terrified he would follow his primitive instincts, physical urges Pip couldn't possibly understand or control.

*He is your husband,* a wicked voice in her head reminded her.

"No!" she shouted as she jerked her mouth away from his. "Stop, Pip! Please let me go!"

He released her so fast she lost her balance. Staggering backward, Kathryn squeezed her eyes shut and crossed her arms over her chest. She rubbed her shoulders where he had grasped them with such force, fiercely denying the heat that had flared inside her. When she opened her eyes, Pip was gone.

Kathryn let out a shuddering breath and walked over to right the piano stool. She ought to have prepared herself for something like this. Several times in the past three days, since that night he played for her so intimately, she had caught Pip staring at her with a kind of longing. Once since then he had tried to speak to her about something, but then abandoned the effort after a few aborted sentences. How earnest and troubled he had looked. No wonder.

Kathryn pressed her fingertips to her mouth and pressed her lips together, trying to supplant the feel of Pip's kiss.

He obviously possessed a man's needs, and legally she was responsible for fulfilling them. But allowing Pip to exercise his husbandly rights seemed wrong. Totally wrong. In his mind, Pip was still very much a child, and Kathryn knew he would never understand the intricacies of a marital relationship. He might not have enough wit to control his passion once it was unleashed. Every female within walking distance might be endangered.

Jon would be abashed if such a situation existed when he returned. In fact, he would probably be furious with her. And as to Jon, where the devil could he be keeping himself all this time? She hadn't seen or heard from him since he left for London with Pip's harp. Maybe he wouldn't return until the time came to claim her money.

Oh, she wished he would come home and help her deal with Pip. Perhaps he could explain in a way Pip could understand that one shouldn't give way to those physical urges that plagued the body.

She could use a little of that admonition herself. It didn't help matters to see Pip running about with all those healthy muscles exposed. The very sight of him did strange things to her insides. How had she ever believed time and familiarity would take care of the problem? Both things exacerbated it.

Kathryn shook herself, burying all thoughts of the incident, and returned to her schedule of cleaning. Pip would have forgotten all about it when he returned. They would have a nice supper of the cold meats Grandy had delivered this morning. She would make applesauce again. Afterward, she would tidy up the kitchen, retire to her room and listen for Pip's music.

Perhaps tonight he would feel like playing. He had removed all his papers and put his instruments away, probably troubled by the loss of his harp. Her explanation of that had fallen on deaf ears. She hadn't heard a note from him in three days, and was beginning to worry about it.


Jon stalked through the woods to the lake. Without a pause, he stripped off his breeches and dived in. The water was too damned cold for a pleasant swim, but it certainly served his purpose this morning. God, he had nearly done the unthinkable. Come so close it scared him to death. Poor Kathryn must be in hysterics about now. He could imagine her terror—expecting rape at the hands of an imbecile. And she'd done nothing to warrant that attack. Nothing!

Anger and desire proved a horrible combination, one he'd have to purge. But how could he? He wanted her so fiercely, even at his calmest. When he saw her toiling like the lowliest kitchen wench, he wanted to lash out. Somehow make her stop. She ought not to take on the cleaning of an entire house! He should to be able to hire someone to do all that, while Kathryn sat sewing and planning menus or doing whatever the hell gently bred women did.

But how could he ever take care of Kathryn, when he hadn't even the means to look after himself? All those years spent developing his gift should have included some practical lessons in dealing with real life. He couldn't blame

*Maman* entirely for the lack. He'd allowed her to insulate him from reality.

The tension in his body remained, in spite of his vigorous exercise. Without the release of his music, his emotions crowded inside him like an explosive mixture ready to detonate. That frustration, added to the dangerous situations that plagued his mind, allowed no possibility of peace.

Kathryn's uncle and that wretch who wanted to marry her were undoubtedly looking everywhere for her. They would be itching to annihilate him, the fortune seeker who had wrecked their scheme. Jon wished she hadn't mentioned Lyham in her letter to Rupert Wainwright. If they thought to check the listing of peerages, they might put two and two together. Any property-title searching they made in connection with that would lead them directly here.

And there was always Bunrich. How long until he appeared again with his hired muscle-heads? Best to expect that any time now, though he probably still had a few days to worry. Jon climbed to the bank and dressed quickly, ignoring the cold. He would have to arm himself from here on. The thought of killing again, even in defense, troubled him. However, he knew he could do it if it became necessary. If Kathryn was threatened.

Right now, he probably ought to try to ease her mind about the only threat she knew about. He strode to the edge of the woods and broke off several stalks of Queen Anne's lace. He looked around, saw nothing else in bloom to pick, and loped off toward the house.

When he entered, he heard the wet slop and swish of her cleaning rag. "Kathryn?" he called softly. He said nothing else until she had abandoned her chore and joined him in the doorway. Then he ducked his head and shoved the weeds toward her clasped hands. "Sorry. I'll be good."

The wary look in her eyes melted into relief. She accepted his offering and smiled up at him. He watched her swallow hard. Her voice broke a little when she whispered, "Oh, my sweet boy. Thank you."

He pulled one of her hands away from the weed stems and ran a thumb over her blistered palm. "Don't work."

She laughed and closed her hand, squeezing his and shaking it playfully. "I'm almost finished in there. You go about your day, and don't worry about me. We'll have a nice clean house within the week. Won't Jon be surprised when he comes to visit?"

She tugged her hand away and reached up to brush the hair off his face. "You're all wet, darling! Dry off and find yourself a shirt, hmm? Can't have you taking sick."

"Shirt," he parroted, brushing a hand over his bare chest and nodding. The guilt got worse every time he said a word, so he tried not to say much. If he told her the truth, she would run. Possibly right into the greedy arms of her uncle and his cohort.

*Ha! You like the attention, Jonny. You like being her Pip.*

*No,* he argued with himself. *She pushed me into this corner.*

*A corner you like. A corner you never occupied before. A corner where someone wants to protect you against the world.*

"All right!" he said, almost shouted, shoving a hand through his wet, tangled hair.

"Fine, darling. Run along then. And put on your shoes, too. The weather's too cool now to run barefoot," she said, with an affectionate pat on his arm.

He trotted off toward the stairs, waited until he heard her resume her scrubbing, and turned back down the hallway and into the study. Quietly he opened the middle drawer of his father's desk and unlatched the small secret compartment at the back. In moments he had the revolver loaded and was tucking it inside the back of his waistband.

"What do you think you're doing with that?"

Jon nearly jumped out of his skin. He whirled around and faced her, not daring to speak. *Caught. What now?*

"Give me that...*thing!*" she demanded, pointing and

striding forward like a little general. She held out her hand, palm up. "Hand it over."

"No!"

"Give it to me, Pip! You cannot play with that. It's dangerous."

"Mine," he said stubbornly, trying to edge around her toward the door.

She stamped her foot and blocked his way with her body. "You hand me that gun! This *instant!*"

With a sigh, Jon reached behind him and pulled out the weapon. He snapped open the cylinder and let the bullets fall into one palm. Then he carefully placed the pistol in her hand and dropped the ammunition into the open drawer. "I can shoot," he said reasonably.

"And just what did you plan to shoot?" she asked with an admonishing glare.

"Rabbits," he explained.

"There will be no shooting, Pip. Not of rabbits or anything else, do you hear?" She slid the weapon into the pocket of her skirt. "Jon's a fool if he allows this, and I won't be a party to it. Grandy brings us plenty of food without your having to hunt. Now, there's an end to it. Go and put on your shirt."

She stepped out of his path and pointed to the door. Her brown eyes snapped, and her lips were pinched together with anger.

With a careless toss of his head, he marched from the room, holding on to his dignity with clenched fists. God's foot, he wanted to spank her. Maybe he should go ahead and tell her who he really was, take the gun away from her, and... Then what? She would storm away from here so fast he would choke on her dust. Where would she go? She had no money yet. Apparently no friends she could turn to, or she certainly would have done so before coming here. Kathryn was his responsibility now. His wife. He would have to maintain this fiction until he had eliminated the threat of danger.

And how was he to handle Bunrich or her uncle when they arrived, if he had no weapon? He supposed he would have to steal the gun back after she went to sleep. A slow smile crept across his face, and he smacked a fist in his palm. She wouldn't let Pip have the pistol, but she would have to give it up to Jon. He laughed aloud as he sprinted across the yard and headed for Grandy's cottage, where he had left his suit and cosmetics.

Kathryn shook her head as she watched Pip scamper across the clearing and disappear into the trees. The sound of his laughter drifted toward her on the crisp autumn breeze. He had already forgotten the shirt and shoes. And the gun, thank God. Her heart ached for him, for what he might have been, but for that random accident that had affected his mind. How hard he tried to please her when he chanced to think about it. She supposed the childlike stubbornness was normal under the circumstances.

She loved his innocence, his joie de vivre, his sweet smile. With a sigh, she brushed her hand over the gun in her pocket. She also loved the fact that he needed her, but wondered how she would handle all those needs. One need in particular. Bedding with her husband was simply out of the question. She must take care that no further opportunities arose to stir his latent lust.

To give him credit, he had stopped immediately when she protested his kiss. Pip would never hurt her. Even before she got to know him well, she had never feared that.

Kathryn touched her lips again with the tips of her fingers. If only...

Several hours later, as she finished scouring the ballroom floor, Kathryn heard a rider approaching. When she peeked out the window and saw who it was, she ran at full speed toward the front door. "Jon!" On down the front steps she hurried, and caught one of his gloved hands in hers as soon as he dismounted. "Oh, Jon, I'm so glad you came!"

"Trouble?" he asked, with a tilt of his head and the customary smirk on his heavily powdered features.

She ignored the expression. "No, not exactly. Well, yes."

"What is it then? Pip up to some high jinks?" The question seemed an idle one. In any event, he didn't wait for an answer to it before he changed the subject. "Come round to the stable with me while I unsaddle the Imp."

Kathryn followed, still holding on to his hand. "I think you should talk with Pip, Jon. He's... Well, you see..."

His bark of laughter interrupted her. "A bit randy, is he?" Jon shook his head, still grinning. "Happens to us all sometimes. You must understand, Kathryn, for all his deficiencies—" he tapped his forehead with the hand that held the reins "—Pip is no longer a child."

"He *is* a child!" she argued. "You know he ought not..."

"Why ever not?" Jon asked casually. "He's had a tumble or two before. I assure you, he knows exactly what to do."

"How awful!" Kathryn shouted, jerking her hand from his. "You've encouraged him? You've actually allowed such?"

"Yes." Jon stopped walking and faced her directly. He was no longer smiling. "Pip may have a dent in his head, Kathryn, but his other parts are undamaged, as you have probably guessed by now."

Kathryn's mouth worked for several seconds before any sound came out. Outrage choked her into silence.

"Oh, come now, Kathryn. You're near twenty-five, not some simpering little innocent miss who's never—" He stopped and slapped a hand over his mouth. His smile escaped it, as did his words. "Lord love you, don't tell me! No, it can't be! You're a virgin? Ha!" He bent double on another crack of laughter.

When he straightened and saw the pistol, his eyebrows

and hands flew up at the same time. "Christ, love, don't shoot!"

Kathryn pulled back the hammer. "I ought to blow that smirk right off your face, Jon Chadwick." Knowing full well the gun was empty, she enjoyed his terror. "Now, will you stop poking fun at me and agree to speak with Pip concerning this?"

Chadwick nodded frantically, but the laughter in his voice belied any fear. "I promise! Better than that, I'll take him over to Bonham village and pay Coralee Mason to see to him."

"Who's she?" But Kathryn knew the answer.

"A woman who handles such matters for a few coppers."

"A whore?" Kathryn gritted her teeth. "I really ought to shoot you where you stand. You won't expose that boy to some diseased trollop, Jon. I won't have it!"

The ice of his eyes melted into a warm summer-sky color. His hands lowered, one of them enclosing the barrel of the pistol. The sudden softness of his voice reassured her. "Neither will I, Kathryn, and thank you for caring." He slipped the weapon from her hand and tucked it in the waistband of his trousers. "Don't worry, I'll have a word with Pip. He won't trouble you with anything like that again."

"He had the gun loaded, Jon," Kathryn said, introducing yet another problem he needed to solve for her. "You mustn't allow him to take it out. Will you keep it with you?"

"Of course," he said, drawing her into his arms and patting her back. "This has been a trial for you, hasn't it?"

Kathryn nodded against his chest, feeling tears creep out the corners of her eyes. She sniffed. "I wanted you to come home."

"I'm here now. I'll take care of things for you."

She drew back and looked up into his eyes. "Jon, he

isn't writing at all. He's put the ladies away, and refuses to play. Has he ever done that before?''

Jon sighed and tucked her hair back behind her ear. "Sometimes. It's all right. Pip will be fine, Kathryn. He simply needs to get away for a while.''

"Away? Where would he go? I assumed that he never left here.''

"We need to talk about that. Why don't you go inside and put on some tea? I'll take care of Imp and be along in a few moments.''

Kathryn wondered if Jon's whole life had been like this. He came and went, performing for a living, returning periodically to smooth out Pip's life. That was probably why he had no wife, no family of his own. He was probably older than Pip by a number of years. What a grave responsibility he had assumed, just to right a stupid mistake his father had made, probably with some village girl, when Jon was only a boy.

Jon had a wicked sense of humor and an exasperating disposition, but he could be kind. She had to admit, his arrival provided a huge sense of relief. For a few days, at least, she would have someone to share in the care of her husband.

The teakettle had just begun to steam when Jon arrived in the kitchen. Kathryn busied herself measuring out the leaves and pouring in the hot water. "How was London?" she asked, to reopen their conversation.

"Unremarkable as ever. I sent your letter.''

"Humph. I would love to have been a fly on the wall when Uncle Rupert got it.'' She took a seat across from Jon in one of the wobbly chairs and waited for the tea to steep.

Jon removed his black coat and threw it across the bench by the window. "That's what we need to discuss.''

"Tell me first where you intend to send Pip.''

"Actually, the subjects are related. Pip will go to Grandy's for a week or so, in the event your uncle comes looking for you and makes trouble.''

''Grandy won't take proper care of him,'' Kathryn said, shaking her head. ''I can't allow it.''

Jon set two mugs on the table and began to pour the tea. ''She minds him well enough. Pip needs a change of scene when he hits the doldrums. This is the way we handle it. And he shouldn't be around here if your uncle shows up unexpectedly. Surely you can see that.'' He dropped four lumps of sugar into his cup and shoved the sugar tin toward her.

Kathryn noticed that he turned his tea into syrup, just as Pip always did. ''You think my uncle might hurt Pip?''

He took a sip of tea and lowered the mug. ''I think your uncle might kill him. Wainwright won't want to give up one hundred and sixty thousand pounds any more than you do.''

''Murder, though?'' Kathryn whispered. ''I can't believe that.''

''He conspired to drug you, marry you to his accomplice and steal your fortune. An angel he ain't.''

''Maybe I should leave before he finds out where I am,'' Kathryn suggested.

''Have you somewhere else you can go?'' Jon asked, leaning forward as though his life hung on her answer.

''No,'' she admitted. ''Or else I wouldn't have come here.''

''I deduced as much. Unfortunately, there's not enough money to set you up anywhere for that length of time. We must face him here, then, if he comes. There's another threat you ought to know about, Kathryn. One I should have made known to you before you entered into all this.''

''Another threat?''

''I owe a fellow a bit over five thousand quid, and he has already been here once to collect.'' Jon pushed back from the table and started to pace the confines of the kitchen.

"Five thousand pounds? What on earth for?"

"Gambling debts."

"You gamble? Oh, good Lord…" Kathryn heaved out a harsh breath and crossed her arms over her chest. Damn the man! With all the repairs needed here, all the necessities he and Pip lacked, how could he have risked so much? "Trying to live the gentleman's life, eh? I should have known."

Jon stopped pacing and looked down at her. She could see anger, and also a deep hurt, in his eyes. "You know nothing!"

She ignored that. "So, what may we expect when this man returns for his winnings?"

Jon sighed and ground a fist into one palm. "I expect you to hide yourself and stay hidden, no matter what happens. Bunrich won't come alone, and he leans toward violence."

"That's why you wanted the six thousand from me, isn't it?" Kathryn felt so disappointed in Jon. She had hoped he had some character buried underneath that foppish facade, but apparently he didn't. "So, just pay him off when we get the money and then stay away from the card tables."

"He might not want to wait. What is it, two months, until your birthday?"

"Closer to six weeks now. What will he do, Jon? You'd better tell me so I can be prepared."

"He'll try to take the Strad in lieu of payment. I've a sneaking suspicion he has a hot buyer for it and plans to get a good deal more than five thousand."

"The Strad?"

"The violin."

Kathryn's mouth dropped open. Her heart rate doubled. "God in heaven, Jon, you have a *Stradivarius?* A *real* one?"

Jon nodded. "She was a gift to a great-grandfather of mine back in 1714, when he lived in Italy. They say he was a friend of Antonio Stradivari and received my little lady from the old man himself. Whether that tale's true or not, I mean to keep her.''

''Of course you must keep her!''

He smiled at her then, a sweet smile that warmed her all the way through. Kathryn remembered another occasion when Jon had abandoned his mocking long enough to grace her with it. Her wedding. She suddenly recalled that same night when Pip had played for her and smiled just so. The two men were so profoundly different, and yet they shared so much. Smiles. Music.

''You let Pip use the Strad?''

''That lady binds us together, Pip and me. She makes us one for the briefest of times.'' Jon knelt before her chair and took her hands in his. ''Can you understand, Kathryn? The sounds start there in the head and heart of the child, unencumbered by all the rules that govern musical fashion or the wants and needs of others. The magic flows out into the lady, and she holds it for me, releases it at my command. At my will, Kathryn. She is my talisman, the key to expressing something that demands a setting free.''

Kathryn slowly released the breath she was holding. She did not know this man at all. How could he switch so rapidly from cynical sarcasm to earnest explanations of this so-called *magic?*

''Are you mad, Jon?'' she asked with a soft smile of her own.

''Yes.'' He sat back on the floor and rested his face in his hands. A small, self-deprecating chuckle erupted. ''I think I very well might be.'' Then he shifted to prop his elbows on his knees and his chin on his palms. ''But I won't let anyone hurt you, Kathryn. I promise you that. Not Bunrich or your uncle. Not Pip. Not even me, selfish profligate that I am. Will you trust me to that?''

Kathryn inclined her head and studied this new Jon. How could she ever have thought him a fop, even briefly? He seemed the essence of everything masculine, sitting there on the floor in his pretentious black clothes and rice-powder mask. For a fleeting second, she wondered what life might have been like had she accepted his offer of marriage, instead of insisting on a fruitless union with Pip.

She shook her head to break the spell. "I'll trust you more if you know how to load that gun. The ammunition's in the desk."

He rose gracefully and took the weapon out of his inside coat pocket and spun the cylinder. "Never threaten a man with one of these unless you intend to use it," he warned.

"Are you a good shot?" she asked. "I heard about your duel, and that you chose swords. You're said to be the best in France with a blade."

The deep music of his laughter filled the kitchen. "What a joke!" he gasped when he could finally speak. "What a rich rumor, that! Would you like the true story?"

Kathryn laughed with him, unable to resist the contagion. "It would probably make my dreary day. Was there no duel at all, then?"

"Oh, yes! There was one, if you could call it that." He chuckled again and flopped down in the chair to toy with the gun as he continued. "Happened one night after I had done my Mozart monkey tricks at some nob's salon. There we were at table, pigging down oysters, as I recall. Sieur Charles Chaveau trilled some offhand remark about *Maman*. I took offense on her behalf. Never mind that his jest was right on the mark about her—I was spoiling for a fight."

"How old were you?" Kathryn demanded, interrupting him.

"A stupid seventeen! Can you imagine it? I slapped the man right across the mouth with my serviette. He kicked back his chair and demanded satisfaction." Jon leaned back his head and stared at some image on the cracked ceiling. "He chose swords, at dawn. I had been thinking along the lines of fists, immediately."

"You were afraid?"

"Terrified! You see, I have an unnatural horror of blades of any kind. Even a dinner knife gives me chills."

Kathryn scoffed, waving away his pronouncement. "You're jesting."

"No, no, it's quite true, and there's a good reason for it. Once, when I was eight, right at that I-won't-do-it-even-if-you-beat-me stage, I refused to perform at this huge birthday fete *Maman* had arranged. She stared at my hands as though she loathed them. Said that if I didn't intend to use the bloody long-fingered things, they might as well get chopped up for finger sandwiches."

He laughed, but Kathryn noted a distinct lack of real humor in it this time. She could only see the top of his head as he continued, "She was holding a dinner knife at the time. I had the worst nightmare of my life that night."

"That she cut off your fingers?" Kathryn whispered, horrified.

Jon nodded. Then he raised his head so that she could see his eyes. Slowly the merriment returned. "So. To the duel. My second was Long San. He was my bodyguard." One eyebrow cocked up in a conspiratorial expression. "Now, Orientals have this high regard for death by a blade, you see. Think it's quite the thing. He was getting paid to keep me alive, though. 'Go for gut, Jon-San! Is big target!' Long advised me."

Kathryn giggled in spite of herself.

He held out his hands, palms up, and wiggled his fingers. "These buggers were all I could think of at the time. I'd never really watched much swordplay, but I knew that blades do slide down blades, and my fingers would be at the hilt, just waiting. I managed the *en garde* thing. At least I knew that much of proper form. Then I just lunged before the poor sod had a chance to strike another pose. Got him right on the bottom rib, I think."

"You pinked him!" Kathryn said, trying to stifle an outright guffaw.

"Oh, yes! I pinked him. However, I didn't know a jot

about first blood. I thought I had to kill the devil to win! I went after him again, but Long San grabbed me from behind.'' Jon threw up his arms, grinning at the memory. "Ah, success. *Maman* kept her honor. Long San kept his job. I kept my fingers. It was grand.''

Kathryn wiped her eyes with the back of her hand. "What a story! So I don't suppose we should count on your expertise there. But can you shoot?''

Jon sobered a little and spun the gun around with his finger. "Oh, yes. I can do that.'' He looked up at her with a devilish gleam in his eyes. "With either hand, quite accurately. I'm ambidextrous, you know.''

"You can write with either hand?'' Kathryn asked.

"Both at the same time on separate texts, in fact. Benefit of a two-tracked mind. Comes from the music, I suppose. Thinking treble with one, bass with the other.'' He grinned. "Do I amaze you?''

"You amaze everyone, and you know it,'' she said with a grin. "That's the trouble with you, Chadwick. No humility.''

He rose and bowed from the waist. "I'd thought to leave that to Pip, poor fellow. However, since you require it of me, I shall *humbly* absent myself and make his visiting arrangements with Grandy.''

"You're excused. Supper at dark, and don't be late.''

Jon strode to the back door, his bearing as arrogant as ever. Then he turned, all evidence of his jocularity vanished. "If you hear someone—anyone—arrive, Kathryn, you must hide yourself immediately. Promise?''

"Yes,'' she agreed. "Be careful, Jon,'' she added, but he had already gone.

# Chapter Seven

The day crept along like a crippled beggar, dragging Kathryn in its wake. She quivered with energy and had nowhere to spend it. Now she wished she hadn't worked quite so prodigiously the past week. Timberoak was as spruced up as she could make it without funds to refurbish. Nothing more could be done for the house until she came into her wealth. In desperation, she chopped fine the remains of the breakfast sausage, added raw vegetables, threw in a goodly dash of pepper and set it on to stew.

Jon still had not returned when the day dwindled enough to make Kathryn light the kitchen candles. Hodgepodge soup would wait indefinitely, of course. Uncle Rupert's cook ofttimes kept a pot on for days, throwing in the leftovers as they became available, serving it up whenever she or Uncle came in hungry at odd hours. It wasn't as though she needed to hurry the meal, but she knew Pip would be ravenous by now. Perhaps Jon had decided they should eat at Grandy's house, wherever that was.

She had taken a bath first thing after Jon left, emptied the water and tidied up the kitchen. Decked out in Pip's old robe, she had spent over an hour cleaning her riding habit, the only decent garment she had left. Housecleaning chores had ruined the one day dress she had stuffed in her valise the afternoon she escaped London.

Dressing for dinner in a riding habit? Cooking up a mess of pottage for the great Chadwick? And married to a simple musician! Life got a bit more bizarre each day. At times she felt she rather like Mr. Carroll's Alice, who had tumbled down the rabbit hole.

The sound of an approaching rider snatched her away from her fanciful thoughts. *Uncle Rupert? The creditor Bunrich?* With a quick breath, she blew out the candles and ran to crouch in the darkness between the pie safe and the dry sink.

"Halloo the house!" Jon's voice rang out as the hoof-beats thundered right up to the back door.

Kathryn relaxed and let out the breath she'd been holding. Grabbing the edge of the sink, she pulled out of her hiding place and felt her way to the table to relight the candles. Visions ran through her head of having to do this time and again until she turned twenty-five and settled all their problems. Her anger found a target.

"Where have you been? I distinctly told you…"

Jon threw up his hands in surrender. His grinning rose-colored mouth taunted her. "Lord save us all, you sound exactly like a wife! But then, you are a wife, aren't you? I suppose it's to be expected." He tugged off his leather gloves and tossed them on the table. Swirling out of his black caped cloak and tossing it over a chair, he sniffed the air with relish. "Garbage soup! Marvelous, I'm famished. Hurry it along, would you, dear? I have to be off as soon as I've eaten."

Kathryn trembled with fury. If she could have lifted the pot, she would have drowned him in the stuff. "You're leaving again? And where do you think you're going?"

He settled himself in one of the chairs and pulled up to the table, obviously expecting to be served posthaste. With a flourish, he unfolded his frayed serviette and placed it on his lap before answering her. "To town. Lady Beralind-Moss has a birthday cirque tonight, and I'm to be the chief clown. You'll be safe enough for the few hours I'm to be gone. There are too many hidey-holes in this warren for Bunrich to bother coming at night. He knows he'd never find me. I don't think we need worry about your uncle floundering around in the dark, either. Just keep your ears tuned for new arrivals, and you should be fine.''

*Town!* Kathryn dismissed her anger at his plans in light of that. She needed some personal items she had left behind at Uncle Rupert's. Most especially the jewels that her mother had abandoned and her father had left Kathryn in his will. If luck smiled, her uncle would be out and she could retrieve the pieces from his safe in the study. Assuming he still had them, of course. How could she have been such a fool and trusted him so blindly? Well, he had trusted her a bit farther than he ought to, given his treachery. She knew exactly where he kept the key.

"I'm going with you, Jon."

He shook his head. "Not a prayer. I'm riding, and I only have two hours to get there. Fortunate the weather's so fine, eh? Could I have my soup now?"

"Get it yourself. I'll saddle my mare."

He grabbed her arm as she passed him on the way out. "You are not going, Kathryn. It would be mad to go into London with your uncle looking for you. You're to stay here and conceal yourself if you hear anyone coming. I wouldn't leave you alone, but we need the money." His fingers loosened on her sleeve, and he smiled down at her. It looked forced. "I'll come home straightaway. Will you miss me?"

She snatched her arm away and brushed her wrinkled sleeve. "Of course not. I'll be right behind you."

"Little fool! I have a performance. I haven't time to worry about you tonight. Suppose your uncle catches you, then what? You expect me to face him down?"

Kathryn pulled a wry face. "You can choke him to death with your rice powder." She almost laughed at his outraged expression. "Don't worry, Jon. You dazzle everyone at the birthday crush, and I'll take care of my business alone."

"Business?" he asked with a look of concern. "What business?"

She relented. "There are some things I need from my uncle's house."

He shoved back his chair and went to the stove to ladle himself a bowl of soup. "Why don't you simply sign over your inheritance to him while you're there? It will save him the trouble of selling you for only half of it."

"Not to worry. I have a key to the servants' entrance. Uncle won't even know I've been there. Go ahead and eat. I'll be ready when you are." Kathryn shot him a triumphant smile and skipped out to the stable.

She had Mabel saddled and was ready to go when Jon emerged from the kitchen. Without a word or an offer of assistance, he promptly mounted and galloped down the lane to the road. Kathryn scrambled onto the mounting block, climbed up and seated herself. Clicking to Mabel, she urged the mare to hurry and catch up.

"You really won't need to fret about me, Jon. I've been racketing around London for over a year now, and—"

"Quiet! Can't you see I'm practicing?" he snapped.

"Practicing?" Kathryn frowned at him, wondering if the man truly was off his bean. "In your head?"

"Hush!"

For two hours, they rode in silence. The only sounds were the creak of leather and the clink of harness. And maybe the music running round in his head, she thought with a roll of her eyes.

When they reached Mayfair and stopped under a street lamp, Jon finally deigned to speak. "Meet me here in precisely one hour and forty minutes. Have you a timepiece?"

She held up her locket watch. "It's five of ten."

He pulled on a length of gold chain and clicked his pocket watch open. "I make it ten on the mark. You're slow." He pinned her with a hostile glare. "Be on time, or I shall leave you behind. And if you're caught, don't expect me to extract you from old Wainwright's clutches. I haven't even the vaguest notion where he lives.''

"My hero," she crooned sarcastically. With a jerk, she reined Mabel around to depart.

"Kathryn!" he called after her, "You have a care!"

"Have a care!" she mimicked under her breath. "Thinking about his six thousand pounds, no doubt." She urged Mabel to a faster trot and never gave Jonathan a backward glance.

Within a quarter hour, she had reached Auverne Street and the impressive brick house that had never quite seemed a home. A sense of excitement gripped Kathryn as she made her way around to the back alley. Quickly she slipped from the saddle and tethered Mabel to the high wrought-iron fence.

The gate to the garden creaked as though it had never felt the touch of oil. "Please, please, everyone be gone," she prayed in a whisper. The door to the stable was closed, and she dared not peek inside to see if the carriage was there. Sidling through the privet hedge Kathryn stopped just outside the kitchen entrance and listened. Silence. Cook would have gone home by now. Thank goodness none of the servants lived in. Kathryn took a deep breath, fished the key out of her reticule and inserted it in the lock. It swung inward without a sound.

She waited just inside, willing her ears to catch any indication that the house was not empty. Nothing. Quietly she crept to the servants' stair and proceeded upward in total darkness. Not a creak emerged. With a sigh of relief, Kathryn opened the door to the upper hallway and hurried to her room.

Satisfied—and not a little smug with success—she moved around the moonlit chamber. Packing took less than ten minutes, since she took only what she could stuff in a pillow slip—two lightweight wool dresses, more underthings, and her sensible pair of low-heeled walking shoes.

That done, she left her chamber and stole down the stairs.

No light came from beneath the door of the study. Uncle must be at his club tonight. She smirked at his pretensions. Probably deluding himself that he was at White's or Boodle's. The upper middle class had had to organize their own men's establishment, though. No matter how rich a merchant or man of business became, he could never buy his way into any of the gentlemen's hallowed sanctuaries. Yes, he was likely at Dysart's, playing at faro.

Kathryn risked lighting a candle. Quickly she retrieved the safe's key from its secret cranny in her uncle's desk. No trick to it, she thought. Uncle could only blame himself for preaching to her how curiosity made or broke a reporter. The small safe opened readily, and she removed the hand-carved rosewood box her father's solicitor had once given her. Realizing the need for haste, Kathryn didn't examine the contents, but summarily dumped it all into the pillow slip along with her clothes. She tied the top of the bundle into a knot, stuck the box back into the safe, locked it and replaced the key.

What a walk around the park, she thought, amazed at her unqualified success. She blew out the candle and opened the door.

"Well, well, well. Welcome home, my dear!" Uncle Rupert smiled. She couldn't see the smile, but could certainly hear it in his drawl. Moonlight filtered through the front windows and outlined his dark, looming form.

She made a dash for it, but he caught the back of her dress and swung her against the wall. "Do come in and give me a travelogue, Kathryn. How was the honeymoon?" He snatched her around rather roughly and shoved her back into the study.

Fright and frustration pinned her there in the darkness as the key snicked in the lock. She tightened her grip on the pillow slip, weighing it as a possible weapon. Too light. What then?

Kathryn sensed he counted heavily on her fear to hold

her immobile. "I came back for some clothes," she ventured.

He struck a match and lighted the candle she had left on his desk. "I wonder what else you came for?" he snarled. Without pausing, he pulled open the secret compartment, took out the key she'd just put there and opened the safe. He saw the jewelry box and nodded, apparently satisfied when he saw that it remained where he had put it. He relocked the safe without checking the box's contents.

Kathryn recovered her breath. "My husband is returning for me within the hour." She smoothed out her skirt with one hand, still gripping the pillow slip with the other. At the first opportunity, she meant to dash out the back and run for it.

"Ah, the husband. We shall await him here, I think. How negligent of you not to bring him by to meet me. Ashamed of the family, are you?"

Kathryn wondered if he knew she had overheard his and Randall's plans for her. It would do him no good now to harm her, since he was not next in line for her inheritance. Father's man of affairs had made it quite clear that whatever her father left her would go directly to specific charities if she died without issue. Pip was the one in danger, not her. If Rupert and Randall managed to eliminate her husband, they could still put their wretched plan into effect.

She ducked her head for a moment to think. She had better make it very clear that Jon was not the man they sought, in the event he decided to come looking for her. "My husband is—"

"The earl of Lyham." He interrupted her softly, as though speaking to himself. "And so, you are the countess."

Kathryn straightened, almost dropping her sack of treasure. "*The earl of Lyham?* Me, a countess? That's absurd!"

His wide-eyed gaze pinned her with its intensity. "You really don't know? How can you not know?" Then he began to nod slowly, pursing his lips. Suddenly he threw back his head and laughed. "So he fooled you! Here I thought you'd gone after his title, but the rascal has duped *you!* Wed you for your money, as though you had access to any! Probably thinks you'll get mine eventually." He slapped his thigh and laughed even louder.

Kathryn fought her confusion. Pip, an *earl?* Nonsense! Or maybe not. She had heard something once about Jon's father having a title, but hadn't taken it seriously for a moment. Obviously, Uncle Rupert had. It would be possible to verify, if one had the correct name and reason enough to investigate. She had written Pip's name when she sent the announcement, and her uncle had no reason in the world to lie about this. She must play for time to think.

"I don't know where you got this ridiculous notion, Uncle, but I assure you my husband is not an earl, of all things!"

Rupert's laughter died, and he sat down in the chair across from her, leaning forward on his knees with his hands clasped together. "Listen to me, girl. This man has perpetrated an evil design, tricked you into this marriage. He believes you'll be wealthy someday because of me. Our Randall has made discreet and very thorough inquiry, since we received your letter."

Kathryn considered his words. He had made no mention of the funds her father had left in trust. So he had no idea that she had overheard him discussing her inheritance with Randall. There might be a way out of this yet.

He clucked his tongue with a sorrowful expression. "Devious of him to use his title as his surname, but Randall and I discovered there is only one Lyham heir left. Your husband inherited the earldom from a brother who died some years ago whilst abroad. But Jonathan Chadwick— your 'Nathan,' of course—never stepped forward to claim the title. He never publicly announced his brother's death."

What did this mean? Was Pip the brother who supposedly died? Had the family concealed the older boy's deficiency by pretending his death? To what purpose, if Jon never tried to assume the title? "I suppose you are going to tell me why he neglected to claim what was his," Kathryn said with a studied blink.

"The family was virtually impoverished even before that. Your husband was just a boy then, but a very talented boy. Couldn't afford to give up performing, you see. And the countess squandered whatever moneys he managed to glean from that. Ran up terrible debts at the tables. When his mother died five years ago, he wisely dropped out of sight. Just disappeared. Only this summer he resurfaced, no longer a child prodigy, but a man with a mission. You went from the pursuer to the pursued, my dear."

Kathryn tried to control her erratic breathing. No wonder Jon chose to disguise himself with powder. He had simply picked up where his brother had left off after that unfortunate accident rendered Pip incapable of performing in public. Jon would have been a fool not to do that, if they were so strapped for money. Her uncle was waiting for her reaction. She nodded doubtfully. "So, this plan of his was to pick about for a rich wife?" Kathryn wondered what her uncle hoped to gain from telling her all this. What was done was done, wasn't it?

"He wanted to marry money, of course," Rupert agreed. "But since he's posing as a mere younger son, he had no recourse but to settle for the daughter of a rich cit. Or in this case, the ward of one—namely, you. No one knows of the former earl's death except his old solicitor, who was paid off and sworn to secrecy. Doesn't do for a nob to play tunes for his supper. Your fine earl would be laughed out of town. Ridiculed into obscurity."

"How would Randall Nelson have unearthed such a tightly held confidence, I wonder?" Kathryn asked, figuring her uncle might be fabricating this whole thing simply to turn her against her husband.

"Randall became acquainted with their old solicitor's clerk. Paid him an outrageous amount for the information. You should thank Randall for his concern on your behalf.

The lad's fair mad about you, Kathryn. He will still want you, even after this fiasco.''

Kathryn shook her head with exasperation. ''None of this will serve you, Uncle. I know it's all a pack of lies. There's nothing you can say that will alter the fact that I am married! I intend to *stay* married, and there's nothing you can do about it.'' She stood, clutched her stuffed pillow slip under one arm and marched to the door. ''Now unlock this, and I shall be on my way.''

He followed her and opened the door. Before she could clear the portal, he had twisted her free arm behind her back and forced her toward the stairs. ''You'll remain here for the present, until I can think how to extract you from this…situation.''

Kathryn struggled all the way to the second floor, kicking backward, to no avail. Screaming wouldn't help; there was no one near enough to hear. Even should they, no one would dare interfere in a family altercation between guardian and ward. Not a soul in London, save Jon, knew she was a married woman.

When they reached her room, Rupert thrust her inside. She stumbled against the bed while he snatched the key from the inside lock. He slammed the door shut. Then came the click that sealed off escape.

His muffled voice reached through the solid oak panel to infuriate her further. ''Think on what I've told you, Kathryn. I shall have Randall bring proof tomorrow if you like. We'll rid you of that leech you've wed, one way or another. Sleep well.''

Kathryn slammed the bundle she carried against the bedpost, wishing it was Rupert's head. How dare he lock her in like some naughty child! She'd show him, by God!

She raced to rake the curtains aside. Her window faced the front of the house, and the brick wall below it dropped straight away, without even a ledge to cling to. Too far to jump with nothing down there to break her fall.

Kathryn lit a lamp and checked her timepiece. Jon expected her to meet him in half an hour. She'd have to hurry to make it to their rendezvous on time.

Damn! The blasted window always stuck. Every time she wanted it opened, she'd had to ask for help. It didn't budge now, either. Well, then, making a rope of the bedsheets was out of the question. Kathryn huffed out a breath of disappointment.

Quickly recovering, she found a paper and pencil. She carefully slid the paper under the door and poked the pencil through the keyhole. She would dislodge the key, and when it fell on the paper, she could draw it back under the crack below the door. It had worked in the last adventure novel she read. The pencil slid straight through without a hindrance. With outside help, in fact. It vanished, snatched from her grip.

The paper also disappeared, and she heard chuckling from the corridor. "Give it up, girl. You're going to stay in there until I prove to you what a mistake you've made. Bad marriages can be undone. Randall and I will help you."

Kathryn hit the door once with her fist, and winced. He would hang about out there all night unless he believed she'd given up. "Oh, all right then! Have it your way!" But not this time, she thought to herself. Not while there's a breath left in my body. "And you may tell Randall he's not to consider this a surrender to his suit. I'm merely curious as to what you've found out about this husband of mine. There had better be an article for the paper in all of this. And I *demand* you use my real name this time."

"There's my girl. I knew you'd see reason."

His footsteps grew fainter and died away. Kathryn flew to the bed and stripped it bare. With shaking fingers, she made knots to do a sailor proud. Securing one end to the bedpost, she coiled the rest beside the window and began riffling her dressing room for her basket of household medicines. Sticking plaster might work. She pressed it onto one large pane in long strips until the glass was covered. The rounded butt of the heavy porcelain water pitcher made a soft crunching sound as she shattered the glass panes to harmless fragments that clung to the adhesive. With satisfaction, Kathryn watched it buckle outward and fall to the ground.

A squeal of elation almost escaped her as she threaded the makeshift rope through the hole. She hiked up her skirts and shed her petticoat and bustle so that she could squeeze through the opening. Just in time, she remembered to don her gloves, the thick leather ones she saved for bitterly cold days. Her heart almost stopped when she stepped through the window and put her full weight on the coiled sheets.

"I won't think about this. I'll just do it," she whispered to herself. Hand over hand, feet braced against the rough brick wall, Kathryn had made it almost within jumping distance of the ground when low, rumbling laughter froze the blood in her veins.

"Well, well, well. Wonders never cease!"

She fell. Strong arms caught her up against a hard, unyielding chest.

"What the hell are you doing here?" she squeaked.

"Playing hero, it would seem," Jon said with a cynical smile. "What took you so long? I was about to knock on the front door and see if you needed help with your bags." He eyed the white sack she'd tossed out the window before her descent. "I could have managed that, I think."

"Put me down and let's go. Mabel's tied around back."

She groaned when he set her on her feet. He scooped up her pillow-slip sack and gathered Imp's reins in the other hand. "Mabel, you say? I hope this is your mare we're setting free, and not some unfortunate housemaid. I'd offer to let you ride pillion, but anyone who risks Imp's back takes their life in their hands. But that's no novelty for you, is it? Spit in the face of death all the time, don't you?"

"Shut up, Jon. You've got enough to answer for without hurling insults at me." They reached Mabel, and Kathryn waited for Jon to offer her a leg up. He did so without delay, and handed her her things. She marveled at his economy of movement as he mounted his stallion. For such a large man, the wretch was incredibly graceful. With that white face and black cape, he looked like some predatory creature of the night. Kathryn shivered at the thought. Without comment, he swung the cape off and settled it around her shoulders.

"Might we stay at your rooms here tonight?" Kathryn asked. "I have business in town tomorrow."

"*Stay?* Someone sucked your brains out through your ear, didn't they?" he remarked without slowing down.

"I have jewels to sell, Jon. You know, those sparkly things that might save your precious hide if we can get a decent price?"

He reined in, almost causing a collision. "Where are they?"

She held up the pillowcase and he reached for it. "Oh, no, you don't," she warned, snatching it away. "I'm going to deal for these myself."

"You wouldn't know what to ask," he scoffed. "Or *whom* to ask, for that matter."

Kathryn didn't even attempt to hide her smugness. "I have connections in this town you couldn't begin to match, Jon Chadwick. You put me up for tonight and, with any luck, tomorrow we'll ride home solvent."

Jon's smile appeared hesitant. "Why, Kathryn? Why would you do such a thing for me? Voluntarily, I mean? You don't really owe me anything. At least not until you get your fortune."

"Call it an advance, if you like," she said. "We'll have enough to deal with when my uncle comes looking for Pip. If this Bunrich you mentioned does you any damage, there won't be anyone to protect my husband but me. It only makes sense to pay the fellow off and reduce our worries by half."

Kathryn witnessed something very like humility stealing across his face before he turned to ride toward the theater district where his rooms were located. Maybe it was a distortion under the gaslight, but she didn't think so. The very thought of a humble Jonathan Chadwick stretched credulity to the limit.

Later, in his Spartan rooms, Jon built a fire in the small coal brazier and she heated a tin of beans. They ate in preoccupied silence, he with the fork and she with the spoon, sharing the one plate he owned.

When they had finished, she washed the utensils and settled herself on the divan. Her uncle's revelations troubled her, no matter how diligently she tried to dismiss them. They must be based on the fact that the Lyham title did exist and a Chadwick held it. Rupert would not tell a lie so easily disproved.

She might now believe that Jon was the heir, if only she hadn't watched him add "Lyham" to the marriage certificate under Pip's name. He knew very well she would assume it to be the surname. Was there another, older brother who had died? Was Jonathan Chadwick the bastard? It was time to get a few answers.

When he brought her a pillow and blanket from the bedroom, she accepted them with a murmur of thanks. Then she broached the subject directly. "Jon, is there any truth to that tale I mentioned once about your being titled?"

"Don't be absurd," he said in a scoffing tone. "Do I look noble?"

Kathryn shrugged. "Did you have an older brother who died?"

He stared at her for a long moment before his gaze slid away. "Ah, yet another rumor making the rounds?"

He looked downright guilty. According to Uncle Rupert, there had been two legitimate Chadwicks in line for the Lyham title. One reportedly had died years ago. Only two possibilities occurred to Kathryn. Jon, a bastard, had reversed roles with Pip when their older brother died. Or, if there had been no older brother, Jon must be the true second son. In either event, Pip had to be the rightful earl.

Education might offer a clue as to Jon's legitimacy. "Where did you go to school?" she asked.

"I didn't. *Maman* hired a tutor who traveled with us." He looked wary and started to leave the room.

"Wait a moment. Couldn't we just talk for a while? I'm afraid the night's happenings have me too keyed up to sleep."

Looking resigned, Jon sat down in the overstuffed chair opposite the divan and crossed his hands over his stomach. "All right," he conceded, but the guarded expression remained.

"So, did your tutor teach you music?"

"God, no!" he laughed, relaxing a bit with the change of subject. "*Maman* wouldn't have stood for any competition in that area. Poor old Mr. Horvel did well to drag me away from her for an hour a day and force-feed me a bit of reading and mathematics."

"That's all?" she asked, abashed. Even a second son rated better than that.

Jon tilted his head in consideration. "Well, I learned geography firsthand from our rather nomadic existence. I have four languages other than English, gleaned from living where they are spoken. And I may very well be the foremost expert in international politics." He laughed again. "Nothing bores me more, but brilliant conversation was part of the game, and one must have a subject on which to speak."

"Other than music," she said, nodding her understanding.

"That's too personal to discuss with strangers." His mouth curled up in that sardonic way she'd come to expect. "I'd as soon speak of bodily functions, religion, or intimate relationships."

He dragged out the last two words. Kathryn ignored his licentious tone. "I see," she mumbled, and cleared her throat.

With a trembling finger, she tucked an errant strand of

hair behind one ear and changed the topic yet again. He could be such a provoking tease at times. "So, your parents? I assume they both have...gone on?"

He ducked his head, pretending to examine a spot on his waistcoat and picking at it with his thumbnail. "Father died in my eighth summer. Mother passed five years ago."

"How sad for you," Kathryn said softly, noting that Jon did not appear overly sorrowful to have lost his mother. Perhaps she hadn't been his mother at all. "So there you were, with Pip to manage, and her debts, as well. I wonder which you minded most?"

He straightened immediately and scowled at her. "Is this how you interviewed those people you destroyed, Kathryn? Did you sharpen your poison pen while they reminisced? Put words in their mouth?" He stood and faced away from her. "God, and I thought we were becoming friends!"

"I thought so, too," she said sadly. She had struck a nerve. Her insinuation that he resented coping with Pip made him furious. Surely no baseborn son would go to such lengths to look after a legitimate sibling in Pip's condition. Jon had to be his younger brother, and he must have done his duty the best he could. That would explain why he had never tried claiming his brother's legacy. Shouldering the burden of supporting and protecting Pip could not have been easy.

"Jon, I meant no insult. You accepted your responsibilities, and I cannot help but admire that."

What did the truth about the title matter, anyway? So what if Pip was an earl? He could never claim a place in society as a lord. Of course, Jon had lied to her about Pip's legitimacy. That petty falsehood irritated her, but it changed nothing.

Jon had employed no deceit when he arranged her marriage to his brother. It had been her idea altogether. He needed money, and he had been very direct about it from the outset. She would honor her agreement to save him from Bunrich. He *was* her brother-in-law, and basically a good man.

Best to let it go for now. Perhaps once Jon trusted her enough, he would confide in her.

"Go on to bed, Jon. You look done in, and I suddenly feel very tired myself."

He turned and stared at her for a full minute, as though searching his mind for something he needed. She watched his mouth open to speak and then clamp shut, abandoning the effort. With a protracted sigh, he walked quietly into the bedroom and closed the door.

# Chapter Eight

Jonathan never asked to see the jewelry Kathryn had taken from her uncle's house. The more he thought about it, the less he wanted to do with any of it, the jewels or her inheritance. This whole matter of using Kathryn's money dragged on his conscience like a loathsome chain. He told himself it would only be a temporary imposition, a loan until his opera succeeded. But he saw *Maman* in himself and it made him ill to see it.

For the first time, he wondered if his mother had ever felt such guilt at using him. True desperation could alter one's scruples. He was going to have to draw the line somewhere.

He escorted Kathryn to a shop she'd selected on Redweskit Street. Patiently he waited just inside, by the window, while she conducted the transaction.

She looked wonderful in her simple blue woolen gown. Her silken hair draped over her shell-like ears and swirled around in a perfect braided oval at the nape of her neck. Sedateness became her and, in its own way, enticed him. The very thought of Kathryn decked in diamonds and swathed in satins seemed ludicrous; it would be like gilding an already perfect rose. In her natural state, she would probably devastate a man's senses.

He wouldn't be that man. Never in a million years would

Kathryn choose him as a lover, and he could only praise her for that bit of wisdom. When he turned, his reflection in the shop's window mocked him; the powder, the long-haired wig, the expression of hauteur. Hell, he looked like a primped-up whore, rigged out this way. Felt like one, too; one who sold himself for public acceptance of his music and a fistful of money to pay gambling debts. He had deceived Kathryn for the same reasons and that reinforced the image.

The man who really lived inside him was even worse than the one she thought she knew. He wouldn't have her meet that man, who was woefully undereducated, reckless and coarse. And, worst of all, obsessed with sounds in his head that stole his sanity for hours on end. Better he should project those attributes onto Pip, who could safely indulge, with the excellent excuse of idiocy.

*Maman* had taught him how to disguise his faults so that she could peddle his talent without embarrassment to herself. But she had never let him forget his true nature and how much she loathed it. No, Kathryn might have gotten brief glimpses of his real person through her encounters with Pip, but at least that alter ego of his had a very good reason for his shortcomings. An imbecile could be what he was and endure nothing worse than pity. Kathryn might despair of the mercenary Jon and sympathize with the slow-witted Pip, but by maintaining the fiction of duality, he at least avoided her full-blown hate.

And to think, he had almost spilled it all to her last night. Thank God he had reconsidered in time. The mere thought of seeing his mother's scorn resurrected in Kathryn's eyes made him shudder with dread.

Suddenly, Jon made a decision. He would not take anything from Kathryn Wainwright. Christ, he was almost twenty-five years old. He had survived thus far without duping a defenseless woman, and he'd be damned if he would resort to it any longer. A man had to draw on his honor at some point.

Bunrich and the debts be damned. Jon knew he could simply kill him, of course. The thought had crossed his mind. If a man came to one's home intent on mayhem, a defense should be expected, shouldn't it? But, as heartily as Jon disliked the bully, the matter of honoring the family debts stood in the way. Bunrich did hold the markers. Jon knew he must give up the Stradivarius and settle things once and for all. It was the only solution.

He leaned against the wall of the shop and watched Kathryn haggle with the clerk and then the owner of the shop. Jon couldn't hear their words. She seemed competent to handle matters, he thought as he saw her accept a jeweler's loupe and examine several of the pieces. Her shoulders dropped slightly, and she shook her head. Moments later, she accepted the stack of bills the man counted out, stuffed them in her reticule and turned to leave.

Her frown when she rejoined him bespoke failure.

"Trouble, my dear?" he asked as they exited the jeweler's.

"I only got four thousand," she admitted, tugging on the edge of her glove. He noted that her hands were trembling. "I really thought they were worth more."

"He cheated you? I should—"

"No!" Kathryn grasped his arm to keep him from re-entering the shop. "Monsieur Dernier's perfectly honest. I inspected the flaws myself. It seems my father hadn't much expertise in selecting stones. No wonder Mother didn't take those with her when she left. She probably knew more about the value than he."

She sighed dispiritedly. "Will Bunrich accept this much on account, do you think?"

Live coals in his stomach couldn't have discomforted him more at the moment. Why didn't she hate him? She ought to hate him. Instead, she treated this as though it were her problem, as well. "I can't take your money, Kathryn. I thought I could, but I can't." He leaned over and cupped his hands to offer a boost onto her mount. When he felt her hand on his shoulder, he straightened abruptly.

"Of course you can," she said. "Those pieces meant less to me than they did to the woman Father bought them for. Why shouldn't the useless things help my present family out of difficulty? I think it's fitting they should."

Her generosity shamed him, but it angered him, as well, now that he had made up his mind not to take advantage of her. And he was angry with himself for this latent streak of goodness. What a rotten time to get gallant. Jon again offered her his hands and propelled Kathryn up to her saddle. Then he mounted Imp and they rode out of London side by side for the silent trip home.

By the time they reached Timberoak village, Jon had decided to make a clean breast of it. Kathryn had the money from the jewels and could afford to keep herself somewhere safe from her uncle until she inherited her father's fortune.

Now was the perfect time to tell her. She had the money in her reticule, a decent mount under her, and a good four hours of daylight left for travel. He took a deep breath and drew to a halt in the road near the smithy's.

She slowed, as well, and then stopped, looking over her shoulder. "What is it?"

"Kathryn, I have a confession to make," he announced. "I have deceived you, and I need to make it right. To tell you the truth."

Her sudden laughter confused him. "Oh, Jon, I've been hoping you would finally break down and tell me on your own. It's all right, though. I already know." Kathryn nudged Mabel forward, and he urged Imp to a walk beside her.

The spurt of relief he experienced proved to be short-lived. He realized that whatever it was she had guessed at couldn't be the full truth, or she would have broken something over his head already. "You know about the business with Pip? That is, that we are the same?"

She nodded and seemed not even vaguely surprised.

"'That Pip's not your half brother at all? Yes, I figured that out. Uncle told me about the title and the supposed death of the heir. I realize you had no choice but to take the measures you did. You mustn't worry that it makes any difference to me. Come, let's hurry home. I think we'll see some rain in the next hour or so." She sped to a quick trot, leaving him to trail behind her.

Jon pondered her words, unsure what to add. How could she dismiss the whole situation just like that? It didn't matter to her that Pip didn't exist? That her marriage was...to him! She *knew* she was really *his* wife? He stared at her back as she rode down the lane and approached the house.

No, it couldn't be this simple. There was a misunderstanding in this somewhere. He blew out a fatalistic breath, reined up in front of the stable and dismounted. Once they were inside and settled, he knew, he'd better insist on a little clarification of what she thought she knew.

"Jon, horses!" Her frantic whisper grabbed his attention, and then he heard it. Several riders were coming, and swiftly at that.

"Get in the house and hide. Your uncle may have followed us. Here, take the gun. Don't come out of hiding until I call you."

"But what if it's Bunrich? You have to give him—"

"Devil take the money! He'd never take less than the five thousand, anyway. Can you shoot that thing?" She nodded. "Go, then! Hurry!"

Jon shoved the horses into the stable and barred the outer door. When he turned, Kathryn had disappeared. He prayed she had sense enough to conceal herself well. If it was Bunrich, it would never do for that rascal and his minions to get their hands on a woman they thought belonged to him. He ran around the side of the house and stood on the front steps as the riders approached.

Jon stood waiting as Bunrich dismounted. The same two oafs accompanied him, clenching their meaty fists in anticipation, obviously eager to exercise more of their muscle.

Three of them might prove hard to handle if things got messy. He wished Long San were here to back him up, but that luxury was a thing of the past. He stood fast and forced a smile. "Well, Ned! Back already?"

Bunrich stopped at the bottom of the steps and rested his hands on his hips. He looked every inch the prosperous merchant he was. "Chadwick? I almost didn't recognize you. Gracious, don't you look all the rage! Or is that supposed to be some sort of disguise? Isn't he pretty, lads?"

Jon inclined his head. "Why, thank you." He appraised each man with a lazy look, trying to discern whether they carried weapons and where they might be concealed. "You had a rather quick trip."

"Oh, trains are wonderful things. And expensive, Chadwick. As is my time. How thoughtless of you to waste my resources, when yours are so limited. Especially *your* time. You have very little left."

"So you plan to kill me, then?" Jon asked, as though his life meant nothing. At the moment, it certainly wasn't worth much to anyone but himself.

Bunrich grinned, showing a gold tooth near the back of his mouth. His heavily waxed mustache twitched. "I'm thinking about it very seriously. You may, of course, redeem yourself somewhat if you deliver what I need immediately."

"You know I haven't got the money, Bunrich. Five hundred's about the best I can do today." Jon spoke reasonably and without anger or sarcasm. He held out little hope that the man would respond favorably.

"That will do for the trouble your futile errand caused me, and the Stradivarius will suffice for the debts you owe." Bunrich took a step forward and his men closed in beside him. "Get it for me, Chadwick. *Now!*"

"You never wanted the money, did you?" Jon asked, playing for time.

Bunrich laughed bitterly. "That fiddle of yours is my ticket to a thriving future, if you must know. A fellow I know would move heaven and earth to get it.'' He smirked. ''At least he's willing to pay handsomely for me to move them. Now, if you would be so kind?''

Jon nodded. Overcoming all three men would be damned near impossible. Even if he succeeded in breaking a few bones and besting them all, they soon would be back with the law. If he killed them—assuming he could—he'd be hard put to explain three deaths to the authorities. Bunrich did have a legitimate claim, and a perfect right to demand payment.

''All right. I'll get it.'' He knew they would follow him inside. He prayed Kathryn stayed hidden and quiet until they left.

The three trailed him to the study. They watched as he opened his father's desk and collected the money he'd gotten from the sale of the harp. ''Here's the money,'' Jon said, holding out the stack of bills. ''The Strad's in the ballroom.''

He led the way, hurrying his steps, wanting the nightmare over so that he could grieve in peace. He figured they would try to beat him a bit before they left. Bunrich would feel he deserved satisfaction after all the delay.

They'd be wise to leave him alone after they got what they came for. Anger heated Jon's muscles, made them twitch and quiver with a need to act. Maybe he would extract a little satisfaction of his own once he'd settled the debt.

''Well?'' Bunrich said.

Jon realized he had stopped in the middle of the ballroom. His feet seemed unwilling to carry out the necessary task. ''In the piano,'' he muttered, and made himself move to it.

With a curse, he lifted the top and reached inside the cavity.

*Nothing! She was gone!*

Frantically he felt about, finding only the frayed piano

shawl in which he had wrapped her. He tossed it on the floor. "Christ, someone's stolen her!"

Bunrich shouted something, but Jon couldn't focus on the words. Someone had taken the Strad! A thief, while he was in London? Kathryn herself? Oh, God, yes! She must have it. Bunrich would take the place apart. He would find Kathryn!

Without further thought, Jon whirled around, head low and leg swinging. He felt his boot connect with Bunrich's head. Leaping aside, he lashed out again and heard a loud "Oof!" Three more times he leapt and shifted, kicking, even using his fists once, in desperation. A massive body crashed into his and knocked him to the floor. Still he fought, battling like a cornered badger.

Heavy knuckles connected with his jaw. Bursts of red light dimmed to black. His last thought was a prayer. *Stay hidden, Kathryn!*

When his senses returned, he realized they had hauled him outside. His mouth tasted of coppery grit. He spat something wet and grainy. Facedown in the dirt, Jon opened his eyes and saw the bloody spittle on the ground beside his face. Refocusing, he noticed the woodpile several feet beyond that.

And a hand gripping the ax.

Bunrich's gravelly voice ordered, "Hold him down, lads. And stretch out his right arm."

*Oh, Jesus, God, no!*

Every nightmare Jon had ever experienced coalesced in that second. Every prayer he'd ever uttered crowded into his mouth and emerged in a soul-deep groan. He felt thighs like tree trunks pin his waist and hips to the ground. A viselike grip twisted his left arm behind him. He forced his eyes open again and saw the blurry image of his right arm stretched out straight beside him; saw and felt it pulsing with terror, like an already disembodied thing.

"Want to reconsider, Chadwick?" Bunrich offered casually, swinging the ax like a pendulum near Jon's clenched fingers.

Jon swallowed the blood in his mouth, certain Bunrich would consider it a sign of contempt if he spat again. Kathryn must have the Strad with her, but even if he knew that for certain, he couldn't risk her falling into Bunrich's hands. *Hands!* He choked at the word, at the image of his own lying dismembered on the ground, at the horrid thought of living on after that.

*Pride be damned.* "The Strad's been stolen, man! I can get you four thousand more," Jon promised, hating his weakness, fighting to keep his voice steady. He might have to use Kathryn's money to survive this, but he'd be damned if he'd send Bunrich looking her. "I'll have it... tomorrow."

"Oh, I think not," Bunrich said conversationally. He swung the blade over the back of Jon's wrist, so close the hairs quivered in the breeze of it. "You'll give me the Stradivarius, I think, especially if you no longer have any use for it. Don't worry, I won't take the whole hand. Couldn't have you bleeding to death. Tell me, old man, how many fingers does it take to draw the bow, eh?"

His fingers, his *life!* Jon grasped at the thin thread of his sanity. Dread, unspeakable horror, clawed at his insides like a wild thing. *Kathryn had the Strad! She had to have it! No, no, he couldn't tell them that.* He must think of Kathryn, alone and defenseless against these three. "I don't have it, Bunrich. I swear!"

"Spread his hand."

Jon bucked upward in panic as a booted heel mashed the back of his wrist. A shot rang out, and his eyes flew open just in time to see the ax fall. "Oh, Jesus God!"

The impact and his roar obliterated the world.

Kathryn clutched the pistol with both hands to keep from dropping it out the window. She fired again for good measure, even though the men were already running. The one she had shot staggered and clutched his right shoulder as his two friends dragged him around the corner of the house and out of sight.

Hurriedly she rushed down the upper hallway to the stairs. By the time she reached the front window of the study, she could see only dust in their wake.

*Jon!* Not even the thought of what might await her could slow her as she dashed through the house and out the back door.

He lay as they had left him, facedown. One arm stretched out at a right angle to his body and the other bent, palm up across his back. Kathryn dropped to her knees beside him and stifled a scream with her palms. The ax head lay only inches from the back of his hand. Three fingers protruded upward from the damp dirt, their middle knuckles buried by the blow of the ax.

Kathryn did scream then. The sound echoed in her head even after she clamped a hand over her mouth. Then she realized it was no echo. It was Grandy. The old woman ran toward them like a runaway mule and collided with Kathryn as she fell to her knees beside Jon.

"Gawd, oh, Gawd, ye shot me Jonny! Oh, Jonny..."

Kathryn sucked in a shuddering breath. "No, no, he's not been shot!" she gasped. Kathryn snatched the woman's kerchief off her head and began the horrible task of cleaning and examining Jon's injury. Her own hands shook so badly, she could hardly control them. Tears flooded her eyes. "Some men came. When they tried to cut off his hand, I fired."

Kathryn swallowed bile and turned her face away from the sight of broken bones and crushed tissue. She groaned through gritted teeth and forced herself to look more closely. "I guess the ax fell blunt side down when the bastard dropped it."

Grandy made a strangled sound, one blue-veined hand pressing her lipless mouth. She recovered more quickly than Kathryn. "Get some spirits. Brandywine or sich. And

a needle and thread to sew up th' split skin. Go, go. Be
quick!'' She shoved Kathryn aside with a pudgy elbow and
gripped Jon's wrist, supporting his dangling fingers with
her other palm. ''Git!'' she yelled.

With a speed she wouldn't have thought possible, Kathryn dashed to the house. She found the old embroidery
basket she had recently appropriated; Jon's mother's, she
supposed. Was there any brandy? No, but there was that
bottle of whiskey in the pantry that she had hidden from
Pip. She grabbed up a small stack of clean dishcloths and
barreled back out to the dooryard.

Within moments, she knelt again, offering the supplies
to Grandy. The woman grunted and took only the bottle.
''Thread 'er up, lass. How's yer stitchin'?''

''Fair,'' Kathryn muttered, watching as the old crone
doused Jon's mangled hand with the liquor and cleaned
away the blood and ground-in dirt. Kathryn turned away
and heaved when Grandy began manipulating the bones
back into place.

''Jonny can't play nothing if we muck this up,'' she muttered. ''Thread th' needle,'' Grandy demanded. ''An'
steady them hands o' yers.''

Kathryn complied. How she managed, she couldn't have
said afterward. Grandy held his ring finger securely against
a small, flat piece of wood from the woodpile while Kathryn stitched the ragged tear in the skin.

She had chosen the smallest, thinnest needle she could
find, and the finest silk, scarcely the thickness of a hair.
The sun beat down on her neck as she bent to the task.
Though the day had dawned chilly, at the moment it
seemed the height of summer. The sweet, metallic odor of
his blood mingled with that of sweat and a nearby pile of
horse droppings. Her own pulse thundered painfully in her
ears. Blood seeped around the stitches, blinding her to what
she was doing. Grandy washed it away with another slosh
of the liquor. Kathryn worked on, matching tissue and skin
as best she could, alternately cursing and praying.

When she had finished his ring finger, she rethreaded and proceeded with the next. Thank God the ax had turned, or it would have severed his fingers completely. As it was, one rough edge of the blunt side had apparently landed solidly between his middle knuckles and the base of his fingers, breaking three. His forefinger, though badly bruised, seemed intact. She made quick work of the last repair and, with a shuddering sigh of relief, sat back on her heels.

Grandy examined the tiny stitches. "Might do. Might not. Could pull out when the swelling gets worse. And it will." She poured more whiskey on it. "Take off yer corset."

"What?"

"Rip out one o' the stays wi' them scissors."

Within seconds, Kathryn sat stripped to the waist, ignoring the cool September air, and cutting her corset to pieces. While Grandy snapped the whalebone and devised splints, Kathryn sheared her chemise into wide ribbons for a clean binding.

"He hasn't moved," Kathryn whispered, laying her fingers against Jon's powdered throat. The pulse felt weak and thready.

"Aye. Good-fer-nothin' layabout's what he is." Grandy harrumped. "Best see if we can get him to bed, then." She pulled herself to her feet and poked Jon's hip with the toe of her shoe.

"Mind his hand for me," Kathryn said. She managed to roll Jon onto his back while Grandy kept the injury as immobile as possible.

No sooner had she gotten him settled than Grandy squatted in front of Jon and slapped his face. Hard. "Wake up, ye great oaf. How d'ye expect us to git ye indoors when ye lay there like a soggy loaf o' bread? Eh? Git up and coom inside!"

Shocked speechless, Kathryn leaned close to protect him. His eyes opened and rested on her for a moment. Then she watched it all come back to him—the horror, the pain, and the gruesome act that had rendered him senseless with shock.

"It's all right, Jon," she said softly. "They've gone, and it's all right now."

He didn't speak. The rise and fall of his chest looked shallow and jerky. For several seconds he lay there, his gaze now focused somewhere over her shoulder. Dark strands of his hair stuck to the dried blood from his split lip. Suddenly, in one surge, he pushed himself up with his left elbow. He rolled sideways onto his knees and got to his feet. His body swayed. Kathryn tried to help, but he shoved her roughly aside.

Grandy held out the whiskey bottle, and he snatched it from her. Helplessly, she and Grandy watched him stagger toward the open back door and disappear inside. Kathryn noted he had never looked at his bandaged hand. Not once.

"Best get some clothes on," Grandy suggested, pointing at Kathryn's bare breasts, "and I'd be hidin' that gun if I was you." She turned away toward the path through the woods.

"Wait! Grandy, don't leave!"

"Ye can tend 'im. I'll get ye some food and stuff."

Then Kathryn remembered Pip. If he was here, at least he could fetch and carry while she looked after Jon. "Where is Pip?"

The old woman grinned and shook her head. "Ye'll be seein' him soon enough, I reckon." She cackled merrily as she waddled off and disappeared into the trees.

"Crazy old witch!" Kathryn cursed under her breath. She crossed her arms over her nakedness and hurried in after Jon.

This morning had been bad enough, but she couldn't have imagined a worse afternoon. Unless, of course, Jon's wound had been fatal. That thought triggered her imagination. Even now, he might be upstairs with the pistol, intending to... Kathryn broke into a run, dashed into the house and took the stairs two at a time.

The weapon lay right where she had left it, on the window seat. She stuffed it under the cushion. Relief immobilized her until the breeze from the open window reminded her of her nudity. Kathryn inserted her arms in her sleeves and pulled the bodice of her dress together. It fitted too snugly without her corset, but at least she was covered.

The water pitcher stood half-full, and she picked it up, along with the small stack of facecloths she kept for her morning toilette. Judging from the sounds she had heard below, his damaged lip and the swelling under his eye, Kathryn knew the men had beaten Jon before they dragged him outside. He would simply have to swallow that pride of his and accept her help, whether he wanted it or not.

She entered his room and set the pitcher and towels on the lamp table by the bed. Jon lay propped against the headboard, his bandaged hand obscured by a pillow and his left lifting the bottle of Scotch to his lips. It sloshed as he righted it.

"That's good, Jon. I think you need that. Why don't you have another sip and then let me clean that cut on your mouth? My, that swelling looks..."

"You have her? The Strad? She wasn't in the grand."

"Of course. I found her when I was cleaning the piano yesterday and moved her up here. She's fine, Jon. I laid her in the bottom of the chiffonier where it's nice and dry."

"Bunrich wants her. You need to get out of here," he said in a deadly-quiet voice. He swigged again, swallowed audibly, and winced. His sigh sounded more like a groan. "Take the Strad and your money and leave. Now."

"I shot him, Jon," she said. Her voice hardly broke at all. "I'm sorry I didn't kill him. I hit his shoulder, though, so I think we have a few days before he recovers enough to come back."

"Leave me the gun. They'll kill me next time, but not before I send Bunrich to hell." He drank again, leaving only a trace in the bottle. His head collapsed back against the headboard, and his face twisted with anguish. "Ah, God, Kathryn! Please go."

Kathryn ignored him and wet a cloth in the pitcher. When she touched his cheek, he dropped the bottle and grabbed her arm. His bloodshot gaze held hers for several seconds, and then he clenched his eyes shut. "How many?" His strangled question didn't need explanation. "Tell me how many he... It hurts so I can't tell."

"They aren't cut off! They're not!" she hurried to explain. "The ax turned when he dropped it. Three were broken. Grandy set them, and I put in the stitches."

Pained laughter rumbled up out of his chest and exploded into the room. She watched while he shook with it. Exhaustion finally stopped the awful sound, but he still chuckled silently. "Only crushed, eh?"

"I think they'll be all right," she said hopefully, patting the hand that gripped her arm. "At least you still have them."

Jon moved his head slowly, side to side, and pushed out the words on a lingering sigh. "And if any of it putrefies, I'll lose the whole hand."

"That won't happen. I promise it won't happen, Jon."

"No matter," he said, his voice slurring. "Can shoot with my left. You, get out. They'll kill you, too...or worse." His eyes closed more naturally now, and his breathing evened out to near normal.

Kathryn watched until she was certain he slept. Considering the amount he had drunk, she knew he wouldn't wake for some time. She thought of washing his face and undressing him so that he could rest more comfortably. But he certainly wouldn't thank her if she disturbed him now, when he had just escaped the pain. She satisfied herself by slipping off his boots and covering him with a blanket.

She had no intention of reliving the afternoon's events, but forgetting proved impossible. Thank God he'd given her the pistol, though things might have gone better if he kept it himself. If she hadn't fired at them, what more might they have done to Jon?

Could he have satisfied them with the money? With what he had in the desk, added to her four thousand from the jewels, he'd only have been five hundred short. Surely he had offered it when they threatened his hand. Bunrich must have insisted on the Stradivarius. That would certainly explain things. Jon wouldn't give that lady up under any circumstances. He'd die first.

Or would he? He must have gone to the piano to get the violin for Bunrich, if he knew it had been moved. Jon would have guessed immediately that she was the one who had taken it. Why hadn't he gone looking for her and the Strad, if he was willing to give it up?

Suddenly, she knew. Jon had protected her by not revealing her presence in the house. All of this was her fault. If she had left the damned violin where he put it, Bunrich would have it and none of this would have happened.

Now Jon had lost the use of three fingers and taken a severe beating, and was planning murder unless Bunrich killed him first. All because of her interference. No wonder he wanted her to leave.

# *Chapter Nine*

*No*, Maman! *I'll play. Please! I promise!* The nightmare woke him. Jon sat bolt upright with a guttural cry and grabbed his right hand to his chest. The pain of his own grip forced him backward in a near faint. He gasped for air. *God curse it, the damned thing hurt!*

His head pulsed as though it might erupt at any moment. Sharp, stabbing pain accompanied every attempt to draw a breath. Ribs in his lungs? Perhaps through his heart. Good, then. Dying meant relief. Long San had said so in his last moments. Even *Maman* welcomed it when she lay so ill. Living would be the trial. The pain he could endure, but living on after... Oh, Christ!

His left hand stirred over the right one he had clutched in terror. Nausea flared with the fresh agony. His *fingers.* Kathryn said three broken. Crushed. She lied. He knew they were gone, all of them. He had seen it in the dream. One by one, *Maman* had cut. *Don't think. Don't move. Die.* That's right, he'd stop breathing.

He tried. He really tried.

"Jon?"

He sucked in a whoosh of air. *Maman!* Damn her black soul. Wait, there was real softness in the voice. Not *Maman's* slurry French Jean, but good old English *Jon.* Kathryn. He released the breath and drew another. Just one more lungful, just to hear Kathryn's voice again, and then he would...

"I heard you cry out, Jon. What can I get for you?" she asked. He felt the stir of her breath on his cheek, and then her fingers brushed it lightly. "Oh, my dear. You hurt, don't you?"

"Don't touch me," he muttered through gritted teeth. Anger snaked through him, wrapped around him and squeezed like a bloody python. Why did she seduce him with this kindness, make him crave it more than peace? He breathed again, blaming her for his urge to do so. He wanted to die, damn her.

"Grandy brought you something for the pain," she whispered. "You must be in agony. Wait a moment."

Jon heard the clink of metal against glass. Then something touched his lips. He drank, amazed that he could feel anything so mundane as thirst. His stomach rebelled at the bitter draft, but he managed to choke the stuff down.

"There, there," she crooned, "you'll feel better in a moment."

"Liar!" A creeping languor stole through him, dulling the sharpness of the blades slicing through his head and hand and side. Bearable devastation, but only just. It ceased to matter so much as the minutes crawled by. He floated away, wondering idly where the current would take him. Hell, probably. But he didn't much care.

When Jon woke the next morning, harsh reality hit him dead-on, with nothing to muffle the blow. Lord God, he wished for the fog of yesterday, painful as it had been. The clarity of his thoughts disturbed him more than the dream had done. Bunrich had destroyed his fingers and would be back for his head. And the Strad, if he could find it.

Kathryn had to get out of here immediately. "Kathryn!" he shouted.

The hurried patter of bare feet on the hall floor reassured

him that she was all right for the moment. She came to his bedside at a run, wearing only her nightgown and wrapper.

"You're awake! How do you feel?" Then she ducked her head, struggling to catch her breath. "Stupid question, I know."

Jon slid his legs off the bed and sat up. "Get your clothes on and ride to Lakesend. I'll send a note with you to Lockhart. He'll put you up until I can think of something else."

"The vicar? No, I'm not going anywhere unless you come with me. We could go to Grandy's, I suppose. I don't even know where her house might be, so I doubt Bunrich could find us there." She tried to shove her shoulder under his arm when he stood up and accidentally brushed against his bruised ribs.

Jon pulled away, holding his bandaged hand high to keep from bumping it. "Christ, woman, will you get out of my way?" He headed for the necessary behind the screen in the corner. "I suggest you leave," he said as he reached for the front of his breeches.

Her eyes rounded, and her mouth made a perfect O. The door slammed behind her and he heard her call out, her voice dwindling along with her footsteps on the stairs. "I'll bring you coffee and some water to..."

"Wash," he finished for her as he relieved himself. His face felt gritty, coated with a paste of powder, tears, blood and dirt. The residue of laudanum lay on his tongue like river scum. Dried blood caked one corner of his mouth, and one of his molars felt a trifle loose as he probed it with his tongue.

Pain pounded through his right hand in tandem with his rapid pulse. Jon forced himself to look at the bandage for the first time. Had Kathryn lied? Wouldn't it be shorter by a few inches if he had lost them all? What did it matter? Smashed or severed, one or all five, he would never play again.

He looked away and down, trying to rebutton his trousers. Dexterity, even in his good hand, seemed to have deserted him completely. After several futile attempts, he gave it up and let his breeches drop. He stepped out of them, thankful someone had already removed his boots. Carefully he wormed his way out of his coat and waistcoat, wincing as he drew the sleeve over the narrow, stiff bandage. Clad only in his shirt and drawers, Jon shuffled back to the bed and sat there until Kathryn returned.

This time she knocked.

"Come," he muttered gruffly.

She opened the door and then stooped to pick up something. When she entered, she carried a bucket in one hand and a mug in the other. "Your coffee," she said, handing him the smaller container.

The sweet, strong brew rushed over his tongue and down his throat as he gulped it. The heat burned away the taste of the drug and provided a jolt of needed energy. He set the cup aside and wiped his mouth and lower face with his hand. It came away covered with yesterday's grime.

Kathryn had set the pail on the bedside table and was wetting a cloth. "The water's warm," she said. "Here, let me wash your face."

Jon noticed she still hadn't dressed. He took the cloth from her before she could touch him. "I can manage. You go and get ready while I clean up. I'll ride with you to Lakesend." The very thought made him ache all over with dread, but one way or another he had to get her away from here.

"Ride? Don't be a fool, Jon. You're so sore you can scarcely walk across the room."

Jon dropped the wet rag, grabbed her shoulder and shook her. "Damn it, woman! Bunrich could be back here at any time. And you will *not* be here when he does! Now, get out of here and go pack!"

She put her hand over his and patted it. "All right. But could I ask you something first? It's important."

He sighed and let his fingers trail down her arm. "What?"

She wriggled out a comfortable spot right beside him on the edge of the bed, as though it were the most natural place in the world for her to be. Jon almost missed her question. "Did you ever actually see the markers Bunrich said he bought?"

That was the last thing in the world he'd expected her to ask. "No."

"If he bought five thousand worth, would you owe anyone else?"

"No," he said thoughtfully. "No one. Why?"

"How do you know Bunrich really bought them?" Her delicate brows arched over dark eyes sparkling with excitement.

Jon's train of thought wavered at the sight. He shook his head to clear it. "Why would you think he didn't?"

"Because," she said, obviously pausing for effect, "*if* he had bought them all up, *why* would there be three letters posted from London late yesterday requesting payment of you?"

Shock almost numbed him. How stupid! He'd never even asked to see the markers. He'd just assumed... "It's past the first of the month," he mumbled, and then raised his voice and looked at her in wonder. "It's past the time I always pay them! For five years, I've never missed a payment. Kathryn, you know what this means?" He laughed bitterly and fell back on the bed, ignoring his aches for the moment.

She nodded vigorously. "Bunrich tricked you—a blatant case of fraud." Her mouth stretched into a wide and open smile. "You can have him arrested, Jon, for that and for assault!" She slid off the bed. "I'll go fetch the constable."

"No, wait!" Jon rolled to his left and sat up again, reaching for her arm. He looked directly at her, searching her eyes. "You aren't going to leave here, no matter what I say, are you?"

"Certainly not to hide in Lakesend," she admitted, still smiling.

He sighed and shook his head. "Then let's not be hasty about this. If we have Bunrich taken up—assuming he could be found and our old constable could manage an arrest—the incident will make the papers." He snorted with disgust. "Jonathan Chadwick's forced retirement will be prime news, won't it?" He nodded in answer to his own question. "Then your uncle and fiancé will know exactly where to find you."

She reached up and gently touched his battered face; it was a tender gesture he'd already grown to crave. "But I'm already married, Jon. There's not a thing they can do to alter that."

"Except kill your husband," he corrected with a wry twist of his lips. "And I'm not exactly in the best form to prevent that." He held up the hand wrapped in white and glared at it.

Kathryn began to pace the floor, yet it didn't seem to indicate helplessness or even frustration. She was thinking again. Bless her heart. What had he ever done to deserve this kind of solicitude? Maybe that was the deal; the fingers and his magic, in exchange for her brief touch of warmth. Maybe it was worth the trade-off. God really did have a sense of humor when it came to giving and taking away. He'd lose Kathryn's regard, of course. No woman could love, or even continue to like, the man he really was. But for now, he would wallow in her concern while he could.

Kathryn stopped and turned to him, her gaze direct and intent. She grasped his bare knees with her hands, leaning close enough for him to kiss, if he dared. He loved the way she touched him without thinking about it. The familiarity of the gesture warmed him all over.

"Jon, listen to me. We're going to have to do something drastic, something you might find deceitful in the extreme. Maybe even distasteful," she warned.

Her earnestness piqued his curiosity. Kathryn deceitful, distasteful? He raised a brow in question.

"You're going to have to pose as my husband," she said

with a decided nod. "Yes, I think it may work. We must announce it in the papers as soon as we possibly can. To-day, I think. Uncle wouldn't dare make an attempt on your life then. Not after everyone in London hears you are the earl and that we're married."

"But, Kathryn, we *are*—"

"I know. I know," she said, interrupting him. She released his knees and turned away to pace again, gesturing impatiently with one hand. "We are *not* married, but who would contradict it? Pip? He doesn't even understand that he's my husband."

Jon sighed when the truth dawned. There had been a gross misunderstanding, all right, one he needed to set straight right now. "Kathryn, listen to me. Pip does not exist."

She patted his shoulder absently while she focused on the floor. "Yes, I know. You've done your brother the best turn of all by pretending his death so everyone believes that. He'd never have managed with the title. People would have laughed and made him dreadfully unhappy if you'd allowed him claim it."

Good Lord, wherever had she gotten such a notion? And why wouldn't she listen to him? "Pay attention, Kathryn! I pretended to be Pip. It was all a ruse."

She nodded again, excited instead of troubled by his words. "Yes! And you must continue the charade, only you need to go the whole distance now, use the power of his title. Claim it publicly for yourself! You are to be the earl of Lyham!" She paced to the window and back, her hands clasped beneath her chin. "Neither Uncle Rupert nor Bun-rich would dare threaten you if you do that. We shall all be safe! You, Pip *and* me. If I pretend to be your countess, they won't dare harm me."

Jon tried to make sense of what she thought she knew. "You think I faked the death of a brother? To hide him from the public?"

She gave a negligent little wave with one hand. "Don't

worry, I told you that I understand why you did it." Then guilt flooded her expression. "It isn't too wrong for us to use his title, is it, Jon? You don't think Pip would mind if he were able to fathom it all, do you?"

Jon shook his head, laughing, speechless at the absurdity of her whole misconstruction.

"Fine, then," she announced with a satisfied clap of her hands. "Everything's settled. I shall do the write-up of the wedding and take it into town today. You should be safe enough for the present. I seriously doubt Bunrich will be able to..."

This had gone on long enough. Jon could hardly bear to disillusion her, but his conscience hurt nearly as much as his injuries. He caught her clasped hands in his good one and squeezed. He locked on her wide-eyed gaze and held it fast. "Kathryn, you must pay close attention. My older brother did die. He went to America adventuring and he died there. The title is truly mine, but it's as impoverished as a beggar's pocket. Empty. Without any power at all."

When she said nothing and her expression didn't change, he continued, trying to make the situation crystal clear. "There is only me, Kathryn. I'm the only Chadwick left, bastard or otherwise. There is no Pip." She nodded once, still expectant, but not as upset as she should be. He sighed heavily and tried again. "You are wed to me, Kathryn. You are my countess, for whatever that's worth. Do you understand? *I* am your husband."

She pulled her hands from his and tapped his cheek softly. "That's *perfect!*" Then she hurried to the door. "I'd better get ready to go, or we'll never get the announcement in tomorrow's editions. We'll make a splash in town with the four thousand from Mother's jewels, make ourselves very visible as a couple. There's great safety in crowds, don't you think?" She blew him a kiss and swept off down the hall.

Jon looked down at his hands—the left one perfect except for its tremor, and the right one swathed like some swami's turban. Regardless of Kathryn's assurances earlier, he could still end up an amputee. But he knew without doubt that he must use his one good hand and all of his wits to protect her as best he could.

Bunrich wouldn't be daunted by his worthless title, and Jon doubted Kathryn's uncle would, either. Maybe if he had some influence or real wealth behind it, they might think twice. But, as things stood now, he was just as vulnerable to murder as the next man. Bunrich would return, out for revenge now, as well as the violin. And Rupert Wainwright would come from yet another direction, probably arrange some sort of disaster to widow Kathryn so that he could carry on with his plans for her.

Kathryn was right in one respect; they would be safer in London. At least he could mount a better defense there than here in this isolated ruin. The old constable hereabouts was so useless, he had trouble finding his teeth in the morning. Better to be under Scotland Yard's jurisdiction if the worst occurred. He would apprise the Yard of the whole situation, and hopefully they would protect Kathryn afterward, if he should be killed.

The music was already dead, of course. He might as well be, too, but he wouldn't seek death. Not yet, anyway. Protecting Kathryn headed his list of priorities just now, and her immediate safety meant having a husband at hand.

The first order of business had to be establishing honesty between them. He had to show her the truth about Pip, since she'd misconstrued every admission he made. She still saw the mask of Jon, the face powder, the dark head of hair and the facade of intelligence. She would have to see to believe.

Slowly he got to his feet, yanked off the wig and struggled out of his shirt. A good scrubbing should do the trick. When she saw the blond Pip with Jon's mangled hand and cynical eyes, she would know the truth. He dreaded her fury, her embarrassment, the humiliation she would feel, but he couldn't live with the deception any longer.

Soaking a cloth in the lukewarm water, Jon soaped up

and scoured off the gritty, tear-streaked powder, dirt and blood. He dunked his head in the water and scrubbed his scalp, then slicked the wet strands back as best he could. Avoiding his eyes in the mirror, he lathered his face and scraped off a day's worth of beard.

When he'd finished, he felt too much like Pip to do Jon justice at the moment. Exhausted, aching and slightly sick to his stomach, Jon lay down to recoup what strength he could before facing the ordeal ahead. Before facing his wife with the irrefutable proof that she *was* his wife. God, how he dreaded this.

Kathryn rushed her toilette, a bit concerned whether she looked elegant enough to portray a countess. The riding habit looked a bit worse for wear, but it would have to do.

When she had cleaned the desk in the study last week, Kathryn had discovered a sheaf of expensive writing paper bearing the Lyham crest in one of the drawers. Today, writing with a flowing, ornate hand, she made announcements to rival a calligrapher's efforts. On a plain sheet, Kathryn composed a very newsy article for *About Town,* K. M. Wainwright's final hurrah as a reporter.

There now, she thought, tomorrow all of London would know her as Lady Kathryn, the new countess of Lyham. And the exciting events in the life of the earl, the great Chadwick, composer extrordinaire, would astound everyone. Regardless of antiquated ideas concerning noblisse oblige, Kathryn didn't believe using a title would rule out Jon's composing. Why, she knew of businessmen, physicians and even one news editor who held titles in today's enlightened society.

She went upstairs to say goodbye and see how Jon was feeling before she left him. When she peeked in, he lay fast asleep. His face was half buried by the pillow he had drawn over his head to block out the light from the window. The soft snores drew a smile from her. He seemed to be recovering nicely thus far. She was glad Grandy had waited around to change his bandage after he took the laudanum last night. Tomorrow, perhaps he would feel strong enough to ride back to London with her and consult a physician to see whether the fingers were set properly.

Kathryn wasn't worried that Bunrich would be back today. He'd be busy dealing with his own wound. With luck, she should return this evening with the worst of their problems solved.

All the way to London, Kathryn worried about Pip. She had no choice but to trust Grandy to keep him with her at the cottage. The old woman had sense enough to keep him well away from Timberoak after she and Jon left for London. Anyone found there might suffer when Bunrich came back looking for Jon.

Maybe the law would find Bunrich before that could happen. Even if Jon reported the assault and the attempted theft of the Strad, Kathryn doubted much would be done about it. Jon had no solid proof against Bunrich. The accusations of a musician who owed five thousand pounds probably wouldn't count for much. But if Jon didn't owe such a grand amount, if he gave every appearance of sudden wealth, and if he wore the title of earl, well, then...

All they needed was a few weeks' time, until her inheritance came through. Then she could settle everything once and for all. The three of them could retire here to the country, repair Timberoak to its former stateliness and lead a life of comfortable leisure. Meanwhile, she meant to surround Jon and herself with so many people, neither Bunrich nor her uncle would dare make a move against them. She patted her reticule and smiled. Her four thousand pounds would go a long way toward that end.

By four o'clock that afternoon, Kathryn felt she had accomplished a good day's work. She had hired an industrious lad to deliver the marriage announcements to all the major newspapers. The Chadwick article for her uncle's newsheet she meant to take care of herself.

A visit to Mr. Grange, an up-and-coming young solicitor

of excellent reputation, had resulted in the rental of a modest but perfectly suitable furnished house in Cronynfield Square. Grange had also arranged a generous payment from Kathryn's funds to the three creditors Jon owed. With the cheques, Grange included word that Lord Jonathan intended to settle all debts in full within the next two months. So the news would go out, via the London grapevine, that the new earl of Lyham was practically solvent. Merchants would scramble to offer credit.

Kathryn counted on the hope that Uncle Rupert hadn't made her disappearance known to the staff at *About Town.* As the owner, he visited the paper only once a week, for staff meetings. Herman Block, the editor, earned his weekly pay twice over. Kathryn approached the offices and slipped in through the employees' entrance.

She greeted one of the copyboys and handed him the article she had written about Jon. "Hullo, Frank. Uncle wants this to run in the morning edition." She said it off-handedly, as though it were of little importance to her personally. "He specified lower front page unless Mr. Block has something he deems more newsworthy." She grinned at the young man and wiggled her eyebrows. "However, I don't think he will."

"Is it the thing on Chadwick you were working on?" Frank asked as he fiddled with the folded paper. "You're almost too late to get the type set up for the next edition."

"Take the time," she advised with a conspiratorial wink. She thumped the edge of the article. "I'll leave it to you, then. Regards to Mr. Block." With that, she skipped toward the back exit and hurried out.

The laugh she'd been holding in erupted as she mounted her mare in an unladylike scramble. Uncle's reaction over his morning tea would be worthy of the front page itself. She only wished she could be there to witness it.

"Come on, Mabel," she said, urging the mare to a trot. "Let's go home."

The sinking sun threw a red blanket over the clouds as

she cleared the city. Riding alone in the dark held little appeal, even though she had the pistol in her saddle pack. Her way lay through open country, with few places for robbers to hide, but one never knew. Kathryn approached a couple in a landau taking the road toward Lakesend and asked if she might ride along beside them for protection as far as Timberoak village.

The well-dressed couple looked askance at a young woman traveling alone. "Are you in some sort of trouble, miss?" the gentleman asked her.

"No. Well, in a way I suppose I am," Kathryn admitted, with a look begging sympathy. She decided now was as good a time as any to begin spreading the news. "You see, I had word that my husband suffered an accident at home, and I couldn't delay long enough to secure an escort." Then she clapped a hand to her cheek and shook her head in dismay. "Where are my manners? Why, I must be more upset than I thought." She stretched out her hand to the man with a belated introduction, "I am Lady Lyham."

"Lady?" the man questioned, with a sharp perusal of her dusty, wrinkled riding attire.

"Yes," she agreed smiling sweetly. "Wife to Lord Jonathan, earl of Lyham." The words made her feel uncomfortably warm in all the wrong places. She supposed it must be guilt.

"My...my lady, I do beg pardon," he stuttered, and then raised her hand as near to his lips as he could manage from the carriage. "I am Squire Farrell of Blythe Close, Lakesend, and this is my wife, Eloise." The portly young woman bobbed several times.

"Charmed," Kathryn crooned. "So nice to meet neighbors. We must get together one of these days under more propitious circumstances, but now I'm dreadfully anxious to get home."

"Oh, oh, yes, of course, you must be distraught," he agreed. "Hope His Grace's accident's not serious. Would you care to share our carriage, my lady?"

"No, thank you. I prefer to ride, sir, but you're very kind to ask. Might we hurry along?" Kathryn had given the two enough fodder to chew for the time being, and didn't want to answer any more questions than she had to. This chance meeting had served her well, if the squire and his lady were the least bit prone to gossip. The marriage, as well as the existence of a new earl, would be all over the county by tomorrow.

The carriage rolled to a stop on the outskirts of Timber-oak village. "I do hope you find His Lordship's accident minor," the squire repeated as he offered his hand to her in parting. "I should be happy to see you directly to your house." He did, in fact, look eager to do so.

"Thank you for your concern, sir, and for the escort thus far. It's only a short way home, and the hour grows late for you, as well. Do take care." She directed her gaze to the shy young woman, who had yet to say a word. "Mistress Farrell, I should be delighted to continue our acquaintance one day soon. Perhaps over tea?"

The woman nodded, mouth agape and eyes wide. She reminded Kathryn of one of the Trafalgar Square pigeons.

"Farewell, then," Kathryn said brightly, and quickly trotted Mabel down the main street past the smithy's and the old Hare's Foot inn. When she glanced over her shoulder, the squire and his wife still sat there staring after her as though she were some sort of apparition. She waved and kicked Mabel to a gallop.

On the way down the lane, it suddenly occurred to Kathryn that she might have made a terrible mistake. Until this moment, she had completely forgotten about Reverend Lockhart, who had performed the marriage ceremony. The Farrells might be—very probably were—friends of his, members of his congregation. What would the good vicar have to say when they told him they'd met the countess of Lyham, who was wed to Lord Jon?

Strange, now that she recalled the wedding. Neither Jon nor the vicar had mentioned the word *proxy* in relation to the marriage. Of course, the name on the certificate was J. Nathan Chadwick, Lyham, which made Pip her legal husband. Did the Reverend Lockhart know all about Pip, or had Jon concealed the truth from the vicar, as well? What a muddle. Jon would simply have to straighten this out himself when it became necessary.

She had more immediate problems to consider.

First of all, Jon would need his hand tended and a bit of reassurance. Then she would prepare a hot bath and a meal of whatever Grandy had left in the kitchen and get a good night's sleep. Tomorrow, if he had recovered enough, she and Jon would go back to the city and begin the masquerade that would ensure their safety.

# Chapter Ten

The moon slanted eerie shadows across the face of Timberoak Manor. A right proper setting for ghosts, Kathryn thought with a shiver. She eyed the creeping tendrils of ivy as the curling leaves swayed in the night breeze. A small animal screamed from the wood, causing Mabel to whinny and fidget.

No light shone from the ballroom or the upstairs window of Pip's room, where she had left Jon sleeping. She rode around back to the stables and breathed a sigh of relief when a wavering glow emanated from the kitchen. Perhaps Grandy was there to share a cup of tea with her. She needed one, after the grueling day she'd spent.

Kathryn lighted the lantern in the stable and quickly saw to Mabel's comfort. Then she washed her hands in the watering trough and picked up the leather pack containing the pistol, her reticule and the papers from the day's transactions.

"It's only me!" she called out as she approached the back door. Without waiting for an answer, she pulled it open and stepped inside.

The sight that greeted her stole her breath. Several cigar stubs and a nest of gray ashes nastied the plate serving as a candleholder. A smelly funk of stale smoke competed with whiskey fumes, making the room stink like a crowded alehouse. The lone occupant appeared to be a dedicated customer.

"Pip! What the devil have you done now?" She marched toward the table that separated her from her errant spouse and slammed down her pack.

"Where did you get this?" She snatched up the bottle of whiskey, definitely not the one they had used to douse Jon's hand. Jon had polished that one off last evening. Apparently the contents of this particular bottle had been depleted quite recently, by her heavy-lidded husband.

Candlelight silvered the little she could see of Pip's eyes. He leaned into the table, bare chest braced against the edge, chin cradled in the palm of his left hand, which also held a new, unlit cigar. Hair trailed about his face and over one side of his forehead in damp, curled strands. His face and body glistened with sweat. He hadn't spoken or moved yet and was obviously quite drunk.

Kathryn felt too exhausted to deal with Pip in such a condition. Damn it, she could wring Grandy's neck for allowing this. Surely the old woman knew enough to keep liquor and cigars out of his reach. Perhaps she'd brought them for Jon.

Kathryn sighed and sank onto the chair across from him. "Oh, Pip, whatever am I going to do with you?"

He tilted back his head and regarded her with a glassy blue stare. One corner of his mouth kicked up in a half grin. "Is that a rhetorical question, Kathryn, or are you offering me a choice?" He raised his right hand from his lap and rested it on the table.

Kathryn gasped at his words and again at the sight of the unraveling bandage. She jerked her gaze from the hand back to his face, noting that his lip wasn't pouting after all, but swollen. From Bunrich's beating? "Jon?" she asked uncertainly.

He tossed the hair back from his face. "If you like."

"Your...hair... Your... I thought you were Pip!"

"A recurring mistake of yours, darling," he drawled.

Then he reached across the table and snatched the bottle from her hand. Before she could object, he upended it and gulped down the last swallow of the whiskey.

Kathryn watched the muscles working in his neck. "Jon, I really don't think you sh—"

"Should drink? Why the hell not?" He slammed the table so hard with the empty bottle, a crack shot up the side of the glass and it fell apart in his hand. He spread his fingers wide, let the remaining piece drop. "A done deed, I'm afraid."

"Quite," she said softly, examining his features with a disbelieving eye. "Without the... You look so much alike. I never dreamed..."

Laughter boomed off the kitchen walls like thunder. Tears rolled down his cheeks as he leaned back in his chair. Then, as suddenly as it had erupted, the false mirth was gone. In its wake lay a look of desolation so profound, Kathryn wanted to weep. "Oh, Jon," she began, and reached out to comfort him.

He simply looked at her waiting hand, his resemblance to Pip so exact she could scarcely believe it. When he spoke, his words seemed more strangled than slurred. "I wish...wish you could forgive me." He shook his head, causing his hair to curtain most of his face as he bent forward. "I know you won't, but I need... Oh, God, Kathryn, please don't leave me." He leaned over the table and laid his forehead to the surface.

Kathryn brushed a hand over his head just as he began to snore. The poor man had to do something for the pain, and she supposed whiskey served as well as, if not better than, laudanum. He would have a devilish headache in the morning, but maybe that would take his mind off his injuries. Maybe she should try to get him back upstairs. Sleeping on the kitchen table couldn't be very restful, and she needed him recovered as quickly as possible. They should get to London no later than tomorrow night, if he could manage to ride.

Kathryn moved around the table and tugged him into an upright position in the chair. "Come on, Jon. Wake up." She supported his head when it lolled back against her chest and looked down on his face. He had worn a wig all this time. A further affectation she hadn't even guessed at. Without thinking, she cradled his chin in one hand. The faint rasp of his whiskers tickled her palm. For a moment, she studied the smooth unlined skin around his eyes. He looked years younger without all that garish powder. *Young as Pip.*

A frisson of foreboding rippled through her and her hand tightened its grip on his face. She used the other to sweep the clinging strands of fair hair away and noticed a tiny, flat mole near the hollow of his throat. Exactly like the one she had remarked the night Pip played his harp and asked her to sing. Her wedding night. The breath rushed out as she stepped away and let his head drop back unsupported.

She stared at him in dawning horror. Words crashed in on her like thieves breaking through a door, sacking her reason, stealing her senses. *Pip doesn't exist. Both the same. I am Pip. A ruse. Recurring mistake. I am your husband. If you like.*

Oh, sweet Jesus! Kathryn grabbed the back of an empty chair and slid onto it to keep from falling. "Nooo…" she moaned, and clasped her hand to her mouth to stifle a sob. Feelings collided and tore her this way and that. She wanted to scream with anger and cry out her grief. There was no Pip! No sweet, gentle boy. Just greedy, conniving, cynical Jon.

"Damn you!" she cried.

Only by sheer force of will did Kathryn keep from kicking over his chair, leaping on top of him and tearing out his hair by the roots. The bloody *wretch!* How he must have laughed at her! She jumped to her feet and sent the leather pack and shards of the whiskey bottle flying with one sweep of her arm. "Damn you to *hell!*"

Kathryn directed her murderous impulses upstairs, where

she began stuffing her clothes into her valise. She didn't dare return to the kitchen, for fear she might kill him. Flouncing around, kicking at everything in her path and cursing aloud slowed her efforts to pack, but she couldn't seem to stop railing.

The rage slowly subsided as exhaustion set in. She flopped down across the bed and pressed her hands to her eyes. Rational thought finally nudged past her fury. Why had he done this? Money?

Kathryn recalled the first episode of his deceit. Jon couldn't have known she would follow him to Timberoak that night in search of a story for the paper. He had known nothing about her inheritance then. He'd had no reason at that point to arrange such a deception, to pretend to be Pip. At least not for gain. She had given him the idea herself. Her own assumptions had fostered this whole ridiculous act.

But why? Why had he gone along with it? Why had he gone to so much trouble to continue the charade? Well, she supposed he had been embarrassed that night when she surprised him, being caught as he was. Even now, despite her anger, the picture of the great Chadwick sprawled on the floor of that cavernous old ballroom, writing opera in his underwear, made her want to laugh. She had to admit, if she'd known who he was at the time, she might have made that discovery into a fine little comedy for public consumption. All of London would have wept with glee on reading it. Small wonder he hadn't owned up to who he really was, especially when she provided him with the perfect escape.

Then, later, when she turned to him for help in hiding from Uncle Rupert, he had wanted her money. He had volunteered to marry her immediately, without a thought to concealing the reason. She was the one who had insisted on marriage to poor, helpless Pip.

*The marriage!* Kathryn sat up straight and gasped with sudden realization. Oh, no! *Jon* was her husband! Well, she couldn't—no, *wouldn't*—excuse that rotten piece of work. He had deliberately, coldly, set out to trick her to get her money. She fumed anew, pounding the nearest pillow until her fists hurt. Burrowing into it, her face buried, her guilty conscience rose up like a wicked little troll and tweaked her soundly. Somewhere deep inside, she had wished for it, wanted Jon to be the one she was wed to instead of Pip.

Kathryn always tried not to lie to herself, but this time she had suppressed the truth with a remarkable vengeance. Her desire for the man she thought was Pip had seemed a near perversion, given his supposed mental state. Her lust for Jon, of course, she had believed downright adulterous. Right now, if she allowed for perfect honesty in her self-examination, Kathryn knew she felt relieved to be free of the guilt on both accounts. At least her body's base longing centered on only one man. Not that she would ever give in to it; certainly not *now*. Not after all he had done.

Thankfully, Jon hadn't acted on her weakness of the flesh and consummated their union. Marriages could be undone, and this one certainly would be annulled as soon as she turned twenty-five. She'd hold to her bargain with Jon and give him his bloody six thousand pounds. And, by God, he'd give her the protection of his name and title until she was through using it. He owed her that.

Her chest began to ache somewhere in the vicinity of her heart, now that her outrage had dulled. Kathryn mourned for the boy she had come to care for, the boy who had never really existed. And she despaired over the arrogant, deceitful man who could stir her to fever pitch with no more than a suggestive look. Somehow that man seemed less believable to her than Pip.

Who *was* the real Jon Chadwick?

Kathryn sighed into the pillow and wiped her eyes on the edge of the linen cover. She sniffed loudly as she pushed herself to a sitting position and began to undress. No use tearing off into the night with no real direction. She must gather her wits.

Tomorrow they would proceed as planned. The remainder of the four thousand from her mother's jewels was enough to take her out of the country until her birthday, but that would leave Jon to face his devils alone. And, wretched charlatan though he was, Chadwick was still her husband.

For the time being.

The hammer inside his head woke him. Jon stirred at the godawful racket and immediately froze. The cricked muscles of his neck protested any movement at all. His stomach gurgled alarmingly, and he thought his eyes might roll out of their sockets if he opened his lids. Christ, what had he done to himself?

After several interminable moments, he realized he couldn't remain motionless forever. With pitiable effort, he forced his head upright and squinted at the sunlight spilling through the kitchen window. Damnation, he wished death had hauled him off last night. Hell had to be better than this. He dragged his feet under him and pushed up from the table with his good hand.

Kicking aside the broken glass with a stockinged foot, he stepped over the leather saddle pack, groaning at the sight of it. Uh-oh. Kathryn was back.

Now he vaguely recalled a row of some sort when she'd come in the night before, but he'd been too far gone for much of it to register.

At the moment, he didn't care what had happened. His mind felt fully occupied just with making his way to the door. Pissing in Kathryn's kitchen loomed as a real possibility if he didn't hurry.

When he'd relieved himself on the weeds by the back door, he eyed the horse trough by the barn. Staggering toward it, he leaned forward to immerse his head. That wasn't enough, and it hurt like hell to bend over. He stood straight, threw a leg over the side and slid down into icy water, clothes and all. The creeping numbness felt like heaven.

Maybe he could drown here. He bent his knees and lay farther back so that the water covered his head completely. Umm.

Old self-preservation nudged him up for a breath, and he sputtered a curse. The water clinging to his lips tasted moldy. He spat with disgust. When he had soaked enough to ease his aches, Jon got his feet under him and heaved himself out of the trough.

By the time he reached the kitchen again, he felt slightly better than a day old corpse.

"God have mercy! Have you lost your mind?" Kathryn's stridency cut through his recovery like a hacksaw, shattering any hopes of a peaceful convalescence.

"If you possess any compassion for a fellow human being, Kathryn, kindly lower your voice to a screech," he whispered. He wiped the stagnant water off his face with his left palm. "And I'd walk on my knees through that broken glass for some coffee."

She sputtered and gasped, flinging her hands out as though seeking a balance. Jon squeezed his eyes shut and leaned against the doorframe, bracing for her next outburst. Instead, the room grew quiet, and her words barely broke the silence. "Sit down, Jon." He dragged his feet toward the table and lowered himself to the chair where he'd spent the night. Elbows on the table, he braced his heavy head on his palm.

The sounds of pouring water and striking matches told him she had discovered a streak of pity somewhere in that termagant's soul of hers. Thank God. "Sorry, Kath," he managed as he drew in the smell of grinding coffee beans.

"Yes, well, you should be! Look at that bandage, soaked through. And you'll likely catch your death of the pneumonia, or some foul disease from that putrid water in the trough."

Jon dredged up a weak smile. She still cared. "Horse spit never hurt anybody."

"Take off those wet trousers while I fetch you a robe."

"Wait, you needn't," he said when she started toward the door to the hall. "I'll go upstairs and change."

She shot him a cold look, her chin raised and her eyes narrowed to brown slits. "Dress for town, then, and shave if you can manage. You don't want me at your throat with a straight razor after all that happened last night. I'll see to your hand when you come down."

"Town?" He noticed for the first time that she was dressed in her riding habit. "Today?"

Her expression remained the same—frigid. "Yes, the marriage is to be announced in this morning's papers. We must see to our wardrobes and get the house in order for curious guests. We're bound to be overrun with them once the word is out."

"Guests?" he repeated, trying hard to comprehend what she might be talking about. He must have missed more than a brief argument about the evils of drink last night.

"Go and change first, and then we'll talk," she ordered, turning away to check on the coffee.

Jon shook his head to clear it, but the action had little effect other than to compound his headache. Unwilling to cross her when she was obviously cross enough, he decided his most prudent course at the moment was to follow orders. She hadn't mentioned the Pip business again, so he had no idea whether or not she'd gotten that straight in her mind. Considering the condition of his hangover, he certainly didn't relish asking about that now.

He supposed she still must be angry about finding him deep in his cups when she returned. Well, what did she expect? She had deserted him at the lowest point in his life, after all. Just taken off to London as though getting his fingers smashed were nothing out of the ordinary.

A bone-shaking shudder coursed through his body and left his knees weak, but he had almost gotten used to the feeling. It came over him every time he thought of his fatal wound, just pulsing there at the end of his right arm. Kathryn wouldn't realize the injury was fatal, though, so he could forgive her a little for the desertion. What signified only ruined fingers to her meant death to him; the death of all he had been or ever hoped to be.

He drew in a deep breath and stretched his chin up, trying to summon the will to face the immediate future. Whatever Kathryn had planned for them in London, he would cooperate with until she was out of danger. Someone had to look after her until she could inherit and establish her independence. That much he could do.

If anyone tried to harm her, he would simply kill them. As a soldier, he had killed before, and while he hadn't particularly relished killing, he had been devilishly clever at it. Bunrich certainly deserved to die, no question about it. Kathryn's greedy uncle probably did, as well. Removing the threats to Kathryn seemed to be the only reason for his existence now.

He suddenly wished he had granted her the first interview she asked for. He wished he had admitted his powerful attraction for her before the need for deception arose. He wished he could have finished the opera, made a small fortune on it and courted her like a normal man. Trouble was, he had never been normal, and now never would be. Perhaps everything had worked out the only way it could have done, but the regrets would haunt him as long as he lived. Perhaps, if the gods finally turned kind, that wouldn't be overly long.

Kathryn uncovered the basket Grandy had delivered before dawn. She fried the eggs and sliced the bread into chunks. Just as she poured the coffee, she heard Jon's boots clump heavily down the stairs. At least his feet weren't dragging, she thought.

When he appeared, more about him looked changed than his clothes. For one thing, the customary powder was missing. And he'd left off the dark wig. His wet hair lay neatly slicked against his head, smelling of his sandalwood soap and free of its usual queue. A small razor nick marred his strong jaw. The pale blue of his irises enhanced the network of red around them.

He had dressed casually in a clean, slightly frayed lawn shirt and a serviceable gray tweed jacket. A maroon silk cravat hung loose about his neck. His black riding pants fitted like a second skin, molded over muscles that flexed admirably with every movement. She wondered how in the world he had managed to get them on with only one hand working.

The clothes had hung in the wardrobe of the room she'd always thought of as Pip's. This outfit must be all he had left after yesterday's altercation ruined his suit. He made a disreputable-looking earl this morning, quite a match to her rumpled countess.

"Eat first, then I'll redress your hand," she said, and promptly took her own seat. He complied, wolfing the food much as the mannerless Pip had always done. Oddly, that comforted her a bit.

They completed the meal without further conversation. Kathryn cleared the table and assembled the bandages and healing potion Grandy had included in the morning's basket of food. When she had everything laid out, Kathryn held out her hand. "Let's get on with it." She didn't relish seeing how the expected swelling of tissue had affected her latest needlework, but there was no one else around to do it.

He shrank back in his chair, holding his right hand cradled in his left. The blue eyes darkened, and he pressed his lips together. He looked so much like the Pip she'd loved, it made her want to cry.

"Come now, it must be done, or you could suffer an infection."

Slowly, reluctantly, he released his right hand and inched it toward her. The trembling caught at her heart, but she resisted offering sympathy. She didn't want to feel sorry for him. She wanted to hate him.

Making her voice as matter-of-fact as she could, Kathryn

explained what she was doing. "First we'll get this wet wrapping off and give your hand a good wash. Be very still." His harsh intake of breath almost stopped her, but she persevered.

A quick glance showed him turned away with his eyes clenched shut. "Look, Jon," she said encouragingly, knowing that the longer he avoided seeing the damage, the worse his imagination would make it.

There was a great deal of bruising and the fingers were indeed badly swollen, but all of them seemed perfectly straight. It would be impossible to tell whether they were set correctly, or if he would have proper use of them, until the bones healed and the swelling receded.

"Don't move your hand," she warned quietly as she gently lowered it into the pan of warm water she'd prepared. When he had soaked for several moments, she lifted the hand out and patted the excess water away from the uninjured parts with a clean cloth.

He might have been a statue carved in stone. As far as she could tell, he hadn't breathed. And he still hadn't looked. "This may burn," she warned as she dribbled Grandy's concoction over the stitching. He grunted, and his body jerked involuntarily.

"How...how many?" he asked through his teeth in an agonized whisper.

Kathryn sighed and looked up from his hand. His eyes were so tightly closed, she could barely see the lashes. "I told you before. Three were broken, one badly bruised, maybe cracked. See for yourself, if you don't believe me."

His lips came uncurled and he sucked in a deep breath, letting it out with a shudder. She waited expectantly as his eyes opened and cut to the side. His glance was quick and furtive, his nod the same. "All right, finish." He breathed the words out in a rush and swallowed hard. He looked slightly green.

In moments, Kathryn had replaced the cleaned bits of the whalebone splint and rewrapped his hand in fresh strips of linen. "All done. You were so brave, I wish I had a sweet-meat to reward you."

That got his dander up, as she had known it would. Sympathy wouldn't do right now. He shook with anger, but at least that was better than wallowing in self-pity. Men could be such babies.

"You think this a bloody joke, do you?" he shouted.

"Of course it's not a joke. But it could have been worse! Good Lord, Jon, people come back from wars with whole limbs missing, eyes blinded, paralyzed, crazed beyond hope. Here you've a few fingers out of order, and one would think the world stopped turning, that your entire life is over."

"It *is* over," he replied in a deadly-calm voice. "At least, life as I know it. You know as well as I that these..." He nodded toward his hand and swallowed hard. "The nerves and bones were crushed. They'll heal stiff, useless. The music's gone." He leaned forward and rested his arms on the table, glaring at the bandage. "Well, not gone, exactly, but dammed up inside my head with no way to get out."

Secretly she feared he was right about the extent of his injury and the outcome. "Even should that prove true, Jon, you are more than the music," she said in her firmest voice. "You are *more* than that."

He met her eyes then, and she could feel his anguish. "Kathryn," he began, his voice steady now, "I do thank you for trying, for shooting Bunrich when you did and tending to me afterward. I'll repay you for all of that if I possibly can."

"Damned right you will," she said, busying herself with clearing the table so that she wouldn't be tempted to show any pity. In his state of mind, he didn't need that. But in spite of her residual anger at his tricking her, Kathryn had an overwhelming urge to take him in her arms and comfort him. She hardened her heart as best she could by recalling how devilishly he had maneuvered her into marriage. "Go collect your music and instruments now and let's be off."

Half an hour later, Kathryn had their horses saddled, with her valise and pack strapped across the back of her mare. She returned to the house to help Jon carry out his things.

She found him sitting cross-legged on the floor in the middle of the ballroom, clutching the lute to his chest and staring through the floor-length windows at nothing. Kathryn felt tears rise, burning her nose and the backs of her eyes. Jon was wrong; Pip did exist. He was right here, a lost soul with no answers.

Pity was one thing, compassion another. With a soft cry, she went to kneel beside him and pulled his head to her breast. "Oh, Jon, please don't grieve so. You still have the music. It's still there, and you'll find a way to share it. I know you will." She threaded her fingers through his hair and clutched him to her heart.

He pulled away from her and gently laid the instrument on the floor. "Right, of course. I might push a bow with two fingers. If the others don't rot, and take the hand, as well."

"That won't happen," she assured him, clutching his forearm gently. "I told you I won't let it. Your hand will be fine and you *will* play again. You will!"

When he turned to her, she saw the battle in his eyes. Desperate hope warred with dark certainty. "I need… I can't shake this…horror," he whispered, "that there's nothing left."

She enfolded him in her arms and kissed him gently, moving her lips over his, trying to soothe. His tense mouth softened under hers, opened, and grasped more than she'd offered.

Under his unexpected onslaught, good sense deserted her and she responded in kind. She couldn't seem to get close enough, taste him enough, give him enough. Desire, long suppressed by guilt, reared with a suddenness that broke all restraints.

His left hand burrowed through her hair, loosening it, gripping it, shifting her head to match the frantic slanting of his mouth over hers. He tasted of mint, male heat, and undiluted passion.

Jon nudged her backward until she lay beneath him on the floor, writhing to bring her aching need in closer contact with his. He groaned and shifted his lower body against her until she parted her legs to cradle him. "Please," he breathed into her mouth, and thrust his tongue inside, filling her, giving her a gentler preview of what she knew must come. Soon.

Kathryn closed her eyes and arched her body in assent. A wordless sound of approval vibrated between them, its source in question, its meaning mutual. She felt his total weight on her as he withdrew his hand from her hair and snaked it between them to drag up her skirts.

As his mouth left hers and sought her neck, a brief flash of reason streaked through the fog of her passion. *You will be married for real. No way out of it. You'll be his.*

Desire argued hotly. *He needs this. I need this. Desperately.*

Fierce hunger slammed through her when he found her mouth again. Reason be damned. Kathryn wanted him, all of him, in all his guises—charlatan, rogue or backward boy, she didn't care any longer. When he braced himself away from her on his right elbow, she added her hands to his eager one and stripped away the clothing between them. Her legs struggled and kicked away her pantalets while he cursed his buttons loose.

Suddenly he was there, sinking into her, stretching urgently into depths she hadn't known were there. A brief flash of pain glided effortlessly into delicious friction. Kathryn cried out and lifted her hips, clutching his with an alien urgency. He rose and fell against her, grasping her mouth with his until she felt engulfed, possessed so fully she felt one with him.

Through the haze of gathering ecstasy, Kathryn could

have sworn she heard his music, a wild, torrid rhythm building to an overpowering crescendo. Her body shook with it, shuddered with pleasure so deep and profound it hurt.

His harsh gasps mounted into a primal growl as he plunged a final time, held rigid against her and then seemed to melt over, around and inside her. His heart thundered against her flattened breasts. She thought her own heart had probably stopped.

Kathryn dragged her hands from his bare hips, up around his narrow waist, and linked her fingers to hold them there. By rights, she ought to be furious with him and with herself. Perhaps a part of her was, but satisfied languor kept her still and unwilling to let him go. He made no move to leave her.

Finally, his lips stirred slightly against her ear. "Oh, Christ, what have I done?" came his breathless, agonized whisper.

"Become a husband," she mouthed soundlessly. The swell of her joy surprised her.

## Chapter Eleven

Kathryn kept a tight rein on Mabel as she and Jon entered the environs of London proper. Carriage traffic seemed light for midafternoon, but the mare acted skittish after having walked for most of what should have been a two-hour trip. Both mounts loved a good gallop, but Jon refused to take the chance of a spill when he was laden with his precious ladies.

One lady in tow thanked God the others were so valuable to him. Kathryn didn't think she could have ridden this far even at a walk if she hadn't been on a sidesaddle. Her back ached from being pressed into the ballroom floor. And other, less mentionable places suffered worse than surface bruises. She longed for a tub full of steaming water and a lengthy stay—alone—in a soft feather bed.

Jon avoided her eyes, and all but the most necessary conversation. She couldn't decide whether he was embarrassed about showing weakness in front of her with regard to his injury, or about tumbling her on the floor as though she were a lusty parlormaid. Probably both, now that she thought about it.

She was a bit uneasy with the tumbling part herself. How tempting it was to blame Jon for what happened, but she *had* kissed him first. He'd obviously regretted what they'd done the second it was over. Kathryn wasn't quite certain how she felt about it yet, but regret wasn't exactly upper-most in her mind.

When Jon had finally disengaged himself from her, he'd struggled to right his clothes, refusing her help. Then he had stalked out of the room and up the stairs without a word. By the time she had put herself back in order and repinned her hair, he had returned with the Stradivarius.

Kathryn had watched him stow the three instruments in their respective cases and slip his stack of music into a leather folder. With only his left hand for gripping and his right elbow for bracing, both tasks had proved laborious. "Take those two," he'd ordered without looking at her, and marched out with the music under his arm and the Strad in his hand. She'd carried the lyre and lute to the horses and assisted him in fastening all his treasures to Imp's sad-dle by means of stout leather straps.

Kathryn had related the events of her trip to London and the location of the house she had rented for them. Jon had merely nodded, lips firm and eyes straight ahead. She'd wanted to smack him then. She still did, for reasons too numerous to list.

As awkward as it might prove, she wanted him to ac-knowledge what had happened between them in some way other than this abominable silence of his. She needed some clue as to how they might proceed from here. It wasn't as though she expected an avowal of love, or anything, but the wretch could at least have said thank-you. As it stood now, she experienced the worst of both his personas: Jon's jaded haughtiness and Pip's childish pouting. He gave whole new meaning to the word dichotomy.

His sharp turn out of Trafalgar Square dragged Kathryn back to their present situation. "The house doesn't lie in this direction. Where are you going?"

"Scotland Yard," he snapped.

"Now?" Kathryn turned Mabel and accompanied him down Whitehall. "We really ought to settle in and then find you a doctor. Why must we do this now?"

"In the event your uncle isn't overawed by my useless title and decides to make you a widow right away."

She had nothing to say to that. It was a distinct possibility, and the more people who were aware of it, the better.

The huge government building at #4 Whitehall looked forbidding, just as she was sure it was meant to be. Jon dismounted and hired a lad to watch their horses while they conducted their business inside. She went about the task of unlashing the instruments as though it were an everyday chore. Jon cradled the Strad and music in his good arm and stood aside as an exiting policeman held the door for them to enter.

"May I assist you, sir?" asked one of the young men at the entrance desk.

Jon might not be dressed for the part, but his voice rang with all the authority of an aristocrat. "My name is Chadwick. I should like to register two complaints, fraud and assault against my person. Also, there's the matter of a murder I should like to prevent."

The young officer's jaw dropped. His wispy mustache quivered uncertainly. "Murder, sir? May I ask who the intended victim might be?"

Jon's left brow rose in a quelling expression. "Not unless you will be in charge of the case."

"Uh, no...no, sir, not I. You should see Chief Inspector MacLinden. Would you follow me, please?"

Kathryn fell in step just behind them as they strode off through a maze of corridors lined with offices. The place looked rather clinical and smelled of old books and cigar smoke. They trudged up only one flight of stairs, and their guide halted in front of a half-glass door.

An impatient voice answered the timid knock, "Yes, yes, come in. Ah, Timothy, who have we here, then?"

"Uh, Mr....Chadwick to see you, sir."

Kathryn couldn't conceal a smile when she saw their inspector. He was so obviously Scottish, the epitome of what one would expect in the august environs. She guessed him to be just under sixty, only a shade taller than she, and sporting a set of old-fashioned dundreary whiskers that still held hints of red. Bright green eyes raked Jon with a quick, assessing look.

He had risen immediately as they entered and braced his square, capable hands on the edge of his littered desk. "Lord Lyham, what may I do for you?"

Jon betrayed his surprise with a small drop of his jaw. He frowned at the inspector's small bow of deference. "Do you know me, sir?"

"Aye, in a manner of speaking," the Scot said, chuckling. He bowed a bit lower in Kathryn's direction, "My lady? Won't you please be seated?"

"Thank you, Inspector." She set down the two instruments beside a comfortable wing chair and then settled herself for the interview.

Jon took the matching chair, rested the Stradivarius on his lap and turned his narrowed gaze on the curious young man who had shown them in.

"That will be all, Tim," MacLinden said, verifying Jon's wordless dismissal. "Now then, milord," he said, "what brings you here?" He backed up, sat down, and leaned forward on his desk in apparent anticipation.

"I never mentioned my title, Inspector."

The bushy eyebrows drew together, and one side of the fellow's drooping mustache rose. "Well, I knew yer father well enough, and you're his spit an' image, if you don't mind my saying it." The grin widened, showing slightly crooked teeth that only enhanced his charm. "Yer da served as leftenant in my company back in '56. Dragoons, y'know. Mere lad then, but a fine officer, all the same." He reached for a folded news sheet and swiveled it around so that Jon could see the front-page article. "And I'll admit the morning papers gave me a wee clue, as well."

Kathryn suffered Jon's suspicious look and then watched him scan the bold print. *Chadwick: Lord of the Ivories.* The masthead read *About Town.* She smiled with satisfaction.

So Uncle Rupert hadn't found out about her article before it went to press.

"Congratulations on your marriage," MacLinden said sincerely.

Bright red color suffused Jon's face. Well he ought to blush, she thought, recalling this morning in the ballroom, when he had made theirs a marriage in fact.

Jon muttered a negligent word of thanks and then launched directly into his complaints against Bunrich. MacLinden listened intently, scribbling hastily in a small, dog-eared notebook he'd fished from his pocket.

Only when Jon stumbled over the episode with the ax and its results did the Scot show any overt reaction. "Good God, smashed? Have you seen a doctor?" The green eyes darted to Jon's bandaged hand and back to his face. He stood immediately and snatched his bowler from a nearby rack. "You come wi' me, lad." Without waiting for an answer, MacLinden rounded the desk and picked up the instrument cases Kathryn had set by her chair. "Well, come on, then!" he barked, and headed out the door.

Jon looked at her as though she had an answer for the man's abrupt behavior. "Better go," she said, shrugging. "He's got your ladies."

They hurried after MacLinden, who took the stairs like a fellow half his age. When they reached the front desk, he ordered his carriage brought round on the instant. Everyone within earshot jumped and scrambled into action. Within moments, he had Kathryn and Jon ensconced in his coach, with their horses tethered behind.

"May I be so bold as to ask where we're going?" Jon inquired, with a touch of the old Chadwick sarcasm.

MacLinden ignored his tone. "St. James. Two of the best doctors in London."

"Thank God," Kathryn muttered.

"Now see here, MacLinden," Jon objected, "I haven't even finished telling—"

"Stow that for now," the inspector said, pointing to

Jon's hand. "First things first. We'll get down to business after we've seen about those fingers of yours."

He began an excited cataloging of Dr. Neil Bronwyn's accomplishments and continued with praise for the man's wife, one of London's few female physicians. "They're primarily research now, y'see, but Neil's done more surgery than most who specialize. Battlefield, y'know. Can fix anything, I daresay. Saved my arm in Salamanca back in '57. That's how I met him. Anyway, you'll need a statement of the damage if you're to bring a charge against this Mr. Bunrich."

Jon never got another word in. Kathryn listened quietly, amused at MacLinden's lack of deference to Jon's title. She was vastly relieved that this doctor friend of the inspector's would soon relieve her of her duties as makeshift nurse.

"Ah, here we are," MacLinden said as they stopped in front of a grand Italianate mansion. He led them up to the massive front doors and rapped the knocker soundly.

A young lady of about fifteen years swept the door open almost immediately and threw her arms around the inspector's neck. "Uncle Lindy! What brings you here this time of day?"

She straightened suddenly when she noticed Jon and Kathryn. "Oh, pardon me, I didn't realize you'd brought guests. Come in, all of you, we were preparing tea. You'll join us, of course." She reached for Kathryn's hand. "I'm Helena Bronwyn."

"This is Lady Lyham," MacLinden offered belatedly, "and His Lordship, the earl of Lyham. And this saucy miss—" he kissed the girl's rosy cheek "—is my favorite goddaughter."

The girl bobbed slightly, tossed her red-gold curls and winked one dark blue eye. "He says that about all four of us. This way, please. Leave your things there on the credenza," she said as she led them through an elegant marbled entry into a sumptuous dining room. "Mama, Uncle Lindy's brought Lord and Lady Lyham to tea! I'll set extra places.'' She scampered off through what Kathryn assumed was the door to the kitchen.

A small, slender woman of around fifty skirted around the table to greet them. Kathryn felt an instant affinity. The lady doctor's infectious smile carried an impish quality, further enhanced by her feathered cap of reddish curls.

''Forgive our informality,'' she said, extending her hand to Jon, who dutifully bowed and brushed his lips over her knuckles.

MacLinden cleared his throat. ''Lord and Lady Lyham, may I present Lady Elizabeth, countess of Havington.''

Kathryn gasped and dropped a curtsy. Why hadn't she made the connection? Lord, the Havingtons were famous! Of course, she hadn't exactly run in their exalted social circle, except on the three occasions when she'd attended those musical evenings. They obviously hadn't been present or she would have remembered them.

The countess laughed at her surprise. ''Lindy was shameful not to tell you beforehand. Neil came into his title long after he had begun practicing, you see. I was his research assistant at the time. I'm afraid we were too firmly entrenched in our profession to give it up. We raised a few brows at first, but now no one seems to mind.''

Then she took Kathryn's hand and drew her toward the door they had just entered. ''Why don't we all repair to the study until tea's ready. Neil's probably engrossed in some eye-straining treatise, and he needs interrupting.''

Jon protested, ''No, please, we can return another time.''

''Nonsense! It's no bother at all.''

The earl of Havington looked even less deserving of a title than Jon did, if attire counted at all. His shirtsleeves rolled to his elbows, gold-framed glasses perched below the bridge of his nose, he rose hesitantly to his stockinged feet. The man stood every inch as tall as Jon, and his physique looked every bit as trim. The inspector had mentioned serving with him in the Crimea, so Kathryn suspected they were of an age. The earl, despite his silvery hair and sun-lined face, carried his years very lightly. Kathryn thought him one of the handsomest men she had ever encountered.

MacLinden reached up and clapped him on the shoulder. "Neil, I've brought you a patient."

"The earl of Lyham," Lady Elizabeth added with a moue of amusement, "and his lady wife. They may or may not have Christian names?" She cocked a sandy brow at Kathryn.

"Kathryn," Kathryn supplied with an embarrassed smile, "and Jonathan." She inclined her head toward Jon. "Chadwick," she added.

"Aha, Jonathan Chadwick!" Lady Elizabeth exclaimed. "This morning's papers! Of course! We heard you'd returned to London and were giving private concerts. I recall seeing you in Milan when you were a child. What a virtuoso you were, even then. I especially loved that violin concerto you performed. Don't you remember, Neil? But this is marvelous!" Then her bright gaze dropped to his bandaged hand, and concern wrinkled her forehead. "Or perhaps not. What has happened to you?"

MacLinden launched into a concise explanation, and Kathryn could see Neil Bronwyn's interest heighten with every word. The moment he had the essential information, he ushered them out of the room, across the hall and into a spotless laboratory. He seated Jon under a bright electric light and began to unwrap the hand.

Jon offered no objection, but Kathryn knew by the tense set of his shoulders that he was on the edge of losing his composure. She stepped closer and rested a hand on his back. His muscles flexed under her palm.

The doctor held the fingers directly between him and the strong light. "Look correctly set, but with all the puffiness, it is hard to tell. With that blunt blow, there could be loose bone splinters."

Bronwyn looked up and held Jon's somber gaze with one of his own. "I believe we should open up these three to check that, and take a look at the tissue damage, as well.

We could wait until the swelling subsides, if it does, but that will be too late. If we don't make certain of proper blood flow, you will lose the fingers through necrosis. That could result in loss of the entire hand eventually. The nerves are very probably damaged, but if we can save the fingers, you may have some mobility. They will be stiff, but at least you'll have them, if all goes well.''

Jon swallowed audibly as Kathryn squeezed his shoulder. She winced at the shudder she felt beneath her hand. How he dreaded the thought of a blade of any kind near his fingers—especially now, after what had happened. His voice sounded scratchy and choked when he asked, ''Wh-when would you do it?''

''Now.'' Bronwyn turned to his wife. ''Get ready, Bettsy, and tell Helena to bring the water.'' He turned to Kathryn. ''You scrub up, as well. Do you know anything of ether?''

Kathryn shook her head vehemently. ''Please! You can't ask me to...''

The doctor pinned her with a glare. ''I'm not asking you, Lady Kathryn. I'm telling. Get your hands washed and assist me. You'll be the anesthetist.''

Kathryn listened carefully while the doctor delivered her instructions. She concentrated on the number of drops she dripped slowly over the gauze mask covering Jon's face. Her fingers felt the pulse in his neck, and she counted as Havington ordered. She marked the rise and fall of the bare chest, glancing warily at the two heads bent over Jon's right hand. She prayed.

After what seemed hours, the earl ordered her to stop the ether drip and remove the pad.

The countess motioned her toward a wooden chair and took up Kathryn's place behind Jon's head to monitor his vital signs.

Inspector MacLinden nudged her shoulder and put a glass in her hand. The brandy slid down her throat with a comforting burn and pooled in her stomach. Kathryn could feel the warmth spread outward through her bloodstream. She curled her own fingers and then straightened them, palm up, tracing the barely visible veins, imagining the liquor suffusing them so easily.

The doctors revived Jon without much effort, but he was so dreadfully sick! Kathryn groaned with sympathy as she watched him heave and retch with the aftereffects of the ether.

When Lord Havington and Inspector MacLinden had helped Jon to a comfortable bed in a small room off the converted conservatory they used as a lab, the earl ushered her out of the room to speak with her out of Jon's hearing.

"Remarkably, there's no sign of infection yet. As I feared, there were bone shards to remove. None of the breaks were clean ones, and they won't heal as such breaks do. Parts of the bone will be missing, you see. I managed to coax open the major veins, however the extensor tendon, which controls the small finger, was nearly severed. The state of all the nerves is anyone's guess. The other tendons should recover partially, at least. The digits will be stiff, hopefully not completely useless. We must insure he moves his hand as little as possible for a few weeks. Once he's over the effects of the anesthetic, I shall dose him with a bit of morphine for the pain."

"Is there any possibility he could ever regain good use of the fingers once they've healed?" Kathryn asked.

The doctor sighed and shook his head, running a long, slender hand through his silvery hair. "To be perfectly honest with you, there's very little chance of that, given the extent of the damage."

Kathryn squeezed her eyes shut and pressed her fingertips to the bridge of her nose. "His days of performing professionally are over, aren't they?"

"Yes, I should think so." He sighed. "I'm very sorry."

Kathryn nodded. Jon had known all along that was the case. She had stupidly tried to create hope where none existed.

Somehow she would have to put aside her anger at her husband's trickery and try to help him adjust. She owed him for giving her sanctuary when she was desperate. And if she hadn't removed the violin from its hiding place in the piano, Jon would have given it to Bunrich and avoided this tragedy. She was responsible. Once he got past the shock of the situation, he would realize that and might not want her around, anyway. Until then, she must do everything she could to further his recovery, both physically and emotionally.

Her vision fogged with tears, Kathryn followed their hostess down the hall as ordered, and mechanically sat down for the delayed tea. All her thoughts, however, rested uncomfortably with the man lying on the narrow bed in the laboratory.

Jon refused the tincture of morphine when Neil Bronwyn offered it. "Don't bother with that now, sir. I need to speak with the inspector. It's important." He turned his head to MacLinden. "My wife's uncle is scheming to take control of her inheritance. He means to force her into a marriage with his partner, a fellow named Randall Nelson. He'll have to get rid of me first, and I believe he'll try to do just that. Kathryn overheard him planning."

"That's all very interesting, milord, but you must know I'm powerless to arrest a man simply for making the plans. Has he attempted anything against you yet?" MacLinden dragged out his dog-eared notebook and busily scribbled away.

"Not yet. That's why I agreed to bring Kathryn to town. If Wainwright succeeds in eliminating me, she will need official protection."

Neil Bronwyn interrupted him. "Seems to me you are the one needing the protection."

Jon frowned at the doctor. "I'm in no position to ask any favors here, but my pride seems to have gone the way of my music. Please, I implore you both, see to my wife's safety. She has no one else.''

MacLinden patted Jon's shoulder and stuffed the notebook back in his pocket. "Not to worry, lad. After I have a talk with this uncle of hers, he won't entertain another thought about interfering with his niece or yourself.''

"And you'll see to Bunrich's arrest? When he reads of the marriage, he may go after Kathryn to get at the violin,'' Jon said, anxious to have every threat removed as soon as possible.

MacLinden pursed his lips and shook his head. "I've been thinking. We could have a slight problem there, I'm afraid. Though the incident took place out of my jurisdiction, I could call in a few favors and have him taken up. But the man was shot, you say. If he has a jot of sense, he'll use those two thugs of his to swear against you and your lady. A magistrate might think his shooting injury worse than what he did to you.''

"What about fraud, then? He lied about my owing him the five thousand quid,'' Jon said.

"Your word against his. You have one witness, your wife. He has two. There's no guarantee you'd be believed. Trend now is to lean over backward not to show favoritism to the upper classes.'' MacLinden raised a busy brow and inclined his head. "And you certainly are established as a member of the upper classes, as of this morning's papers.''

Jon released a worried sigh. "Bunrich will seek his revenge. I know him. Even if I give the blighter what he wants, he'll still seek satisfaction if he figures out who shot him.''

"I expect you're right about that,'' MacLinden agreed. "Even if I can't arrest him, nothing says I can't keep him under close watch once I locate him. Same goes for Rupert Wainwright.''

"Thank you,'' Jon said, and closed his eyes against the excruciating pain flaring all the way up his arm. At least he had done what he could, for the present, to arrange for

Kathryn's protection. "I would like to speak with my wife. Alone, if I may?" he asked.

"Of course," the doctor agreed as he stood to leave. "You're sweating like a racehorse. At least allow yourself a bit of laudanum, if you won't have the morphine. I'll mix some with tea and have your wife bring it in."

Jon nodded, thankful for the relief provided by their promises and the repeated offer of a painkiller.

"You're a very lucky man, my lord," MacLinden said, chewing thoughtfully on his unlit pipe.

"Right," Jon said with a snort of derision. "Problem is with the *sort* of luck, isn't it?"

"I was referring to your lovely wife. I suppose you're entitled to a bit of self-pity about your unfortunate injury, but I shouldn't cling to it, if I were you," the inspector snapped. He waved the pipe at Jon when he had snared his full attention. "I can't help but wonder at your stoicism in refusing the morphine, and then this urgency in setting up for your lady's welfare. You aren't thinking of doing something foolish, now are you?"

Jon's laughter tasted bitter as he focused on his newly wrapped hand. "Think I'll swallow a bullet, Inspector? Over this? Don't be absurd." He realized too late that his choice of words had given away his earlier thoughts on the subject. Thoughts he'd rejected.

The rustle of skirts prevented MacLinden's response, and Jon was glad. He suspected the impertinent old fart was about to deliver a stern lecture on the value of life. God forbid. He didn't feel his own worth a toot on a penny-whistle just now.

"Jon?" Kathryn rushed to his side and knelt by the bed, where she deposited a small tray.

"I'll speak with you tomorrow," MacLinden said, then threw Jon one last, warning look as he left the room.

"Sit up a bit and drink this," Kathryn said, holding a cup to his lips. "There's no reason you should suffer. Lady

Elizabeth insists we stay the night, so you might as well rest."

"Good of her," Jon said with a forced smile. "Tomorrow I should feel well enough to see about this house you've taken. Tell me, do you like it well enough to live there after you inherit?"

"I suppose so. It's small enough to require little upkeep, and yet it's in a very acceptable location. If it suits us as well as I think it will, we could purchase it."

"*We?*" Jon asked. "There will be no *us,* Kathryn. Not after all this is settled and you no longer need me."

Her brows drew together in confusion. "But after what happened this morning, we can't very well…"

"Dissolve the marriage?" He squeezed her hand. "Don't worry. It's quite possible. You can cite the fact that I deceived you about my identity." A sudden thought reared its troubling head. "And if there should be an…unfortunate result of our mistake that precludes an annulment, I shall provide you sufficient reason for divorce."

"Adultery?" Kathryn whispered, drawing back from him. She looked stricken.

"I believe that's the only grounds, other than insanity. If you like, we could go with that instead. God knows it's close enough to the truth at present."

He noticed her bottom lip trembling before she bit down on it. He was making a complete muddle of this. Now he had hurt her feelings. "Look, Kathryn, public opinion of divorce is not what it once was. You'll live it down. One day you'll find someone you feel a *tendre* for. Someone deserving."

She said nothing, and he couldn't see her eyes, with her lashes lowered as they were.

"Kathryn, I am truly sorry about what I did to you. I had no right. Please know that I regret it with all my heart."

Her chin came up with a jerk. "You have made that abundantly clear, my lord! Nonetheless, I shall see you get a proper settlement. I believe six thousand was the sum agreed upon.'' She sniffed violently. ''Perhaps I should deduct a fiver for services rendered, just to ease your conscience.''

Jon knew she felt used, hurt by what had passed between them. He cursed the selfishness and desperation that had driven him to take her innocence. If only he could bring himself to confess the driving need and overpowering desire for her that he had felt, she might feel less humiliated. He still needed and wanted her, if he was honest about it. Their present situation didn't allow for any declaration of that nature, however. She would probably view it as an attempt to secure the whole of her fortune for his own use. He would know it for exactly what it was; a last-ditch effort to grasp what he had never had and had never been worthy of in the first place.

''Kathryn, please don't turn bitter about this. I don't want your money. I'll admit I did when I proposed, and even after we married, but not any longer. I decided against taking anything from you the morning you sold the jewels. I tried to confess what I had done, but you refused to listen to me.''

''A rather belated attempt to set things right!'' she said accusingly.

''Story of my life. I was never very apt at doing what I should when I should do it. Usually had to be coerced.''

He began to feel the deadening effects of the medicine now and leaned back to close his eyes. His hand and arm ached, but the sharpness of it dulled even as he thought about it. The god-awful tension in his head and shoulders eased into lethargy.

She scoffed and got up from her position by the bed. ''I suppose you'll solicit my sympathy now and blame your behavior on your unorthodox upbringing!''

''No, probably inborn. Always was a rotten child.''

''Speaking of a child,'' Kathryn said, her voice falling to a low murmur. ''Would you be content to leave one, in the event I have conceived?''

Jon grunted noncommittally. He tried to consider his feelings about that through the gathering fog of the drug. "Shouldn't matter. Didn't to...the others."

"Others?" Kathryn asked.

She sounded rather shocked, he thought, but maybe she ought to know it all. Wasn't as though she'd write about it in that blasted newspaper now.

"Jon, I asked you a question! You have fathered children?"

"Ummmm," he said, nodding. "All over the place. Oldest ought to've come up to scratch if he's ever goin' to. No mention, though. May be a girl." The idea made him smile.

She shook him by the shoulder, and he tried to focus on her face. Her eyes were so round...almost black...so pretty.

"How many, Jon? How many children?"

He shrugged and settled more deeply into the comfortable pillows of drug-induced apathy.

# Chapter Twelve

**K**athryn stared at Jon, unwilling to believe the shocking revelation that he was a father. And had apparently made more than one woman a mother. If she had thought him irresponsible before, she now knew she'd barely scratched the surface of his reckless behavior. He had abandoned his own children. Just as her mother had abandoned her. She grasped his chin between her fingers and pinched him awake. "*Why,* Jon? How could you do such a thing?"

"Hmm? What?" he mumbled sleepily.

"How could you beget those babies and then just leave them?"

"Rich," he said, and closed his eyes again, as though the word explained everything. "Very," he added with a sigh.

She shook him again. His eyes flared open and rolled a bit. "Listen to me! The mothers were rich? Is that what you mean?"

"Umm-hmm."

Oh, God, this was worse than she'd imagined. He had bedded rich women for profit? "I can't believe you took *money* for that!"

"*Maman,*" he mumbled, and tried to turn over.

Kathryn released his chin and pressed her fingers over her lips to hold back a vile word she'd never uttered before.

Was he trying to absolve his guilt by saying he took the money for his mother? How low would the man stoop? Or had he even been a man at the time? Youth wouldn't excuse him, of course, but she wondered how old those children were now, those poor fatherless children.

One thing she did know; she would never get to the bottom of this baby business unless she did so now. He would never volunteer information like this unless he was drugged or drunk. She shook him harder this time, for the laudanum had done its work well. "Jon! Pay attention, Jon. When did this happen? How old were you?"

"Twenty...four," he mumbled.

"Not now, *then!* When you took the women to bed for the money. How old were you?"

He licked his dry lips and inhaled deeply, letting it out through his teeth. Speaking seemed a great effort, but he made it. "Fourteen...fifteen."

"Sweet Mary!" Kathryn exclaimed.

"Nah, not sweet," he protested, his chest buckling with an inaudible chuckle. "Not Mary. Greedy...Mary."

"Go back to sleep, Jon," Kathryn said softly and pressed her palm to his cheek to turn it away from her. "I don't want to know any more."

He complied before she had finished the sentence. She sat down on the floor beside his low cot and rested her head on the side of the mattress. What in heaven's name was she supposed to do about this? Perhaps Jon looked on her as just another customer, another wealthy female to love for money and then leave. Possibly with a child. He probably knew no other way to relate to a woman. Well, if she happened to be with child by him, unlike the others, this one would at least have his name.

Kathryn had to admit that having a baby appealed to her, despite the circumstances. All her maternal instincts had blossomed unexpectedly when she undertook the care of Pip. Whether he'd truly needed her or not, she had felt needed at the time. The experience had given her a focus outside herself and had satisfied something deep within her that she hadn't even known was there. A child of Jon's would definitely be beautiful, and probably enormously talented, as well. She could certainly afford to give it a good life, with or without its father's presence.

Then let him leave when the time came. She wanted nothing more than to be rid of him. What kind of influence would he be on a child, anyway? No woman in her right mind would keep a husband who admitted his lack of morals with such candor. No, his youth didn't excuse all that he had done. He'd been old enough for some time now to find and recognize the children he had fathered. Jon Chadwick was no better than the mother who had walked out on her without so much as a backward glance. Neither of them considered a damn thing but their bloody music. Their *careers*.

So be it. She and Jon had made a deal, and she would hold to it. His name and protection until she turned twenty-five, in exchange for the sum of six thousand pounds. Fair enough. Then he could go on his merry way and scatter bastards to the four winds, for all she cared. Her heart felt cracked along its seams, but that had happened before and she'd survived. She would this time.

A quiet tread drew her attention. "I'll have another cot set up in here, if you'd like to stay with him tonight," Lady Elizabeth whispered.

"No, I think not," Kathryn said, not bothering to lower her voice or disguise its acidity. "If it's not too much bother, ma'am, I think I should like a hot bath and a bed as far away from this room as is possible."

Kathryn avoided being alone with Jon for the next two days. Accompanied by Lady Elizabeth and young Helena, she shopped for an appropriate wardrobe. Modistes and shopkeepers virtually begged her to establish accounts at their places of business. At her request, the earl of Havington's own tailor visited Havington House and measured Jon for new suits and formal wear.

On the evening of the second day, Neil Bronwyn sent for Kathryn to attend him in his study.

"Milord? Helena said you wished to speak with me?"

"Close the door and sit down, Kathryn." His expression hovered between sadness and exasperation. "We need to straighten out a few matters before you and Jonathan leave in the morning."

Kathryn had no intention of discussing any personal problems with Lord Neil. Despite her gratitude and instant liking for the gentleman, her attitude toward her husband must remain her own concern. Lady Elizabeth had already approached her about it, when Kathryn's avoidance of Jon became too pointed to ignore. She supposed the woman had enlisted Lord Neil to pry. If she had to anger him to put him off, she would. "If you will draw up our bill for the medical services, milord, I shall..."

"Bother the billing. Sit yourself down, girl, and wipe that defensive expression off your face. If you're going to act like one of my pouty-faced brood, I shall treat you as such." He leaned forward over his desk and clasped his large hands together. "Your husband is my patient, and I'm worried about him. You should be, too, but apparently you are not. Now, out with it. What has fostered this coldness I sense between you?"

Kathryn braced her shoulders and looked him straight in the eye. She had dealt with overbearing men before. So many, in fact, that she wondered if there were any other kind. "The state of my marriage is no concern of yours, Lord Havington."

His face softened into a wry half smile. "Of course it's my concern. We are all concerned, about you, as well as Jonathan. I know I'm overstepping my role here, but Elizabeth and I have reared six children who are almost of an age with you and Jon. How can we ignore the situation, when the very problems you suffer seem to have generated right under our own roof? You cared very much about Jonathan the day Lindy brought you to us. Something took place after the surgery to change that. You must know that if he said anything untoward to you then, the drug had to be responsible.'' He reached out as though he would take Kathryn's hand, but she looked away, refusing. ''Kathryn, I want to help if I can. Jonathan is despondent.''

She tossed her head and scoffed. ''Jonathan is *impossible!*''

He nodded. ''To one extent or another, most persons of his genius are.''

''Most persons of his *profession* are!'' she retorted, unable to conceal her anger.

''Composers?''

''Entertainers!'' She threw up her hands. ''They're all the same! Every one of them. Selfish to the extreme, and inconstant. Unable to face the consequences of their actions. Totally irresponsible. Uncaring!''

Havington rested his elbow on the desk, tapping his lips with a finger as he thought for a moment. ''You know a great deal about them, then? These *irresponsible* entertainers?''

''Assuredly! My own mother was one, though I'm loath to admit it.'' Kathryn cut through the air with the back of one hand. ''She's busy cavorting about Italy right now, without a thought to the family she deserted. Doesn't even know her husband's dead, I'll wager. And she isn't the only one kicking propriety in the teeth. Surely you must have read my exposés in *About Town?*''

''Ah, now I see. K. M. Wainwright, eh? Yes, I have read your columns. But there are good and bad in every profession, Kathryn. Surely you can't tar the whole theatrical community with that same brush?''

Kathryn's wrath escaped the thin grasp of her control. ''Oh, can't I? That *despondent* husband of mine is a prime example!'' She narrowed her eyes and shook her finger at the earl. ''Do you know he has a brood of children strewn across the world and not an inkling as to how they fare? He admits he doesn't even know their gender, much less their names! How's that for profligate?'' She slammed herself against the back of her chair and crossed her arms over her heaving chest.

The doctor hadn't even the grace to look shocked. He merely steepled his fingers under his chin and regarded her with those midnight eyes of his. "You discovered this the day you came here?" She nodded. "While he was under the influence of the laudanum?" Again she bobbed her head. "Don't you think you should allow him to give you a more coherent explanation, Kathryn?"

"What's to explain? He admitted it outright, clear as day!" Why was he taking Jon's side in this? Just like men. They stuck together like nettles.

"It appears to me you have two choices, young lady." He paused a moment, until he had her undivided attention. "You can either come to some understanding with your husband and make your peace with his past errors, or you can leave him at this most vulnerable point in his life. He believes he has lost his music, and he equates that music with what he is as a man."

"That's absurd." Kathryn scoffed. "He has an estate to rebuild and duties to fulfill that go with his title. You and I both know he can still compose, whether or not he ever plays another note." In spite of her vehement denial of the doctor's supposition, an odd sick feeling swirled in the pit of her stomach. "You must make him see that...."

"No, my dear. *You* must make him see." The doctor pinned her with a stare. "You are his wife. *Sickness and health, better or worse...* Remember all that bothersome stuff you promised?"

Kathryn nodded in reluctant agreement, feeling roundly chastised. Lord Neil was right. Jon was her responsibility. Like it or not, like *Jon* or not, she knew she must do what she could to roust him out of his doldrums. If she didn't, that made her no better than he was. She grimaced at the thought. Well, she had wanted a child to look after. Pity the one she'd gotten had to be the same age as she. "Looks as though there is a Pip after all," she muttered.

"I beg your pardon?" Havington questioned as they both rose and headed out of his study.

"A private jest," Kathryn explained over her shoulder as she took her leave of him. "On me," she added to herself.

The morning move to their rented house went smoothly enough. Mr. Grange, the young solicitor Kathryn had hired, had arranged for a cook and a maid. In the interest of economy, Kathryn had not requested personal servants for either Jon or herself. Now she wondered whether she'd made a mistake in not hiring a valet for her husband. She didn't relish helping him dress. Or undress. So far, however, he had managed on his own.

The Havingtons planned to host a soiree two days hence. The event, to be held in Jon and Kathryn's honor, was to serve as the newlyweds' formal introduction to society. She'd expected Jon to protest, but he'd seemed apathetic when the countess announced the plans. Apparently Havington was right about Jon's despondency. His unnaturally quiet demeanor and the doctors' worried looks had begun to frighten her.

Conversation since the arrival at the new house had been desultory at best. Their talk centered only on trivial household matters; she suggesting, he agreeing without any discussion. After their first dinner in their new home, Kathryn attempted to draw him out of his silence and see whether she could generate some sort of interest in his future. "So, do you think you might take a whirl at the House of Lords eventually? You once told me you were an expert on world politics."

"Superficial knowledge. All gained from gossip and the broadsheets." He placed his serviette very carefully beside his plate and pushed slowly away from the table. Every move he made since the day of the operation had seemed calculated and precise. His words, the same.

Kathryn began to long for the self-effacing wit, the recklessness, even the biting sarcasm, that had made Jon what he was. Some inner imp prodded her to see whether he had lost all that. "Poor Chadwick," she crooned while she swirled her wine, "Soap bubbles for brains."

To her surprise, he accepted that without comment. He did, however, respond with a question. "Where did you study?"

"Oxford," she answered, encouraged that he would care enough to ask. And a bit proud of her accomplishments, odd as they were.

One dark brow shot up in surprise. "They allow women?"

"Yes. I enrolled immediately after Father died and went to live at Lady Margaret Hall. I lettered in the arts, became a real bluestocking." She grinned. "Does it show?"

He inclined his head. "You were very fortunate. I envy you the opportunity."

Kathryn laughed. "*You* wanted to live at Lady Margaret Hall? Lord, the girls would have *loved* that! I expect you would have been their favorite classmate, though I doubt you'd have had enough energy left to study."

"You mock me," he said, softly but without any rancor.

"No, silly. You're a handsome man, and they were a rowdy little gang beneath all their town polish. That's all I'm saying. No, you'd never have lacked for company at Lady Mag's!"

He looked up at her from beneath his long, sooty lashes. "Would you have kept company with me, Kathryn?"

If she hadn't detected the note of sad yearning buried just beneath the surface of his question, Kathryn might have thought he meant the question to be suggestive. "Yes," she said seriously, "I probably would have."

"Because of the music," he stated.

"No, Jon. You do play beautifully, but..."

"*Did* play, Kathryn. I *did* play beautifully," he told her. Then he bit his lip, worried it for a moment and then looked directly into her eyes. "Didn't I?"

"Of course. You know very well how wonderfully you played, but music isn't everything." Suddenly, she wished the table were not between them. His despair threw a pall over everything in the room, dimming the luster of the silver, the glow of the candles, the sharp, sweet scent of the roses.

"That's what this happy little conversation's all about, isn't it?" he asked. "Lord Neil thinks I'm about to stick my old spoon in the wall over this?" He held up his bandaged hand and laughed bitterly. "Don't worry, I'll be around for as long as you need me."

Kathryn didn't like the way he said that. "And then what? What will you do?"

"Enlist," he announced, and reached for his wineglass. When he had emptied it, he set it down with a thunk. He mimed shooting a pistol with his left hand. "Behold the warrior."

"The *army?*" Kathryn couldn't mask her disbelief.

"This trigger finger works. Why not?"

"You know nothing about it!"

He rose from the table and went to stand by the window, looking out into the night. "As a matter of fact, I do. I've served four years already. This time I'll be taking orders instead of giving them. Commissions come dear."

Kathryn threw down her napkin and stalked across the room. "You are a bubble-brain! I was teasing earlier, but you really *are!* Well, you are not going to do it, do you hear? I won't let you put yourself in front of a bullet just to indulge this stupid streak of self-pity!"

He turned to face her and looked quite at peace with his decision. "Don't be silly. There's not even a war at present. And I promise I won't go until everything's settled for you."

She rolled her eyes and groaned. "You won't go at all!

Your place is here, taking care of your estate and seeing to your family!''

"Family?" He gave her a puzzled look. "What family?"

"Me!" she declared, pointing forcefully at her chest. "You aren't running away this time, Jon Chadwick, so you just put this *army* nonsense right out of your head."

His eyes looked tired as he regarded her for a few silent moments. The only sound between them was the rasp of her angry breathing. When he did speak, his voice sounded weary. "You think there might be a child, don't you?" She didn't answer, but held his gaze with hers. "I'm very sorry, Kathryn."

Kathryn turned away from him and clasped her arms over her chest. "Is that what you said to all those other women you left carrying your babies?"

The silence drew out to an impossible length. When she turned around, he was gone.

Jon kept to his room except for meals during the days following. When obliged to endure his company at the table, Kathryn proved unfailingly cheerful, given her low opinion of him, Jon thought. She really did have a good heart.

Had he been in his right mind, he'd never have mentioned his offspring. He couldn't recall exactly what he had said about them but it couldn't have been much, considering how little he knew. Whatever he had let slip must have been lurking there in some dark corner of his mind. All too often that misspent time of his youth haunted him. She seemed to have gotten the main truth of the matter, though, so he saw no point in enlightening her further. Details would only make the truth uglier, few though he had to relate.

He spent the time between meals and most of the night hours transcribing his scribbled code into proper notes on score sheets. If only he could hear the music played again and know whether it was truly worth the effort. He needed that reinforcement badly, but knew there was no way to get it. Perhaps, someday, someone would play the score and wonder who the hell Jonathan Chadwick had been. That was about the best he could hope for.

At least Kathryn had left him alone once she realized what he was doing. He'd grown tired of her forced efforts to rally his spirit. It was not that she didn't mean well, but she was only acting on orders from Neil Bronwyn. Jon knew they thought he was suicidal. Dying held no appeal, though it was true that living offered little more at this point. He simply existed in a sort of limbo. Writing the music down only provided something to occupy his mind and ensure his privacy.

Later, once he'd gotten used to relinquishing his primary reason for being, he would try to dredge up something that might fill the awful gap in his soul. Right now, he just couldn't imagine what that would be.

On impulse, he added a trill to one measure and then wondered whether it would sound too contrived. Just as he paused to hear it in his head, Kathryn swept into his room without knocking. "Time for your bath. I've laid out your evening clothes. You needn't hurry, though. We've about two hours before we must leave."

"Leave?" Jon laid down his pen. "Oh, it's the Havingtons' thing tonight, is it?"

"Yes, had you forgotten?" Her voice sounded altogether too bright, its gaiety as pretty and false as a silk flower. "He's sent Jenkins round to help you shave and dress. I'm afraid I'd be a poor hand at it, since I've never acted the valet for anyone. You've done very well for yourself thus far, but tonight you'll have all those studs and buttons and links and... "

"Stop nattering on, then, and send him up." Jon congratulated himself for biting back the bitter words that had leapt to mind. He'd never had anyone help him deck out since he came out of short coats. The need only emphasized how damned helpless he was. Oh, he knew it would only be temporary. Once he got the splints off his hand, he could probably do most everything he'd done before.

Everything except play.

Well, at least he was off the hook as far as playing for the audience tonight was concerned. Unexpectedly, this brand-new realization cheered him as nothing had since the injury. The more he thought about it, the more excited he became. No one could expect him to perform. Odd it had never occurred to him that there might be a bright spot in all this. For the first time in over a week, he smiled. Really smiled.

His good humor increased as Jon allowed Havington's crinkle-faced old valet to shave him and assist him in dressing. The full-length mirror reflected a man Jon hadn't seen before. He wore a tailored white shirt with tucks. The white set off his natural complexion, free of its layer of chalky powder. No need to worry about blushes tonight, he thought as he smiled at his new image.

Over the ebony evening coat, Jenkins slipped a black satin sling and cradled Jon's injured hand inside it up to the elbow. The man flicked an imaginary speck of lint off one shoulder. "There now, milord, you'll not have the wrapping on your hand distracting from your attire. May I say you look quite dashing?"

"You certainly may, and take credit for it, as well. Thank you, Jenkins. I don't know when I've ever felt this well put together." He noticed the man glance at his sling and chuckled. "Literally!" he added with a wink, and they both laughed at the macabre little joke.

Something inside Jon shifted. He thought it might be the barrier he had recently erected against feeling. In one way, he hoped so, since he didn't like himself very much as a do-nothing dullard wallowing in self-pity. But in another way, he wondered whether his moods might continue veering too swiftly to control. Right now he seemed to be soaring; satisfied with his own looks for once, delighted to be attending a party for the first time as a real guest, and eager to see Kathryn. The sudden, unexpected euphoria frightened him a bit. Was this at all natural?

Kathryn was waiting at the bottom of the stairs. Jon drank in the sight like a draft of champagne. "Ah, Kathryn, you take my breath away. Just look at you!" He grasped her gloved hand in his and turned her about. "Beautiful."

In truth, she presented a vision Jon hadn't expected. He had always thought her lovely, but in a quiet, unstudied way. Tonight her hair captured the light in its ringlets and formed a wavery halo on her crown. Several gilded curls trailed down one side of her neck and tickled the top of her half-exposed bosom. Her skin shone like the finest pearls as it curved beneath the soft rose satin of her gown. The graceful draping of the skirt emphasized her slender waist. "You are striking. An *incomparable,* as the old folks used to say!" He flashed her a delighted and sincere smile.

He didn't miss her flicker of confusion. So she wondered, as well, what had caused such a rapid upswing in his mood. Jon admired the way she quickly recovered her aplomb. "You look rather handsome yourself." Her voice sounded as natural as rain in April, as sweet as the lilac scent she wore. "Shall we go, then? Perhaps we should try and arrive first, since we are the guests of honor."

Once in the coach, Kathryn eyed him warily when she thought he wasn't looking. When he did glance her way, she made a great fuss about straightening her skirts and set about making conversation. "You look so different without the powder and wig. Are you changing your image, then?"

"The dark wig was to prevent me looking like a corpse. Light hair, light eyes, white face. Ugh!" Jon ran a finger across his forehead. "Glad to get rid of it. And now I can sweat tonight without accumulating paste. I only wore the powder to hide turning red. Thank God I shan't have to worry about that anymore."

Her curious stare prompted him to explain. "I blush furiously when anyone applauds, you see. Always have," he elaborated. "Most embarrassing."

"And you don't think you will be blushing tonight?"

"No, no, that's the marvelous thing about all this, don't you see? I won't have to *play*. I can't tell you what a relief that is." He thought of something he hadn't considered and turned to her in his excitement, grasping her hand to his chest. "And the insults to everyone, Kathryn! I should stop being so beastly! Don't you think? They won't expect that now, will they?"

He noticed that her eyes narrowed for a second before she could drum up a wide smile. The lightness in her voice sounded manufactured. "Well, it's a good thing you kept the scarlet ribbon, or no one would believe you are you."

His laughter spilled forth in great gusts, reverberating off the walls of the carriage. Jon felt every bit as mad as she must think him, but he could remember only one time ever when he'd experienced such a feeling of incredible joy—on the floor at Timberoak with Kathryn in his arms. In belated thanks for that fleeting moment of bliss, Jon captured her head with his left hand and kissed her soundly on the mouth. Lord, he felt wonderful, and at the moment, he didn't care in the least why that was so.

The receiving line had proved a nightmare, Kathryn thought. Jon's sudden affability threw the elite into a tizzy after his weeks of condescension and outright belligerence. They obviously expected him to revert at any moment and say something truly outrageous, something in keeping with the Chadwick they knew. Relief when the last guests had gone through sent her straight to the rum punch.

Kathryn downed a cup quickly and drew in a deep breath to steady her fractured nerves. As soon as she spied her host, she signaled Neil Bronwyn with a quick little wave. She watched him extricate himself from a group of men and wend his way toward her through the crush. Across the room where she'd left him, Jon seemed involved in a spirited discussion with Lady Tremayne and another older woman whom Kathryn didn't recognize.

"It's going rather well, don't you think?" Neil asked as he joined her by the door to the hall.

"I need a word with you, milord. *Now,*" Kathryn said, tugging on the hand he had offered her. She virtually dragged him down the hall and into his study. "Shut the door," she ordered.

The doctor did as she asked and then motioned her to a chair by the fireplace. "What's happened, my dear? You seem upset."

Kathryn wrung her hands and paced, realizing she forced him to remain standing until she sat, but she couldn't seem to be still. "It's Jon, sir. He's acting so strangely I can hardly credit it. Did you notice? Positively effusive, first at home, then in the carriage, and even in the receiving line. Offering to fetch drinks, even talked of dancing! It's unnatural." She shook her head and worried her bottom lip. "What's wrong with him?"

He frowned. "Nothing, I should think. He's charmed the whole crowd in less than a hour. Everyone's remarking on the wonderful change your marriage has wrought in him."

"Listen to me, sir. This attitude is not normal for Jon. You haven't seen him in public as an adult, have you?"

"Well, no," he admitted, glancing at the closed door as though it were the patient himself. "Several people have remarked on his former arrogance. Perhaps he's merely putting forth his best side."

"Ha!" Kathryn threw up her hands in frustration. She strode over to stand toe-to-toe with the earl. "On the way here, he thanked God he could no longer *play!* Tell me that's sane. You yourself said his music was everything to him and that I should expect he'd be depressed. Well, he was. Up until the time he came downstairs tonight."

Kathryn grasped his arm, digging her fingers into the superfine of his sleeve, trying to impress on Lord Neil how worried she was. "Sir, he has closeted himself in his room day and night, only coming out to eat. And even then, he ate almost nothing. He's worked like a demon possessed, writing his music down. I had to drag him away from it to dress for this fete of yours. Once he'd done that, it was as though he turned into a different person—the one you see tonight. Do you think he might be mad?''

The doctor placed a hand over hers and studied a spot on the carpet for some moments before he asked. ''Do you love him, Kathryn?''

She rolled her eyes and gave an unladylike snort. ''Ours was a marriage of convenience. Or *inconvenience*, if you want the truth.''

''That's not what I asked. Do you love him?''

Kathryn turned away, releasing his arm to hug both of hers around her middle. ''Sometimes.'' The word slipped out, sounding forlorn. God, she felt forlorn when she realized what she'd said was true. She had admired him, babied him, hated him and comforted him. And loved him, for goodness' sake. She loved Jonathan Chadwick.

She felt the doctor's strong arms encircle her and his chin rest on top of her head. The vibration of his deep voice against her back soothed her jangled nerves. ''Kathryn, dear, if you love him, then you must give him something more important than his music to live for. Jon is trying very hard to discover whether he can survive without the essential core of himself right now.''

''He really believes there is nothing else in him, doesn't he?'' she whispered.

''I'd imagine for most of his life he's been taught that's all he is—his mind a repository where arrangements of beautiful sounds are stored, his body an instrument for their release. How can he not believe that, when it's all he's ever known?''

Kathryn whirled around to face him, breaking his gentle hold on her. Without thinking, she grasped the lapel of his coat as though it were a lifeline. ''What if he's right, Lord Neil? What if it's true?''

Neil Bronwyn sighed and cupped her cheek in his large, long-fingered hand. ''If you do anything to reinforce that belief, Kathryn, I think Jonathan will be truly lost.''

# Chapter Thirteen

Kathryn kept a careful watch on Jon from a discreet distance after she returned to the ballroom. He laughed often and imbibed all too freely of the champagne.

Dancers whirled in a huge waltzing circle between them, lending a macabre sort of gaiety to the situation. Then her gaze locked on one couple in particular. "Uncle Rupert!" she exclaimed, clutching a hand to her chest. He nodded and grinned at Kathryn over his partner's shoulder just as the dance ended.

Kathryn waited where she was. There was little point in trying to avoid a confrontation. She wasn't even certain she wanted to. When he had returned the young woman to a group of ladies standing nearby, he accepted a drink from a passing waiter's tray and approached. "Well, niece, you've managed to inveigle yourself into high circles, haven't you?"

"What are you doing here?"

He brushed his palms over the lapels of his evening coat. "Invited, of course. I am your only family, after all, and the party seems to be in your honor."

Kathryn glanced around the room for help in the event her uncle tried to drag her away. Inspector MacLinden stood nearby, looking a bit rumpled in his finery. He saluted her with his crystal goblet and winked. Ah, she thought, so that was the plan. The inspector obviously wanted to see how her uncle would react around her. Know the enemy, or some such idea. Relieved, Kathryn made herself smile. "I hope you've decided to accept my marriage."

Rupert's eyes narrowed with what could only be malice. "Why not? It's nothing to me." He cleared his throat and looked toward Jon, who was circling the dance floor in their direction. "Your friend from the Yard spoke to me about what you think you overheard. Such outlandish accusations, Kathryn. I'd not have believed it of you."

"I heard what I heard." Kathryn felt her stomach squeeze.

"And can never prove a thing, my dear. I've told the inspector that you are a bit off balance and prone to wild fantasies. Goes with being a writer, you see." He chuckled and raised his glass to her. "A female writer, at that. Unstable."

Kathryn looked over at MacLinden again. He was watching their conversation intently. She felt reassured of her immediate safety. "Surely you have abandoned that ridiculous scheme of yours."

Rupert inclined his head and pursed his lips. "No need for it now. Neither you nor that moneygrubbing husband of yours will see a farthing of the inheritance. Depend on it."

He looked entirely too pleased with himself. "Uncle, what have you done?" Kathryn asked, not really expecting him to answer.

But he did so with a gloating smile. "Though *you* haven't access to the money yet, your representatives can effect the disposition of funds for you, provided they agree that your suggestions for investment are sound. In this case, I'm told they did just that. Even checked with me to see whether I concurred. That letter you sent to your father's solicitors took care of the entire amount. Don't you recall?" He grunted a nasty laugh under his breath. "Told them to sink everything into the Witwatersrand gold fields for you. Bright move, that.''

"I never sent them a letter! What are you talking about?'' Kathryn grasped his sleeve.

He began peeling her gloved fingers away as though they were repulsive leeches. "Seems you promised the old fellows a right hefty return for their troubles if they'd expedite everything. Soon as all that South African gold's shipped in, they'll be incredibly wealthy. If it ever is, of course. They have absolutely nothing to lose. And everything to gain.''

"They...they couldn't have! No one but the foolhardiest of gamblers are putting their money there!'' Kathryn felt the cushion of promised security collapse. Somehow, her uncle had colluded with her father's solicitors to divest her of her fortune before she came into it. Only weeks until her birthday. So close.

"Why, Uncle? What could you possibly hope to gain from doing such a thing?''

His smile was smooth as good sherry. "If I can't have it, you little nitwit, neither will you. I can just envision my brother writhing in his crypt. He should have left everything to me.''

Jon joined them just then and slid a proprietary arm around her. She looked up at his expectant face and stumbled through an introduction. "My uncle, Rupert Wainwright. Uncle, this is my husband, Jonathan Chadwick.''

"My lord,'' Rupert acknowledged, with a sardonic twist of his lips and the barest nod of his head.

Jon smiled. Kathryn felt his fingers tense on her waist. "Ah, Mr. Wainwright. Kathryn has told me so much about you, I feel we know each other already. Come to wish us happy, did you?''

"If you can be so with your useless title and her worthless stock, then go to it.'' With a smirk and a satisfied nod, he ambled away toward the dance floor.

Jon peered down at her, his confusion evident. "What did he mean by that? What stock?"

Kathryn turned toward him and rested her forehead against his shoulder, uncaring how inappropriate it might appear. She swallowed hard to stifle the sob at the back of her throat. His arm tightened around her for a moment and then released her so that he could lift her chin. With one finger, he wiped just beneath her eye. "The old bounder's upset you. How?"

"Will you get me out of here, Jon? I feel...ill."

His face darkened as he glanced toward the door and back at her. "I'll kill the son of a bitch! What did he say to make you cry? Has he threatened you again?"

Trent MacLinden interrupted quietly, "Follow me, both of you, unless you happen to relish that rapt audience you're creating."

Jon steered her in the inspector's wake as they left the ballroom and made their way to Havington's study. The earl had followed them, and he closed the door just as Kathryn turned around.

All three men tried to speak at once, and Kathryn threw up her hands for silence. "Wait, please. No questions yet." She covered her eyes with one hand and took a deep breath. Then she looked directly at her husband. "My uncle has sunk every cent of my inheritance into the South African gold fields. Witwatersrand, he said. Apparently, if he can't have the money, he's determined that we shan't have it, either."

MacLinden broke in. "How could he do that? I mean, if you couldn't touch it until your birthday, how could he?"

"He forged a letter with my signature to my father's solicitors. From what he said, I gather that the funds could be invested so long as Danly and Ross agree my plans for it are sound. Apparently, they did. They have nothing of theirs at risk and—if, on a fluke, the investment proves sound—everything to profit. God only knows what percentage Uncle promised them in my name."

Lord Neil pounded a fist in one palm. "It's out and out madness! Everyone knows that South Africa's a disastrous gamble. With all the conflict down there, steady mining's impossible. Even if there are tons of gold to be had, it will be impossible to get it out. They've done her out of her inheritance, all right, through either stupidity or greed, certainly fraud. I say throw the idiots in jail."

MacLinden nodded. "Aye. I can arrest 'em. But it isn't hard to predict what they'll say, that the lady must have changed her mind, heard the investment's unwise and only wants her money back. After all's said and done, I'm afraid all you'll have is a fistful of paper giving you shares in the African mines. Wainwright would no doubt vouch for the solicitors and swear he saw you sign the letter. Hard to discredit him before the court, when the man has nothing to gain either way the venture goes."

"What am I to do, then?" Kathryn demanded. "Just let him get away with this? It's an act of vengeance against my father and against me!"

"It's an outrage," Lord Neil declared. "Lindy, you'll check this out first thing in the morning, won't you? See what's to be done?" MacLinden nodded.

Kathryn noticed Jon had said nothing. He simply regarded her with a bland expression. She wondered where all his concern for her had gone in the space of a few minutes. Well, what did she expect, when he'd just been done out of his six thousand pounds? He was probably furious now that he had married her for nothing. "I'm so sorry, Jon," she said sincerely.

"I expect you are," he agreed in a flat monotone.

She wished she knew what he was thinking. She hoped he wasn't back to considering some harebrained idea of making her a soldier's wife. Not while she drew breath. Kathryn went to him and latched on to his arm while she directed her words to Lord Neil. "Thank you both, sir, Inspector, for wanting to help. Would you please excuse us? Jon and I need to go home and discuss this."

"Of course," Havington agreed readily. "You will let us know if there's anything, anything at all, that we can do until we get this straightened out?"

Jon had seemed terribly preoccupied since she delivered the news about her inheritance. She hoped he wasn't lapsing into another bout of melancholia. They made their way around the edge of the dance floor with the intention of leaving. "We'll work this out, Jon," she said.

He turned his head smartly, as though he'd forgotten she was there. "No doubt. Do you realize who your uncle is dancing with?"

Kathryn looked, curious as to why Jon would care. Uncle Rupert seemed to be enjoying himself enormously. "Camilla Norton. We attended school together. Her father's Magnus Norton, the financier."

"Yes, I have met her. And the old rogue's grievously ill, I hear. She's betrothed to Sean Wilder. Do you know of him?" he asked, and a smile flooded his features when Kathryn nodded.

Everyone knew Mr. Wilder. Rumor had it that he'd been born and reared in Whitechapel, that East End hell populated with the offscourings of society. No one dared speculate aloud about just how he had won his current wealth. Wilder's uncanny resemblance to Prince Edward, a man over twenty years his senior, made one wonder whether a portion of it hadn't come out of royal pockets.

"Why do you ask?" Kathryn knew Jon was up to something. He fairly twitched with contained excitement.

He pulled her to the nearest wall and stationed her against it. "I need you to do something for me. Catch your uncle's eye as soon as the dance is over and get him to follow you onto the terrace. Make certain he notices me speaking with Wilder before you go. Can you do it?"

"Of course, but why?"

"Just do it," he said, still smiling, his gaze fastened on the dancers. "Don't worry, I'll join you immediately after you leave the room."

Before she could question him further, he left her to wade through the crowd toward Sean Wilder. Kathryn frowned at the thought of Jon consorting with the man. When the music ended, she held up a tentative hand and beckoned to her uncle. He did the pretty with Camilla, then strode confidently toward Kathryn, wearing a smug expression.

"Could I speak with you outside?" she asked. Then she threw a look across the room. "Jon will join us in a moment. He had to speak with Mr. Wilder about something."

A shadow dropped across Rupert's face as he took her arm. "If your young buck thinks to frighten me by flaunting any sordid connections, he is wasting his time."

Kathryn said nothing as she accompanied her uncle through the French doors and onto the flagstone terrace. Before they managed to find a secluded spot, she heard Jon's silky voice behind them. "I should keep walking toward the back gate if I were you, Wainwright."

Rupert turned. "What? Leave the party?" He laughed and shook his head. "But I'm having such fun, Chadwick. What a mix we have tonight, eh? All your hoity-toities and all Kathryn's common chums. I commend the Havingtons for their democratic airs, but then, they always were a bit strange." He rocked back and forth, heel to toe to heel, supremely self-satisfied. "I noticed the little byplay with Wilder. But of course you intended that. Planning to hire him to get a bit of revenge?"

Kathryn watched Jon pretend to consider before he spoke. "Never crossed my mind." He looked up with an innocent expression Kathryn could only have described as Early Pip. "Kathryn and Sean's intended, Camilla, were once school chums. I simply thought he and I should get better acquainted. Can you imagine Wilder's horror at learning what my wife recently overheard? No? Well, it seems her uncle had it in mind to waylay an heiress, drug her and arrange a quick marriage to secure the fortune she would soon inherit."

Rupert shrugged and tugged at his waistcoat, smoothing the brocade front with a well-manicured hand. "I'm certain Wilder's heard worse. Probably done worse. Why ever would he be interested in your troubles?"

Jon smiled serenely. "Oh, he wouldn't, of course, unless he assumed they were his."

Her uncle's hand froze over his stomach, and his eyes locked with Jon's. "*Camilla Norton?* He thinks that I—?"

Jon aped Rupert's former shrug and cocked his head to one side. "Well, her wealthy old father is at death's door, they say. And you did dance with her. Twice that I recall." He motioned toward the glass doors, where couples were swaying to another waltz. "You're certainly welcome to go in there and try to correct his assumption."

"You fool!" Rupert growled, grasping Jon's sleeve. "The man will kill me!"

"No, no, I shouldn't think so," Jon offered in a voice rife with sarcasm. He surrounded her uncle's wrist and squeezed until Rupert's fingers turned white and uncurled. "But he probably wouldn't quail at having it done."

Kathryn watched her uncle back away toward the garden gate leading to the alley. With a wordless promise of hateful retribution, he finally turned and stalked off into the night.

Kathryn felt chilled that her husband could so coldly manipulate a man into doing murder. "Will Mr. Wilder really try to have him killed, Jon?"

"No reason for him to. I merely congratulated Sean on his coming marriage and mentioned that you and Miss Norton were acquainted. I rather like the fellow, by the way."

"You lied!" Kathryn exclaimed with a relieved sigh.

"Not technically, if you'll recall. I simply presented a hypothetical situation."

She had to smile. "You're splitting hairs. All the same, I admit I like to see Uncle Rupert sweat. The wretched man has made a pauper of me, hasn't he?"

Jon sighed and took her arm to lead her back inside.

"The remedy for that may take a bit more doing. Shall we go home?"

Kathryn nodded and stole a sideways glance at him. He looked exhausted.

By the time they arrived at their town house, Kathryn feared something inside Jon had snapped. He appeared to have retreated completely from the world around him, so fierce was his concentration. As soon as he had closed the front door behind them, he slid a commanding hand under her elbow and guided her into the front parlor.

Kathryn shivered. "It's cold in here, Jon. Why don't we go upstairs now and sleep on this? I don't think we can resolve anything tonight."

He ignored her suggestion and set a match to the fire that had been laid in the hearth. When it flared to his satisfaction, he seated her on the divan and dropped down beside her. When his knee brushed hers, he carefully added distance between them.

The small act of propriety emphasized the formal tone he employed when he spoke. "We must assume that your uncle has successfully rid you of your inheritance, just as he claims. I was down there during my stint with the army, and the situation in South Africa doesn't bode well for any mining successes. At any rate, we need funds to go on. I've been thinking about it."

Kathryn leaned forward expectantly, encouraging him to continue. "Have you something specific in mind?"

"Yes. But I'm going to need your assistance, Kathryn," he said. "You deal with people more skillfully than I. And I suspect—no, I pray—that you have a better head for business."

Her heart leapt in her chest. He did have a plan. Kathryn didn't care how far-fetched it turned out to be; at least he hadn't lapsed into a blue-deviled megrim as she'd first thought. "I'm fair with figures. Please, go on," she urged.

"Do you read music at all?" he asked.

"Yes. My father never allowed it at home, but it was

required that I learn at school. Do you need me to help you transcribe?" She wondered where he was going with this. "I can't play, Jon, if that's what you have in mind," she clarified.

"Can't or won't?" he asked with a sidewise glance.

"Won't." She cast him a pleading look. "I told you I never play or sing, because my mother—"

"Bother your mother! This has nothing to do with her," he stated flatly. "I can't afford to hire anyone, and you know I'm unable to do it myself." He reached for her hand and examined it as though he'd never seen one before. "Kathryn, the music I've already written is all we have between us and poverty at the moment. Unless you want to live hand-to-mouth, as I've been doing at Timberoak these past months, you'll have to cooperate."

Kathryn thought long and hard as he traced circles on her palm with his thumb. She wasn't certain just what he was asking of her. "You don't expect me to perform in public, surely?"

"No, never that. I only want you to help me adjust what I've done so far. Just play what I've written while I record the changes. Then," he said with a strained smile, "we must find someone to publish the sheet music."

He sighed and gave her hand a quick squeeze. "Popular music's all the rage now. A few of my melodies will lend themselves rather well to that, I think. Of course, nothing in the libretto's of any use. It's written in Italian, and we'll need English rhymes, don't you think? Something maudlin and sweet?" He looked infinitely sad over this compromise he intended to make. "You have a clever way with words. Do you think you could you write love songs?"

This was the last thing she had expected. Or wanted. "Your opera? Good Lord, Jon, you can't think to sell it piecemeal?" He nodded with what looked to be forced enthusiasm.

"I won't allow you to do that. We'll find some other way."

He scoffed gently, still rubbing her hand. "How? No one's willing to back an entire production anyway. Have you any idea of the expense involved? Stage sets, costumes, orchestra, cast? That's leaving aside promotion and advertising, rental on the opera house, and so on and on. A veritable fortune."

"I have it!" Kathryn exclaimed, turning her hand so that she grasped his. "Not a full-scale production, then. What about an *oratorio?*" She wriggled with excitement. "That could work! Don't you see? That will eliminate sets, choral ensemble, and any number of expenses. We only need hire a couple of sopranos, a tenor, a basso profundo. What do you think?"

He pursed his lips and shook his head. "Still too costly."

Kathryn hated to admit he was right. They had very little left from the sale of her jewelry. The amount wouldn't begin to cover the outlay they'd need. They would be fortunate to stretch the funds to cover living expenses. She had counted far too heavily on receiving her inheritance in a few weeks.

She began thinking aloud. "All right, let's evaluate. Our assets are these—your incredible talent, foremost."

"For what it's worth, thank you."

Kathryn ignored the sarcasm. "And your current reputation."

"Meaning?"

Her smile grew wicked as she cut her eyes to capture his curious gaze. "Oh, your former snootiness and my glowing influence on you, the new bridegroom. They loved you tonight, you know. You were the soul of charm, the exact opposite of your old self. The change in Chadwick is the new *on-dit.* We're going to use that."

"I don't understand."

"First, you're wiping your feet all over the population of London, literally thumbing your powdered nose at them. And then, lo and behold, you do a total about-face when you fall in love. Isn't that romantic? They're already eating it up after tonight's soiree at the Havingtons. Our stage is set."

"Stage? What are you talking about?"

She grinned and pinched his cheek with her free hand. "Our stage, my friend, will be all of London! Perhaps all of England and the Continent, as well, if we're lucky. You are going to be famous beyond your wildest hopes. And rich."

His confusion etched frown lines on his smooth, tanned forehead. "You'd better explain a little further. I think you left me back there thumbing my nose at someone."

Kathryn giggled and gave him a slight shove. "Go find the music for the thing you played for me on the Strad that first night. Only that. Well, come on!" she ordered, getting to her feet and tugging on his hand.

She watched him saunter to the door. There he stopped and turned, as though to pose a question, but apparently thought better of it and went on up the stairs. Kathryn couldn't stifle her excitement and did a little swaying dance across the parlor. She shrugged off her cloak and pulled back the stool of the grand piano. The thing was old, maybe out of tune, but it would serve.

When Jon returned to the parlor, she halted in the middle of running the scales and held out her hand for the sheaf of music. "Thank you. Now run along to bed. You look tired."

He snorted with an inelegance that reminded her of Pip. "If you think I'm leaving now, you must be crazy. At least tell me what you're going to do with this." He thumped the corner of the thick parchment. When she said nothing, he added, "I won't sleep a wink unless I know. Tell me and, if you make any sense at all, I promise I'll leave you alone with it."

Kathryn took a deep breath and dragged her forefinger across the ivory keys, landing on high C. "All right. As succinctly as I can. First of all, we'll do love lyrics for this piece. Marcus Brothers at *Tit Bits* will probably print the sheet music for me in exchange for a front-page story on the Chadwick transformation.'' She cocked a brow and clicked her tongue. ''*Voilà!* Free publicity. Free sheet music. How's that for ingenuity?''

He nodded a little uncertainly. ''Then?''

''Rumors. K. M. Wainwright, female scandalmonger, meets her nemesis. Gives up her semisecretive career. Jonathan Chadwick temporarily abandons a lifetime of classical training to pen a love song to his bride. Who is the most besotted, the infamous lady news writer or the haughty composer? Everyone will see it as our just deserts, our comeuppance, our salvation. You swept me off my feet,'' Kathryn said, pursing her lips invitingly, ''and I landed in your lap. An unwitting love match!'' She laughed at the way his mouth dropped. ''Silly, of course, but trust me—London thrives on the ridiculous.''

Try as she might, she couldn't sit still. Sliding off the piano stool, she tapped him on the chest with the music. ''We build it up, surround it with a bit of mystery—did I tame you first, or vice versa? Make everyone clamor to hear what you've written for your cheeky new wife.

''Then, we find a good dramatic tenor and someone to play. We allow a solitary performance at the biggest to-do we can arrange. Perhaps the Havingtons would agree to host another. The entire population will be wild to have a copy of the song once some of them hear it and the word gets around. The cits will go benders over the tune, as well, since I'm one of them and you wrote it for me.''

She told him the best part. ''If we can bring this off, you can keep the rest of the opera intact. With the money from this *one piece*,'' she said, shaking the paper under his nose, ''we can finance an oratorio. Perhaps even the opera itself!'' Kathryn paused for him to consider. ''Well, what do you think?''

''You really believe this one's that good?'' he asked. Kathryn couldn't help being amazed at his self-doubt.

''It's wonderful! The music is so touching that my lyrics

won't matter.'' She trained her eyes on the page of bold notes she was holding, to avoid his piercing gaze. The mere memory of his playing it for her sent a trickle of heat throughout her body. "It's very moving, Jon. At the risk of sounding suggestive, I felt as though you made love to me as I listened that night.''

"So did I, Kathryn," he whispered, taking the music from her hand and laying it on top of the piano. Once he'd done that, he threaded his fingers through the curls at the back of her neck as he drew her mouth to his. "God knows I wanted to.''

She expected a soft kiss and got it. What she was unprepared for was the barely constrained passion behind it. She sensed he battled a tremendous need, one that mirrored itself in her own wild yearning. The heated urgency of the feeling overwhelmed her. He drew his injured hand from between them and pulled her close with the other. With a groan of encouragement, Kathryn embraced him and opened her lips under his.

Jon's tongue invaded, swept her mouth in frantic exploration as though the meaning of his very life lay inside her. When he drew back for breath, his voice sounded pained, "Kathryn, maybe we shouldn't..."

"Why not?" she moaned.

"I forget," he breathed raggedly against her lips before he claimed them again.

Kathryn was lost. Nothing mattered, not past deception, nor doubts for their future. Now, at this moment and right here, Jon Chadwick belonged to her, and she meant to have him.

# *Chapter Fourteen*

There was no stopping now. Kathryn held fast to Jon's mouth as she fumbled at the waist of his trousers. His hand dropped from her hair to the hooks at the back of her neck. Kathryn purposely ignored how expertly he undid them one-handed. She tugged out his shirttail and started to work on his studs, popping them out until she reached the barrier of the sling hanging about his neck.

Jon released her from everything but his heated gaze and ripped the black silk over his head. "Upstairs?"

"No!" she murmured, and returned to her task of undressing him. Before she knew it, she was down to her shimmy and corset, while Jon stood bare-chested. He kissed her again, sweeping away any errant streaks of caution waiting to surface. She felt his long fingers surround one breast and leaned into his grip. Her own hands slid inside his unbuttoned trousers and pushed downward.

Dimly she wondered at his intention as he backed up and lowered himself to the piano stool. He untied and dragged down her pantalets. She kicked them aside, holding to his wide shoulders for support.

"Astride," he ordered, and pulled her toward him, edging his knees between her own. Kathryn felt the ridge of his rampant arousal against her core and reached frantically to guide him inside her. "Yes!" She breathed the word as she lowered her body, filled to capacity and momentarily satisfied. "Oh, yes…"

Jon leaned back against the keys, unaffected by the discordant sound his elbows made. "Ride," he ordered as the sound died away.

She rode. His groans and her murmurs of pleasure mingled with the steady bump of his arms against the keys at his back. Suddenly he snaked his left arm around her waist and surged up powerfully against her. Kathryn felt his pulsing tremors become her own. Wave after wave of ecstasy washed through her as she clung to him, twisting and writhing, reveling in the cacophony of sounds that they produced along with the odd piano notes.

"More, Kathryn…again." His voice penetrated her even as his body had done. Strong fingers gripped the top of her hip, forcing her down as he ground upward. Like a rapid series of lightning bolts, his movements ignited explosions she could never have imagined in her wildest dreams. Heat rushed through her veins and consumed her. With a final cry of joy, she fell against him, gasping.

His breath rushed out against her ear. *"Bravissima."*

She lay on top of him, still joined, her silk-clad legs hanging limp on either side of his hips. Tears rolled over the bridge of her nose and disappeared into the crisp mat of hair on his chest. Even if she could speak, what did one say at a time like this? She barely had strength to sniff.

Jon's lazy drawl solved that dilemma. "I don't think we can sleep like this, love. At least *I* can't."

"Mmm."

"Three octaves worth of ivory are permanently embedded in my back." His chest shifted ever so slightly beneath her flattened breasts. "And if I move my feet, the stool will roll out from under us."

Slowly, Kathryn sat up and lifted away from him. The dismounting proved as inelegant a movement as she had ever made in her life. The wretch had a smile on his face, but at least he had the good grace to keep his eyes closed.

Her legs almost buckled under her when she stood. Horrified, she glanced down at herself and quickly tugged her chemise up to cover her breasts and down to shield her to the knees. The twisted corset bit into her ribs, preventing a deep breath.

Well, if she looked disreputable, Jon looked even worse. His starched detachable collar and crushed cravat hung askew about his neck. The rest of his magnificent, sprawled body lay bare down to his trousers, which tangled around his ankles like soft black manacles. He opened one eye. "You realize this is one of my better arrangements for the piano."

Kathryn covered her mouth and spoke through fingers that trembled. "How dare you make jokes! I never meant this to happen. Not again."

Jon pushed himself to an upright position and swiveled the stool around so that she faced his back. When he finally spoke, his voice sounded harsh. "Well, it's not as though I planned it."

Kathryn noticed he didn't exactly apologize. At the moment, she cared very little about that. What happened had been as much her fault as his. They were both idiots.

She only wished he would hurry and make himself decent. Staring at that finely muscled backside was making her ache again in places she shouldn't. All right, she would admit to wantonness where he was concerned. Facing a problem was the first step toward solving it. She wondered what fool had said *that?*

With effort, she tore her gaze away from him and began snatching up her scattered clothes. When she had them bundled, Kathryn hurried from the parlor without speaking or looking at him again. She was not going to want this man anymore. She wasn't, and that was all there was to it. And she was not going to love him. She would stop that immediately.

There was no point in trying to arrange an annulment. The debacle in the ballroom at Timberoak had already prevented that. And divorce was no option, no matter what he said.

They might have to stay married, but she didn't have to love him. Desiring him could hurt her just as badly as loving when he took it into his head to return to his former ways. No doubt he would, too, once he recovered a bit more. Maybe he wouldn't even need to wait for that. He'd certainly performed with alacrity tonight, in spite of his injury and depressed state of mind.

How could she deal with a man who scattered his seed around like pennies for the poor? He had proved his worthlessness as a father. And as a husband, he would never be faithful. If she kept an emotional distance between them, perhaps she could turn a blind eye to his future antics. Many wives were required to do that, so she had heard. But if she allowed herself to love him, or even to make love with him occasionally, Kathryn knew she wouldn't be able to ignore it when he strayed. She couldn't share him. Loving or needing Jon Chadwick would prove devastating. Out of the question.

But if they could agree to be friends... Could she maintain a platonic relationship with a man like Jon? There were qualities about him that she admired, besides his awesome talent and physical beauty. There was his sense of humor, irreverent and intermittent though it was. He acted protective toward her. And sometimes sensitive. Could they build on that?

Kathryn had to admit that everything had gone extremely well tonight when they were discussing the business of his music, before their acrobatic act at the piano. He had considered her ideas without putting them down automatically just because she was a female. Perhaps they could construct a friendship on that. They would simply have to, Kathryn thought, or spend a lifetime going their separate ways, avoiding each other altogether.

With the financial problems at hand, added to the danger of Bunrich's possible retaliation, avoidance didn't seem a prudent course of action. Surely they could put aside the complications of marital intimacy and establish some sort of camaraderie.

Friends it would be, then, she decided. She'd put the idea to him first thing in the morning. And no more of tonight's nonsense. She would make that perfectly clear.

Jon slept like the dead. Even after he awoke and doused his head in a basin of icy water, the pleasant grogginess remained. He scrubbed a towel over his face and then ruffled it through his hair.

He couldn't remember ever feeling quite this way, so peaceful and numb. Well, perhaps not numb, he qualified, but certainly relaxed and free of pain. Even his fingers didn't hurt this morning. He had an almost irresistible desire to rip off the splinted wrappings and flex them, at least the ones that would flex.

Shaking off the impulse, Jon ran his left hand over his face to see whether he could decently skip a morning shave. The cool scent of lilacs and Kathryn herself clung to his hand, a persistent reminder of why his tension had lessened to nearly nothing.

What in God's name had he been thinking of, to take Kathryn on a piano stool, as though she were some dancehall doxy? He had no business taking her anywhere at all, for that matter, even though she was his wife. Suppose he had saddled her with a child? She wasn't wealthy, like the others he had left in that situation. How would she manage alone if he landed in debtor's prison? There were still the debts to pay, even if Bunrich didn't own the markers. No, he should have denied himself, or at least have taken the precaution of withdrawing early.

The memory of Kathryn's lithesome body and eager willingness made it impossible to prolong any regret for the act itself. She was nothing less than marvelous. How responsive she'd been, even though neither episode of their lovemaking had been anything a new bride should have to endure. Poor thanks she got for trying to help him work through his angst. But it had been bloody marvelous, he admitted with a heartfelt sigh. Both times.

Jon backed up and sat down on the bed. He kicked idly at the pile of clothing he'd dropped on the floor last night. Maybe her attempted "help" had caused him to treat her the way he had. Maybe he'd thought that sex was the only area he could ever hope to control between them. Obviously, she fully intended to take charge of his so-called career. And their finances. Kathryn was a forceful woman, used to having her own way.

*Just like* Maman, a small voice warned. Tenseness returned.

He stood up and kicked one of his shoes across the floor. "I won't have it," he growled. "Never again."

Jon dressed as quickly as he could and headed for the stairs. If she thought she'd lead him about like some overgrown puppy, he would have to set her straight right now. No one, certainly no woman, was going to take over his life again. He had only allowed *Maman* do it because he'd promised his father. But no such deathbed vow made him prey to Kathryn's machinations. Just because he desired her more than anything else in his life, that was no reason to let her take the reins and crack the whip.

Fine, then. He'd make it clear as brook water that he could damned well decide for himself what to do with his music. And everything else, as well, by God. So long as she remained his wife, it was her duty to come to heel.

The music arrested him at the top of the stairs. He froze at the sound. His hand gripped the newel post until his knuckles turned white. Slowly, he lowered himself to sit on the top step and listen.

For a moment, his anger dissolved like sugar in hot tea. He had never heard another person play his work before.

The introduction went down well. Yes, it worked almost as effectively on keys as it had on strings. Her expression was good, and not a note had been changed, either. Timing off, though, just a hair.

Conflicting emotions triggered an unsettled feeling in his chest and stomach. Pride in his own invention struggled with fury that another, even Kathryn, would dare usurp his magic. Jon beat back his arrogance and forced himself to listen objectively.

*Impossible.* Now that her sweet, clear voice and unfamiliar words began twisting through and around his notes, Jon suddenly felt invaded in some horribly intimate way. In his rational mind, he realized that Kathryn had succeeded at the improbable; she had blended his complicated composition with a popular theme that might captivate an audience. But in his heart, he felt much like a painter whose untrained patron had painted a tacky barn in the middle of his delicate landscape. Or put a chipped straw bonnet on his *Mona Lisa.* Christ, he wanted to break something. Preferably, her lovely neck!

But he waited, fuming, until she reached next to the last measure. Then he rose and charged downstairs, feeling damn near murderous. *How dare she do this! Bloody little thief!* He halted in the doorway to the parlor, just as she struck the last chord softly. She hadn't realized his presence yet, so he stood and watched her. Now she would smile to herself, he thought, congratulate herself for watering caviar down to tasteless fish soup.

She burst into tears. Arms propped against the sheet of music in front of her, forehead on her wrists, she wept like a child just bereaved of both parents.

Too shocked to move, Jon felt rooted to the floor. It wasn't as though he hadn't seen women cry. Hell, he'd even seen *her* cry. But never in his life had he ever seen anyone quite this beset. Great soul-wrenching sobs, noisy sniffling and moans of what sounded like utter grief poured out of her as though some dam had burst inside. In spite of his anger over her prostituting his music, Jon was moved to do something. Anything. Question was, what? Wait for her to stop, he decided.

But she didn't stop. On and on it went. Her body shook and trembled, and the noise grew worse. Lord, the little fool would make herself ill. What the devil had come over her, anyway? One moment pouring out some nonsense about beguiling hearts and love lasting unto death, and the next she'd flown apart in all directions.

God save him, this had to cease. With several quick strides, Jon crossed to the piano, grasped her nearest shoulder and gave her a shake.

To his surprise, Kathryn swiveled abruptly and threw her arms about his waist. She muttered against his stomach between gasps, but the words were jerky and incoherent. With a one-handed effort Jon managed to disentangle himself and pull her up and off the piano stool.

"Come over here," he ordered gruffly, and pushed her toward the settee. She collapsed onto it and leaned her head against his chest as soon as he sat down. "Calm down, Kathryn. Stop this caterwauling and tell me what's wrong with you." He figured the events of the past couple of weeks must have caught up to her all at once. That must be the case.

After more loud sniffs and a couple of sobs, she managed to breathe more or less evenly. Jon stuck his fresh handkerchief in her hand and watched her blow her nose. When she finally looked up at him, he felt his heart catch. Poor little waif. Dark circles lay beneath her eyes, and the weeping had mottled her lovely face with angry splotches of red. "I ca-can't...do it," she wailed, and was off again.

He drew her into his arms, wondering just what she meant by it. That she couldn't write lyrics? Well, there was an absolute given. Or perhaps she meant what he hoped she meant; that she couldn't stand bastardizing his composition the way she had done.

Jon sighed and patted her tousled hair. Bless her heart. Now that he began to consider it from her point of view, the task she'd set herself had been impossible to start with. At least she had tried, he had to give her that.

Judging by her state, she had come back down after he retired and worked on it all night long. The poor chit was exhausted, as well as frustrated by her inability.

"Now, now," he crooned against her ear, "if you can't, then you can't. We'll find another—"

She sat back and beat her fist against his chest. "Yes, that's it! Another word. Nothing rhymes with *beloved!* You have to help me. I can't do it. God knows I've *tried!*"

He pushed back and stared, mouth hanging open for lack of a foul enough epithet. Choking was too good for her. *"Beloved?"* he thundered. "That's what this is all about? You can't find a rhyme for *beloved?*"

She jumped up from the settee and started pacing. Her slender fingers crooked upward as though trying to draw something intangible out of the air. "One word, Jon! Only that one word, and it would be perfect!"

"Perfect? *Perfect?* Good God, woman, it's abominable! *You* are abominable!" Jon quickly stood and shook his fist under her nose. "You can't sing, your playing is atrocious, and you sure as hell can't write!" He accidentally nudged the leg of the piecrust table and winced at the crash of knickknacks tumbling to the floor.

She halted, dumbstruck. Her wide eyes looked blackened by a beating. Slowly she drew her hands up to clasp her shoulders, a self-protective gesture. "Oh..." she whispered. A small shake of her head loosed what was left of her chignon, and the golden strands scattered around her. "Ex-excuse me." With hurried steps, barely shy of a run, she headed for the door.

Jon caught her by the arm. "Wait, Kathryn. Please wait. I didn't mean that," he said, appalled at how stricken she looked. When had he ever been that vicious? He'd never attacked a person's inner self that way. Never. A sword thrust, a bullet through the heart, was kinder, and he knew that better than most. "Kathryn, I'm sorry, truly. I suppose I'm jealous. Yes, that's it, of course. Inexcusably jealous."

She stared at the floor beside his foot. The muscles of her arm were taut as bowstrings under his firm grasp.

"Your voice is beautiful, and you play quite well," he offered softly, honestly. "I swear."

Her gaze crept up to meet his. "And the words?" she asked tentatively, chewing on one corner of her lip.

He had to smile. "Maudlin. Sappy. Only a cut above Browning's. I loathe her poetry."

Incredibly, she laughed. "So do I."

"It shows."

With a trembling hand, she brushed the hair back from her face and slumped slightly. "Sorry I acted so missish. I'm just so exhausted I can't seem to think anymore."

Jon slid his arm around her shoulders and guided her into the hall, toward the stairs. "Quite all right. Letting off steam's good for you, I expect. Why don't you go up and rest? We'll go over it later, when you feel better. Then we'll see what can be done. Hmm?"

She came close, stood on tiptoe and brushed her cheek against his. "I...I do understand what your music means to you, Jon. Everything's such a muddle, isn't it? I'll figure out something, though. Try not to worry." Before he could think of anything to say to that, she had already disappeared into the upstairs hall.

Had he just been manipulated? He could have sworn he was in control of the situation there for a moment.

Jon pondered the situation over his third cup of coffee. The cook made disgruntled noises as she puttered around the kitchen, obviously put out by his prolonged presence there at the table. He ignored her and added an extra sugar cube to the strong, hot brew.

Maybe Kathryn had employed tears to trick him into accepting her ideas. Perhaps she did intend to manage whatever gains they acquired from the song. If he let her, she would probably want to direct the whole of his opera if it ever got to the production stage. He'd let have her way for now. She seemed to know what she was doing as far as printing this one song and marketing it. Business tactics eluded him. Of course, *Maman* had never allowed him to develop any. He'd never published his work, and he had no earthly idea how to go about it. Might as well make use of Kathryn's knowledge there. But when it came to their personal life, Jon knew, he had to draw the line.

Another demanding termagant like his mother was not to be borne. His wife had much stronger weapons at her disposal than *Maman* had possessed. Unless he intended to relinquish all right to call himself a man, he would have to learn to ignore those tears of Kathryn's and stay out from under her skirts.

For the present, he would allow her to use her knowledge and get the music printed while he observed very carefully how it was done. And from here on out, any tricks worked on his compositions would jolly well be his own. If he had learned anything at all in the past four years of relative independence, it was that he possessed adaptability.

He downed the last sugary dregs of his coffee on his way to the parlor. If he remembered right, she needed a sight more than a rhyme for *beloved* to make the damned thing work. If the masses wanted heart-wringing drivel, he could bloody well do that as well as the next man. Or woman.

Kathryn heard voices as she came downstairs around noon. The gravelly voice of Inspector MacLinden reached her before she could make her presence known. "Looks bad, son. We might get a conviction if I haul her solicitors into the courts, but we'll court hell getting a pound of her money back. I think Wainwright must have infected the old fellows with a case of gold fever. They might even have acted in good faith, if you want the truth of it. He did present a letter with your wife's signature and, however fraudulent, he has a witness that she signed it."

"Inspector?" Kathryn said, by way of announcing herself. Both men rose wearing woebegone expressions. "It's hopeless, then?"

MacLinden inclined his head and sighed. "Unless the mining company in which they invested your money produces and can manage to transport the gold out of the country."

"And that's hardly likely, is it?" she asked, knowing the answer already.

"Yes, but not totally impossible," Jon said. "We'll have to let the investment stand, in any case. I could travel down there and see what might be done."

"No!" Kathryn said, grabbing his arm as though he meant to leave on the instant. "You'll do no such thing!"

MacLinden added his objection with a firmness that Kathryn appreciated. "She's right, lad. Your presence wouldn't change anything. I've asked around of investors in other companies. A few have realized limited profits, but don't get your hopes up."

Jon raised one eyebrow and pursed his lips. "Most have gone bust, haven't they?"

"Yes," the inspector admitted reluctantly. "Almost all."

"It's Baumgartner Ore we're dealing with, you say?" Jon asked.

"You know the company?" Kathryn asked.

Jon ignored the question and kept his conversation directed toward the inspector. "Where are the stock papers? Does Wainwright have them?"

"No," MacLinden said. "You may pick them up from the solicitors' offices. After Lady Kathryn's birthday, of course."

"Good, we shall do so. Now then, as to our other problem. Have you discovered the whereabouts of our estimable friend, Mr. Bunrich?"

"Not a clue. His antiquities shop remains closed, and none of his people have seen or heard from him." MacLinden admitted. "Since all his deeds against you took place outside London proper, the Yard has no real jurisdiction. My orders to put him under watch when he's located are strictly a preventive measure. Seems he's gone to ground, assuming our little lady didn't finish him off with your pistol.''

"We can always hope," Jon remarked dryly. "But I doubt we're that fortunate. He will have guessed by now that I know the truth about his not really owning the markers. Either he'll give it up, fearing arrest, or he'll strike when we least expect it and try to steal the Stradivarius. I'm certain now he never intended to accept any payment, even had I managed to come up with it. He has an eager buyer for the violin, probably someone who has promised him future business if he obtains it.''

MacLinden smiled. "Lord Havington has it, as well as your other instruments, secured in his vault. Not to worry. Bunrich would be foolish to approach you again. Considering what I've learned of him, he's nobody's fool.''

"If you do find him, won't he have to answer for the assault?" Kathryn asked.

"If you insist on that, it would only endanger you. He could demand your arrest for shooting him, as I said before. There was no one else to witness the event except for his two henchmen. You must know how they would testify.''

Kathryn's anger welled up and exploded. "I don't care! How can you allow that man to go free after what he did to Jon? For heaven's sake, he almost destroyed my husband's livelihood!''

She felt Jon's firm hand on her shoulder. "Calm down, Kathryn. The inspector is doing all he's able.''

Even through her distress, Kathryn noted a new tone of self-assurance in Jon's voice. He met her questioning gaze with one that showed no trace of worry. At times like this, she recognized neither Jonathan the arrogant nor Pip the humble. Who was this new fellow who had taken up residence in her husband's body? She rather liked him, she thought with a smile.

"I really ought to be going," MacLinden said with a

shrug of apology. "Both of you take care, and notify the Yard immediately if Bunrich should turn up. We can at least keep an eye on him."

Jon silenced Kathryn the moment she opened her mouth to object that the notification might come too late to prevent further disaster. His voice seemed calm as a prayer. "Thank you, Inspector, for everything. I believe I can handle things from here on, but I promise to keep you informed." He left her sitting there on the parlor settee while he walked Inspector MacLinden to the door.

Jon seemed so different, Kathryn thought. Perhaps he had simply had time to come to terms with the change in plans for his music while she rested.

"Now then," he said as he returned to the parlor and shut the door behind him, "you and I have plans to complete, my dear."

Kathryn knew she must make her feelings about their union absolutely clear, this very moment. She might never be able to muster the courage to approach the subject later. Especially when this newly regained confidence of Jon's wreaked havoc with her body's needs. He was terribly appealing at his worst, and this looked as though it definitely might be one of his better days. With a sharp intake of breath, she prepared to speak.

He interrupted. "There can be no further incidents like last evening." Kathryn noted the blunt determination in his voice as he continued. "If we are to succeed in this endeavor, nothing personal must get in our way. Do you understand what I'm saying?"

Kathryn raised her chin and stared at a spot on the wallpaper just past his left shoulder. Damn him, that was supposed to be *her* line. She had expected him to argue when she refused him his rights, but apparently he didn't even want them.

## Chapter Fifteen

W hy should she feel such disappointment that he had reached the same conclusion as she? Because his reasons were vastly different, Kathryn told herself. She wanted to keep their marriage platonic, because she couldn't deal with his probable inconstancy, couldn't bear to share his body with another, probably *many* others. His reason was that he simply didn't want her. Well, he would never know that it mattered to her. Not in this lifetime.

"You're quite right. Intimacy will only muddle our thinking," Kathryn affirmed with a succinct nod. "Distract us from the goal, as it were. I agree completely. Last night was only—" she gave a negligent little flick of her wrist "—a result of my confused state of mind. My uncle upset me, was all. Normally, I would never have allowed…"

"No, no, of course not. A trying evening all around…for both of us." He shifted his weight from one leg to the other and fiddled with the sling he had replaced on his arm. "Now that we have, ah, recovered, I see no reason to flay ourselves over a moment's aberration."

Her brows flew up before she could stop them, or the word that burst from her lips. *"Aberration?"*

Instantly he assumed a contrite expression. "I didn't mean that! Not in that sense," he hurried to say. "Only that it was out of the ordinary… Uh, that is…"

"Never mind," Kathryn said, throwing both palms up to make him stop. "I know what you mean. Both incidents are best forgotten." She shook her head and tried to manufacture a smile out of feelings not in the least amused or anywhere near content enough to warrant the expression. "We're adults, not mindless adolescents, and therefore should be perfectly able to conduct a businesslike relationship when it's to our advantage to do so. And it is. To our mutual advantage."

Jon reached for her arm, but apparently rethought the gesture and jerked his hand away. "So, it's agreed."

He blew out a deep breath from between lips gone tight. "Now, would you like to hear the revised lyrics?" With exaggerated gallantry, he adjusted the stool and waited for her to sit. "I hope you won't mind, but I decided to translate the original words from Italian, after all. Changed a few, of necessity, so that they produce a sort of rhyming cadence. When you play it, slow the intro a bit and mind the grace notes I've added." He inclined his head and shook it, slightly apologetic, as he pointed to the score. "Had to substitute for two of the high notes, there and there—easier for the average voice without great range, you understand."

"Very practical of you," Kathryn conceded. The easier the song was to sing, the more people would sing it. And buy the music.

As to the other change, she knew he had hated her lyrics. Well, she would be just as honest if she disliked his. But infinitely kinder about it, she decided, feeling smug.

The music, familiar after her long stint at the piano last night, flowed smoothly, despite the minor changes he had made. When his voice lifted to accompany the notes of the first stanza, Kathryn raised her eyes and marveled at the feeling he injected into it. Into her. Her fingers stumbled a bit on the lead into the second verse, but quickly recovered.

The breath stuck in her throat and her heart seemed to pound right out of her chest as he sang. Low and melodious, love and passion rolled from him in measured yet increasing waves of heat. Beautiful, seductive, glorious heat. How the devil her fingers managed to connect with the keys, she couldn't have said. By the time she reached the finale, a trilling, sensual promise that led past the song itself, Kathryn quivered with response. "Lord," she whispered without meaning to as she struck the final chord. "Oh, my Lord."

He smiled. After a truly pregnant pause, he spoke. "Like it?"

"Love it," she answered on a helpless, drawn-out sigh. The stool seemed to vibrate beneath her bottom, sending frisson after frisson of pure unadulterated lust through a part of her anatomy too weak to escape it. "It's...quite dangerous." The thought slipped out in a whisper.

Jon threw back his head and laughed—a provocative, full-throated laugh that sent tremors through her brain and all the way down to her toes. Kathryn shook her head to clear it and leaned her elbows on the music rest. "You're a bounder, Chadwick. Not a female who hears this will be safe."

He propped on the edge of the grand so that their faces nearly touched. The breath from his chuckle stirred the curls on her forehead. "Have 'em rutting like sheep in the springtime, eh?"

Kathryn pushed back on the rolling stool and closed the piano. "Don't be coarse, Jon," she said, but couldn't stifle a grin.

"Sorry. I have a coarse nature," he explained ruefully. "*Maman* despaired of me before I left the nursery."

Kathryn abandoned the piano now that her legs had grown steady and went to recline comfortably on the settee. She hid a little start of shock when Jon came over and sat down beside her. He fully extended his long legs and crossed them at the ankle. Did she dare pursue a personal line of conversation, now that he'd opened it? Well, shouldn't a wife, even a platonic one, at least be curious?

"Your mother. What was she like?" Kathryn asked, keeping her tone light.

"Dreadfully devious, if you must know," he said. His eyes focused on his shoes. "Pushy. Mercenary." He sighed, a forlorn sound. "I suppose she had to be. We had to eat. She made me perform, you know, or I'd never have done it."

Kathryn nodded, trying to convey understanding. "My father insisted I learn Latin and Greek. I hated every minute." Maybe if she gave tit for tat, he would open up to her. She really needed to know more about his single greatest sin. Perhaps find some excuse for it, if she was to really like him as a person. "Did she mind your having lovers when you were so young?"

He straightened immediately, resting his elbows on his knees and glaring directly at her. "I wish I'd never mentioned that. You're not going to let it go, are you?"

"Well, if we're to be friends, I didn't think you'd mind my knowing. I simply need to understand how you could bring yourself to leave children of your making." She saw his nostrils flare with increasing anger. His eyes shot sparks she knew would ignite fairly soon now. Carefully, she softened her voice, placating him. "You see, my mother left me, and I've never quite fathomed how a parent could do that. You must have had good reasons, though. I don't believe you're unkind."

He pushed up from the settee and walked to the fireplace, resting his left arm on the mantel and staring into the grate. "I didn't know about them until it was too late."

"Too late for what?" she asked, trying not to allow her own indignation to surface. "Recognition? Acceptance? Surely it's not too late for that, even now."

"Neither was or is possible under the circumstances," he said, hesitating before he continued. "The...the mothers are women of means." He turned and glanced at her, probably to check her reaction. "Wealthy. Highborn." Again, a pause. "Married."

"Oh!" Kathryn said, soundlessly. His expression betrayed the old disillusionment his mother had fostered, and she wanted to comfort him. Not wise to do that, however, given their new agreement and the present state of her nerves. "So you didn't know they were married at the time?"

He laughed, but it sounded incredibly bitter. "Oh, yes. I was well aware of it. But tell me if you know one lad who has just discovered his role as a male who would deny a worldly woman's advances. Husband be damned, he thinks, this woman wants *me!* Only later I found out it wasn't me they wanted. Not me at all." He spat bitterness with every syllable.

"I don't understand," Kathryn said, thoroughly confused. "If not you, what did they want?"

"My babies, Kathryn." He ground out the words, turning on her like a wounded animal. "They wanted my progeny, little replicas of the boy genius that they could parade around Europe to stir up the envy of their music-loving friends. They wanted what my mother had—a performing pet."

"Oh, Jon!" Kathryn whispered, horrified.

"And they paid for the privilege!" he added. "They paid a bloody good fortune, each and every one, damn their eyes. They paid my mother like the thrice-cursed pimp she was. Are you happy now you know? Are you proud to call yourself wife to the great Chadwick, consort to the richest whores in Europe? A rented stud at fourteen?"

Kathryn grasped the arm of the settee with both hands to keep from running to him. "You were just a child then. You can't possibly blame yourself!"

"No? Who gets the blame, then? *Maman?*" He struck the mantel with the side of his fist. "Oh, I blame her, right enough, but I was the one crawling in and out of beds like a satyr on the loose. Only later, years later, did she tell me, in a fit of pique, that they had given her money. And why." Jon leaned back against the wall beside the hearth. "And then it was too late. Too late to go back." His voice dropped to a rasp, hardly audible at all. "Christ, it breaks my heart to think of them. To know that three children might be suffering all that I—"

Unable to stand it another moment, Kathryn found herself rushing to him and folding him in her embrace. She kissed the side of his neck and hugged as hard as she could. "It's all right. It's all right." She soothed him as she had wanted to do when he was Pip. He didn't resist. "It might help if you talked about them," she said encouragingly, resting her face against his chest.

He grasped her so tightly, she could hardly breathe. "Acknowledge them, if only to you, eh?" His long sigh stirred her hair. "Why, Kathryn?"

She patted his back gently. "I don't quite know. Perhaps you've kept it all inside you too long. There are only three, you say?"

"Only?" He scoffed. "Well, there were just three that *Maman* taunted me about." He muttered a low curse so foul Kathryn's ears burned. "Mary, countess of Bouvain. She was the first. Paris tour, in May of '79. Later that year in Milan—after a Christmas concert—came Sophia." His short laugh was bitter. "She called herself my birthday gift. I turned fifteen in her bed."

"Another countess?" Kathryn asked.

"Mayor's wife."

"And the other?"

"Elspeth Koenig. Heidelberg, the following spring. *Maman* and I were their houseguests at Professor Koenig's invitation." Jon snorted with disgust. "I wonder now if the old fellow set things up himself. God, I was so stupid! So bloody young and stupid."

Kathryn nestled closer, trying to give comfort to the boy he had been. "You never sought them out on later tours? To find out the results, I mean?"

"I couldn't bear knowing," Jon whispered. "Knowing and not doing...something. I wish I could explain," he said, his voice rough with anguish. "I have no right to know. Or to upset their lives. Expose them as bastards. What could I offer them but ruin?"

Jon made no move to push her away, but he grew still and passive in her arms. She could feel him distancing himself from her, as though he sensed her need to offer more wifely comfort.

"I misjudged you again, Jon. You truly are a selfless person," she said, leaning back to meet his sorrowing gaze.

"Not selfless," he corrected her with a patently false smile. "Just ill equipped to be a better father than the ones they already have." He did set her away then and gently brushed her cheek with the backs of his fingers. "There is no way to solve the dilemma, Kathryn. I've had six years to think on it since *Maman* told me, and there is no solution."

"Well, then," Kathryn said with a brisk nod, "I suppose we'd best dwell on what we *can* remedy, hadn't we? Why don't you go and ask Cook to hurry luncheon while I begin a neater copy of your score and lyrics? I have a printer to visit later today."

She smiled innocently at his look of confusion. The poor dear couldn't understand how she could dismiss the subject of his children so readily. Just as well he didn't.

The instant Jon left the room, Kathryn snatched up a sheet of paper and pen from the top of the piano and began to write.

"Let's see now," she mumbled under her breath. "Lady Mary, countess of Bouvain..."

During the next two weeks, planted rumors about the song mushroomed. Tidbits about its romantic inception appeared in all the news sheets, increasing interest in a possible performance. But *where?* Kathryn let the public wonder. They gossiped about whether the haughty Chadwick planned to make a real cake of himself over his wife, of all people? Had he truly composed a love song specifically for *her,* that cheeky little cit who wrote for newspapers? How droll. Her brainstorm had worked out just as she planned. Even better.

The steady stream of curious visitors leaving cards, and the stack of invitations arriving daily, certainly boded well for the future success of their project. Kathryn smiled as she sorted the missives into piles according to their importance, as she did every morning.

Not much in the way of other correspondence, she thought, searching for one letter in particular, from the Continent. Silly to be so impatient; the investigation might take months. Wouldn't it be wonderful, though, to be able to set Jon's mind at rest on the welfare of his children? Then he could fully enjoy all the hoopla that was bound to occur after tonight's performance at Havington House.

Thank God interest in Chadwick's unusual choice of a bride hadn't abated during the two weeks required for arrangements and the printing of the sheet music. The piece, which Jon had titled "Love's Tribute," had yet to make its splash in the sedate stream of London's elite. However, word of it flew around parlors and drawing rooms. Anticipation had reached fever pitch. The public was primed. Kathryn's dedicated advertising campaign had seen to that.

She couldn't resist reaching for the copy of the music she kept on her desk and admiring it again. Sally Gillem, the young and talented wife of *About Town*'s engraver, had done the marvelous artwork for it on the sly. Kathryn had hated to call in the favor, but Sally's husband would never have gained Uncle Rupert's attention if Kathryn hadn't recommended him for the position last year. Sally's illustration, of a handsome man at the keys holding his beloved enthralled, perfectly depicted "Love's Tribute." The dark brown ink on frightfully expensive buff linen paper lent class to the work, Kathryn thought proudly. Sally's scrolled border and calligraphy greatly enhanced the cover, as well. It was a masterpiece, inside and out.

Wistfully she brushed her finger over the title and the

name below it. This might be all she had left of Jon one day. Judging by his current attitude, he obviously didn't intend to carry on their life as it stood now. Once they had settled all the problems that held them together, she imagined, Jon would make arrangements for them to separate. He had even mentioned divorce several times in passing, as though they had already decided upon it.

Kathryn had remained mute on the subject. Even if they were not to have a normal marriage, she couldn't imagine life without him now. And in a rare moment of honesty, she admitted to herself that she wanted to be Jon's wife in every sense of the word, despite his wandering, irresponsible ways. Given half a chance, she might bring him around and make him want her again, even if he didn't love her. Maybe she could even keep him faithful most of the time. That would be more than many married couples had going for them.

He dutifully gave her adoring looks during their appearances in public. However, she knew he was merely setting the stage for their introduction of the song, just as she'd advised. Only during those times, with scores of eyes watching his tender regard and her response, could she allow her true feelings for him to show.

In private, even the promise of a platonic friendship had rather fizzled. Perhaps he felt uncomfortable with her knowing his long-held secrets. She wished she could reassure him, tell him to let go of his guilt, but he'd never do that. Jon couldn't forgive himself. Unless something came of her master plan.

Since he had confessed everything about the children, she and Jon had existed as virtual strangers. They shared polite, nearly silent meals, avoided private discourse of any kind whenever possible, and never dared to touch. Uncomfortable as the situation was, Kathryn dreaded the day when they could afford to live apart. Would he insist on it?

She wanted Jon more than she had ever wanted anything. The simple sound of his voice sent desire humming through her veins. She suspected that he might desire her a little, but he seemed determined not to commit himself, even to a mere physical relationship.

"Tonight's the night," Jon said softly.

Kathryn jumped and then turned with a hopeful smile.

"Our big premiere," he clarified, as though she might have mistaken his meaning. For a second, because of her wishful thoughts, she had.

"Lady Elizabeth's in a dither," he said. "Havington House is decked out like the queen herself's expected. Lord Neil and the inspector wisely retreated to a pub before I left." With a wry little chuckle, he inclined his head toward the sheet of music she held. "Still gloating over your bargain there?"

He looked downright approachable for a change, at least not half as distant as he had in the previous weeks. She glanced down at the printed piece. "Don't you love it?"

"Very high tone," he agreed, inspecting it again. "You may have overestimated sales, however." He nodded at the huge carton in the corner of the study containing stacks of the print run.

"Not on your life!" she exclaimed. "That's only half the copies. The rest have already gone out to retailers around the city. Have to be ready for the demand tomorrow." She grinned and thumped her copy. "So, how did the practice session go?"

Jon stretched out on the small settee and rested his head against the lacy antimacassar. "Wonderful. Couldn't have asked for better. Mrs. MacLinden plays beautifully, and Scotty's voice can make a grown man weep. I still can't believe our good fortune. Who would have thought old Lindy had such talent tucked away at home?"

"Mrs. MacLinden performed Lady Macbeth once at the Lyceum, did you know? Before that she did musicals. Lady Elizabeth raves about her. She told me that Scott inherited his mother's voice. He's very good, then?" Kathryn smiled at Jon's enthusiastic nod and turned back to straighten a stack of invitations. "I don't know how we shall ever thank them properly for offering to perform."

"Things are going entirely too well," Jon remarked. "I keep waiting for the ax to fall."

Kathryn jerked her head around to stare at him in disbelief.

He laughed. "Sorry. Wouldn't think I'd ever use that figure of speech, would you?" He held up his damaged hand and stared at the wrapping.

"How…how is it?" Kathryn asked hesitantly. This was the first time in a long while that Jon had given any indication he wanted to speak of his injury.

"Neil says I may leave off the splints in another week."

"Does he think maybe you'll be able to…?"

He shook his head, silencing her. "It's strange we've heard nothing of Bunrich since it happened."

She shuddered and pushed up from the heavy oak swivel chair. "You don't suppose he really might have died of the wound I gave him?"

"No, I shouldn't think so. MacLinden says his shop is still deserted and the man's nowhere to be found. He's biding his time, I expect, but he won't let the incident pass. Even if he's given up on getting the Stradivarius, he'll seek some kind of retribution. I'd bet on it."

Kathryn hated that their first meaningful conversation in a fortnight had taken such an ominous turn. "Must we spoil today by thinking of him?"

"Slay one dragon at a time, eh?" he said with a soft smile. "You're right, of course. We'll concentrate on duping London into making us rich first and then worry about the rest. Your uncle seems out of our hair for the present. At least he hasn't tried to kill me yet. Dodging Sean Wilder must be keeping him occupied."

Kathryn raked her bottom lip with her teeth and slowly shook her head. "Something's not quite right about all that investment business, Jon. Do you really think he would simply throw away all of my inheritance like that, simply to keep it out of my hands? Somehow, I doubt he would do that without some eye to profit for himself. Knowing Uncle Greedy-Fingers as I do, simple vindictiveness just doesn't make any sense.''

Jon's brow furrowed as he pursed his lips for a moment. ''That bothers me, as well. MacLinden accepts it all as a done thing, but I think there's more to your uncle's trick than meets the eye.'' He stood up and brushed an impatient hand through his hair. ''As you said, we may as well focus on today's—or rather tonight's—project and let tomorrow take care of itself.''

Kathryn agreed. Perhaps if the song proved to be the rousing success she envisioned, the loss of her inheritance would cease to matter. And Ned Bunrich would think more than twice about meddling further in the affairs of the wealthy earl of Lyham.

What a performance! Jon gulped a huge draft of cold air, his first since leaving the Havingtons' door. He held the chilled breath in his lungs, certain that if he let it go, he would explode with pure euphoria. For the first time ever, he'd been able to watch close at hand, as a member of the audience, the reaction to his music. Mrs. MacLinden had outdone herself at the keyboard. Scotty's voice had moved them to tears. After a pause of deathly silence at the end, the applause had been thunderous.

It was over. No, he thought as he quickly handed Kathryn into the closed carriage, it was just begun.

As soon as he slid onto the seat, he turned to her. ''Well?''

Kathryn let out a gleeful screech and threw her arms around his neck. She bounced up and down with excitement. His laughter gusted out against the top of her carefully constructed mass of curls as they swayed together, hugging like delighted children.

''You did it!'' she yelped as he crushed her to him.

"*We* did it!" he corrected. "*We*, Kathryn! They loved it, didn't they? Don't you think?"

"They were wild for it! Absolutely mad!" She reared back, tilting her ecstatic face up to his. "Did you hear them? Did you hear? God," she exclaimed, collapsing back in his embrace like a boneless rag doll, "you'll be rich! Famous!"

"Or *infamous!*" Jon declared wryly as he stretched his arms wide across the back of the carriage seat. "After those ghastly articles you planted in all the papers, I've precious little privacy left."

"Oh, but it was good! Everything I had printed about you made you out to be the hero of the century—the best composer, the best earl, the…"

"Best lover," he finished, and rolled his eyes comically.

"Well, you are!" she said, crowing with delight. "Certainly the best I ever had!"

"The *only* you ever had," Jon declared with another burst of happy laughter. "Rowdy minx."

"Shameless romantic!" she countered, giggling.

"Not guilty! You, you're the one!" Suddenly, caught by the look of her in the warm light of the coach lamp, Jon no longer felt the urge to laugh. His gaze locked on hers. The sparkle in her eyes shone like diamonds on ink.

"Kathryn," he whispered as he reached. "Do you know what you do to me? I've tried…really tried, not to…"

Her eager mouth, hot against his, fed the hunger that reared up and gnawed inside him like some great frantic beast. Helpless against it, he abandoned her lips and scraped his teeth over her chin, along her neck, devouring the taste of her. Kathryn's hands snaked under the lapels of his coat, and he shuddered with anticipation. Through his shirt, her nails dug into his chest, coaxing, pleading, demanding.

The beast raged lower, concentrated its attack, forcing them together in a snarl of feeling so intense, Jon gave himself up to it. Urgent moans and gasps against his ear, sharp-edged sensations at his lobe, drove him higher, twisted his body in line with hers. "Oh, God," he groaned as the lower point of the stiff corset beneath her dress raked his arousal. The unexpected contact distracted his monster long enough for Jon to realize that the rocking coach no longer aided his motions. *Home. Well, hell.*

Kathryn's breath hissed out between her teeth as he released her and sat up. They shared a guarded, guilty look, until her half of it grew into a wicked smile. Even painful frustration couldn't keep him from returning it. Helplessly, they laughed together.

Jon leaned back against the seat, shaking his head in wonder. This was going to be one of those times held in the heart, never forgotten, always savored. So many emotions had coalesced in the space of a carriage ride—joy, fear, hope, disappointment, excitement, need. Even anger, though that was pretty much self-directed for what he'd nearly done to Kathryn. Again.

"We're going to have to talk about this," she said softly, still smiling with what could only be seen as enticement. "Perhaps change some rules," she added, as though he hadn't grasped her pointed invitation.

Well, Christ thump it, he had had it with playing the martyr. It wasn't as though he hadn't tried to give her a way out of this cockeyed relationship. If she didn't care whether he was deserving of her, why the hell should he mind? "Your brains are all in your knickers, girl, you know that?"

One brow rose, and she flashed her dimples. "You show me yours, and I'll show you mine!"

His beast growled with enthusiasm. "Race you inside!"

## Chapter Sixteen

Despite Jon's challenge, they exited the carriage and made it up the walkway with a modicum of grace, all for the benefit of Havington's borrowed driver and footmen.

Jon felt tense, expectant and full of himself as he reached the front door. He had a wife, a real wife who wanted him as much as he wanted her. Deep down inside, he knew he didn't deserve Kathryn. But, by God, he meant to have her now that he was certain that was what she wanted, too. Not just tonight, but every night hereafter. So what if she was a forceful woman? He could deal with that. Hadn't he resisted her these past two weeks? And yet she hadn't tried to manipulate him, as he expected her to. Not once.

It helped tremendously that her feelings for him weren't entirely physical. She cared about him and had proved it time and again. Still, at this moment when his body craved her closeness, he wondered if he'd even care if it was strictly lust she felt.

"Oh, my God! Jon, look!" Her horrified gasps jerked his attention away from the business of locking the door behind them.

The foyer lay in shambles. Someone had deliberately turned over the vase of mums by the commode and up-ended the fern stands beside the parlor door. Water puddled on the highly waxed floor, while flowers and fronds lay crushed flat into the Oriental runner. Pushing Kathryn behind him, Jon rushed into the parlor and found even worse chaos.

"Who would do such a thing?" she whispered.

Jon bent to retrieve the metronome that lay like a broken soldier on the battlefield. Cradling it in the curve of his arm, he surveyed the wreckage of the room. Nothing seemed intact. Papers from the desk covered the floor, trampled with soot from the hearth. The new music sheets from the carton by the door had little left to identify them. Only a few charred corners survived the stacks of ash in the fireplace. He looked inside the old grand piano, which now stood open. Its wires had been severed.

"Bunrich," Jon said, nodding toward the burned music and the damaged piano. "Likes to strike where it hurts worst. Sort of a trademark of his, isn't it?"

"Could he still be here?" Kathryn whispered.

"No. The ashes are cold. I expect he waited outside for everyone to leave. Cook and Tansy would have left immediately after we did. No point in taking any chances, however. We're going back to the Havingtons' until morning. I doubt the upstairs suffered any less than this." He took her arm and ushered her back toward the parlor door. "Since Lord Neil's carriage is gone, we'll have to hire a hackney. I just hope we can find one at this hour."

"Not necessary," Bunrich growled as he stepped into the doorway, blocking their exit to the foyer.

Kathryn squealed, jumping backward. Jon used her momentum to thrust her away from him. She hit the side of the desk with a grunt. Jon's gaze was riveted on the barrel of Bunrich's pistol. "So you've come for the Strad again."

"No use for the damned thing now. My client died," Bunrich said with a sneer. "Of old age, I might add, while I fiddled around with you. Since making mincemeat of your paw didn't dent your good humor, let's see how you enjoy watching your little tart suffer. The bitch put a bullet in me." He shrugged and winced.

"Let her go. She had nothing to do with it."

"Nice try. My man saw her in the window with the gun." He waved the revolver toward Kathryn and flashed her an evil grin. "Remarkable shot. Pity you weren't a little faster."

"Or a little closer to the heart," Jon remarked, and took a step forward, noting with relief that his approach changed the pistol's direction. He allowed his gaze to wander past Bunrich. They were there in the shadows of the stairwell, the two heavyweights. He could sense them waiting.

Without warning, Kathryn dived and struck Bunrich's wrist with both fists. The gun discharged into the carpet and tumbled under the desk. "Get down!" Jon yelled as he attacked. Weight centered on his left foot, he caught Bunrich's midsection with the heel of his right. An automatic chop to the neck sent the man sprawling.

A huge body barreled through the doorway and leapt over Bunrich, brandishing a long, wicked blade. Jon dodged the slash and kicked again, feeling the satisfactory crunch of his leather sole against a knee. The brute issued a scream cut short by a solid thunk. No time to consider the source of that sound. The other man had already hit him like a speeding train, taking them both backward to the floor. Jon curled his legs in front of him, pushed up and upended the hulk over his head. Rolling to his feet, he faced a rocking, bellowing, knife-wielding target.

This was a rotten time to realize he hadn't lost his fear of blades yet, Jon thought. He bounced back, arching his body to escape the slash of the knife. As the man followed through with the swipe at him, Jon bent left and planted a foot in the man's gut. With a loud *whoof,* the fellow dropped. Kathryn loomed over the kneeling man with a bronze bust of Mozart and dealt him a blow that would have felled an ox. The brute toppled from his knees to lie prone on the floor.

The loud bong stirred Jon out of his shock. "What the hell are you doing?"

She looked up, breathless and red in the face. Curls tumbled around her shoulders, several hairpins swinging like delicate pendulums. Sweat beaded her brow and upper lip. "Finishing him off," she gasped as she raised her weapon again.

"Give me that before you kill him," he grumbled, reaching out to snatch the statue from her hands. "Why can't you just stand back and act the lady for once? Finishing him off, indeed!"

She stepped over her victim and stood toe-to-toe with Jon. Looking down at her, he noticed her bottom lip quiver. Poor little thing, he thought. Poor, brave girl. He started to apologize for snapping at her when he noticed she was raising her skirts. "Kathryn, what—?"

The sharp toe of her dancing slipper caught him right on the shin. "Damn!" he shouted, and grabbed his leg, hopping to keep his balance. Limping over the bodies and debris, Jon rushed after her as she tore through the foyer and flung open the front door.

He saw her poised on the front step, fingers curled to her lips.

"Jesus Christ!" he groaned, unheard, hands flying to his ears, while she emitted the longest, shrillest, most bloodcurdling whistle he'd ever heard in his life.

"Here's your *lady,* you ungrateful wretch!" she announced as she flounced back inside. The watch arrived in less than two minutes.

Kathryn studiously ignored Jon throughout the questioning, giving the officers succinct answers in a loud, clear voice. She looked on without a wince as the policemen bound Bunrich and his minions and carted them away. If her insides were churning like breakers on the coast, she wasn't about to let Chadwick know it.

If he still thought her some missish, weepy standabout, he could bloody well think again. Hadn't she shot a man for him? Hadn't she doctored his mangled fingers without fainting? Hadn't she dragged him through his melancholia? Now, tonight, when she simply tried to keep the odds in his favor during the fight, he'd turned on her. Had actually accused her of being *unladylike,* as though that counted for anything. Botheration, men were so stupid.

She shot him a murderous look. He returned it with interest.

"That's all for tonight, my lord, my lady," the elder officer was saying. "Milord, if you'd come round to the Loman Street Station first thing tomorrow and prefer the charges, we shall get these fellows before a magistrate as soon as may be."

"Of course," Jon answered. "Good night, Officer, and thank you for your speedy response."

"Oh, we'd heard the report of the pistol, but your whistle gave us the proper direction. Powerful sound, that! *Quite* loud." The officer shook his head in admiration.

"Quite," Jon agreed with a quirk of his brow, and closed the door. He turned slowly to face Kathryn fully, as though struggling to keep each movement under strictest control.

Kathryn waited to see what he would do. His expression looked so furious, she fought the desire to run.

"You kicked me!" he snapped through gritted teeth.

"Yes," she admitted with a defiant lift of her chin. Arms crossed over her breasts, Kathryn silently dared him to retaliate.

"If I had two good hands, I would turn you over my knee and blister your bum!"

She sniffed and tossed her head. "If you had two good hands, I'd not have needed to interfere in your little games."

"My God, girl, you scared me out of my wits! Do you know what might have happened if that bloke had raised up with the knife before I could...?"

"You were afraid for me?" she asked, softening a bit. Had all that bluster been concern for her, instead of anger at her assertiveness?

"Hell, yes, I was afraid for you!" he shouted, throwing up his hands, mindless that his bandage had unraveled and was swinging to and fro like a party streamer. "You simply don't stop to think of consequences, do you? You just barge right in swinging, or shooting, or...or whistling, for God's sake! Can't you even *try* to act genteel? Do you even know *how?*"

He quickly stepped backed when she picked up the front of her skirts. Oh, she thought about it. She wanted to kick him again, even more than she wanted a shot of brandy, but prudence won out. With a loud "Humph" and an effort at a dignified exit, she spun around and headed toward the back of the house.

"Where do you think you're going?" he thundered, and stomped after her.

"The wine cellar," she threw over her shoulder. "I've decided to get roaring drunk. We, who have disavowed *ladyhood,* salute you! Ingrate."

"I'll bring the glasses!"

"The glasses are shards!"

"The bottle it is, then!"

Kathryn halted at the door to the cellar. "Well, make yourself useful," she ordered, pointing to the rusty lock.

"What do you mean? Don't you have a key?" he asked, shifting impatiently while she lighted the oil lamp in a nook beside the door.

"Mr. Sevier put up the house and furniture to be let, not his bloody wine cellar. Now give it a kick."

"You asking me to break the lock?"

"Oh, for pity's sake, spare me the outrage. Everything else breakable in the place is already broken. Kick open the damned door!"

Jon kicked. The aged lock popped off, and the door swung in with an eerie creak.

As they descended, light from the lamp spilled into a cozy room that contained a good-size table and two short, straight-backed chairs. Racks upon racks of surprisingly dust-free bottles lay cradled in their niches.

Jon strode into the room, snatched up the nearest bottle and shoved it at her. "Have at it," he said, nudging the decorking device that lay on the table.

Kathryn hung the lamp on its hook by the door and set to opening the bottle. That done, she raised it to her lips and drank deeply. With a strained cough and a wince, she passed it to Jon. "Wine?"

He spun one of the chairs around and straddled it, leaning his forearms across the back of it. Only then did he gulp a slug and follow with a wry face and a shudder. "Piss or vinegar, not sure which!" He handed the bottle back.

"Over there," she said, noticing two wooden boxes stacked in a corner. "Perhaps that's the brandy. Recognize the stenciling?"

Jon followed her finger. "*Smythe's Imports.* Let's see." He got up and pulled open the loosened lid. "Struck gold! Here we go." He pulled out a dark bottle and returned to the table.

Kathryn opened it, took a tentative sip, and rolled her eyes. "I wonder how they ever let this stuff get out of France. Taste!"

He did and smiled, mood seeming to mellow with the slow burn down his throat. For several silent moments, they passed the bottle back and forth, simply enjoying the brandy and the moment. Kathryn saw it as a kind of celebration. They had just overcome one of their dragons, cheated death, as it were. And they'd beaten near poverty, as well, tonight, with the almost certain success of his song. Jon looked preoccupied, probably thinking the same things, she decided.

"We're going to be all right now, aren't we?" she asked, taking another sip.

Jon came around the table and leaned over her, sealing her nearly numb mouth with his own. "Better than all right, love," he assured her as his lips broke free. "Once you promise to let me handle things.'' Jon drew her up from the chair into a fiercely intimate embrace, hips grinding against hers, which were braced against the edge of the table.

"Handle what things?'' Kathryn asked, scarcely able to draw breath as arousal rushed through her. Her knees felt boneless and her head spun with brandy and mind-numbing desire.

"You, for starters,'' he muttered against her mouth. "Let me handle…you.'' His agile hand made short work of the covered buttons at the back of her already ruined evening gown and found a whole different problem underneath.

"Curse it, get out of this thing! I forbid you to wear it.''

"God bless you,'' she muttered, and reached for her corset laces. With her frock and dress-improver pooled around their feet, Kathryn sighed her relief and began tearing at his clothes. She found it incredibly hard to concentrate as he alternately pulled at and caressed over her silken chemise and pantalets.

"Kiss,'' he whispered harshly, then found her mouth. Probing, biting softly, searching out every hidden place within, he took her mouth with a hunger that drugged her senseless. The spreading flames trailed down her neck to her breasts, lower, drawing eager sounds, pleas and demands, from her throat. She writhed against his hips, absorbing the pleasure of his own deep groans.

Slowly he rose, brushing his bared chest against hers, sweeping the fire along every nerve ending. "Up,'' he grunted, and flung a mound of her ruffled clothing on the tabletop. She lay back on her dress and petticoats as he climbed above her. His shirt hung from his shoulders like a parted curtain, exhibiting a tempting array of straining muscles all the way to the unbuttoned flap of his trousers. And below.

Kathryn had never imagined such wild, overpowering need. Such craving emptiness. Her hands worked the closely fitted clothing down his hips and then clutched him to her with an imperative tug on both his bare cheeks.

He filled her with one hard thrust and froze for a second. When she opened her eyes, he held her gaze with one that burned itself into her mind for all time. "Here," he whispered. "Here is the magic." Then he began to move.

Spellbound, lost in the throes of love's dance, Kathryn sensed the melody in his mind, felt the resounding accompaniment with each rise and plunge of his body. Building...increasing...faster and faster, until the final chords crashed down with a finale so fierce it swept away reality. She was barely aware of Jon's rumbling roar and his eventual collapse.

Then he moved to her side on the table and drew her to him, as though he feared someone would come and take her away.

"Jon?" she questioned in a whisper as the world around them settled back into place. His intense hold on her increased.

"They could have killed you," came his tortured voice, the words tumbling out in harsh, accusing tone. The arm around her tightened further. "Why the hell didn't you run when I...?"

Gently she covered the half-wrapped hand that grasped her lower jaw between his thumb and forefinger. "Why do you hate it so when I try to help you?"

"Try to help?" He ground out the words in fury. "You always take charge! Always!"

"Oh for goodness' sake, Jon, don't be a fool!" Kathryn struggled away from him and raised herself on one elbow. "It was not some sort of competition. I wasn't about to stand back and allow him to put a bullet through you!"

He seemed not to hear her at all. "You wouldn't even wait for me to call the watch when it was over. Whistling down the night like a loudmouthed street urchin! God, women don't whistle, Kathryn. They just don't. It's undignified!"

She grinned down at him and dropped a laughing kiss on his nose. "So is sprawling about in a wine cellar with your trousers round your knees. Get up, *my lord,* and fetch me my knickers."

Jon laid his arm across his eyes and groaned. "You are impossible."

"Better get used to it if you plan to live happily ever after," she advised.

His arm fell away from his face, and he grasped her busy hand. His eyes looked a stormy gray as his gaze locked on hers. "Do you really think we could do such a thing?"

Kathryn recognized the grudging hope underneath the sarcasm in his voice, and her heart soared. "Probably not. I expect we will forever be at loggerheads over something or other."

"Forever? You plan to stay? When everything's settled, I mean. You don't want the divorce?"

"Divorce?" Kathryn asked on a disbelieving chuckle. "Surely you don't think for a moment I took you seriously? I figure if we stay married long enough, we'll eventually get round to the marriage bed!" She thumped the table. "Wouldn't that be a novelty?"

After a moment's tense silence, he laughed. "You're a cheeky piece of work, Wainwright."

She slapped him lightly on his hard belly with the back of her hand. "Merchant's daughter," she declared proudly. "Good common stock."

"Nothing common about you, Kathryn," he said, brushing her curls off her brow. "Nothing at all. You're truly most *uncommon.*"

He traced her lips with his thumb and smiled sweetly. "Except for that bloody whistle of yours."

Kathryn couldn't help the shivers of anticipation running through her as they mounted the stairs to the bedrooms. Would Jon share her bed tonight, now that he knew she wanted to stay with him? He'd said nothing more about it once they began to dress in the wine cellar. She had giggled

when he stuck her corset under his arm and firmly refused
to let her have it back. His answering smile had looked a
bit grim.

If he was somewhat chagrined over their recent intimacy,
at least he wasn't haranguing aloud about how it was the
greatest mistake in the world. Kathryn thought privately
that it was the single most thrilling experience of her life.
Their tryst at the piano had been quite a happening, but he
had shadowed that afterward with his open self-reproach.
This time she had sensed his hope that they might eventually make something comfortable out of this marriage of
theirs. Hadn't he almost said as much? Well, to be quite
honest, she had said it for him. Perhaps her wishful thinking
had gotten away with her.

If she could entice him—this time in a less spontaneous
way—to recognize their mutual needs once they reached
their rooms, Kathryn thought he finally might accept the
permanence she hoped for. He might not offer love, but
he'd admitted they had magic together. Wonderful, musical, transporting magic. Her body still sang with it. Wanted
an immediate encore, if the truth be known. She smiled and
shivered at the wicked thought.

As they ascended, dawn peeked through the long glass
lights of the upstairs hall windows. The servants would
arrive soon, she thought with disappointment. Her sigh rent
the morning stillness. Well, there was always tonight.

They stopped at the door to his room. He reached for her
hand, and before he spoke, she read the question in his
eyes. Wonderful, silvery eyes, faintly shadowed with doubt
as he raised a brow. "Coming in?"

Kathryn nodded and squeezed his hand. His dazzling
smile nearly blinded her. Nothing grim about it this time.
He shoved the door open, still watching her face. Kathryn
glanced past him into the inner sanctum and froze. At first,
the memory of his room at Timberoak flashed to mind.
*Bachelor chaos.* Then she remembered the past night's
events and gasped. "Oh no!"

Pushing past him into the room, Kathryn halted at his writing table and then rushed to the fireplace. "Your score! Oh, Jon!" she wailed, covering her mouth with her hands. "He's burned your entire score!"

All thought of intimacy forgotten, Kathryn sank to her knees and wept with grief for him. He would be devastated now. Nothing, not her love or her concern or her encouragement, would ever be enough. He had lost the one thing he held most dear. His opera, his life's work.

*His opera.* Jon knelt beside Kathryn and stared at the grate while she sobbed inconsolably. Gray ash lay stacked as it had formed, ready to disintegrate at a touch. All his scribbles, all his translated pages. Everything, ashes. Well, not everything. Not the notes in his mind. Given time, he could probably re-create most of it.

But, strangely enough, he knew he didn't really want to. An overwhelming sense of release rocked him suddenly. The feeling wasn't new. He had experienced the same thing the night he realized he didn't have to perform anymore.

In the blink of an eye, everything came clear, as though a murky veil had lifted somewhere inside his head. All these years, he had been living *Maman*'s dreams. Playing in public certainly hadn't been his idea. Hers. Writing the opera had also been her notion, come to think of it; a last-ditch appeal before she died, for him to scrabble together the fortune she had lost. She had always scorned popular music, thought it plebeian and beneath their notice.

Hell, truth told, he liked "Love's Tribute" far better now than he had in its original form. He liked the genuine, heartfelt acceptance of it by the listeners at the Havingtons. Not one person had mouthed the high-flown tripe usually accompanying an opera's debut. They'd truly liked the music and the lyrics. And he knew why. It bespoke the honest emotion he'd felt when he wrote it, that night after meeting Kathryn at the Ballingers'. Hadn't she permeated his mind as he composed the notes? Hadn't the final lyrics, embarrassingly sentimental though they were, restated his feelings?

The thing had not been constructed for universal appeal, as an opera should be. It did not pretend to raise any social issue or to enlighten the masses. It spoke directly from one man to one woman. The song appealed on a very personal level, and he liked the idea enormously. He wanted to do that again. And again.

Jon admitted that perhaps part of this new attitude had to do with rebellion against *Maman*'s preferences and prejudice. But he knew most of it stemmed from the fact that he and Kathryn had collaborated on the effort. "Love's Tribute" was theirs. The opera no longer mattered at all.

Jon felt liberated, quit of his past, delighted with the present and deliriously eager for the future. A shout of triumph might not be appropriate, however, when his wife looked so distraught.

"It's all right, Kathryn," he said softly as he sat down on the floor and drew her into the circle of his arm. "Don't cry." She wept harder, soaking his rumpled shirtfront. Jon smiled and patted her tangled hair. He would let her grieve a few moments longer, he decided. She was, after all, weeping for him. No one else had ever done that before, and the sound of it stirred an unaccustomed warmth in the center of his body. Warmed him straight through to his soul.

God, he could write a barrelful of songs about it right this minute. Happy songs.

"Now, now, that's enough of that," he admonished, finally setting her away and wiping her tears with his thumb. "Look at me, Kathryn. See? I'm fine with this. Truth told, I never liked opera much anyway. Maudlin old fat ladies screeching like banshees. Tenors taking eons to die while they gasp out a song. Dreadfully tedious!"

"Oh…Jon. Please…don't pretend. You needn't."

"Pretend? *Moi?* Nah," he said, chuckling as he inclined his head toward the fireplace. "There's much better stuff where that came from!" He sat back and crossed his legs before him, wiggling out a comfortable spot on the carpet. Taking both her hands in his good one, he leaned forward. "Now then, what would you think of an operetta one of these days? Gilbert-and-Sullivanish sort of thing?" His enthusiasm grew as he thought of it. "Light, funny, maybe add a couple of those sappy things like 'Tribute' for the ladies!" He thumped her slumping shoulder. "Happy ending, too. What do y'say?"

She looked wistfully into the grate at the heap of destruction. Then with a shuddering, indrawn breath, she turned back to him. "I say you're the bravest man I've ever known, Jon Chadwick, and I think I love you."

His heart stopped. He knew it did. Blood swept to his lower body, halted in its round-trip and grew hot with inaction. She couldn't mean that. He knew she cared about him, even desired him, but... A figure of speech, surely. *"Love?"* He choked the word out, widening his eyes to take in every nuance of her expression.

"Maybe," she qualified, worrying the corner of her lip. "I'm not certain I know exactly what the word means, but it feels right to say it, you know?"

Jon recovered a little, but he couldn't simply dismiss the fact that she had said what she had. "What do you think it means?"

"Well, there's concern. Real caring," she amplified. "And lust, which we've pretty much established."

"Without question," he agreed, no longer trying to ignore the greediness below his belt.

"And then there's that powerful—"

A scream from below rent the air, fairly shaking the upstairs windows.

"Cook," they said in unison, scrambling to their feet.

"We're not through with this conversation," Jon declared as he dusted the seat of his pants. "Not by a long chalk."

Kathryn had already headed out the door when she

whirled around, ran back and planted a hurried kiss right on his open mouth.

Jon licked his lips as she dashed downstairs to explain the night's destruction to their outraged help. All things considered, he decided, this was a great way to start one's day; a willing wife who possibly loved him, an exciting new direction for his music, and their threatening dragons all but slain.

God, he felt like a new man.

# Chapter Seventeen

God, she felt like an old woman.

If only they hadn't been interrupted, she and Jon might have stolen a short interlude in which she could have put off thinking of all this.

Kathryn raked a hand over her forehead to wipe away the perspiration, if not the worry. Her sleepless eyes stung with fatigue. She counted the money again. Only sixty pounds, not counting the funds she had set aside to complete payment to the Sampsons for their errand on the Continent. She couldn't use that hundred for bills, though, for the couple might return at any time and expect to be paid. Or they might wire for extra funds to complete their task. At any rate, unless residuals from the sale of "Love's Tribute" trickled in during the next week, she and Jon might be begging for meals and a roof over their heads.

Neither of them had gotten to bed after their discovery of the mess upstairs. She had left him there while she went down to calm the cook. Shortly afterward, she and their two domestics had begun clearing away the wreckage.

Jon had appeared an hour or so later. Nattily dressed and groomed, he'd excused himself for a few hours. She knew he'd gone off to the police station to institute charges against Ned Bunrich and his men. But that shouldn't have taken him the better part of the day. Where in the world could he be? She hoped to goodness he hadn't decided to go shopping afterward.

With a long-suffering sigh, she tucked the money away and lay back on her bed. Havington would make them a loan, but she knew Jon wouldn't countenance asking. Male pride and all that.

A persistent knock on her door roused her. Dashing the sleep from her eyes, Kathryn cursed herself for leaving Cook and Tansy to finish cleaning downstairs. "Just a moment," she called.

"Pardon, my lady, but there's company in the parlor," Tansy shouted through the door.

Just what she needed with Jon gone, the house topsy-turvy and her half-asleep. "Coming." She slipped on a fresh morning gown and buttoned it hastily as she stepped into her shoes. A quick glance in the mirror made her roll her eyes in dismay. Snatching out her hairpins, she brushed the flyaway mass back and secured it with a netted snood. Presentable, she thought, but only just.

One guest stood in the middle of the foyer near the parlor door, as though she'd conjured him up from her earlier thoughts.

She halted at the foot of the stairs, searching the man's kindly face for signs of bad news. "Mr. Sampson? How...how did it go?"

He grinned. "Successfully, my lady. A tad beyond your expectations, I should think." A nod toward the closed parlor door set her in motion, but he stopped her halfway. "You might want to see these first. Replies to His Lordship's three inquiries," Sampson explained with a wry quirk of his gray mustache.

Kathryn reached for the missives and opened them, mindless of the fact that they were addressed to her husband. Since she had faked his signature on the inquiries, she had no qualms about opening their replies.

"Good Lord," she whispered after she read the first. She stared up at Mr. Sampson in wonder. Shuffling that one to the back of the stack, she scanned the next letter, and finally the last short message. Her gasps and the rattling of paper were the only sounds in the house. "I can't believe this," she said finally, and clasped the letters to her bosom.

Sampson laughed and inclined his head toward the door. "You will, my lady. Believe me, very shortly you will."

Jon's step was light as he entered the house. In fact, everything about him felt light. Bunrich and his muscle-heads were locked up right and tight. And Rupert Wainwright had proved remarkably easy to dupe. If what MacLinden said was true, the man should be arriving in America in a few days. Just as Jon had hoped he would, the old bastard had swallowed the whole tale about Sean Wilder seeking revenge. Kathryn's uncle had sold out the newspaper to Randall Nelson and booked passage last week. There had been no sign of him since. Too late, Lindy's investigation had revealed that Baumgartner Ore, the mining company old Rupert formed to swindle Kathryn out of her inheritance, was owned by none other than Wainwright himself. With the man out of the country, they couldn't sue or arrest him for fraud. At least he was gone. And with profits mushrooming from "Love's Tribute," it wasn't likely they would suffer terribly from losing her fortune.

"Kathryn? Where are you?" he called, laying his gloves and hat on the hall table.

"In here," she answered from the parlor.

On entering, Jon stopped short at the sight of the two persons ensconced on the settee. He glanced around the room. A bonnet and cap rested on top of the piano, two short cloaks on the stool, and several small traveling cases near his feet.

No one said a word. He looked at Kathryn for an explanation, but didn't really need one. The little duo was self-explanatory.

"Jon, I'd like you to meet—" Kathryn began.

"I'd like a word with you. In the foyer, if you please?"

"But you don't under—"

"Oh, yes, I do. I understand perfectly well what you're about. The idea occurred to me, as well, but it just won't do. Come." When she hesitated, he insisted, "*Now*, madam!"

He strode through the door, held it open for her, and then closed it again, drawing her a little away from it lest they be overheard. "Kathryn, you must know we can't be responsible for those children in there. If you want me to take on students to bring in money, at least you might have chosen adults for day classes. Residentials are out of the question in a house this size. What the devil are you thinking? At any rate, I'd never teach beginners."

"You'll teach these," Kathryn declared with a sly grin.

"Prodigies, are they? Lord God, that's even worse!" He slapped his forehead and rolled his eyes.

"Not prodigies, dear, but they are extraordinary."

He shook his head and sighed, resting his hand on his hip. "Kathryn, I know you mean well, but we really can't do this. We don't even need to, now that I've worked things out financially. You must contact their parents immediately and send them home."

"They are home, Jon," she said, still smiling. "These are your children. *Yours.* And now, as of today, *mine*, as well."

Kathryn's words finally registered. He felt his heart leap and his knees go weak. For a long moment, he just stared at her, disbelieving. His voice rasped out in a croak, "The...the babies? *My* babies?"

"Yes," she said, embracing him.

"But how?" He felt numb, terrified, relieved, overjoyed, all at once. Then a measure of reason returned. "Oh, my God, Kathryn, what have you done?" He pushed her away from him, horrified.

"I've found the children, Jon. I thought you'd be happy." She looked a bit desperate, but not half as desperate as he felt. How could he send them home, now that he'd seen them?

Jon shook her shoulder in frustration. He knew she'd only meant to help, but he had to make her understand the cruelty of her act. "Kathryn, don't you realize that *I* could have found them myself? Have you never asked yourself why I haven't done so? I could have sworn we had spoken of this! I left them to their mothers so they would know the acceptance of a family and have all life's advantages." A worse thought occurred. "God above, Kathryn, you didn't have them kidnapped? Tell me you didn't!"

"Of course I didn't. I merely sent someone to discover how they were getting on. You told me how their mothers wanted them to emulate your career, so I issued an invitation for the children to study with you next summer. You have agonized about their well-being, and I wanted to ease your mind. Perhaps have you meet them, if only as their music master." She pulled a stack of letters from her pocket and held them out to him. "You'll want to read these later, but I'll give you a quick appraisal of the situation.

"Your eldest, Étienne, was abandoned by his mother for her Spanish riding instructor two years ago. Her husband knew all along the child was not his own, but was kind enough not to turn a seven-year-old onto the streets after the woman left. The count agreed to the boy's leaving, delighted to be rid of his embarrassing presence. Hence, we now have a son. Permanently."

Jon could only manage a nod, his mind whirling with guilt. Why? Why had he simply assumed the boy had been accepted as legitimate? "The others?" he asked, afraid to know.

"Señora Sophia Purpura thanks you for remembering her fondly, and for the kind offer to tutor her progeny. However, much to her regret, she has never borne any children."

"Thank God." Jon ran a hand over his face and sighed. "The little blonde is Elspeth's?"

"Yes. Elspeth's husband died last year, and she has recently remarried. She insists on your taking custody of Lisl, but wishes to see her daughter once each summer to determine her progress." Kathryn's lips were pinched, and she frowned as she continued. "Elspeth sends her regards and hopes Lisl won't disappoint you, as well."

"Devil Elspeth!" he spat. "Unnatural bitch!"

Kathryn rewarded him with a bright smile. "Just so. Will you come in now and meet them properly?" she asked gently, and steered him along beside her.

"Wait!" he said, pulling away from her hold. "What must I say to them? I have to think!"

"No. You have to let them know they're wanted here, Jon. You must do it immediately, or they may not believe you, after that entrance and exit you just made. They have precious little reason to think they're welcome anywhere at all."

"I've done this to them," he whispered, pounding his chest with his fist. "My poor babies."

Kathryn soothed him with a touch, much as he imagined her doing earlier with those poor, unfortunate children in the parlor. "Everything will be all right now, Jon." She straightened his cravat and patted his face. "Smile when you go in."

Jon sniffed, wiped his eyes and straightened his shoulders. This might prove the most difficult performance of his life. He marched into the room and stood before four little wary eyes the exact pale blue of his own.

Feeling like a looming great hulk, he knelt in front of the settee, turning first to the lad. *"Comment allez-vous, Étienne? Parlez-vous anglais?"* He wondered if the boy's English mother had bothered to teach him.

*"Oui,"* the boy answered. "I mean, yes, *monsieur*...sir."

*"Bien!"* Jon offered a soft smile. His son. His Étienne.

Big for nine years old, wavy gold hair, a shade too long, wide eyes, and such a vulnerable mouth; a blushing replica of himself at that age. How had he not seen that at first glance? Jon cleared his throat. "Out of deference to those present, we shall speak English, then. All our private conversation—men's business, as it were—shall be conducted in French, though, eh?"

The boy nodded hesitantly, obviously confused by the offer. Jon patted his son's sturdy knee and turned slightly to the girl.

"*Wilkommen, Liebchen,*" he said, taking the tiny clasped hands of his youngest. She looked like a china doll, with her cloud of ivory curls and her rosebud mouth. Her little cheeks were wind-kissed and rosy. How alone she looked. How frail.

"*Veilen Danke, mein Herr,*" she said in brusque German. Her strong voice belied her fragile appearance. "I know your language. *Mein* old *Vater* was a professor of the English at the *Universität,* and I learn everything. *Mein* new *Vater* is a *Dummkopf. Mutti* says I must not say this, but true is true."

"*Ja?*" Jon said, squelching a laugh at her cheeky revelations. "And what else does *Mutti* say?"

"She say I must be *gut* here. I must practice wery much."

"You like music, do you?" he asked conversationally.

"*Nein,*" she announced with a pout.

"Then you shan't play a note. The piano's *kaput,* anyway."

Her smile fairly glowed. She wriggled with pleasure and squeezed his hand. Jon lost his heart, or what was left of it.

"Now then," he said, sitting back on his heels. "I have an announcement to make. I hope you two will be as pleased to hear this as I am to say it." He looked up at Kathryn for reassurance, and then regarded the children in turn. "I'll speak plainly to you both. I am your natural father, and I have wanted you with me for a very long time. Kathryn brought you to me and would like to be your mum, since your other mothers are...so busy.'' He'd had no idea how to phrase that, since Étienne's mother had abandoned him outright, and Lisl's had sent her packing. He searched their eyes for signs of rejection. ''Will you let us love you and care for you as parents should do?''

The two sat silently, hands folded politely in their laps while their little behinds squirmed restlessly. Regardless of their former situations, they must be terrified, dumped in an unfamiliar country with strangers. Jon sighed. This wasn't going as smoothly as he wished. He tried again. ''Haven't you any questions to ask me? Étienne?''

''I am a bastard, sir.''

''Not any longer. You are my son. I would be happy if you, and Lisl, would accept me as your father.'' Étienne shrugged with typical French nonchalance, but Jon could see the nervous twitching of one small boot. ''Haven't you anything else to ask?''

''If your stables are very cold, sir, may I have two blankets?''

Jon squeezed his eyes shut and swallowed hard. ''Oh, my boy. You'll not be staying in anyone's stables, ever again. Your room is above stairs, next to my own.''

The wide-eyed youngster nodded, raking his lower lip with small white teeth. Then he darted a look at the little girl sitting next to him, as though wondering how she would fit into the new scheme of things.

Jon followed the boy's gaze and smiled gently. ''Now to your sister. Lisl, have you a question, *Liebchen?*''

''*Ja,*'' she answered boldly. ''May I have a dog?''

Jon's surprised crack of laughter made them both jump. Then their wide gazes darted from him to Kathryn, who had nearly doubled over with mirth.

''Yes, yes, yes,'' he groaned when he could speak at last. ''You certainly may have a dog, sweetheart. Lots and lots of dogs!''

He reveled in the delighted giggle of his daughter and the slow-forming smile of his son. Kathryn had knelt beside him and rested her head on his shoulder.

The import of what she had done here dawned on him. Controlling his life again, taking over. But if he lived to be a hundred, he would never take her to task for it. Not for this.

Jon remembered Kathryn's gentleness with him as Pip, her joy in cleaning and cooking for him, her soothing touches and motherly smile. Her soft discipline. He recalled her quick responses when he was hurt, her sympathy and love. *Love.* She might not be able to put a definition to the term, but he knew without a doubt that she loved him and that she would extend that love to his babies. His fine, marvelous babies.

"One thing you should know, both of you," he said, holding up a finger for attention. "Your new mother and I wish something from you in exchange for our love and care."

They stilled immediately, their excited chatter about pets halted in place by the qualification he had added. Their wariness alerted him that his children had probably paid dearly for their daily sustenance during their short lives. Étienne had likely earned his way as a stable hand. And Elspeth had obviously tried to force on Lisl the heavy mantle of musical genius.

Étienne glanced at Lisl. Assuming his role as older brother and spokesman, he turned back to Jon and asked quietly, "What is it that you require of us, sir?"

Jon shook his head sadly. "Well, son, your mother and I need hugs, you see? We've made do with one another thus far, but it seems we need more. When you are ready, of course. We'd not like to ask too much, too soon." Jon didn't even try to hide his eagerness.

Étienne bit his lips together, looked briefly at Lisl and back again. The boot twitched almost frantically. "All right," he said, almost inaudibly.

Jon held out his arm, and the boy slid from the settee to kneel on the floor beside him. "Come to Papa, lad." For a span of moments, nothing existed for Jon but the feel of those strong little shoulders under his hand, that tousled fair hair tickling his nose as he kissed it, the quick, shuddering breaths against his shirtfront. "My fine, fine son," he said in a choking voice. "How I have missed you all these years."

When Étienne pulled away, Jon saw him dart a glance at Kathryn. She smiled brightly, dark eyes sheened over as she reached for the boy.

Jon turned his attention to the girl, who sat motionless now on the edge of her seat. Lisl regarded him with her fair head cocked to one side.

"How about you, love?" Jon asked softly, holding out his arm.

She pursed her rosebud mouth before answering in her clear, strong voice. "I believe I shall wait for the dog."

## *Chapter Eighteen*

Kathryn felt inordinately proud of herself as she readied for bed. Matters hadn't turned out exactly as she planned, but she had certainly gotten her money's worth out of the venture. Mr. Sampson, a friend of Inspector MacLinden's and a recently retired detective, had used his initiative, thank God. He and his wife had removed the children from untenable situations and brought them home to their father.

The letters with Jon's fake signature that she sent to the mothers had been worded so as not to reveal his paternity in the event the women's husbands examined them. She had believed Jon's former lovers would leap at invitations to develop and refine any talent their children might have inherited. At the very least, she had intended to find out whether his babies were happy and well. Then he could cease feeling guilty. At most, she hadn't expected them to arrive until summer for music lessons.

Now she was the mother of two. And Jon's happiness at instant fatherhood warmed her as nothing else had ever done. Throughout the evening, he had surrounded the two with all the paternal love he had hoarded in his heart for so long. Kathryn smiled as she remembered the children's reactions. It had been like watching rosebuds bloom.

The pragmatic little Lisl still seemed a bit suspicious of her sudden good fortune. Apparently she had never kept a nursemaid for any great length of time and wasn't particularly close to her mother. Kathryn suspected the girl still grieved for the old professor she had thought was her father. The man must have doted on her.

Lisl had fallen asleep instantly when Kathryn tucked her into bed. A quick peek into the only guest room revealed Étienne sprawled on top of the coverlet of one of the two large double beds. He and Jon lay side by side, as though they had collapsed during a conversation. In repose, their features looked nearly identical. She covered them with a blanket and left them to their rest.

Today had been devoted to establishing their family. Tomorrow would be time enough to set ground rules and address problems. Kathryn didn't delude herself. There would be problems. Finances, foremost. They had just increased to a family of four. They would need a housekeeper now, perhaps even a larger house. And, if tonight's supper was any indication, at least twice as much food. Their remaining sixty pounds seemed pocket change in light of all that.

She crawled between the sheets of the bed in Jon's room and smiled wearily. Lisl had the room where Kathryn had been sleeping, and Étienne occupied the only guest room. At least now she and Jon wouldn't have the dubious luxury of private bedchambers. Perhaps tomorrow night Jon would join her here. Mama and Papa together. Could they truly become the loving family none of them had known thus far?

Kathryn snuggled under the covers that held Jon's special scent, determined to count her blessings. She wouldn't allow any worries to dim the pleasure of this exceptionally wondrous day.

"Come on, little mother. Wake up," Jon said, shaking her shoulder gently. Before she opened her eyes, Kathryn felt his lips brush her brow, then skim lower to find her lips for a hasty kiss. "The nestlings are chirping for their morning worms. They're settled with a cup of chocolate for the moment, but Cook has breakfast nearly ready.''

She blinked up at him and frowned. "How are they?"

"Chattering like magpies!" he assured her, laughing. "Battling for supremacy already. That Lisl's a corker, isn't she? Giving Étienne fits, but I suppose sisters are supposed to be like that."

Kathryn braced herself up on her elbows as Jon slid off the bed and held out her robe. "Well, come on, then! I have business to attend to in town after we eat."

"You're going to see how sales on the sheet music are going, I hope. We are desperately in need of funds."

"And we shall have them," Jon said. "I'm off to collect some of the consignment proceeds this morning. I made the rounds of the music shops yesterday, and sales were exceeding our hopes. I ordered more printed up and made arrangements for the next effort."

Kathryn shook a finger under his nose and grinned. "No fair, you having all the fun. You might have let me in on what you planned to do!"

He inclined his head in a travesty of a bow while his jaw clenched and his brows met in a frown. His expression of anger surprised Kathryn. Where had that come from, and why ever should he be disturbed with her? She had only been joking. And he was the one acting so high-handed.

"Why didn't you tell me about your investigation of my children, if you're so hell-bent to share plans?"

Kathryn couldn't argue with that, even if she did resent his accusatory tone. "All right, you have a point. But everything turned out well. Better than you could have hoped!"

"Yes, fortunately it did," he admitted as he took her arm and led her out to the stairs. "I'm grateful for that, but perhaps we need to set a few rules for our future machinations."

Kathryn looked directly into his eyes, noting his tightly controlled ire. He had no right to be angry with her, when she had done him such a good turn, bringing his son and daughter to him. "Rules, Jon? I can't imagine you conforming to rules, even your own."

His expression grew steely as he looked down at her. "I've discovered there needs to be some regulation in a man's life. I know you believe me an undisciplined scoundrel, but I have lived by someone else's guidelines almost all my life. First, my mother called the tune, and when she died, the army. It's only in this past year that I've allowed myself to run wild. Disciplining oneself is difficult when one's never had it to do, but I am learning. You have given my life new direction, Kathryn, and I thank you for that." His eyes glinted like blue steel. "But I cannot—will not—live under your thumb as I did *Maman*'s. I make my own decisions, and I do not plan to answer to anyone for them, not even you."

She saw how seriously he meant the words. Jon had undergone a metamorphosis in the past few weeks. He bore little trace of the old Chadwick now, though there were times, like now, when she could see that arrogance reassert itself. She also glimpsed Pip on occasion, that sweet guilelessness that had drawn out her maternal instincts. But he seemed a different man altogether most of the time, more thoughtful and composed than he had been. And at the moment, altogether too autocratic to suit. Maybe she could understand that, though, given his background.

Slowly, determinedly, he seemed to be gathering purpose, taking control of his life. And of *her*. She rankled under rules, especially someone else's. He would have to know that right now, at the outset. "Well, if you plan to issue any edicts to me, Jon Chadwick, you can bloody well think again!"

He laughed bitterly. "Perish the thought! I still carry bruises on my shin from my attempt. All right, we've both transgressed and are luckily no worse for it. Consider us even. Now, if you *please*, my lady," he said with exaggerated courtesy, "would you *mind* attending breakfast?"

Kathryn pulled her robe close around her and let him lead her downstairs to greet their children. The morning's conversation hadn't gone exactly as she would have wished it, but at least the lines were clearly drawn. She was not to meddle in his affairs, nor he in hers. Fair enough.

No real harm had been done thus far. Jon admitted he was glad she had brought the children home, despite the fact that he'd had no say in it. And he had done exactly what she would have done with the business about the music. Instead of wrangling over who usurped the power in their relationship, they ought to be sharing, as they had done when developing the song project.

Relinquishing any amount of control came hard for Kathryn, she admitted. After all, ordering her own affairs had always been her primary goal in life. If Uncle Rupert and Randall Nelson hadn't planned to physically overpower her, she would never have sought help from any man. And even then, she had chosen to marry the simple Pip, just so that she could manage her own future without a man's high-handed interference.

Given his past, perhaps it was doubly difficult for Jon to give up any independence at this point. Kathryn understood that. Silently, she determined to establish a real partnership between them, to stifle her own take-charge attitude, and to make him feel a part of every decision she made.

Two weeks later, Kathryn wondered whether she was truly designed for the roles of wife and mother. The children were demanding little creatures and filled her every waking moment. Jon spent much of his time with their friend Lord Neil, ostensibly to learn something about the responsibilities inherent in an earldom. She supposed that was necessary, since he hadn't been trained for the task. As for her own duties, there were clothes to buy, lessons to teach, manners to improve, quarrels to resolve and questions to answer. Though she loved the two little ones and enjoyed the business of motherhood, other things had not evolved the way she hoped.

Her primary worry was that Jon held himself from her in the ways that mattered most since their argument. And she could not, for the life of her, determine why. It could hardly be that she had failed with the children. Étienne and Lisl had settled in and made themselves right at home. And his song was a success, so their financial problems were practically alleviated. "Love's Tribute," rang out from every parlor across the country, if sheet-music sales were any indication. Well, every parlor except their own. The only musical notes she'd heard since the song's debut at Havington House had come from the expert hired to replace the piano wires Bunrich had damaged.

Perhaps Jon missed his music. If that was the case, she had no idea how to compensate for that. They never spoke of it, or of his injury. Something was definitely wrong.

He treated her with polite deference and consulted her on all matters pertaining to the household and the children. On the surface, he was a wonderful husband. As to fatherhood, he seemed torn between sharing in their childish escapades and establishing himself as a stern patriarch. His inconsistency didn't seem to bother the children nearly as much as it worried Jon. She wondered perhaps if that dilemma alone was not enough to exhaust him for other things. Maybe he was simply pouting about their fight.

Now and then, when he thought she wasn't looking, she would catch an expression of longing on his handsome features. Whether that longing signified renewed desire for her, Kathryn didn't know, but she certainly wouldn't offer an overture to resume their lovemaking. Pride was an awful thing, but Kathryn couldn't battle hers down enough to risk rejection.

She wondered whether he wanted another child. She knew now that he was going to get another one whether he wanted it or not. Kathryn hugged the knowledge to herself, waiting for a further sign that Jon might want to resume their closeness. She found it devilishly hard to discuss the matter with the polite stranger he had become. Impossible, in fact. News such as that should be shared in the privacy of their bed. Unfortunately, he hadn't come to it.

He had taken over the second bed in Étienne's room, muttering something about the boy's nightmares while he moved his things out of the master bedroom. Kathryn didn't believe that fabrication for a moment.

She considered that Jon might be trying to make a point concerning their former argument over control. Instinctively she knew she mustn't approach him about it, or he might accuse her of, heaven forbid, "directing his life." The decision to resume relations must be his. She would wait.

The flowers arrived that afternoon. Kathryn and the children scurried to find places to stack the huge arrangements of hothouse blooms around the parlor.

"Where do you suppose all these came from?" she asked lightly, searching in vain for a card on the last arrangement.

"From me!" Jon exclaimed from the doorway.

"What's the occasion?" she asked, plucking out a broken fern frond.

"Finding our children, music sales through the ceiling! You name it, we celebrate it! Who's for dinner at Chez Louis?" He strode forward even as he spoke, and kissed her soundly on the mouth. Étienne giggled and Lisl grunted with disgust.

"Jon! The children," she admonished, reluctantly pulling away. Secretly, she thrilled at his gesture, his first kiss in two weeks. Perhaps he had only been too distracted for affection.

"How could I forget the *children?*" he exclaimed, and promptly stepped over to buss Lisl's cheek. He ran a hand over Étienne's head and then drew him close for a hug. "What have you rascals destroyed today?"

As the children launched into separate accounts, trying to drown each other out, Kathryn noticed that Jon's surface brightness slipped a bit. She couldn't pinpoint exactly what alerted her—a cloud in the silver eyes, the forced set of his shoulders, a chuckle that didn't quite ring true. Something was amiss, more amiss than usual.

"Why don't you two run along and see what you might wear tonight? I'll be along to help you choose in a few moments, after I speak to Papa."

They scampered out, still arguing. Kathryn reached for Jon's hand. "Tell me."

"What?" Jon said, his smile stretching wider.

"You are trying too hard, Jon. What's wrong?"

He sighed and sank onto the settee. "Don't badger me, Kathryn. Lord, you certainly know how to wreck a good mood."

"There's no need to pretend, Jon. All that cheeriness of yours is patently false, and you know it. What has happened to upset you?"

If she thought he would try to maintain his carefree facade, she was wrong. Apparently he had assumed it for the children's benefit. He removed his left hand from his face and stared straight into her eyes. "Neil removed the splints."

Before she could form a question, he carefully slid his unbandaged hand from the black silk sling and held it out. Kathryn hadn't seen the hand in its entirety since shortly after Neil operated.

"It...it looks good," she said. It did look fairly normal. No swelling remained, and the scars where she'd stitched the split skin were only slightly reddened. "Does it hurt?"

"No," he said softly, glaring at the hand. He swallowed hard. Kathryn watched the working of his throat above the starched collar of his shirt. "As a matter of fact, it feels rather...dead." He rushed on, obviously struggling to inject the former lightness into his voice. "The whole thing, that is. Not just the fingers. All of it. Quite numb."

Kathryn had to admire his attempt to conceal his feelings, even if it wasn't working. "What did Neil say about that?"

"He pricked it with his little pin, of course," Jon said, taking a deep breath. "There is some sensation where I should feel it, but the muscles won't—" he looked away, around the room, anywhere but at his hand or at her "—won't quite work."

Suddenly his words rushed out as though he couldn't contain them. "Hard to admit how I hoped, you know? It was stupid, of course, but in the back of my mind, I just *knew* I could make them move when the time came. All of them." He got up and paced to the window. "This is…damned hard, Kathryn. I don't mean to take on so about it."

Suddenly, he turned, tightened his lips and then forced them into a determined smile. "You're not to worry about it, you hear? Everything will be just fine. *I* will be just fine, once I get things in perspective." He shook his head as though to clear it. "And I will. It isn't as though I *have* to play, now is it? God knows I always thought I hated it anyway. Perhaps this is some sort of comeuppance for all that grousing I did." His quick laugh rang cold in the warmth of the parlor.

Kathryn hurried to him and slid her arms around his waist. "I love you, Jon. *You,* not the music! I know it matters to you that you think you can't perform anymore, but you have so many other talents besides that." She searched his face, hoping what she said would sink into his troubled mind.

She grasped his chin with her fingers and shook it gently. "Listen to me. Hear what I'm saying. You can still compose. You can do wonders for the community at Timberoak, now that you have the funds. You are a marvelous father to Étienne and Lisl. We will work through this loss of yours, Jon, and come to terms with it. We will keep you so busy, soon you won't miss performing."

He shook his head, dislodging her grip on his face. "It's not the performing, Kathryn. I won't miss that. It's the playing for myself, don't you see? I need to play for *me*. I *need* it."

"I'll play for you, Papa," said a small, manly voice from the doorway.

They whirled around, surprised to see the children standing hand in hand, bickering forgotten, faces earnest.

"Me, too," Lisl said, her huge, light eyes mirroring Jon's sadness. "I shall learn to like it."

"Thank you," Jon whispered in a choked voice. "That…that will do nicely."

When Jon squeezed her arm and turned away, Kathryn strode quickly to the door and gathered the children, ushering them back upstairs. He needed some time alone to come to grips with his disappointment. But Kathryn blessed the children's offers and the good fortune that had brought them here to live. At least Jon knew beyond doubt that he was loved. She had finally admitted her love for him aloud. And Étienne and Lisl had shown him theirs.

Jon forced himself to shake off his mood as he bathed and dressed. There was certainly no point to all this groaning about like some character out of a Greek tragedy. What was done was done. Poor Kathryn must be ready to throw up her hands and quit on him. At least now he knew the worst. Even that was better than wondering about it, dreading it. The past two weeks had been hell. It had taken every ounce of his energy to keep calm, not to fly apart, with all he had to face. And to be.

So he'd suffered a few shocks lately. Not as though it were the first time that had happened. Life had to change with the circumstances. At least he wasn't alone now. He would simply do as every man should, see to his family, his home, and concentrate on the ordinary business of life.

His special talent had spoiled him, made him see himself as something extraordinary. Perhaps he had needed a blow like this to bring him to his senses. Well, here it was: one hand rendered totally useless.

Losing his magic for certain forced him to dig deeper into himself. And all modesty aside—as though he'd ever pretended to have any—Jon admitted he found a strength he hadn't known was there. If not for Kathryn, would he have bothered with all this introspection? Hardly.

She had said more than once that he was more than his music. He hadn't believed her, of course, but she'd kept at him. What a treasure she was. And those babies of his, what more could a man ask in life than to produce such wonders as those two? How the devil could he keep a long face with a family like his? Music was only music, after all. Kathryn was right, bless her; he did have more to offer than pretty sounds.

Suddenly, he needed to see her and tell her how grateful he felt for all she had done, for all that she was, for having her in his life. Things would be different from here on out. No more of his ridiculous comparing her aggressiveness to *Maman*'s, resenting her interference. Kathryn was nothing like his selfish mother. Nothing at all. She was his wife, and she had just said she loved him. Why the hell shouldn't he take her at her word? Why the hell shouldn't he take her, period?

Well, oversights ought to be rectified immediately, oughtn't they? He smiled with anticipation, both for the coming night and for the coming years.

## Chapter Nineteen

Jon strode down the hall to the master bedroom and knocked on the door. He heartily wished he had never mentioned going out tonight. Perhaps he could use it to his advantage, however. A bit of subtle courting might not come amiss. Thus far, each of his intimate encounters with Kathryn had certainly lacked finesse. As she had reminded him in the wine cellar, they had yet to make it to a bed.

"Come in," Kathryn called, and he entered with his cravat still in his hand.

Lisl had come to get her bows tied, as well. The overwhelming urge to cancel their dinner out and send the children straight to bed made him smile. But there would be plenty of time later tonight. They had the rest of their lives, after all.

"Ah, don't my women look a picture! Lisl, you look ravishing in blue. Give Papa a kiss and run tell Cook she may leave now since we're going out, hmm? There's my good little *Madchen!*" He flicked her cheek with one finger as she turned to go.

"Étienne, don't gallop on the stairs!" Kathryn called out as the unmistakable clatter sounded through the open door.

"Papa, some man waits below to see Mum! He looks fit to burst, his face is so red!" The boy sucked in a deep breath and shifted from one foot to the other. "Name's Mr. Nelson."

"Randall?" Kathryn asked. "Why would he come here?"

"You're not going down," Jon ordered. "I'll take care of it."

"No, you won't!" Kathryn argued. Then her face softened, as though she'd just recalled something. "We will go together. Whatever he's about will certainly affect both of us." She smiled up at him. "We are a team now, aren't we?"

Jon didn't want her anywhere near a man who had once meant her harm, but he recognized an olive branch when he saw one. He could keep her safe. "Let me get my weapon." He retrieved his pistol from its drawer in the wardrobe, tucked it under his frock coat and offered her his arm. Together they descended the stairs.

"Kathryn!" Randall Nelson halted his pacing of the foyer and greeted her. His expression changed from excited to truculent as he turned to Jon with a faint nod. "My lord."

"Well, Mr. Nelson, what brings you here? Still entertaining notions of acquiring a rich, pretty widow, are you?"

Nelson's head shook erratically. "No! I swear that killing you was never my intent!"

"Like hell it wasn't," Jon said, injecting a warning into his voice. "But the devil will sell ice out of Hades before she'll go to the likes of you, Nelson, whether I'm dead or not."

Nelson hung his head, still shaking it. "Forcing a marriage was Rupert's notion, not mine." He shifted nervously. "I'd never have gone along with it, I don't think."

Jon uttered a disbelieving grunt and shook his head. "*You don't think?* What kind of man are you?"

"Look, I came here to warn you. Rupert's gone round the bend. Mad as a hatter!" Randall looked helplessly at

Kathryn, pleading for her to listen, if Jon wouldn't. "I don't mean angry, Kathryn. He is stark raving crazy!"

"But we thought he'd gone abroad," Jon said. "He booked a ticket on the *Etruria* bound for New York."

"A ruse to throw Sean Wilder off his track. He has been at my house, brooding and hiding away," Nelson declared. "When I left just now, he was making a hash of my study, shouting curses about losing everything. Lord, he was carrying on about events that happened years ago! Your name and your mother's kept cropping up, as though he couldn't distinguish between you, Kathryn. He threatened murder!"

Kathryn grasped Jon's arm so tightly he could feel her nails bite through his sleeve.

Nelson stole a look at Jon and then turned his attention back to Kathryn. "He means to kill you. *Both* of you."

"The authorities would be on him within the hour if anything happened to us. This had best not be some fabrication of yours to frighten my wife," Jon warned, knowing better even as he said it.

"Rupert's too far gone to care," Nelson rushed to explain, "Since he seems to be confusing Kathryn with her mother, I think you should know what destruction he's already wrought. Some of this he'd admitted to me in the past, the rest I gleaned tonight from his ranting. He wrote a letter to your father, supposedly from your mother's paramour. There never was another man, you see. Rupert met your mother first and introduced her to your father. After that, she would have nothing to do with your uncle. He thought if he ruined her marriage, she'd turn to him."

"But instead she ran?" Jon asked, drawing Kathryn closer.

"He…he tried to drug her into compliance, just as he planned for Kathryn, but Maria escaped." Nelson swallowed heavily. "By that time, it was too late for her to return home. Your father would never have believed her. Rupert was combing London to find her. She ran. What else could she have done?"

Jon gathered Kathryn against him and motioned Nelson out with a jerk of his head.

"No, I must tell you the rest," Randall said, standing his ground. "He put it out that your mother was living in Italy with her former agent. He taunted your father with that. Rupert produced another letter, a short note your mother had once written him after she married, begging him to leave her be, saying that she was happy and in love. Only Rupert cut off the salutation, so your father thought the note written to himself."

"Did Wainwright really know where she went?" Jon asked, with a vague idea of finding Kathryn's mother as she had his children.

Nelson brushed a hand over his face. "I think not, or he would have gone after her. But that's beside the point now, isn't it? As to his plans for you..."

"We get the idea. You needn't elaborate unless you know something specific," Jon said, cradling Kathryn as she shivered.

Randall shook his head. "No, but he's in such a state!"

"We'll keep that in mind. You'd better go now."

"All right." Nelson twisted his hat into a shapeless mass. "I hope this makes up somehow for what I—"

"Thank you," Jon said coldly. "Now get out of here."

As soon as the door closed, Jon motioned Étienne and Lisl from the shadows of the stairwell where he knew they'd been listening. "Son, see all the doors and windows are locked. Lisl, Cook's gone home by now. Would you set the kettle for some tea? Under the circumstances, I think we'd best stay home tonight."

"*Ja*, Papa," she agreed. Then her little face screwed into a worried frown. "You won't let that crazy man kill you and Mum?"

"Not a chance," Jon vowed. "Hurry along now."

Jon ushered Kathryn up the stairs, undid her stays and settled her in the bed without a word.

When she finally spoke, her voice was tremulous. "All

this time I blamed Mother and everyone like her! How could I not have known something foul had happened?''

"Even your father believed it, Kathryn. You were only a child, led by his lack of faith in her, by his jealousy.''

She turned away. "I might have wronged innocent people because of that if I'd kept up with those columns. Even you. I hated you at first, just because you shared her love of music.''

"I doubt that was the sole reason," he told her. "At any rate, you know now that people are people, regardless of what they do as a living. Entertainers are no worse or better than nobles or chimney sweeps." He stretched out beside her, propping himself on his elbow, resting his head on his hand. "You mastered that lesson before tonight, Kathryn. I was one of that group you wanted to draw and quarter. You don't hate me any longer, do you?''

She turned and snuggled against him. "You know I don't!''

"So there you are," he said, dropping a kiss on her head. "I'm glad you found out your mother didn't desert you of her own accord.''

"She loved me after all," Kathryn said, weeping softly against his chest. "Don't you think?''

"Of course she loved you," he affirmed, drawing her closer into his embrace. "And I'm certain she still does. Tell you what, first thing tomorrow, we'll set your Mr. Sampson on her trail. Before you know it, we'll have a grandmother for our babies!''

"Oh, Jon," Kathryn said, cradling his face with her hands. "You are so wonderful. What can I ever do to make up for my treatment of you?''

He kissed her cheeks and tasted salt. "Dry those foolish tears, for one thing. My waistcoat's drenched and shrinking as we speak. I'd best go down and see that the children aren't too frightened. They heard every word Nelson said. Will you be all right for a few moments?''

She smiled a bittersweet smile. "You won't...stay in

Étienne's room tonight, will you? You will come back here?''

His heart thudded with pleasure. "If you like."

"I would like," she said.


Étienne was speaking as Jon approached the kitchen. "You needn't worry, Lisl. Papa won't let anything bad happen. He was a soldier once, you know. A crack shot, he said."

Jon stopped just outside the door to hear Lisl's reply. She heaved a sigh of exasperation. "Who says I am worried? Papa will take care of Mum. He *always* does what he says he will. *Immer so.*"

Jon knew very well that people who eavesdropped seldom heard good of themselves, but this certainly seemed to be the exception to that axiom. When Lisl spoke again, he couldn't help but listen. "Give me that last biscuit and I'll tell you a secret. You're not to repeat it to anyone. Especially do not let on to Mum we know."

"Here, have half this and give over."

"Mum's expecting," Lisl said in a garbled voice, her mouth obviously full.

"Expecting what?" Étienne asked, his words likewise muffled.

"A *child, Dummkopf*," Lisl explained. "I heard Cook tell Tansy this morning while they folded the wash. Where shall this one come from, I wonder? A girl from Spain would be nice. I should love to dance to those clickety things they play with their fingers."

Étienne issued a rude noise. "A girl? No, I think it should be a boy. Maybe from Russia. We could teach him English!"

"*Ja,* we could!" Lisl replied, excited about the prospect.

Jon leaned against the wall and covered his face with his hand. A *child!* He stifled a surprised laugh. Why on earth hadn't Kathryn told him? He fought the urge to dash upstairs and ask her. But he realized suddenly that he knew why she hadn't shared the news. He hadn't given her a chance.

He had been dwelling only on his own upheavals these past two weeks: his unorthodox marriage, the injury to his fingers, instant fatherhood and learning the duties associated with his title. And he'd been angry with her on top of that. It had never occurred to him that she might need him, his comfort and support, his love. And he did love her. The realization didn't surprise him. Hell, it wasn't even a new thought. He'd just been scared to death of admitting it to her.

Jon sighed, still leaning against the wall. The time had come to settle things once and for all with Kathryn. He accepted his limitations, as far as the music went. Bunrich was locked away and no threat now. And Wainwright soon would be, if he dared try anything havey-cavey. First thing tomorrow, he'd notify MacLinden that the old reprobate was still in town. There wouldn't be much Kathryn's uncle could do with someone from the Yard watching his every move. For the first time since he had met Kathryn, Jon felt their situation secure enough to concentrate fully on their personal relationship.

Thanks to her, the children had settled in nicely. He would soon have enough money from the song to begin setting Timberoak to rights. Together, he and Kathryn had worked out all their major problems. Except one. Nothing ever should have taken precedence over confirming their marriage vows; he knew that now. Kathryn had become the single most important thing in his life.

Now that his priorities were straight, he would make it up to her. Tonight. At the moment, she probably needed a bit of time alone to reflect on what she had learned about her mother. And, of course, he must reassure Étienne and Lisl, get them fed and off to sleep. The thought of Kathryn waiting in bed and wanting him there with her set him in motion.

* * *

Kathryn snuggled down into the comforting softness of the bed, as far removed from sleep as she had ever been in her life. Darkness had fallen only an hour past. She heard the muted sounds of Jon and the children as they went through their nightly bedtime rituals without her.

Thoughts of her long-lost mother had occupied her for the past hour. Now she began to dwell on her own responsibilities as a parent. And as a wife.

Falling in love had proved a frightening experience, and she was still afraid. She had resisted loving Jon as long as she could. Love could die; she had seen it happen firsthand with her father. But had it truly died, after all? She had even thought her own mother's love for her so fragile as to shatter into nothingness. Now she knew better, of course. Kathryn brushed her palm over her still-flat stomach and sighed. A mother's love couldn't die. Perhaps what her father had felt for his Maria hadn't died, either. The man had never been the same after she went away. He had eventually grieved himself to death.

A one-sided love such as hers for Jon was dangerous, however. At least emotionally. She didn't worry that he would leave her. After all, he needed her to look after Étienne and Lisl. Soon he would learn of another, more irrevocable tie between them, the new baby. He no longer spoke of dissolving their union, but Kathryn wondered whether Jon really wanted a true marriage. She could hardly bear thinking that he might simply endure it out of his newfound sense of responsibility. Where had her pride gone, that she could tolerate such a thing?

Was she doomed to suffer what so many wives did, a "convenient" arrangement? That, of course, meant convenience for the husband. The thought made her angry enough to punch her pillow and grit her teeth. She could make him want her. She could entice him into bed and keep him so sated he wouldn't wander. But to what purpose? To suffer heartbreak when he grew tired of her? And he would after a while, if he felt nothing but lust.

Damn, but she hated the loss of control over her life! Love meant sharing herself, her needs, her hopes, her dreams. She didn't know how to do that. For so long, she had been self-sufficient, independent. Now she needed him, a man who felt nothing for her but a bit of gratitude and a grudging obligation. The very thought was maddening.

"Are you asleep?" Jon asked softly, closing the door behind him. Dishes rattled as he set a small tray on the bedside table.

"No," she snapped, still angered by her musings. How dare he be nice to her, when he'd made her love him and wouldn't love her back!

He sighed as he kicked off his shoes and sat down on the edge of the bed. "I brought you a sandwich and fruit. Are you hungry?"

"No," she repeated, and flounced over, giving him her back.

"I do hope all that temper's directed at our crazy uncle Rupert and not at me," he teased. She felt his hand caress her hip and quickly wiggled away.

"Just go. Go sleep in Étienne's room and leave me alone," she ordered, sniffling.

He lay down beside her and pulled her close. "Nah, the little devil snores."

Kathryn hauled herself to a sitting position and pushed his hand off her waist. "That's why you're here? You're tired of his snoring?"

"No. But I *am* tired of pretending I don't want you."

"Well, you can't just come in here demanding your husbandly rights after ignoring me all this time! How do you think that makes me feel?" she snapped. "You purposely tried to shut me out of your life! You made me love you and then thumbed your nose like the spoiled wretch you are!" She shoved at his chest, hoping he would fall off the bed.

He caught her hand in his and smiled up at her. "You're absolutely right."

Kathryn tried to tug free. "And now you waltz in, hoping I'll fall all over you in a mad heat just because you feel randy!"

"You're right again," he said again, kissing her knuckles.

"Don't you patronize me, Jon Chadwick!"

"I'm not going to patronize you, Kathryn. I'm going to kiss you." And he did.

Kathryn struggled for a moment before the feel of his lips registered. Next thing she knew, his arms, both arms, surrounded her like a vise. Her own had somehow snaked around his neck, and she found herself kissing him back.

"No!" she protested, pushing him away, when she realized what she was doing. "You're not going to do this! Not just like that!"

He aped a horrified look, brows raised and mouth a perfect O. Then he shook his head. "By Jove, you're right again! Not 'just like that.' How insensitive of me. We deserve a fanfare, having made it to a bed this time! *Da da da da...da dum!*" He smacked a kiss on her nose. "There you go, love. Now back to business." He buried his face in the curve of her neck and tickled her with his tongue.

Kathryn laughed, her anger dissolved. She had forgotten the reason for it, anyway. "I'm taking this too seriously, aren't I?"

He groaned and flopped back on the pillows, plucking at his buttons. "Not half seriously enough, I'd say. My little maestro's in a bad way, conducting his heart out while everything in the orchestra pit ignores him. You should at least start tuning up."

"Poor fellow," Kathryn said with a giggle, knowing now might be exactly the right time to tell him her secret. "You can stop pouting, *Pip*. There's a reason for my megrims, you know."

His eyes rolled as he sighed. "Ah, so you're going to blame your fit on the nipper, are you? That's silly." A long finger tapped gently at her abdomen before he covered her with his palm. "He's too small to mind an intrusion at this point. Ought to be damned glad his old man loves you."

Kathryn stared at him in awe. "How...how could you know?"

"All-wise, all-seeing," he intoned somberly. "All done up, if you want the truth. Suffering! Are you going to love me or not?"

"Say it again, Jon," she demanded, snuggling closer. "Again."

"Are you going to love me or not?"

She pinched him on the shoulder. "Not that, you idiot! The other, about *you* loving *me*. Do you really?"

"With all my soul," he declared, with a smile that had lost its playfulness. His fingers touched her face as though tracing it into memory, while his soft blue gaze caressed her just as surely. "I do love you, Kathryn."

"Thank God!" she whispered, and abandoned herself to passion.

Jon relished her attack. There was much to be said for an aggressive woman, after all. The hasty revision in his thinking prompted a grin. Kathryn quickly erased that expression when she reached for the buttons on his breeches. He almost came undone.

Adding his urgent efforts to hers, he soon held her close without anything to impede their progress except her nightgown. "Get rid of this thing," he demanded, tugging it over her head and tossing it in the air, "and nothing will ever come between us again."

He hurriedly drew her on top of him, groaning as she guided him into her sweetness. The whole world shrank to the glory of their joining; the smell of her lilacs, the taste of her mouth, the sound of her sighs, the love in her eyes. Jon wondered fleetingly if he would ever know such joy again in his life.

And then she began to move. Ah, how she moved!

He watched, fascinated, as her breasts swayed enticingly

just within reach of his lips. Impossible to resist. He took her into his mouth and drew gently at first, then harder. They would stay this way forever, Jon thought as he tried to slow the rhythm. Her cry of pleasure and her sudden clenching around him caught him off guard, completely destroyed his resolve. Clutching her hips, he bowed upward, mindlessly grasping, desperate to give her more. On the third thrust, she came again, matching him so precisely, he gasped with the wonder of it. Here was perfection; a loving so absolute, he felt tears spring to his eyes. Good God, what had he ever done to deserve her, to warrant this? His heart felt too full.

Exhausted and breathing like a bellows, Jon wrapped her in his arms and held her as tightly as he could without causing her pain. By the time he managed to relax his hold, he knew she had fallen asleep. Still, he couldn't seem to make himself lay her down. For what seemed hours, he remained motionless, Kathryn draped over him like a cloak of peace.

The serene stillness of his soul reminded him of the bucolic life at Timberoak. London was never quiet for long. The faint clattering of a carriage and the clopping of hooves on the cobbles faded to nothing. Distant, frenetic laughter replaced the sound. Not long afterward, a prolonged scream rent the night; probably one of the thousands of prowling city cats. His lazy old Dagnabbit would be in Timberoak's kitchen, curled up and comatose by this time of night.

He, Kathryn and the children really ought to go home soon. His new family, at home. At peace. Jon drifted for a while in soft clouds of blissful imagery, his eyes finally closing.

And then he smelled the smoke.

# Chapter Twenty

"Wake up, Kathryn! Hurry!"

Kathryn came awake slowly, despite Jon's anxious prodding. When she blinked away the sleep, she saw him frantically pulling on his trousers and boots. "What...what's the matter?"

"Fire downstairs!" He shoved a robe in her hands. "Get that on and come help me get the children out. Come on!"

Kathryn shrugged on her velvet robe, already following him out. When he opened their door, smoke billowed into the room, choking them both. Jon grabbed her arm and jerked her to the floor. "Crawl along the wall," he said, coughing. "Keep your sleeve over your mouth and nose."

She followed. Panic rose in her throat, thick as the smoke that prevented her screaming.

At the first door, Jon opened it, dashed inside and was back in a second, a whining Lisl under one arm. Kathryn had already reached Étienne's room. Moving quickly, she opened it only enough for all three of them to crawl through. "Étienne," she called as she reached the bed and began to shake him. "Wake up, darling. We have to get out!"

He sat up immediately and scrambled off the bed, eyes darting from her to his father, who still held Lisl. "Papa?"

"Let's be calm now," Jon ordered, his words quick and

steady. "There's fire below. We can't get out through the lower floor."

"But, Jon," Kathryn argued. "We have to try!"

He lowered Lisl to her feet. "No, the stairs have caught. We'll have to jump for it. Might as well be from here." He was opening the window even as he spoke.

"Jon, are you mad? We can't jump!"

"We'll have to. No time to use your old trick of tying the sheets. Really, it's not so far down." His words grew faint as he leaned out the window. Then his head reappeared and he ran to the bed, snatching off the fringed woven coverlet. "This should serve." He turned to her, his eyes hard in the moonlight. Suddenly, she had a perfect picture of what he'd been like as an army officer, a leader of men. Decisive and direct.

"All right, here's the plan, Kathryn. I'll go first. There's a drainage gutter just above the window here that looks loose at the corner. If I hang on, it should swing me down and break my fall." He shoved the coverlet into her hands. "As soon as I'm down, drop one end of this out the window."

He shifted his focus to Lisl. "Sweetheart, you'll go next, and then Étienne. Slide down the cover as though it were a rope. Just like little monkeys. Can you do that? Fine. The bottom end won't reach the ground, but let go when you reach it. Papa will catch you. Understand, Lisl?"

"*Ja*, Papa. I can do it." She glanced at Kathryn for reassurance and seemed to find it.

"Étienne?" Jon asked.

"Yes, sir. But what of Mum? Who's to hold it for her?"

Jon bit his upper lip, but when he spoke, his voice sounded confident. "Mum will throw down the coverlet, and we'll make a net to catch her when she jumps."

Kathryn's heart nearly stopped. "What?"

"Trust me," Jon said. "This will work. Now there's no time to quibble." He planted a hasty kiss on each of their faces and proceeded to climb out.

Before she could gather her thoughts, there came a rusty creak and a loud snap. Shoving Étienne aside, she looked down. Smoke billowed out of the windows on the ground floor just below, all but obscuring her view. Breath stuck in her throat when Jon released the pipe and tumbled onto a grassy stretch of lawn. *Thank God!*

Hurriedly she threw one end of the coverlet out the window, wrapped the other end around her arm and gripped it with both hands. Bracing her legs against the wall, she nodded to Étienne. "Hurry, help Lisl!"

After several moments of supporting Lisl's struggling weight, Kathryn felt the tension cease. "She's made it!" Étienne crowed.

"Now you." Kathryn encouraged him, deliberately not thinking of her turn at escape. "You can do it."

"Of course I can," he said, looking so much like Jon, Kathryn wanted to hug him for that alone. "Don't be afraid, Mum. We will catch you."

"I know, darling," she said, as brightly as she could. "Now, hurry!" She fought not to dwell on the thoughts of Jon gripping her "safety net" with only one hand, aided only by the dubious strength of four slender nine-year-old arms.

With Étienne down, Jon called up, and Kathryn realized the time had come. She pushed the coverlet out the window and watched it fall. Even when they spread it out, the triangle it made looked terribly small. What if she hit one of the children as she fell? She coughed again. The room had filled with smoke, as had the side yard where they stood. Kathryn put one leg through the opening and drew the other out, as well, until she sat on the window ledge.

"Curl up and land on your side if you can," Jon called up. "Come on, Kathryn. The longer you think, the harder it will be. Jump!"

She aimed her body and flew. Her hip and shoulder took the impact when she hit the ground, but the stretched coverlet had broken her fall. Her lungs struggled to reinflate.

Next thing she knew, Jon had her in his arms and they were well away from the house. He quickly ran his hand over her. "Are you all right? Anything broken?" The children squatted as close as they could, eyeing her with downright fear.

"I...I don't think so," she answered, stretching her arms and legs carefully. She ran a hand over her abdomen and then settled it there. "Yes, I'm fine. Quite all right!" She laughed then, a genuine laugh at herself for being such a coward.

"What a commotion out front! One of the neighbors must have gone for help." Jon commented as he nodded toward the street. "The fire brigade's arrived, though I doubt they can save anything." A figure came tearing across the side lawn as she looked up.

"Is that Lindy? What do you suppose he's doing here?" Jon stood up to greet the inspector.

Huffing and puffing, MacLinden grasped Jon's hand and pumped it vigorously. "Thank...the Lord you...got out!"

"Here, sit down, sir. You're winded. Must be the smoke," Jon said tactfully. "Were you just passing by, or what?"

"No, no. Nelson paid me a visit after he left you, and I decided to check on Wainwright myself. He was missing when I arrived at Nelson's house. Didn't take a quick mind to figure where he might have gone. By the time I arrived, the place was a bloody inferno!"

Kathryn gasped. "Uncle Rupert's responsible for this?"

MacLinden nodded and sucked in another deep breath. "He must have used a month's worth of coal oil all round the place. Devil knows how he got it here so quickly. He must have been soaked through with the stuff once he'd applied it."

"You've found him, then," Jon said with relief.

"Aye," MacLinden said on a long sigh. "He should've thought things out a bit more carefully. Went up like a torch when he struck the first match, I'll wager. He managed to stagger away from the house a ways as he burned. Surprised you didn't hear him screaming.''

"Guess I did, but I didn't realize what it was," Jon said. "Thought it was a stray cat." He ran his palm over Kathryn's head as he spoke, soothing her as he would one of the children after a fright.

She noticed Étienne and Lisl hanging on to Jon's legs like the little monkeys he had mentioned earlier. They eyed the burning house with horror and fascination, probably imagining her uncle's terrible death as the inspector had described it. Kathryn tugged at Jon's hand and whispered, "Could we leave here, Jon?" She nodded meaningfully at the children.

His lips tightened as he looked down. "Sir, I need to get Kathryn and the children out of this night air. Do you suppose you could give us a lift to..." Jon looked momentarily confused. Kathryn suspected he had used up most of his decisiveness for one night. Wearing that current expression, his hair in wild disarray and his body barely covered, he reminded her of Pip as she had first seen him.

"To the Havingtons, I should think," Lindy quickly supplied. "They'll be right put out if you don't go there." He raised one scraggly brow. "And ye do look pretty disreputable to be attempting a hotel."

Kathryn agreed, and they set off for MacLinden's coach.

"Mum, that was a prime jump," Étienne said softly, patting her hand. "I think you are the bravest woman I ever saw."

"Certainly the happiest, my darling," she replied, and looked up to see Jon smiling down at both of them. "You will never meet another woman as happy as I am tonight."

The next two weeks at Havington House seemed like two months. The greater part of that time Kathryn found herself confined to bed. Her jump from a second-story window into that unsteady "net" held by Jon and the children could easily have proved devastating. No one, least of all Kathryn, was taking any chances on her losing the child she carried. The Nipper, as Jon called him, held fast to the womb thus far and showed no ill effects of his mother's reluctant aerobatics.

On the advice of Lady Elizabeth, Kathryn had forgone Rupert's funeral. That had been no sacrifice. Perhaps one day she could forgive her uncle. Now she felt only anger for the man who had destroyed her parents' lives and her childhood through his greed and revenge. Worse yet, he had almost murdered her and her present family.

At the moment, Kathryn worried more about Jon than herself. Each day he disappeared before the sun rose and returned in the evening too exhausted for more than a desultory kiss before retiring. And they were back to separate beds again. She supposed Lady Elizabeth had ordered that, too. Though she hadn't been allowed downstairs, at least the doctors had permitted her up and about in her room for these past two days.

Through her west-wing window, Kathryn watched the sun die slowly, knowing she must wait for several hours yet before Jon came to wish her good-night. If he came at all. Aside from Lady Elizabeth's brief examination early this morning and the maids bringing her meals, no one had come to visit her. Today, of all days, she had wanted company.

"Mum, Mum, you're to go downstairs! And..." Étienne shouted as he burst into the room, red-faced with excitement.

"And wear your new blue gown," Lisl finished, clapping a hand over her brother's mouth.

Before Kathryn could react, Lady Elizabeth's maid arrived to shoo the children out. "Run along now, so's your lady mum can make ready."

"What's all this, Maisie? Am I to go down for dinner?" Kathryn could hardly credit that, since she had had a tray in her room not half an hour past.

"Oh, no, milady. 'Tis a special meeting, and that's all

I'm to say.'' Maisie's sparkling eyes indicated there might be some treat in store.

Kathryn didn't have to ask why. She had grumbled silently all day because no one had recalled it was her birthday. Wasn't as if they all didn't know. Apparently someone remembered after all.

Dressed in her new sarcenet gown, Kathryn descended with Maisie hovering just below her on the stairs. The maid all but shouted for her to mind her step. The agreed-upon cue, no doubt, for her well-wishers to make ready. She smiled with anticipation.

"For she's a jolly good fellow" rang out the moment she stepped into the front parlor. Kathryn laughed aloud with absolute delight. Jon conducted the rowdy chorus gathered around the piano, where Helen MacLinden banged out the chords. Étienne whirled around the room, blowing a noisemaker. Lisl ducked behind a serving cart and swiped a fingerful of icing off the back of the cake.

After all the cheek kissing, felicitations, cake cutting, and opening of presents, Lord Neil seated Kathryn on the settee. "Now for the presentations!" Helen played a fanfare on the keys.

MacLinden stepped forward, bowed and delivered an envelope. "I present your inheritance, milady."

Kathryn's mouth dropped open.

"Rupert Wainwright left no will, and you're his only heir. The Baumgartner Ore Company is yours," he explained. "The funds are still intact, not a farthing spent. Also, half interest in the newspaper, your uncle's house, all moneys and property." MacLinden smiled at Kathryn's speechlessness, bowed toward Lady Elizabeth and stepped aside to give her the floor.

Her hostess grinned down at her. "As your physician, I present you with a clean bill of health, my dear. You may resume *all* your former activities...with the exception of jumping out windows, of course."

Kathryn felt herself blush and darted a look at Jon, who gave her a salacious wink.

Étienne and Lisl stepped forward, and, in a rare moment of cooperation, jointly handed Kathryn a telegram. Étienne explained it. "We present you what you gave to us. A real mum."

"Your mum," Lisl clarified, and then whispered, "Papa and Mr. Sampson helped."

Kathryn unfolded the message and read aloud. "'Dear Kat. Stop. Arriving two weeks. Stop. Forgive me. Stop. I love you. Stop. Mother.'" She burst into tears, grasping the telegram to her heart.

Before she could recover properly, Jon knelt before her and brushed away her tears. "Can you deal with another presentation?"

She nodded and choked back a sob of happiness, wondering how on earth anything could exceed what she'd just received.

Jon rose and accepted his Stradivarius from a smiling Lord Neil.

Disbelief and apprehension stole her breath as Kathryn watched Jon fit the violin beneath his chin and raise the bow. Silence reigned, tense and expectant. His eyes closed tightly for a moment as he adjusted his grip, bracing the end of the bow with his rigid ring finger. He looked up then, drew a soft, mellow note from the strings and smiled at her. "For you," he mouthed silently, and began to play.

Clear, sweet sound surrounded and enveloped her. Poignant strains of yearning and promise curled around her heart and wound themselves throughout her body. The vibrating strings echoed the current gently lifting her to a plane where nothing existed but pure feeling. Time lost meaning as she experienced the magic flowing from Jon's very soul into hers. When the final note softened into silence, she closed her eyes and sighed a fervent thank-you. Whether to God or to Jon, she could not have said.

When she finally looked up, every one appeared stunned.

"Well?" Jon demanded rather petulantly, breaking the spell.

Sudden laughter and raucous applause broke out immediately.

Jon grinned a sheepish grin, promptly blushing bright red.

Neil slapped him on the back. "That completes the presentations, Lady Kathryn. With a sincere wish for your continued health and happiness, we shall bid you good-night!"

She rose and looked at each person gathered there. "This is the best night of my life. God bless you, every one."

Jon scooped her up and swept her away, laughing at Helen MacLinden's snappy little offering of the "Wedding March" from *Lohengrin.*

When they reached her chamber, he set her down. She felt rather shy. Without looking at him, she asked softly, "Will you stay with me tonight, Jon?"

He chuckled as he pushed open the door and ushered her through. "Lady, the entire contingent of the Royal Guard couldn't keep me out of this room. Do you know what hell I've been through these past two weeks? Talk about gnashing of teeth! Lady Elizabeth threatened to lock me in the wine cellar if I so much as touched you below the chin. We nearly came to blows over it!"

Kathryn turned toward him and covered his right hand where it rested on her shoulder. She brushed it gently, touching the last two fingers, which Neil said would remain useless. "I feared you would never play again. I prayed every night that you would."

"I know. It worked." He smiled, slid his arms around her and unfastened her dress. "Do you know what a grace note is, Kathryn?"

"Of course," she replied, wondering what had prompted the question. "It's a small fillip that adds interest to a piece of music…a uniqueness, I suppose." She felt her dress pool around her feet as she watched him unbutton his clothes.

"Exactly," he agreed, shrugging out of his evening coat

and vest. "But it's an insignificant, essentially worthless thing when it stands alone." He looked down at her, a smile in his eyes, and pulled his shirt off over his head. "It borrows its time—its value—from whatever follows it. Without the rest of the measure, it's nothing. Did you know that?"

"I do read music, Jon, even if I'm not proficient." She gasped softly as he untied her chemise.

"The music—my old magic, if you will—is only a grace note to my existence. That's all it is. Nothing more."

She felt stunned. And rather exposed into the bargain when he slid the chemise off her shoulders and pushed it downward. "How can you say that, darling? The beauty of…"

"A bit of beauty when taken in context, I agree. Just like the grace note. But for the first time in my life, Kathryn, I can view the whole of my composition for what it is. The music is only a very small part." He pulled the tie of her pantalets loose and watched them fall.

"Such introspection, Chadwick. I never suspected you were so deep," she said, teasing.

He kissed her lightly on the lips and sighed against them. "Oh, I'm very deep. A veritable well—inexpertly dug, I might add. Almost caved in until you came along and shored me up."

"And what a simile-ridden conversation this is! Perhaps you should have been a novelist or a poet," she teased further. His breathing had grown rather labored with the efforts of undressing.

"Nah. Romantic lyrics are the extent of my writing, I'm afraid." He seemed distracted by the sight of her wearing only her hose and silk slippers.

She backed up the few steps to the bed, putting distance between them. "So your life's a song, is it?"

"Umm," he agreed. "My prelude couldn't have been better. Until Father died, my life was all a child could hope for. Such happy promise for the future of the piece." Then the silvery eyes grew dark. "The measures following that I'd as soon have left unperformed."

"Surely there were some good notes during your travels with your mother," she offered, encouraging him to remember.

"A few," he admitted. "Enough to keep me going, I suppose." He closed the distance between them, kicked off his shoes and stepped out of his trousers.

"There are the children," Kathryn reminded him.

"Ah, the babies," he said with a slow nod. "Deviations from the general theme who will generate their own separate scores someday. For now, they add interest, wonder, sweetness." He sat down on the bed and drew her to him.

Kathryn kissed his cheek. "How lovely of you to think of them that way. And me? Am I but a grace note, or another deviation to your composition?"

He snuggled closer and burrowed his nose in the curve of her shoulder. "You, my love, are my melody. Without you, the whole thing would collapse in a jumble of dark, somber chords with no rhyme or reason for being. An ugly, fruitless noise."

Kathryn held his head to her breast, loving the feel of his warmth and his love. "Ah, so we make beautiful music together. Is that what you're saying in your convoluted way?"

"What I'm saying," he said, lifting his head to hold her gaze with one gone silver, "is that you are my life's inspiration, my magic, my everything."

"Do you feel inspired to join me in an aubade, my lord?" she invited, trying to lighten his suddenly reflective mood.

"A tribute to the morning, my lady?" He grinned Pip's grin, and Kathryn knew she had succeeded.

"We'd have until sunrise to perfect it," she said by way of encouragement.

"All night long." He pushed her back against the pillows and stretched out beside her. "It might even surpass our nocturne in the wine cellar," he murmured as he slid his arms around her.

She raised her chin and chided him with a sidelong glance. "Perhaps, if we slowed the tempo a bit."

He shook his head, pulled her closer, and nuzzled her neck with an openmouthed kiss. "Umm. For the second movement, maybe."

# Epilogue

*August 1890*

The beauty of late summer at Timberoak exceeded all Kathryn's expectations. Workmen had completed most of the renovations while the family had been abroad. The necessary furniture, delivered only last week, would be followed by the rest, which they had purchased on their recent arrival in London. The grounds abounded with wildflowers. These lent a sweetness to the air that rivaled that of the most carefully planned gardens. But the true wonder lay in simply coming home.

Jon had great plans—many already under way—to improve living conditions in Timberoak village. He had promised nearby Lakesend a school, a clinic, and his continuing gift of music for the church they would attend. ''Love's Tribute'' and the two songs that followed were making her husband a wealthy man in his own right, as well as benefiting their neighbors.

Her own unexpected inheritance had financed much of the remodeling on the manor house. Uncle Rupert must have planned to live forever, considering his lack of a will. Kathryn wished he could know that, as his only relative, she had been heir to his wealth.

Ah, now that birthday had been an event to remember. Jon had played his beloved Strad for her that night. The performance had lacked the arrogant fire and boisterous energy of Jon's former efforts, but even then Kathryn had detected a new and more compelling force in his music. The antagonistic dare-you-to-love-it attitude had given way to a mature, irresistible beckoning, a gentle seduction that drew the listener into the heart of his creation. He gave of his soul now each time he played, finally understanding that he could share it without losing it.

Kathryn knew that Jon was only now reaching the full measure of his gift. He knew it, too. Never let it be said that the great Chadwick harbored any false modesty. The rascal had even outgrown the blushing.

She leaned against the doorframe of Timberoak's redecorated ballroom, her arms crossed in front of her, reluctant to enter until Étienne finished his piece at the grand piano. Her mother sat on the new brocade settee, holding the baby. Lisl sang as lustily as she did everything else, accompanying her brother in her husky, off-key, accented voice. Maria joined in, her voice every bit as wonderful as Kathryn remembered, trying to prompt Lisl to the correct pitch. Baby Saskia howled, adding to the cacophony.

"Such a multitude of talent." Jon's wry whisper tickled her ear as he sneaked up behind her. "Fair boggles the mind."

"They are wonderful, aren't they?" she agreed, laughing softly and leaning back against him.

"Ouch, that F sharp," he said, wincing as Étienne erred.

"Do hush, he's doing fine!" The poor lad seemed as tone-deaf as Lisl, but Kathryn had to commend them both for perseverance.

Jon's lips brushed her earlobe again. "While they're so engrossed, what do you say we disappear? I swear I don't remember our being alone since we left England. And certainly not since we returned." He slid his arms around her.

"Well, it was ridiculous to travel all the way to Amsterdam when I was so far gone with child. You had to know I'd deliver Saskia there.''

''Ah, but that was necessary!'' He nipped the curve of her neck—a favorite spot of his, she had learned—and soothed it with his tongue. ''Having an ordinary, English-born child would have insulted our little international family to hell and gone, now wouldn't it? Besides, the tour there certainly didn't hurt sales of the two new songs, did it?'' He pulled her close and rotated his hips against her backside. ''What do you say we slip away before they invite us in there and we *have* to listen?''

''Now?'' Kathryn asked, playing coy.

''Saskia's six weeks old today. I've been counting the days, the hours.'' He caressed her uncorseted waist as he spoke and then squeezed it hard. ''The minutes.''

She rubbed her bustle against him suggestively and covered his hands with hers. ''What exactly did you have in mind?''

''Oh, well,'' he began thoughtfully, ''our new Dutch girl is such an unqualified success, I thought we might go upstairs and make a little Swede or something. We've an open invitation to Stockholm next year.''

Kathryn stifled a giggle as she turned to follow him out. ''Sweden's far too cold in the spring. New York might be nice. What would you think about an American?''

He drew back and gave her a look of wonder. ''Positively inspired, darling! But do you think we could ever teach it English?''

\* \* \* \* \*

**Harlequin Historicals presents an exciting medieval collection**

# THE KNIGHTS OF CHRISTMAS

## With bestselling authors

### Suzanne BARCLAY

### Margaret MOORE

### Debborah SIMMONS

Available in October
wherever Harlequin Historicals are sold.

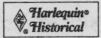

**Harlequin® Historical**

From bestselling Medieval author

**Suzanne Barclay**

comes another tale in her popular
Sommerville Brothers series

**Knight's Rebellion**

Romance and intrigue abound when
an outlaw knight rescues a beautiful aristocrat,
who bewitches his heart!

**KNIGHT'S REBELLION** (ISBN 28991-X)
will be available in November.

# WANT WESTERNS?

**Harlequin Historicals has got 'em!**

In October, look for these two
exciting tales:

**WILD CARD by Susan Amarillas**
A lady gambler wanted for murder falls for a
handsome sheriff

**THE UNTAMED HEART by Kit Gardner**
A dashing earl succumbs to a reckless woman
in the American West

In November, watch for
two more stories:

**CADE'S JUSTICE by Pat Tracy**
A schoolteacher heals the soul of the wealthy
uncle of one of her students

**TEMPLE'S PRIZE by Linda Castle**
Two paleontologists battle each other on a dig,
and uncover their hearts

Four new Westerns from four terrific authors!
Look for them wherever Harlequin Historicals
are sold.

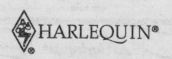

# COMING NEXT MONTH FROM

# HARLEQUIN HISTORICALS

Every month there's another title from one
of your favorite authors!

## October 1997
### *Romeo in the Rain* by Kasey Michaels

When Courtney Blackmun's daughter brought home Mr. Tall,
Dark and Handsome, Courtney wanted to send the young
matchmaker to her room! Of course, that meant the single
New Jersey mom would be left alone with the irresistibly
attractive Adam Richardson....

## November 1997
### *Intrusive Man* by Lass Small

Indiana's Hannah Calhoun had enough on her hands taking
care of her young son, and the last thing she needed was a
man complicating things—especially Max Simmons, the
gorgeous cop who had eased himself right into her little boy's
heart…and was making his way into hers.

## December 1997
### *Crazy Like a Fox* by Anne Stuart

Moving in with her deceased husband's—*eccentric*—family
in Louisiana meant a whole new life for Margaret Jaffrey and
her nine-year-old daughter. But the beautiful young widow
soon finds herself seduced by the slower pace and the much-
too-attractive cousin-in-law, Peter Andrew Jaffrey....

**BORN IN THE USA: Love, marriage—
and the pursuit of family!**

Available at your favorite retail outlet!

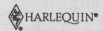